Damien fell through the doc  minute. With a deep breath and : grabbed onto the simulacrum to

The simulacrum *couldn't* move. He barely held his grip, and one of his arms was clearly going to make him pay later, but he stopped.

He looked up at the bridge link and met Rice's eyes.

"They have a six minute recharge on the laser," the captain told him. "It's no Navy gun, but it's plenty for their purposes. We are now out of defenses, so I hope your idea works."

"We'll see," he said quietly, opening a link to engineering. "Kellers?"

"It's done," the engineer replied. "You have no idea how scared shitless I am right now."

"Join the club," Damien told him. "Everyone hold on."

With a deep breath, he placed the runes on his palms on the model, and became the ship.

This was the true purpose of the matrix. He knew it the moment he linked in. Before, only trying to cast the jump spell had linked this completely to the ship. Now, just completing the matrix changed everything.

He saw as the ship saw. Felt as it felt. The scars where the turrets had been burned away hurt as badly as his own strained limbs. The broken engines burned as if his own skin had been seared with fire.

And the *Blue Jay*'s eyes were his eyes. He saw in radiation and heat as clearly as day, and saw the pirate ship closing on them, certain now that it had disabled its victim – so certain they hadn't even demanded their surrender.

This time, he had no intention of scaring anyone off. The simple self-defense fire spell every Mage learned leapt to his mind and power leapt from his hands into the runes of the ship. He sensed the power loop through the ship, repeating and building so quickly no one outside the spell would have sensed it.

Fire lit the darkness of deep space as his magic lit a tiny sun and flung it across the void. His senses and power followed it the entire way, waiting for the pirate to try to dodge.

They never even saw it coming. Super-heated plasma ripped through their hull, tearing a hole through the length of the ship, until the fireball reached the antimatter storage that fueled the pirate's engines.

The ship vanished in the searing white flame of annihilating matter.

ISBN-13: 978-0-9938434-3-3
ISBN-10: 9938434-3-3

Published in the United States of America

Starship's Mage
Omnibus

Glynn Stewart

1

"Welcome aboard, Mage Montgomery," the spacer waiting just inside the starship told him. "Captain Michaels is waiting in his office. If you'll follow me, please?"

Damien nodded as he carefully maneuvered himself through the zero-gravity boarding area. Behind him, a short metal boarding tube linked the central hub of the massive rotating rings of Sherwood Prime to the keel of the container ship *Gentle Rains of Summer*. He checked the personal computer wrapped around his left arm as discreetly as he could, making sure he was on time for his job interview with the Captain.

"Our outer ribs are on a low rotation right now as some of our thrusters are under repair," the crewman warned Damien as he moved towards one of the doors on the outer walls of the main keel. "We're only under about a tenth-gee, so watch your step."

"That will be fine," Damien told the man. He watched the spacer move from handhold to handhold up the ladder to the outer keel, and carefully followed suit. If necessary, he was able to control his own motion even in zero-gravity, but Mages learned quickly that blatant, unnecessary use of magic didn't make friends.

Damien was shorter and lighter than the spacer, though, so he was slower and more careful with the handholds until they reached far enough out on the rotating outer keel for the pseudo-gravity to kick in. He settled onto his feet with a carefully concealed sigh of relief, straightening out his clothes and unconsciously checking on the gold medallion settled into the hollow of his throat.

The medallion announced to all who saw it that Damien Montgomery had the Gift and was recognized by the Royal Orders and Guilds of the Protectorate of Humanity as a Mage. A member of one of those Orders would also recognize the symbols on it marking him as having completed a degree in Practical Thaumaturgy as well as being a fully qualified Jump Mage.

The last was why he was aboard the *Gentle Rains of Summer*. The container ship consisted of a central steady state keel with the boarding pod at one end and the engines at the other, around which four 'outer ribs' rotated to give the living and working spaces with a semblance of gravity. She was a wondrous technological creation capable of accelerating at several gravities while carrying up to twelve million tons of fuel and cargo, but it was the silver runes inscribed throughout the interior of her hull that made her a starship. With those runes a Mage like Damien could jump her up to a light year in an instant.

1

"This is the Captain's office," the spacer announced. He knocked on the hatch sharply, and then stuck his head in. "The young Mage is here to see you, sir."

"Come in, come in," the man behind the desk said loudly as the spacer gestured Damien into the room. "Montgomery, right?"

"That's right sir," Damien answered. "I'm here about the junior Ship's Mage position?"

Most starships that could afford it would have two Jump Mages aboard. A Mage was only able to jump so often without using up so much energy as to fatally burn out their brains, so having two aboard would double how fast the ship would move.

"Yes, yes of course," the captain replied, gesturing for Damien to sit. "I'm Andrew Michaels, Captain of the *Gentle Rains of Summer*. I'm afraid I owe you an apology."

Damien took the offered seat, glancing around the captain's cabin. It had the lived-in look of somewhere the occupant spent much of their time. The bookshelves, filing cabinet, and desk were all worn green ceramics, and the floating projected terminal on the desk was a model older than Damien himself.

The only 'decoration' in the room was a bronze plaque engraved with the silver runes that channeled mana to created magical effects once charged by a Mage.

"An apology?" Damien asked.

"Yes, I'm afraid we couldn't contact you earlier this morning," Michaels told him, to which Damien nodded slowly. Sherwood Prime's internal communications net was oddly spotty for the main orbital dock of a world of two billion souls. "An old friend called me this morning and I've given the Ship's Mage position to her son. I would have let you know in advance, but once we couldn't I figured I owed you an explanation in person."

Damien swallowed. "Thank you, sir," he said politely. He'd figured he'd at least get the interview, not be shut down almost before he'd introduced himself. "Is there any chance you'd be taking on a second junior Mage?" he asked carefully.

The Captain had the good grace to look somewhat sheepish. "I've actually agreed to take on two juniors already," he admitted. "Kyle and Grace McLaughlin, I would guess that you know them?"

Damien nodded his recognition of the names of his classmates. The McLaughlin family were the core Mage family of the Sherwood system, traditionally providing the system's Mage-Governor and generally acting as an established aristocracy. Kyle and Grace were two of six members of the family who'd gone through Jump Mage training with him – he knew them both well and had been 'close' with Grace.

"Thank you for your time, Captain," he said politely. "If you'll excuse me, I'll be heading back to the station – I'll need to see if any other ships have available slots." He knew perfectly well that none did – and if any did, one of the other McLaughlin youths would likely have already snapped it up.

"I know it's a point of pride not to lean on one's parents," Michaels said quietly, "but you really should see if your family knows a ship's crew who owes them a favor."

Damien focused his gaze on the spell plaque above the Captain's head. "I'm a Mage by Right, sir," he said quietly. "My parents were bakers... and died years ago."

Mages by Blood were born to the core families of the Protectorate, the inherent nobility defined by the Compact that ended the Eugenics Wars of the Twenty-Second Century. Mages by Right were identified by the testing every human child underwent at age thirteen. They had all the rights of Mages born of the main families, all of the powers and all of the official support from the officers of the Mage-King of Mars... but none of the family connections.

"I'm sorry," Captain Michaels said quietly.

The young Mage shook his head in response his gaze still on the spell plaque as his Gift traced the lines of power and he read the runes. He blinked at it confusedly. "Um, sir, what is that plaque supposed to do?" he asked, intentionally changing the subject.

"It's a security spell," the Captain explained, seizing on the topic change. "It detects if anyone enters the office with hostile intent."

Damien traced the flow of energy through the runes and shook his head again. "You might want to have your senior Mage look at it," he told the Captain. "The scribe used future-imperative tenses instead of future-probabilistic. It's actually slightly *encouraging* the chance of violence, not predicting it."

He turned his gaze back down to the captain, blinking away the lines of magic. "Magic doesn't predict the future very well, sir. If the plaque was detecting hostile intent, it would be obvious to you well before it triggered an alarm."

Michaels looked at the plaque, and then back at Damien. "You mean I got scammed, don't you?" he asked.

"A little bit, sir," Damien admitted. "Like I said, have your Senior look at it, I may be wrong – I haven't seen a spell like that before."

As he let the office, though, Damien knew the Captain had been thoroughly scammed. He hadn't misread a rune matrix since he'd started studying his gift at thirteen years old.

#

3

The same spacer escorted him out of the ship, but clearly sensed that the young Mage wasn't interested in talking. Damien had contacted Captain Michaels as soon as the posting had gone up on the Sherwood internet – he knew he'd been the first to apply, as the Captain had told him so.

Nonetheless, he'd lost the position before he'd even boarded the ship. He thanked the spacer and crossed back onto the twelve-kilometer long cylinder that was the central hub of Sherwood Prime. He quickly grabbed one of the transit tubes that took civilians up and down the central hub to any of the immense rings spaced evenly along its length, each rotating around the hub to provide the semblance of gravity. The sooner he was off the Hub, the happier he was - he was as comfortable without gravity as anyone born in a gravity well, but that didn't mean he liked it.

His rooms were on Ring Seven. Flanked on either side by multiple similar immense rings rotating around the hub once a minute, the central two rings were generally inaccessible by ship. This made Rings Six and Seven the cheapest places to live and eat on the immense space station.

At age thirteen, every child on a planet under the Protectorate was tested for Mage gift. For the children born to the noble Mage families that served the Mage-King of Mars and bound His Protectorate together, the testing was a formality. For the vast majority of the rest of the population, it was also a formality, but for the opposite reason – children like Damien who had no Mage parents and became Mages were barely one in a million.

Damien found himself wandering Ring Seven aimlessly. He paid for his room out of the small stipend the Mage-King provided every unemployed Mage. While his parents had lived, they'd received a larger stipend – an encouragement to have more children since they'd proven they would likely have Mage children. Damien's younger brother and sister had died in the same crash that had killed his parents, long before either was old enough to be tested.

The discovery of his gift had changed his life, though. The Royal Testers, men and women who reported to the Mage-King, not the McLaughlin's government of Sherwood, had arranged for his education to expand, and for him to eventually attend the elite school of magic that trained the noble children – Mages by Blood, versus Damien's Mage by Right – of Sherwood.

Despite that, the Testers couldn't provide the interlinking web of connections the Mages by Blood – especially the grand-children, nephews and nieces of a man as powerful as the McLaughlin, recently re-elected Mage-Governor of Sherwood for his seventh term.

Lost in his thoughts, Damien realized he'd wandered off of the central concourse, which was brightly lit and patrolled by security even on as cheap and dingy a section of the space station as Ring Seven. He was still in public corridors, but these hallways didn't have wide-open storefronts and bright lights.

Instead, easily a third of the lights were broken, and sealed doors with small nameplates or even just numbers were the only exits. Finally starting to pay attention, Damien realized that someone had scratched out the corridor numbers on the intersection nearest him, and touched the medallion around his throat for reassurance – no matter how run-down the area was, no one was going to attack a Mage.

Conceding that his funk had resulted in his getting very lost, he brought up the map function on his personal computer, a black plastic band wrapped around his left wrist. Its holographic display flickered in the air for a moment, with a small warning in one corner about connection issues, and then identified his location and a route back to his rooms in the main concourse.

"Nice PC," a voice said behind him. "Too nice a PC for so small a bit, don'tcha think?"

Damien slowly turned around to find four large men, the smallest easily twice his own size – but carrying a length of black piping where the others were unarmed. He was hoping that the sight of the medallion would cause them to back off, but the largest man simply grinned at the sight.

"Waay too nice a PC for a tiny Spark, boys," he repeated. "Why don'tcha jes' take it off and pass it over? Avoids anyone getting hurt."

The PC turned off, the holographic display and interface disappearing back into the band around Damien's left wrist as he stepped back away from them.

"None of that now, little Spark," the big thug told Damien. "You PC, you cash, and that lovely gold medallion – or we start breaking limbs. You can't spark with no hands, can you?"

Damien drew on memory for a self-defense spell, reaching for the glove that covered the silver runes engraved on his palms, but a massive fist slammed into his stomach before the glove came off.

"Oops, me fist slipped," the man told the Mage with a grin. "Guess the Spark won't play nice, will he?"

The massive fist wrapped itself around Damien's throat and lifted him off the ground. Damien was small and slight, the man likely lifted arm-bells that weighed more than him.

"Like I said," he said directly into Damien's face, "The PC, the cash, and the medallion."

He reached for the medallion and Damien closed his eyes, finally remembering the spell he was after – and knowing what would happen when the thug touched the gold coin.

The security spell carved into the runes under the collar holding the medallion flared into action as soon as they were forcefully removed from Damien's neck. A blast of super-heated air shot out in all directions, burning the thug's hand and throwing him back with telekinetic force.

Damien hit the ground and released his own spell. A mental baseball bat slammed into the leader's knees, and he heard one of the man's kneecaps *crack* as the spell hit them. His face half-burnt and a kneecap broken, the man fell to one leg with his hands over his face.

Before Damien even started to run, however, the thug was moving again. With one eye closed and his face bleeding from the heat burns, the thug rose on his one good leg and grabbed Damien with both hands. He threw the slight Mage bodily into the wall, crushing the breath out of him.

Still balancing on one leg, the thug slammed one hand around Damien's neck, crushing him against the wall, and then smashed his other fist into the Mage's stomach.

Unable to breathe, Damien began to choke, his vision graying out and pain tearing through his body as the thug struck him again. And again.

Then one of the *other* thugs flew bodily into the leader's back. Still the man remained on his feet, dropping Damien as he turned to see who was interrupting.

Damien barely recognized the spacer from the *Gentle Rains of Summer* before the 'liberated' length of black piping crashed into the leader's head. The thug wavered for a moment, and then the piping slammed up between his legs, and the mountain of a man finally crumpled.

Damien's consciousness crumpled with him.

#

Captain David Rice figured he was about to die.

The pirate ship had been waiting for the container ship *Blue Jay* when they emerged from their second-to-last jump en route to the Sherwood system. Compared to the freighter's four spinning ribs wrapped around its core and containers, the hundred-meter long cylindrical ship was tiny.

Unlike the *Blue Jay*, though, the pirate ship had antimatter thrusters, a Mage who hadn't just jumped, and fusion-rocket long-range missiles. The last were the cause of the muscular captain's sense of incipient mortality.

He stood on the freighter's bridge, watching the display from his ship's cheap but functional sensor suite with one eye, and the video link to the simulacrum chamber at the center of the ship showing his Ship's Mage's exhausted face with the other. The sensors showed the pirate, just less than two million kilometers distant – and the missile salvo it had fired several minutes ago, accelerating towards them at over two thousand gravities.

"Four missiles," his first officer, Jenna Campbell, reported in a strained voice. "RFLAMs engaging."

The ship had two Rapid Fire Laser Anti-Missile systems: defensive turrets containing a dozen rapidly charging gas-chambered pulse lasers. The ship mounted one at the bow, where the four ribs and the central keel combined into the protective shield dome. The second was at the rear of the ship, where it guarded the vessel's immense engines.

"I'll see what I can do," Kenneth McLaughlin told Rice through the video link, the Mage closing his eyes and reaching out. Even from the simulacrum chamber, no Mage could reach very far, and jumps were exhausting. There was no way McLaughlin would save them.

"RFLAMs each got one," Jenna reported grimly. "Two more inbound – *shit*! One's out of the gun's field of fire!"

"Got it," Kenneth said grimly. A third blinking icon on the screen disappeared as the Mage reached out and turned part of the missile into super-heated plasma.

It wasn't enough. The immense, multi-megaton mass of the *Blue Jay* lurched as the last missile slammed into the forward RFLAM turret. Rice expected to die in that moment, only to blink as nothing more happened.

"What the hell?" he demanded.

"Either it was a dud or a straight kinetic," Jenna told him harshly. "Not that it matters – the RFLAM is gone, as is half the bow dome. We try any major maneuvers and we'll open up like a rusty tin can."

"I am not dying like this," Rice told her, engaging the maneuvering controls himself. He took it gently, trusting the XO's assessment, but he slowly turned the ship so her main fusion rockets – and the last laser turret – faced her attacker.

"We're being hailed," Jenna told him. "Playing it."

"Captain Rice," a sardonic voice told him. "I do believe your ship may be a bit banged up! Please don't run too hard, you might hurt yourself."

"Shit, shit, shit, *SHIT*," Jenna exclaimed as the hull lurched again, this time much less noticeably.

7

"What?!"

"Asshole painted us with an x-ray laser while we were busy listening to his transmission," she said bitterly. "Now the *aft* RFLAM is gone."

Jenna didn't wait to play the second transmission; she just threw it on when it arrived.

"In the name of the Blue Star Syndicate, I order you to heave to and be boarded," the voice ordered. "Continue running, and I will put a kinetic warhead through your bridge, and then collect your cargo and bodies from the debris field."

Rice shared a helpless look with Jenna and McLaughlin. If the Blue Star Syndicate boarded the ship, he was dead. If they blew out the *Jay*'s bridge, he was dead.

Now Captain David Rice *knew* he was going to die, and his crew with him.

The Ship's Mage took a deep breath and looked him in the eye.

"Not happening, sir," he said quietly. "Ready the ship for jump."

"You just jumped," Rice told him. "You can't jump for at *least* a few hours!"

Regulations said a Mage should jump every six hours. If you had a strong, brave, Mage, you could jump after three... once. They'd arrived at the final jump zone short of Sherwood barely twenty minutes before.

"I'm sorry David," Kenneth said quietly. "I won't let everyone on this ship die."

The camera to the simulacrum chamber cut out, and David turned back to look at the sensor board and the pirate ship closing. Then the indescribable sensation of teleportation took hold, and the whole bridge faded out.

When it slowly faded back in, the sensors were clear. They were a day's regular flight out of Sherwood Prime.

"Get the camera back," he ordered Jenna. "Kenneth, answer me dammit!" he snapped.

The monitor flipped back on, and Rice swallowed hard. The simulacrum chamber was at the center of the ship. It had no gravity, only the small model that was always, somehow, at the exact direct center of the ship it was a copy of.

One of Kenneth's hands was caught in the model. The rest of him had started to float away when his eyeballs had exploded out of his head.

The *Blue Jay*'s only Ship's Mage, the youngest son of the Mage-Governor of the planet they'd just arrived at, was very, very dead.

#

8

Damien woke up to bright lights and white walls, blinking as he slowly realized that he could breathe and wasn't in pain, both facts a minor surprise after having a human-mountain hybrid try to choke him to death.

He managed to make it about a quarter of the way into a sitting position before a nurse realized what he was doing, arriving in time to stop him from collapsing back onto the clinic bed he was occupying.

As the brunette clad in light blue scrubs helped him upright, he glanced around a room that any citizen of a Protectorate world would recognize. The Charter defined a minimum standard of health care as a human right for governments to provide, and Olympus Mons helped meet that standard by providing funding and a standard pre-fabricated clinic-in-a-box with a certain set of diagnostic and medical tools.

"Hold still," the nurse ordered once she had Damien upright. This was followed by a series of scanners, pokes and prods. Apparently finished, she grunted and disappeared out of the clinic room with a sharp "Stay here."

Still dizzy, Damien thought that might have been the most useless instruction ever. The room slowly stopped spinning while he waited, but the nurse eventually returned with three other people.

Behind the others was the spacer from the *Gentle Rains of Summer*. In front was an iron-haired gentleman in a white lab coat reading over a datapad the nurse had passed him as they entered the room. In between was a tall redheaded woman in the dark blue uniform of Sherwood System Security.

"I am Doctor Anderson," the man introduced himself. "This young lady is nurse Kosta – remember to thank her on your way out."

"You are lucky to be alive, young man," the doctor continued, setting the datapad down next to Damien's bed. "Your trachea was damaged and several of your ribs were cracked. The dizziness will fade, though you will be very tired for a day or two – a normal side effect of the bone-mending process."

The doctor asked him a few questions, ran a more complex scanner the nurse hadn't used over him, and nodded in satisfaction.

"We'll keep you in tonight for observation, but you'll be free to go in the morning," Anderson told Damien. "If there's anything that needs to be taken care of at your home – pets to feed or a girlfriend to let know - let Kosta know and we'll get it taken care of."

"Neither," Damien told him, coughing to clear his throat after he spoke. "Thank you."

"Now, Kosta and I will leave you with Captain Harrison," the doctor continued. He turned to the SSS officer. "You have fifteen minutes," he said sternly, "and then I am kicking you out of my clinic, clear?"

"Perfectly, Doctor. Thank you," the Security officer said calmly.

The doctor shuffled out, and Captain Harrison pulled two chairs up beside Damien's bed, gesturing for the spacer to sit.

"I kept Mr. Casey here around as I figured you'd want to thank the man who saved your life," she said quietly. "Brian Kendall – the thug who worked you over – is known to System Security. Given the number you'd done on him, he was going to kill you. Mr. Casey's intervention prevented that, and his witness statement is going to put him behind bars for a very long time... after the doctors finish fixing his knee. That was you, I presume?"

Damien nodded. "I... didn't think he would keep coming after that," he admitted. "I was trying to calm things down."

"With most thugs, that'll work," Casey told him with a small smile. "But that Kendall... 'e seemed a piece of work."

"Thank you," Damien told the spacer. "I'm not even sure why you were there, but Captain Harrison is right – he was going to kill me."

Casey slipped a small paper envelope from his jacket onto the table by Damien. "The Cap'n wanted to give you a little something for your help with the ward," he told him. "'e sent me after you to hand it over. I, um," he gave a sideways glance at the Security Captain, "pinged your PC for your location... and hurried when I saw where you were."

Harrison was studiously looking at Damien's medical monitor, pretending she hadn't heard the spacer confess to a minor crime. Personal Computers were keyed to a user and contained all of their personal information – accessing one without permission was considered a form of personal assault.

After a moment, the Captain turned her eyes back to Damien and tapped her own PC.

"I need you to give me a recorded witness statement," she told him. "After that, I shouldn't need to call you in for anything, but we'll hold onto your contact information in case. Is that acceptable?"

Damien nodded, and Harrison pressed a button on the computer. "All right, let's get started."

#

It didn't take very long for Damien to give as complete a description as he remembered of the incident. Some of his memories were clouded from being choked into unconsciousness, but at least the start of the encounter was clear.

"One last question for the record," Harrison finally told him. "How many spells do you know that would have killed Kendall?"

Damien blinked, confused. "Sorry?"

"I'm aware of at least some of the spells taught in the self-defense portion of the Practical Thaumaturgy curriculum," she said. "Your response was non-lethal, but you were capable of a lethal response – correct?"

Damien thought about it. He'd learned self-defense spells around various forms of energy manipulation – heat, cold, electricity. Even the straight force spell he'd used could have been more deadly if directed at, say, Kendall's neck.

"At least five," he finally answered quietly. "At most basic, a fire spell would have inflicted significant third degree burns if not killed him."

"Thank you," Harrison said, turning off her PC. "That will be sufficient for the courts I think." She was shaking her head slightly.

"What?" he asked.

"I think you are the first Mage I've ever met to default to a non-lethal level of force when threatened," she told him. "Most Mages go straight for fire or lightning – we spend a good part of the training for the System Security Mages teaching them to use a targeted level of force."

"I thought I could scare them off," Damien admitted. "I was wrong."

"That wasn't your mistake," Harrison told him. "Your mistake was not escalating as soon as you realized you couldn't. Training can fix that – have you ever considered joining the SSS?"

"I'm trained to be a Jump Mage," Damien answered. "That's what I'm going to be – as soon as I find a ship."

The Security Captain looked like she had swallowed something sour.

"Every Mage wants to Jump," she told him. "There are what, ten thousand Mages in Sherwood? Out of two billion people – ten thousand Mages. Everyone, from System Security to the Ship-wrights, to the damned *power company,* needs Mages. They're desperate for anyone who can cast a spell – and you are sitting up on this station, doing *nothing,* complaining that you can't find a place on a starship?"

Damien touched the collar he wore – the product of years of study and training so that he could Jump. Getting into Jump training wasn't easy, for the exact reasons that Harrison had just thrown at him.

"I earned the right to Jump," he told the cop. "You'll excuse me if I don't give up on that just yet."

Harrison took a deep breath. "I'm sorry," she told him. "It's frustrating trying to recruit Mages, and watching there be not enough

11

Mages for anything *except* Jumping – and too many Jump Mages. Just… keep it in mind, hey? You'd make a better cop than most."

"I'll think about it," Damien told her. He even might, if he went long enough without finding work on a starship.

#

It took six hours to get any of the *Blue Jay*'s massive fusion engines working after they'd jumped into Sherwood. Rice had made his way along the ship's zero-gravity core after the first hour to help out – without engines they were dead in space and unlikely to even show up on sensors so anyone knew they were in trouble.

Finally, the Captain was shoulders deep in a maintenance box re-connecting wires when he heard the ship's engineer shout, "That looks like it, Skipper. Get clear, I'm going to open up the hydrogen feeds."

David pulled himself free of the open panel and glanced up at the even blacker than usual face of his senior engineer, James Kellers. "Go for it," he told the man.

"Everyone clear?" the engineer asked loudly. Both of the two assistant engineers responded in the affirmative, and the wiry black man threw a toggle on the datapad he was carrying. The engine room was on the aft end of the gravity-less main core, so they all felt it when the engines kicked. The room had a sudden, very faint, sensation of down.

"Well?" David asked.

"It's not much," Kellers admitted. "We've got the thrusters back at about fifty percent, but the main engines are shot to hell. Call it… two percent of a gee."

"It'll get us inbound – and make it so the Fleet can detect us," David told him.

"And if they do, you should be on the bridge, not immersed in the *Jay*'s guts," Kellers replied. "We can take it from here boss."

Rice looked down at his hands, which were covered in ash from the burnt out conduits he'd been helping replace. It had been years since he'd worked Kellers' job, but he hadn't forgotten which way the circuits went in. He knew from when he'd done that job, though, how filthy his face was after crawling into a burnt out maintenance panel.

"I don't know, looking like this might get help from the Martian boys faster," Rice observed, but he was carefully making his way up the engine room against the very slight pressure of the ship's acceleration.

For once, he'd welcome 'the Martian Boys' – the Royal Navy of the Mage-King of Mars, more commonly simply the Protectorate Navy – showing up.

Given that any Navy ship would have to at least wait until the light-speed signature of the Jay's engine reached them though, he probably even had time for a shower.

"Captain to the bridge," Jenna's voice echoed over the intercom. "Captain Rice to the bridge, ASAP."

With a sigh, David increased his pace up the core.

#

Jenna had somehow managed to get the main view screen for the communicator online, and it was showing an impeccably turned out officer aboard the disgustingly neat bridge of a Navy warship.

"This is Mage-Captain Adrian Corr of His Majesty's destroyer *Guardian of Honor*," the dark-haired man in the dark blue uniform told David as he entered the room and faced the concealed camera over the viewscreen. "You are Captain Rice of the *Blue Jay*?"

"I am," David replied. "I have to say, I'm glad to see you boys so far out."

He counted in the back of his head until the Mage-Captain responded. He made it to four seconds – the destroyer was still two full light-seconds away. Close in interplanetary terms, but still quite a distance away.

"We were doing an outer-system scan as an exercise and one of my officers identified your jump flare," Corr said in his neatly precise tones. The blonde hair, with the slightly angled eyes and the soft accent marked the Mage as a Martian, one of the *old* Mage families. "When she did not see an engine signature, she recommended we investigate. My apologies for the delay, Captain – my first officer believed that even an in-system jump was my decision, not his."

"As you can see, Mage-Captain, the *Blue Jay* is in no state for me to be complaining about any help present."

"Of course," Corr nodded. "My apologies again - are you in need of medical assistance?"

"We have no significant injuries," David told him. "Only minor injuries and one fatality."

"What happened?" the Mage-Captain asked.

"A pirate ship jumped us at our last jump lay-over," Rice answered. "Disabled our defensive turrets, and was preparing to fire into us when our Ship's Mage jumped us."

The Navy Officer's wince, four seconds later, was small but noticeable. "Early," he said. It wasn't a question.

"We will take your ship under tow when we arrive," Corr informed Rice. "I will pass your report on to System Command. We will investigate this pirate."

13

David nodded his agreement. "Thank you," he said quietly.

"We serve the Mage-King of Mars," the Martian Noble told him. "What does his Protectorate mean if we do not protect people?"

#

The *Guardian of Honor* was unable to tow the *Blue Jay* much faster than the battered freighter could move on her own power. While the destroyer's engines were both more powerful than the freighter's and fully intact, the navy ship had done a full sensor sweep of the freighter – and Mage-Captain Corr judged her only capable of surviving about a quarter-gravity of acceleration.

At that much reduced rate, it took the destroyer several days to haul the ship into something resembling real-time communication range of Sherwood. David spent most of the trip on the bridge, watching the battered thermal scanners carefully for any sign of trouble. A million-ton warship was a lot of reassurance, but after watching pirates try to blow his ship away, he figured he was allowed some paranoia.

He'd sent Jenna to get some rest earlier, which meant he was the only one on the bridge when the *Blue Jay* received the first of the two transmissions he was dreading.

The transmission was a video signal, carrying the image of an expensively dressed dark-haired woman with the kind of perfectly imperfect prettiness that spoke of either natural beauty or *truly* expensive cosmetic surgery.

"Office of the Sherwood Governor," the woman announced herself. "Please connect me to Kenneth McLaughlin."

It was phrased as a request, but the tone made it very clear that the woman expected to be obeyed instantly.

"I'm sorry miss, I can't do that," David told her with weariness tingeing his voice that had nothing to do with having been conscious for over twenty hours.

A few moments later, he could tell when his response arrived. The woman blinked, clearly surprised by his response. "And why not?" she demanded sharply.

"Kenneth McLaughlin is dead," the freighter captain told her simply.

This time, he could time the light-speed lag to the microsecond. As soon as his words arrived, the haughtiness took a full-on body blow, and the woman's lips tightened until they were almost white. It took her a few seconds to even minimally re-compose herself.

14

"Hold for the Mage-Governor," she instructed sharply before the screen threw up the eagle and bagpipes of the Sherwood planetary crest.

David waited out the crest patiently. They were slowly decelerating towards the massive station in orbit around Sherwood. Even with the *Guardian of Honor*'s tow, the *Blue Jay* wouldn't dock for another five hours at their current pace. There was no rush.

Finally, the crest cleared to show a man that David had only met once before, though he'd seen the face on dozens of newscasts.

Miles James McLaughlin, patriarch of his clan and seven times elected Mage-Governor of Sherwood, was a tall, steel-haired man with cold blue eyes. He wore a plain black suit, but pinned to the breast pocket of the jacket was a small red ribbon with a golden planet hanging on the end – the Mars Valor Award, given to a much younger Mage-Commander McLaughlin after single-handedly ending one of the nastier anti-pirate campaigns in recent history.

"Where is my son?" he demanded.

"In the morgue of the destroyer *Guardian of Honor*," David told him quietly. "We didn't have the facilities to properly preserve his body." Or the spare manpower to clean up the awful mess Kenneth had left of himself, but the medical team the *Guardian* had sent over had taken care of that too.

"What the hell did you do?" McLaughlin snarled. "I sent my son with you so he'd stay *safe*, not so you'd get him killed!"

"Kenneth saved our lives," David told him. "We were ambushed by pirates – he jumped early, saving everyone else aboard."

"Pirates don't find ships at random anymore. What the hell are you involved in Rice?" the Mage-Governor demanded.

"Your son died a hero," the captain repeated, his voice even quieter. "I have no idea how the pirates found us."

"Heroes happen when other people fuck up," the McLaughlin said sharply. "You won't be dragging any more children of Sherwood into your disaster, Rice. Get out of my system."

The connection terminated, and Rice stared at the screen wordlessly, glad none of his crew had been on the bridge. Getting out of Sherwood wasn't an option, not with no Mage and the damage the *Blue Jay* had taken. Staying in the McLaughlin's system after he'd told you to get out wasn't wise, though.

Before he could begin to come up with a plan the communicator announced the second call he'd been expecting – this one from his insurance company.

With a sigh, he opened the channel.

#

The medallion of a Mage opened a lot of doors – even for an unemployed Mage like Damien. When he'd heard that a new freighter was coming in, he'd made his way down to Sherwood Prime's zero-gravity hub. His medallion had earned him a respectful nod from a security guard as he entered an observation lounge he'd normally be barred from.

There was a neatly marked and signed line between the zero-gravity hub and the luxury lounge. The signs warned Damien, so he was ready when his feet dropped sharply towards the ground when he crossed over the rune-inlaid carpet. Like so much else, artificial gravity could be created with magic, but runes like those woven into the carpet required recharging by a Mage at least once a week. Only warships, with their multiple Mage crews, would expend the resources to have gravity throughout the ship.

Damien reveled in the experience of full gravity for a moment as he made his way to the massive windows. Even the rotating rings only maintained about seven-tenths of a gravity, but this lounge was spelled to Sherwood's nine-tenths. Weirdly, the slightly heavier weight he was bearing was... relaxing.

The lounge was quiet at this time, roughly midnight by the station's clocks, which was likely part of why the gold medallion at the base of his throat had been enough to get him into the lounge unquestioned. Lounges like this were the only ones in the hub with tables and chairs, and he settled into one by the windows.

The windows were impressive. Normally, an 'observation lounge,' even on the hub, was just a set of viewscreens, but the Angelus Gravity Lounge had managed to get itself a place right on the edge of the station's hull – and right above the main docking arms. The owners had then paid an astronomical sum of money to magically transform the complex ceramic and metal composite of said hull to be transparent.

Damien ordered a small coffee from the cute but tired waitress and settled in. From here, he could see the *Gentle Rains of Summer* at a far docking arm, having cargo containers slowly maneuvered into locking positions on the massive ship's keel. Closer, a fast passenger liner, its sleek lines suggesting that it, like the Angelus Lounge, had magical gravity, rested at another docking arm.

Eight of the slender docks were visible from the cafe, half of the civilian docking arms on the Station. The other eight were on the other side of the hub of Sherwood Prime's ever-rotating wheel. Of those sixteen docks, four were full. Sherwood wasn't one of the Core systems around Sol and Mars, but it was a hub of interstellar trade by Midworlds standards, let alone the Fringe further out.

The distinctive star-white flare of an antimatter engine took Damien's attention entirely away from the incredibly good coffee the waitress delivered. No civilian ship used an antimatter torch, and the young Mage stretched his eyes for what he knew had to be out there.

The Protectorate destroyer swum out of Sherwood's corona like a swimmer from the surf, carefully short bursts from its rockets slowing it as it guided its charge home. An even pyramid, one hundred meters on a side, at this distance its hull was a smooth white, the weapons it bristled with invisible.

He was so shocked by his first sight of one the famous Martian ships that he almost missed what the ship was doing. Massive cables, only visible by the occasional glint of sunlight on them, linked the destroyer to a long and rounded container ship. Like the *Gentle Rains of Summer*, this ship had a long solid keel with four rotating ribs arrayed around the keel and cargo like an old egg-beater.

The ship was about a third of the size of the *Gentle Rains*, and even from several hundred meters distance, Damien could see someone had worked the freighter over hard. Scorch marks marred an already dirty gray hull, with the engine so battered the Mage wasn't surprised that the ship had needed a tow.

From the looks of it, the freighter might *need* a Mage but, sadly, he didn't think they were going to be hiring one anytime soon.

Wondering both at the sharp lines of the destroyer and the battered curves of the freighter, Damien sipped his coffee and watched the *Blue Jay* arrive at Sherwood.

#

A full day after finally easing the *Blue Jay* into the docking arms at Sherwood Prime David Rice found himself walking the ship with the insurance agent, a thin man in a cheap gray suit. The agent said very little as they walked the docking arm, viewing the exterior damage from the windows. He occasionally took a picture with his PC, and spent much of his time making notes on a keyboard only visible to him.

When they reached the entrance to the *Blue Jay* so they could survey the internal damage, they were interrupted by the agent's PC buzzing,

"Excuse me, Captain Rice," the man told David before stepping aside to answer the call. Only the occasional small exclamation was audible of the conversation, but when the man returned, his closed exterior was replaced with a wicked grin that belonged on a prank-pulling schoolboy, not an insurance agent of a company notorious for nickel and diming every claim they ever received.

17

"I'm pleased to inform you, Captain Rice, that my superiors have confirmed that the damage to your ship is covered under the piracy clause in your contract," the agent told Rice. "As such, only half the usual deductible will apply as the damage is entirely beyond your control."

"I thought that was what you were here to assess?" Rice asked, and the agent shook his head.

"I'm assessing the value of the damage," the agent told him. "I have no authority on my own to confirm or deny your claim – the branch head retains direct control over all claims related to starship damages."

"Ah," Rice observed. "So if I may ask, what is the joke I'm missing?"

The agent's smile faded slightly, but not completely. "Off the record, my manager is the worst I've ever met for rejecting claims on any grounds," he admitted quietly. "But Mage-Captain Corr called the office and let us know that he and his crew would be perfectly willing to supply their professional analysis of your telemetry data if there was need to support the piracy claim – and then reminded him that the *Guardian of Honor* is slated to be on-station for the next *two years*, so they couldn't even push it off until the ship left. It feels good to watch that tightwad get stuck in a corner."

"I see," Rice agreed, understanding at least part of the other man's thoroughly unprofessional glee, and grateful for the Martian officer's assistance. Without Mage-Captain Corr leaning on the insurance, it would have taken longer to get the claim cleared, and if they'd managed to declare it an accident, it would have doubled how much of the repairs he had to pay for – a difference that would almost have bankrupted him.

"Shall we go see how much we have to fix then?" he asked the agent, gesturing back towards the ship.

#

The rest of the tour with the agent was much more pleasant than the exterior tour had been, as if the certain knowledge that he wasn't going to be forced to screw the ship's crew took a large weight off the man's shoulders.

David was finally relaxed for the first time in days when he settled in at his desk to call the Ship's Mages Guild to post for a new Ship's Mage. The video screen on his desk showed the gold icon of the Guild, the same three stars that every Jump Mage wore carved onto the medallion at their throat and the Guild's Latin motto: "*Per Magica Ad Astra*" – "Through Magic The Stars."

The young woman who answered the call did not wear any such medallion – no one would waste a Mage on reception and booking duty. She did wear a fetching skirt and blouse combination in green and white that accented her black hair in a manner that reminded David it had been two years since his divorce.

"Sherwood Ship's Mage's Guild, Melanie speaking, how may I help you?" she chirped cheerfully.

"Good afternoon Melanie," David greeted her calmly, refocusing his attention where it belonged. "I need to put up a posting for a Ship's Mage position."

Among its many roles and tasks, the Guild maintained the 'job board' on the System communication net. A ship's captain could be fined for posting a Ship's Mage role on a more general classified board, and none of the Jump-qualified Magi in a system would be looking for jobs anywhere else.

"Of course!" Melanie told him. "That will only take a few minutes. Do you have an account with the Sherwood office?"

Of all the wonders that magic had given humanity, one that the Magi hadn't managed to pull off was any type of large-scale interstellar communications. A few facilities, massive monstrosities of runes and power, allowed a Mage to transmit their voice to a specially built, equally massive, receiver, but data transmission of any kind was impossible. It wouldn't matter if David had accounts with every other Guild Office in the Protectorate, he would need an account for Sherwood.

"I do," he told the girl. He'd hired Kenneth in Sherwood, though that hadn't been through the Guild but through a favor to an acquaintance in the government. He reeled off the account number. "Captain David Rice, aboard the *Blue Jay*," he concluded.

Melanie cheerfully started inputting data into a computer below the edge of the screen, and then stopped in confusion.

"I'm sorry Captain," she said slowly. "I've never seen this before, but I have a note here that your ship is blacklisted and I can't authorize any job postings or hiring contracts."

The ground fell out from underneath David in a way the rapid rotation of the *Blue Jay*'s ribs to create gravity didn't explain.

"I can put you through to a manager and you can try and sort out what it would take to get you un-blacklisted?" she offered, still fully in 'help the customer' mode. The girl didn't realize what a system-wide hiring blackout meant to a man like David. The McLaughlin had just killed his ship.

"No," he said faintly. "I will contact them later. Thank you Melanie," he managed to squeeze out before cutting the connection, staring at the screen as it dropped back to an automatic rotation of the cameras around the docking bays, showing him the *Blue Jay* and the other ships in dock.

Miles James McLaughlin, it seemed, did not fuck around. When he'd said that David would drag no more of Sherwood's Mages into his affairs, the Mage-Governor had clearly leaned on the system's Guild to block him hiring any Mage in the system. Since David hadn't committed any of the acts – lack of payment, for example – that would normally result in being blacklisted, he knew it wasn't a Protectorate-wide blacklist. He could send a note on another ship to another system's Guild, hire a Ship's Mage sight unseen and ship them to Sherwood.

The risks and price tag of that option made him sick, and the shifting images on his screen weren't helping. He touched the screen, freezing the picture on a single camera, and then stopped in thought.

Off to the side of the camera view he was watching was the *Gentle Rains of Summer*. Four times the *Blue Jay*'s size and capacity, the ship likely had more than one Mage aboard, and Andrew Michaels was an old friend of David's.

Maybe they could work something out, at least to get the *Blue Jay* out of this ill-begotten system with its vengeful overlord.

#

With his rooms tucked away deep in the cheaper areas of Ring Seven, Damien didn't think that anyone knew where he was staying – he certainly hadn't *given* anyone the name of the cheap hotel or his room number, so when the buzzer for his door went off, he had a moment of panic.

Remembering after a second that he was paid up for a full week and it was unlikely to be the landlord, Damien opened his door. Waiting on him was the last person he expected: Grace McLaughlin, one of the two McLaughlin mages who'd beaten him out for the *Gentle Rains'* junior Ship's Mage slot… and his on-again, off-again lover from the Jump Mage program.

"Hi Damien," she greeted him with a mischievous grin. "Hurry up and invite me in, this is one *shitehole* of a neighborhood you've picked to slum in."

Damien was too surprised to do more than wordlessly step back and gesture her in. The petite redhead ducked under his gesturing arm and closed the door behind her, rapidly finding the room's sole ragged couch and perching on it, eyeing him like a cat with a favorite toy.

"You know, I know you're trying to save money, but would it kill you to have asked for a little help?" she asked him. "I don't know what you're paying, but I'm sure we could have found you somewhere nicer for about the same – the family *always* knows somebody."

"It doesn't work that way for most of us," Damien told her quietly. He'd spent a lot of time around the various McLaughlin scions of his age, and continued to wonder at their view of the world. They weren't *arrogant*, they were too driven to help and serve to be arrogant, but they knew that everyone on Sherwood would happily do them favors at the drop of a hat.

"It works that way for family," Grace told him, locking her gaze on him. "And you went to school with six of us *and* Granddad likes you – you practically *are* family."

Grace, as Damien had not found out until *after* he'd shared her bed, was the eldest daughter of the Governor's eldest son. She was the only adult in the entire *system* that would refer to the McLaughlin as 'Granddad.' Damien wasn't so sure the Governor liked him – he'd barely met the man after all.

"How did you even *find* me?" he asked finally. "It's not like I even told your Captain where I was staying."

"Casey," Grace answered simply. "First rule of being shipboard – the Bosun can *always* find out what they want to know. I asked her, she sent me to Casey, who apparently lifted your address from your PC while he was saving your life. An incident, I'll point out," she said sharply, "that you didn't mention to me, my sister, *or* my cousins."

As usual when dealing with Grace, Damien was starting to be overwhelmed. He was never sure why the woman had picked him to be her lover, though he would never have dreamed of complaining. She ran at roughly twice his speed on a good day.

"Everyone involved is spending a very long time as guests of System Security," Damien told her. "Beyond that, what was the point of telling anyone?"

Grace sighed loudly, and pushed Damien down onto the couch to hop into his lap, snuggling up against him in an *extremely* pleasant way.

"Because, you adorable dolt, we actually care and worry about you when we don't hear a peep for weeks?" she told him. "To hear *about* you getting beaten up from the spacers on my new ship on top of that is not my idea of a good day."

Damien hugged her back, not sure of what to say.

"I'm sorry about the *Gentle Rains*," she continued after a moment, her voice quieter. "I wasn't expecting Mom to call in favors quite that heavily. If it helps, she promised to make sure the next Captain heard about you first."

Arya McLaughlin was, as well as the daughter-in-law of the system governor, Head Administrator for Sherwood Prime. Her prodding ship captains about Damien couldn't hurt him, but he felt uncomfortable at the thought of strings getting pulled on his behalf.

Before he expressed that thought aloud, however, Grace laughed, and kissed him.

"You, of course, have an even greater portion of pure Sherwood Scot stubbornness than any of the family," she told him. "Which is a small, teensy, portion of why I'm spending my last night on the station here."

"You leave tomorrow?" Damien asked, surprised.

"Yeah, we ship out at eleven hundred hours station time," Grace told him. She sat up straight, remaining on his lap but creating some distance between them. "Which, given that I need to be on-ship two hours beforehand, means we only have about twelve hours. I'd better get business out of the way."

"What business?"

She slid a tiny data disk out of her cleavage and dropped it on the side table.

"That's from Captain Michaels," she told him. "It's the contact info for Captain David Rice on the *Blue Jay* – they're the ship that came in damaged from a pirate attack a couple of days ago. Trick is, they lost their Mage on the way in – but for whatever reason, the Sherwood Guild has blacklisted them. Rice can't post for a new Mage."

"You mean…" Damien said slowly.

"Rice asked the Captain if he knew anyone," Grace told him. "Then the Captain asked Kyle and me if we knew you – and I said I was trying to track you down since we were leaving, and he told me to tell you to contact Rice if you still wanted a Jump job."

For a long moment, Damien was silent, looking at the tiny disk on the table. Finally, he looked up at Grace.

"Thank you," he said quietly.

"You're welcome. Now, I believe I mentioned spending the night?" she continued with a familiar wicked grin.

#

Damien didn't get a lot of sleep that night, but when he did wake up, Grace was gone. He wasn't sure when she'd left, but by the time he woke up, it was only an hour short of when she'd said the *Gentle Rains of Summer* was due to leave. Running his hand down the slight indent her body had left in the cheap motel mattress, he realized he could still clean up and make it down to watch the freighter leave.

Making sure to grab the data disk Grace had left with him, he made his way down to the same observation deck he'd watched the

Blue Jay arrive from, slipping into the window table in the Angelus Gravity Lounge in time to see the last lines drop away from the big freighter.

The *Summer* was one of the biggest freighters the worlds of the Protectorate built, rated for twelve million tons of cargo and massing over twenty million tons fully loaded and fuelled. This close to the even greater mass of Sherwood Prime, the immense ship moved slowly, running on secondary ion thrusters to avoid damaging the station itself.

Her gravity ribs locked as she maneuvered out, so Damien could clearly make out the four flattened structures that contained crew quarters, and the hundreds of standard ten thousand cubic meter containers attached to the central keel's cargo spars.

Launching from the central, immobile, hub of the station forced the ship to build up her momentum entirely on her own. It took easily ten minutes before the minuscule thrust of the ion thrusters moved the *Summer* out of the station's safety zone and rotated her to face out-system. Once the ship was in position, the massive fusion rockets at the end of the central keel flared to life. The window between Damien and the rockets darkened noticeably to prevent the light of those miniature suns from injuring the patrons' eyes.

Watching the ship burn away from Sherwood, it finally sunk into Damien why Grace had been looking for him even before her Captain had asked her to. It would be months, even years, before the *Gentle Rains of Summer* returned to Sherwood. If Damien went on another ship, it was exceedingly unlikely that he would be in Sherwood when the ship returned. Last night had been the last time they were likely to see each other.

Damien pulled the data disk out with a sigh and eyed it. The PC on his wrist could read it and place a call. On the other hand, the *Blue Jay*'s dock was only ten minutes drift through the zero-gravity section of the station.

#

"David, there's a young Mage here to see you," Jenna told Captain Rice, sticking her head in the office just off the bridge. The bridge and his office, located on Rib Four, had only had gravity restored about two hours before, and David was trying to catch up on the paperwork his insurance agent was inflicting on him.

David suspected he'd never seen this much paperwork for insurance before because he'd never seen insurance work progress so quickly, but the agent was taking an almost gleeful pleasure in ramming through the *Blue Jay*'s repairs before his superior could find some way to argue against the sworn affidavits of the bridge crew of a Martian destroyer.

"A Mage?" he asked, to be sure he'd heard correctly. His best efforts to try to track down a Jump Mage without going through the Guild hadn't produce much more than vague promises, and his best hope of poaching a junior Mage from someone had just left port, Michaels assuring him that 'steps had been taken.'

"He says his name is Damien Montgomery – and that Captain Michaels sent him," his first officer advised, glancing at the small pile of authorizing data disks on Rice's desk. The stocky blonde flashed a bright smile at her Captain. "I'll send him in, shall I?"

"Any distraction from Mr. Clarke's mountain of helpful paperwork," Rice told her, agreeing with her implied glance. For that matter, David was willing to meet with *any* Jump-qualified Mage, even if they had three heads and only spoke Sanskrit.

The 'young Mage' that Jenna showed into his office a minute later, though, was barely more than a boy. Dark-haired, short and slim, he was probably older than he looked, but David would have placed him at maybe sixteen years old.

"Captain Rice, I'm Damien Montgomery," the youth introduced himself calmly. Instead of the tie that David would have worn with the dark slacks and shirt combination he was wearing, Montgomery wore a black leather collar holding a gold medallion against the base of his throat. As the youth stood across from David, the Captain recognized the tiny three stars carved into the medallion that marked him as Jump-qualified.

"Have a seat Damien," Rice told him. "I'd ask if you were here about the Ship's Mage posting, but I'm afraid there is no posting."

"So I was told," Montgomery said quietly, settling into the proffered chair. "The Governor has blacklisted you. The Guild won't let you hire anyone." He paused, and shrugged. "I'll jump for you."

Rice regarded him levelly.

"As you said, the Guild has blacklisted us," he said carefully. "Our last Ship's Mage died jumping too early to get us away from a pirate attack. Jumping for us may be risky, and will definitely get you in trouble with the Guild. Why?"

The youth shrugged again. "I Jump-qualified in the same year as six children of the McLaughlin clan," he said quietly. "Their families have connections and wealth to buy favors. My father was a baker, and died several years ago."

Rice nodded slowly. "What you're saying, Mage Montgomery, is that we are both desperate?"

"Exactly."

The Captain eyed the young man across the desk for a long moment. To qualify as a Jump-Mage, a Mage had to have made at least twenty supervised Jumps, but he suspected that those jumps were the only time Damien had ever cast the spell. He hesitated to put his life – and his crew's lives – into the hands of a youth with no experience.

"Are you prepared to have me review your Jump calculations?" he asked bluntly. Normally, a Jump Mage's work was extremely private, with no oversight except maybe a more senior Mage. After thirty years on merchant ships, though, David knew enough to at least tell if the calculations were wrong.

Damien paused again; then nodded. "I think that might even make me more comfortable," the young man admitted, looking sixteen again for a moment.

"Fine. You're hired," Rice told him. "Jenna will find you a bunk – we only just got our Ribs rotating for gravity, so you may have to lend a hand cleaning up around the ship if that's all right?"

"There is a lot I can do to help 'clean up,' I suspect," Montgomery told him. "If nothing else, I will need to review the rune matrix before we jump. From what I saw of the damage, I want to be sure it wasn't compromised."

That wasn't a thought that had occurred to David yet, and he shivered at the potential danger. Hopefully the young Mage in front of him knew his job. At best, a compromised rune matrix wouldn't work. At worst… it would scatter the ship in pieces across the full length of the jump.

"What about registering your employment with the Guild?" David finally asked: another unpleasant thought.

"I… would prefer to do that in a system not Sherwood," Damien suggested, and the Captain laughed.

"I think we can both agree to that."

#

Damien took a long, slow look around the tiny room he'd been living in for the last two months. It had never been much of a room, though Grace had managed to add some pleasant memories to the space before vanishing out of both the room and his life.

When he'd left the surface, he'd sold or given away anything large or heavy he'd owned, so it had taken him under ten minutes to pack a single mid-sized bag with all of his worldly belongings. Now, the room was sparse and empty, merely awaiting a simple transmission to the landlord to deliver his last payment and cancel his access code.

Once he left this room, it was done – he was leaving Sherwood, and unlikely to return. Even if he switched ships later on, the

McLaughlin was unlikely to forget that Damien had defied his black-listing of the *Blue Jay* and returning to Sherwood would be unwise.

From the moment he'd tested positive for Mage Gift and his life had changed forever, Damien had known he wanted to be a Jump Mage. He'd failed the entrance exams for the Protectorate Navy – by the skin of his teeth, in a year when no Mage on Sherwood *had* passed the exams – which meant the merchant ships were the only way to Jump.

His family had passed on before he graduated with his degree. Grace had left aboard the *Gentle Rains of Summer*. Nothing held him to Sherwood, but he still hesitated for a moment.

But it was only a moment. He sent the transmission to the landlord, shouldered his bag, and headed for the *Blue Jay*.

#

Jenna was waiting for Damien when he reached the transfer tube onto the *Blue Jay*, a zero-gravity transfer cart waiting by her. She glanced at his single bag and arched an eyebrow at him.

"I brought the cart to help carry your stuff, but I see that wasn't necessary. Light packer?" she asked.

"I lived alone, I didn't have or need much," Damien admitted. "Anything specific I should make sure to have?"

"Not really," the heavy-set officer told him. "Food and such are included in your pay. Grab the cart, let's get aboard."

Damien grabbed onto the cart and pushed it forward, keeping a hand on it as it drifted through the zero-gravity boarding dock. Not much more than a metal tray with clips for keepings objects attached to it, the cart was useful to keeping things from drifting away while moving through zero-gravity zones such as the central hub of Sherwood Prime, and the transfer tube that linked it to the keel of the *Blue Jay*.

"The *Blue Jay* is a *Venice* class freighter," Jenna told him as she kicked off into the tube. "We're rated for three megatons of cargo – three hundred standard ten thousand cubic meter cargo containers at their max mass."

"To carry that, she's almost a full kilometer long, with four rotating gravity ribs. With a crew of eighty-five, we have quite a bit of cubage to give people living space." She paused as they entered the main lock and gestured to a storage rack on the side of the plain room. "Since you've just the one bag, stow the cart there."

Damien obeyed, carefully propping himself as he slung the bag back over his own shoulder.

"Through here is the rear access point for the ribs," Jenna continued, launching skillfully and catching the handle by the open door out of the loading zone. The room beyond the door held four 'elevators' that would spin up to match the ribs, and then slide into tubes heading out to the edge of the ship.

"Your cabin is on Rib Three," she told him, "the same cabin as the last Ship's Mage."

"Don't worry," she said after a pause, "we already sent all of his stuff onto his family."

"What happened to him?" Damien asked, following her into one of the elevators

"We were jumped by pirates," Jenna told him grimly as she carefully oriented herself feet-first towards the outside of the ship before hitting the button to start the tiny cab rotating around the ship. "Kenneth jumped us before he should have and burnt himself out."

Damien wasn't sure if the bottom fell out of his stomach due to the memory of the lectures he'd had on over-exerting his magic, with attendant pictures of the results, or the sudden acceleration induced shift in apparent gravity.

"Are pirates common?" he asked slowly, holding onto the safety railing and determinedly ignoring his inner ear's confusion.

"In the Fringe and the UnArcana Worlds where the Navy is sparse, they can be," she said quietly. "But normally a major Midworlds system like Sherwood is so safe as to be boring."

The sensation of gravity changed again as the elevator stopped accelerating sideways and Damien's stomach lurched as the pod shot outwards towards the rib.

When it finally came to an apparent halt, there was a comfortable sense of about half a gravity of centrifugal force, and Damien breathed a sigh of relief.

"The elevators take some getting used to," Jenna told him with a grin. "But you *do* get used to them."

She led the way out of the elevator, pointing out the stairs leading 'down' towards the outside of the ship. "Each rib is arranged in four decks," she explained. "The outermost deck is storage, systems, and radiation shielding. Quarters are on the inner two decks, and working spaces on deck three. Follow me; I'll take you to your cabin."

Damien's cabin, it turned out, was on Deck One of Rib Three – the innermost deck.

"The ribs are about two-thirds the length of the overall hull," Jenna told him as she led him along the corridor. "Even after curvature, shielding, and the rotation motors, there's about five hundred meters of usable length on each one, so we have no shortage of space. There's a saying in the merchant fleet – 'cubage is cheap, mass is expensive.'"

She gestured at the doors they were passing. "We have individual cabins for one hundred and sixty people, almost twice our crew, but crew are restricted to less than one hundred kilos of personal possessions."

"Do we ever carry passengers?" Damien asked.

"Sometimes," she confirmed. "We keep Rib Four's cabins empty for just that purpose, actually. I'd say we have passengers maybe a quarter of the time – we're no luxury cruise liner though."

She palmed the scanner by one of the cabins and the door slid open. "Put your palm on the scanner," she ordered, and Damien obeyed. After a moment, the device beeped at him.

"It's now keyed to you," Jenna told him. "The captain or I can override it if we have cause, but no one else can enter your rooms."

Damien almost missed the plural until he stepped into the cabin. The room was bigger than the space he'd rented on Sherwood Prime, though it only contained a single, extremely lightweight, couch, an entertainment screen, and a desk.

"Bedroom to the right, bathroom straight ahead," Jenna told him. "You can pick up some furnishings on the station if you want, but, like I said, one hundred kilos max. The Captain and I have the same restriction – mass is expensive," she concluded with a grin.

"Thank you," Damien told her, looking around the living room with a small degree of shock. "Are all the cabins like this?" he finally asked.

"This is an officer's cabin," she admitted. "The crew cabins are only a single room and the workspace requires you to sit on the bed, but they still have the couch and entertainment screens. *Blue Jay*'s first owners outfitted her for the long runs in the Fringe – it makes sense to keep the crew in style if you're in the boonies for months at a time."

The Mage nodded, dropping his single bag – *much* less than a hundred kilos – on the bench, and looking around for a moment.

"Where is the simulacrum chamber?" he finally asked, figuring getting to work was probably a good idea.

Jenna laughed. "You've been on the ship less than ten minutes, and we aren't leaving port for at least three days," she told him. "In any case, I have to get back to the bridge for a conference call with the repair company and our insurance agent. How about you get unpacked and grab a bite to eat, and I'll give you the grand tour at eighteen hundred hours?"

Damien looked around the somewhat excessive cabin and at his tiny bag. Unpacking wouldn't take him long, but he could probably order some useful items through the communications net for delivery if he had three days.

"Call it a plan," he agreed.

Damien took about forty minutes to unpack his few belongings and lock them away in the drawers set into the wall of his bedroom next to the lightweight bedframe. The bedroom shared the front room's lack of any major pieces of furniture, containing only the bedframe and two sets of shelves set into the wall. A handful of the drawers contained the multi-point clips that substituted for hangars when you were traveling in zero-gravity, so he placed his two dress jackets and the eight half-necked dress shirts that were formal wear for mages in them to keep them un-wrinkled.

Fully unpacked, he found himself with over an hour before he was supposed to meet Jenna for the tour of the ship, so he pulled up a map of the ship on the screen in his sitting room and began to study it.

His stomach allowed him long enough to locate the mess hall on Rib Four before loudly growling at him, and he realized he hadn't eaten since before Grace had arrived at his hotel. With a grin at his own forgetfulness, he took mental note of the location of the mess and headed out into the ship's halls.

The half-gravity that *Blue Jay* maintained wasn't much lighter than the inner area of Ring Seven where he'd been staying and the layout of the Rib was straightforward – each floor had a single corridor down the center, and the mess hall spread from one side of the hull to the other at the end of that corridor on Deck Two.

There was no one in the mess hall when Damien entered it, giving him a minute to take in the plain, lightweight table bolted to the floor, and the similarly lightweight magnetized chairs. One of four mess halls on the ship, this one had enough tables and chairs for sixty people – half again the number Jenna said would live on a rib, and almost three-quarters of the crew.

There was a kitchen, set up to function in gravity but be easily secured for zero-gravity, and a number of reasonably high quality food prep units. They were glorified vending machines, but they happily spat out a sandwich and a cup of coffee for Damien with only a little coaxing.

He was half-finished his sandwich when someone else wandered into the mess. A bulky, dark-skinned man with a black turban wrapped around his head, the newcomer flashed bright white teeth at the sight of the gold medallion on Damien's throat.

"So! The Captain did find us a Mage!" the stranger boomed, stepping over to Damien and offering his hand. "I am Narveer Singh, First Pilot aboard the *Blue Jay*. May I join you?"

Damien shook the big man's hand and gestured to the several empty seats at the table he'd taken.

"Feel free," he agreed. "I'm Damien Montgomery – the new Ship's Mage, as you guessed."

"The Captain, he is a lucky man!" Singh boomed as he conjured a stew-like dish from the food prep units. "Rumor I heard was that the Governor blacklisted us!"

"I had my reasons to ignore that," Damien told him. "I also never officially heard about it, so I don't think it counts as breaking it."

Singh boomed laughter, echoing off the previously sterile and silent walls of the mess.

"I like your style, Montgomery!" He told the young Mage. "It isn't disobedience if you didn't hear the order – 'communications failures' are good for that in shuttles!"

Damien was about to ask about the 'First Pilot's role when the ships public address system clicked on with a slightly noticeable, almost definitely artificial, buzz.

"Now hear this, now hear this," Jenna's voice rang clearly throughout the ship. "We have confirmed loading times with Sherwood Prime Docking and will have a twelve hour loading shift commencing at oh-nine hundred OMT. Please secure all items for zero-gravity."

"I repeat: we will have twelve hours of zero-rotation in the ribs starting at oh-nine-hundred Olympus Mons Time tomorrow. That is all."

Singh pumped his fist exuberantly. "Brilliant!"

"What is?" Damien asked, thinking through the announcement. It made sense, though he'd never thought about it, that they'd have to stop rotating the ribs to load the cargo. The *Blue Jay*'s ribs were two hundred meters out from the ship's center, which meant they rotated around the ship three times every two minutes, preventing anyone from attaching cargo to the central keel.

"We have a cargo – with the black-listing, we might not have found one," the dark pilot explained. "The Captain, he is brilliant!" He paused, swallowing down some of his spiced stew. "I'll need to check on the shuttles," he continued after a moment. "We've been using them to help with repairs, but we'll need to get the beasts set up for cargo handling again."

With a shudder at the thought, Narveer Singh started inhaling his food so he could get started. Damien simply watched in amazement and nodded goodbye to the pilot as he left, charging towards the aft of the ships and the shuttle bays.

#

30

"And this is your working area of the ship," Jenna told Damien as she drifted up to a handhold near another hatch. They'd started their tour of the keel of the ship at Singh's shuttle bay at the rear end of the ship and worked their way down the central corridor of the keel in zero-gravity. "The last Ship Mage called it the ship's 'Sanctum.'"

Damien followed Jenna through the hatch and saw that the central corridor dog-legged ahead, around a chamber he knew would be exactly one-hundredth the length, height, and width of the *Blue Jay*'s exterior structure. Even if Jenna hadn't warned him what he was approaching, that dogleg would have suggested he was approaching the starship's simulacrum chamber.

Runes coated the outside of the chamber: swirling patterns of silver inlay that Damien knew cut through the wall and were visible from the inside as well. From here, they linked into other patterns that marked carefully calculated routes out to the outer hull of the *Blue Jay*.

"Your workshop is over here," Jenna continued, gliding neatly up to a side hatch leading off the dog-legged main corridor. "Watch your step," she warned, "Kenneth put in gravity runes, but they've been finicky since..." she trailed off.

"They likely haven't been charged recently enough," Damien told her as he joined her by the workshop door. "Runes like that need to be renewed weekly."

Jenna hit the panel to open the hatch, and it slid aside to reveal what Damien judged to be a relatively standard Mage's workshop – a Wonderland-esque cross between a research lab, a jewelry workshop, and a private office. On the far wall, a centrifugal casting unit occupied the center of a workbench, surrounded by soldering irons and etching tools.

Another wall held a desk with three massive work screens, touch-driven interfaces that were currently combining to show a pseudo-three-dimensional view of the space around Sherwood. The opposite wall held a spectrometer, a microscope, and a set of micro-scale manipulators – for the *really* fine rune work.

The floor plating was the same plain steel as the rest of the ship, but here someone – Kenneth, presumably, or possibly an even earlier Ship's Mage – had inlaid the silver pattern of runes that provided artificial gravity equivalent to the spinning ribs.

Even from outside the room, however, Damien could tell that the runes were almost uncharged, spitting out tiny bursts of gravity that would make the entire room a tripping hazard.

"Hold up a moment," he told Jenna, and focused. He needed to touch the runes without worrying about spinning off, so he oriented himself with the floor of the workshop and slowly created a gravity field underneath himself. He drifted downwards and then settled his feet onto the floor in a comfortable half-gravity before kneeling and removing the glove on his right hand.

As soon as the rune on his palm was within a few centimeters of the runes on the floor, both began to glow gently. Damien focused on that glow, and fed energy into the gravity runes. The glow rapidly spread out from his hand, and Jenna's gasp behind him suggested that it was bright enough the ship's first officer saw it.

After about fifteen seconds, the entire room's floor was glowing brightly to his eyes, and Damien closed his hand into a fist, cutting off the connection between his own power and the runes on the floor.

He rose to face Jenna, standing in his own personal field of gravity as he met the gaze of the officer floating in zero-gravity beside him. "It'll be safe to enter now," he told her. "It doesn't take much to maintain a room this small; it just has to be done regularly."

"You don't actually need to deal with zero-gee," she answered accusingly, reminding Damien of what he was doing.

He released the spell, though without motion he remained standing on the deck initially.

"Not really, no," he admitted. "We're taught not to show off magic though," he explained. "It tends to attract unfortunate attention."

"I can see that," Jenna agreed. "Is there anything you need to check in here?"

Damien took a glance around the workshop. All the equipment looked relatively standard. "Nothing that I can check quickly," he told her. "I'll need a few hours to get used to the gear and the setup before I do much of anything, but you said we have a few days?"

"We do," she confirmed. "Enough of the crew is living aboard that we need to rotate the ribs during the night, so we can only load for one of Sherwood Prime's twelve hour shifts each day. Even with all of their gear, it takes two full shifts to attach three hundred ten thousand ton containers to the keel."

"That'll give me time to review the gear, and go over the ship's rune matrix," Damien told her. He had never had a chance to inspect the rune matrix of a jump ship in detail before. He saw and identified power flows and purposes better than any other Mage he knew, but it still took time to examine as complex a spell as a jump matrix.

"Speaking of which," Jenna gestured carefully towards the simulacrum chamber. "The rest of your Sanctum awaits you."

Damien didn't wait for her to catch up with him once he'd kicked off, and touched the panel next to the hatch. It slid gently open, and he slipped into the only space from which he would be able to jump the ship.

The same runes that coated the room on the outside were visible on the interior as well, continuing up onto the roof and the floor and coating the room on all sides. The inlaid silver runes stood out against the thousands of tiny optical diodes around them that projected the image of the outside of the ship. Right now, Damien saw the docking arms and the base of the hub of Sherwood Prime, but beneath him fell away the black of space, and if he looked carefully up and to the side, Sherwood itself was visible past the bulk of the space station.

In the exact center of the room, unsupported yet utterly incapable of moving from that position, was the simulacrum. Forged by magic from molten silver when the ship was built, it exactly mirrored every part of the ship's exterior. The *Blue Jay*'s four ribs rotated around. Her forward radiation shield still showed the damage where the last repairs were being done. Damien drifted, unthinking, to the model – exactly one-thousandth the size of the ship itself, catching himself on the immobile engines. His hands on the simulacrum, he *felt* the ship, and with the screens around him, he saw what the *Blue Jay* saw.

"This place is always awe-inspiring to me," Jenna said quietly from the edge of the room, and Damien glanced up from the impossibly perfect model of the ship to look at her. "I don't understand *any* of how what you do works, but this room… this is the key to the stars."

"That was the Compact," Damien half-whispered, reveling in the power pulsing around him. "Peace between Mage and Mundane, between Mars and Earth… and in exchange, we gave you the stars."

#

"How's the firewood loading going?"

Captain David Rice turned around, carefully, in the bridge's zero-gravity to face his executive officer.

"I think the company paying for a million tons of premium hardwood would be… displeased if it was used as firewood," he observed drily. "Or were you referring to the forty-five containers of luxury furniture made from said hardwood?"

Jenna shrugged, grabbing a handhold and positioning herself to review the video screen Rice was watching. On it, the dozens of manipulator arms of a major docking station were carefully maneuvering the Protectorate's standard ten meter by twenty meter by fifty meter; ten thousand ton rated mass; cargo containers onto the *Blue Jay*'s keel.

"Did you follow up on the secondaries?" he asked her.

"Yep," she confirmed. "Corinthian is just major enough that people are shipping there, and just minor enough that no one has shipped out for two months."

There were dozens of cargos to be shipped between the worlds under the protection of the Mage-King of Mars, but few of them would justify filling even a three megaton freighter like the *Blue Jay*. The usual policy was to book a standard container, fill it with your cargo, and list it as a secondary cargo on a station like Sherwood Prime. As soon as Rice had the contract to ship a hundred and forty-five containers to Corinthian, he'd had Jenna put in a notice to Prime of which world they were shipping for.

All secondary shipping contracts to Corinthian would now be loaded onto the Jay, along with a massive data upload to be transferred to the other system's communications net. The data transfer fees alone were a hefty part of the freighter's operating costs, but it was the primary cargo contracts that paid the bills.

"How's our young Mage working out?"

"He seems dedicated and smart so far," Jenna told him. "I showed him around Kenneth's lab – he fixed the gravity in about two seconds flat. Last I saw, he was going over the runes in the simulacrum chamber with a magnifying glass."

"He thinks they may have been damaged?" Rice asked, remembering Damien's comment to that effect with a shiver.

"I don't *think* so," she replied. "From what he said, I think it's the first chance he's ever had to really examine a jump matrix, and he wants to make sure it all… 'flows right' was how he described it."

"Good," David let out a breath he hadn't realized he'd taken. "We'll have all of the rest of the repairs finished by the time the primary cargo is loaded. We'll hang out a day or so after that for any new secondaries, but then we need to get to Corinthian."

"That wood isn't exactly going to rot in our hull, skipper," his executive officer pointed out.

"No," David agreed, looking around the empty bridge carefully before continuing quietly. "But I don't think our pirate friends are deaf and dumb either, and I've got an itchy feeling between my shoulder blades. The sooner we're out of Sherwood, the happier I'll be!"

#

The Martian Runic script defines a spell matrix in the same way that a programming language defines the 0s and 1s that allow a computer to function. With seventy-six characters and fourteen different ways of connecting them, the script is complex and difficult to read – and the *Blue Jay*'s jump matrix contained the equivalent of sixteen million lines of code.

Damien read Martian Runic fluently, but he couldn't go over that many runes in detail with less than a month of solid reading. Unlike every other Mage he'd ever known, though, he didn't need to. He saw the flow of energy along the patterns and read the purpose and flow of entire blocks and sub-matrices at a single glance.

On a small matrix, like the 'warning spell' in Captain Michaels' office, he often read the entire structure of the spell, from its triggers to its actions, in a few seconds. Larger spells would take him some time, but it was minutes where another Mage would spend hours.

He'd never done it on a spell matrix as large as the *Blue Jay*'s jump matrix though, so when he hit the first utterly wrong sub-matrix he assumed he was misreading it.

The sub-matrix was at the core of the spell, one of the seventeen that linked into the simulacrum at the center of the ship. The other sixteen sub-matrices fed energy out from the simulacrum, but the seventeenth interfaced with the others and changed the energy flow somehow. On certain criteria, it redirected energy away from the main matrix.

Damien spent an hour reading the runes on the sub-matrix, and then took another long, hard look at the energy flows. Sub-matrix clusters came in primes and squares, so it was theoretically possible that the seventeenth sub-matrix was unnecessary, but it made no sense. Shaking his head, he made a note on the matrix diagram he'd inherited from the ship-mages before him. It was the only current notation on the file, all the previous notes were 'sub-matrix in this location damaged by crate impact, repaired' or similar minor fixes.

Still confused, he moved on, following the rune matrix forward towards the prow of the ship.

#

At the front of the ship, where the lengthy connecting sub-matrix expanded into the runes that covered the inside of the immense radiation shield, he found another 'wrong' sub-matrix. Four of the sub-matrices made sense, channeling the power of the jump spell out into space, but a fifth, again interfacing with the other four, siphoned off energy if criteria were met. The criteria didn't make sense to Damien, the runes basically redefining the standard teleport spell that the matrix would amplify.

From the empty, echoing void beneath the radiation cap, Damien made his way into Rib One, following the chains of runes that linked together the major sub-matrices into the locked down decks. At the far extreme of the rib, the links broke apart to create seventeen sub-matrices, spread along the length of the outer rib, the extreme exterior of the ship. The central matrix, the one linking all seventeen together, was 'wrong' again. Like the runes in the simulacrum chamber and the radiation shield, it channeled away energy on criteria that read like a description of a jump spell.

By the time Damien had followed the rune matrices around to the central part of Rib Two, he wasn't surprised to find almost the exact same rune matrix as he found in Rib One. He noted the slight differences on his matrix diagram. It almost looked like all three of the matrices were redirecting energy towards the same place if it met the same criteria.

In Rib Three and Rib Four, he didn't even try to follow the linking matrices, heading directly to where he knew he would find the strange matrices. Each was basically an 'if-then' line of code, redirecting energy to a single point in the jump matrix if their criteria were met.

He floated in an empty maintenance space on Rib Four with his personal computer up, reviewing his notes on the sub-matrices. The six patterns had more to do with each other than with the hundreds of other sub-matrices and millions of other runes that made up the jump matrix, and they made no sense to him.

All six redirected energy away from the matrix, where the entire purpose of the runes was to multiply a spell that would transport Damien, personally, roughly ten thousand kilometers at best into a spell that would transport an entire ship a full light year.

The calculation he'd set to run finally finished, and the computer spat out an answer – all six runes were directing energy to the same place, likely a seventh and final sub-matrix. If his calculations were correct, it was in engineering.

#

Drifting into the engineering spaces in zero-gravity almost got Damien crushed as a load of containment cylinders of some kind swung through the space just inside the door. Only an instinctive jerk of magic pulled him back from a dangerous collision, and a voice bellowed across the cavernous space at the rear of the freighter.

"*Watch* what you're doing, you dimwits! That's the only damn entrance; let's *try* not to kill ship's officers, eh?"

Damien remained motionless for a long moment as a white-faced assistant engineer caught up to his wayward cargo. The man gave Damien an apologetic glance before regaining control of the floating cart from his datapad. Tiny jets flared on the cart, redirecting the cylinders – which he now noticed had a 'Warning: Explosion Hazard' sign on them – away from the Ship's Mage.

A dark-skinned man, not much bigger than Damien's own slight frame, appeared out of the depths of the engineering space, zipping across the empty space and grabbing a support loop with practiced skill, turning bright blue eyes on the Mage.

"Only one folk on a ship like this wears that gewgaw," he said gruffly. "Welcome to Engineering, Ship's Mage Montgomery. Chief Engineer, James Kellers."

Damien carefully shook the engineer's hand, keeping his feet and spare hand carefully wedged to keep him in place. Releasing the handshake, he looked around the engineering room in awe. There were no rooms, corridors or dividers in the working space at the rear of the ship. Designed to function in zero-gravity, the space around the engines was festooned with hundreds of devices and consoles that he didn't begin to comprehend.

The room stretched to the exterior of the hull on all sides, and on the far edges of the room Damien saw the graceful looping patterns of the runes of the Jump Matrix.

"What brings you to engineering Mr. Montgomery?" Kellers asked.

"Looking in awe, right now," Damien admitted. "I did my jump tests on a much smaller ship, and they had the life support and other equipment separate from the engines."

Kellers nodded. "Probably ex-military," he admitted. "The Navy likes to space important bits out through the keel, minimizes the point failure sources. Concentrating all of the important gear in one place allows three of us keep everything functioning, though."

Damien took a deep breath, inhaling the faint scent of burnt plastic and fused hydrogen. "Is it safe for me to move around in here?" he asked. "I need to review the runes and make sure nothing was damaged when we got banged up."

"The Ship-Wrights had a pair of Mages in here day before yesterday checking all of the runes," Kellers told him, scratching the stubble on his chin. "But if you're careful, you should be fine. My boys are not normally quite that dumb," he finished loudly, glaring at the assistant who'd nearly flattened Damien.

With a nod to Damien, the Engineer kicked off towards one of the many strange machines in the cavernous space. Damien took a moment to orient himself against the map he'd put together on his PC, and then kicked off himself.

The runes he was looking for weren't on the exterior hull, but as he approached the strange device they were carved on, he saw that they were close. A massive block extended in from the 'bottom' of engineering, with grills and strange conduits all over it. The runes ran in from the sub-matrices that connected the matrix to the rear of the ship, and Damien looked at them, tracking their energy.

The links that flowed out to the matrix on the massive metal block were barely even connected to the main spell, tying directly back to the other strange matrices throughout the ship. Whatever the other runes were doing, it focused here.

The runes on the center of the block were different from the other six weird matrices. Those had all been roughly the same, criteria triggered redirects. This just took all of the energy that flowed into it and cast a simple... fire spell?

"Kellers?" Damien called. After a moment, the engineer rejoined him, a worried look on his dark face.

"Something broken in the runes?" he asked quickly.

"I don't think so..." Damien said quietly, eyeing the matrix. "What's this block?"

"Block...?" the engineer said slowly, blinking at the massive piece of technology in front of him before smiling brightly. "Oh, *that* – sorry, I've never heard anyone not know what it is. That's our primary heat exchanger – takes the excess heat from the reactor and life support and dumps it into space. Without it, we'd eventually cook ourselves just with our body heat, let alone the engines!"

The Mage eyed the runes. A spell to create heat in something that had the purpose of getting rid of heat still made no sense.

"How much extra capacity does it have?" he wondered aloud. If this was something wrong, at least it probably wouldn't cause too much damage.

"A lot," the engineer told him. "The only thing on the ship more over-engineered than the heat exchanger is the main reactor core. You could fire one of the main engines at this baby and it would dump the heat to space. Whatever you're thinking, this gear can take it."

Damien nodded, eyeing the runes again. Whatever they did, it clearly wasn't new – the runes had the permanently rubbed-in layer of dirt over them that came from being as old as the ship itself. The jump matrix was a standard set of runes, no one ever changed it. Whatever these runes were, they made sense to experts with a lot more experience than Damien.

But the pattern of energy to them... didn't fit.

#

The strange matrices didn't quite leave Damien's mind over the next few days, but they weren't the focus of his attention as the *Blue Jay* loaded its cargo for its journey to the Corinthian System. He'd helped arrange the loading of supplies onto the freighter for the crew, while keeping one eye on the overall loading process, and spending his spare time checking the rune matrix for any damage.

The last day before they left the station, he and Captain Rice spent three hours going over the calculations for the fifteen jumps it would take them to travel to the other system. They'd worked out a relatively sedate three jumps a day path that would deliver their massive cargo in just less than five days without straining Damien much on his first ever voyage. Including the two and a half days of maneuvering clear of the gravity wells at the beginning and end of the trip, it would be a ten day voyage to cross fifteen light years.

Finally, after three days of chaos, he waited in the simulacrum chamber as the *Blue Jay* began to slowly accelerate out of Sherwood Prime. The chamber had a small platform just 'beneath' the simulacrum in the acceleration-driven gravity, allowing him to keep a hand on the magical token, sensing the gentle rush of power as the freighter accelerated at one-twentieth of a gravity.

Around him, he watched the station rotate around the ship as they spun to face open space. On a part of the bubble of screens that surrounded him he had a video link open to the bridge. Jenna sat at the navigation console, her face composed as she fed the computer the series of maneuvers that would get them clear of the station.

On the screen of the PC strapped to his wrist, Damien reviewed the calculations for the jump. He kept one eye on the world around the ship though, and saw when they were finally clear, the last gantries falling behind them.

A few more minutes passed in silence, and then Rice spoke on the bridge link.

"Link to Sherwood Prime," he ordered. A moment later, a triple click announced an open channel.

"Sherwood Prime to *Blue Jay*, our screens show you clear of the station safety zone," a space controller's voice informed them. "Please confirm."

"Sherwood Prime, this is *Blue Jay* Actual," Rice replied. "We show five kilometer separation, requesting permission to fire main engines at seven hundred thirty eight Olympus Mons time."

"We confirm five kilometer separation and authorize main engine firing," the controller informed him. "*Cair vie, Blue Jay.*"

"*Na h-uile la gu math duit*, Sherwood Prime," Rice replied, the old Gaelic flowing smoothly off his tongue. The channel shut down and his next words were for the crew.

"All hands, hear this, all hands, hear this," he said into the PA. "All ribs are secured, all cargo is secured, prepare for one gravity burn in two minutes."

At seven thirty eight A.M. on the far-away clock of the mountain the Protectorate was ruled from, the *Blue Jay*'s main engines burned to life, the tiny stars sending a surge of entirely non-magical power through the simulacrum under Damien's hands.

Standing on the acceleration platform, Damien breathed deeply, standing against the firm acceleration and reviewing the calculations on the datapad again. There was no computer assistance for the final jump – he had to know the vectors and energy levels in his mind, and move the ship entirely with his magic.

#

The *Blue Jay* accelerated for twenty-four hours, building velocity, and then coasted for another day, drawing clear of the gravity well of the planet behind them. Damien calculated and re-calculated his first jump. Rice reviewed it once more, the morning of the third day.

It finally came down to it late that afternoon. Damien checked the sensor readouts, and they were clear enough of gravity wells for the spell to function.

"Captain, we're ready to jump," he said quietly into the bridge link, and Rice nodded.

"Note for the log," Rice ordered. "It is seventeen forty Olympus Mons Time, and I am authorizing the jump."

"Noted for the log," Jenna replied, though Damien knew the computer would be recording after the phrase 'note for the log.'

Rice looked through the link directly at Damien, holding his gaze. "You may jump when ready, Ship's Mage," he said firmly.

Damien nodded, and turned his attention from the link screen to the simulacrum floating at the heart of the *Blue Jay*. The tiniest of kicks launched him away from the acceleration platform, leaving him floating in zero-gravity, held in place only by his hands on the silver icon of the *Blue Jay*'s essence.

With a deep breath, he slipped the runes on his bare palms into the exact places carved for them on the simulacrum, and let his power become part of the rune matrix of the ship. The screens around him allowed him to see as the ship saw, and now he *felt* the ship.

He reached out with his mind, confirming through the simulacrum what the sensors had already told him – that the space-time here was sufficiently unbent by gravity to allow for a jump.

He touched the reservoir of power in his core, mustering energy up into his hands and through the connection into the ship. The rune matrix greedily sucked up his power, reflecting it around the ship in an ever-building net that was almost blinding to someone who saw the magic in the rune matrix.

Without conscious thought, Damien knew the calculations were perfect, and he held them in the center of his mind.

Then, he released his breath and his power and *moved*. He touched a blip in the probability of reality, and all of his energy fled his body in a single exhalation.

The *Blue Jay* jumped.

#

"How are we looking?" Rice asked Jenna as soon as the indescribable sensation of being transported trillions of kilometers through space in an instant faded.

"Checking position now," she replied, running a series of programs on her console before looking back up at him. "We are bang on target, dead center in jump zone one of the Sherwood-Corinthian sequence."

Rice turned to the monitor showing him the simulacrum chamber, taking in the utterly drained expression on his new Ship's Mage.

"Well done Mr. Montgomery," he told the youth. "Shall we schedule the next jump for oh-three hundred Olympus Mons time?"

That would give the young man over nine hours to rest – nine hours it looked like the Mage desperately needed. He and Damien had scheduled to jump every eight hours, but after the new Ship's Mage's first jump, he figured they could spare the time.

"I'll be ready," Damien promised; his voice soft with fatigue.

"Get some sleep, Damien," Rice ordered. "We'll talk before the next jump."

With a nod, the young Mage turned off the video link, and Rice turned to Jenna.

"Scopes clear?" he asked quietly.

"All clear so far as our sensors can read," she replied, equally quiet. "No one has come through here in a week at least."

Rice considered the screen showing the thermal signatures around them. The thermal scope was the most reliable method of detecting ships, seeing as how any vessel under power blazed like a tiny sun against the backdrop of empty space.

"Three degrees Kelvin as far as our eyes can see," he muttered to himself. "Why does that not make me feel better?"

"Because you're rightfully paranoid, sir," Jenna replied.

"Which is why I want you to send the maintenance 'bots out to check over both of our new turrets," Rice told her.

#

For ninety quiet minutes, Rice slowly relaxed as no sign of pirates or technical difficulties materialized. Both of the new Rapid Fire Laser

41

Anti-Missile turrets checked out as fully functional, and he took some comfort in the fact that he'd paid to upgrade them heavily from the previous weapons. Each of these turrets was rated to take down a four missile salvo like the last one they'd faced on its own.

Ninety-one minutes after arrived at the jump zone, all of his quiet hopes for a peaceful trip shattered as the distinctive heat and radiation flare of an incoming jump appeared on their screens.

"Jump flare!" he barked, grabbing Jenna's attention from her focus on the maintenance 'bots. "Get me something Jenna," he ordered as she pulled up the rest of the sensor suite. Heat would only tell them so much.

"Single ship, three million kilometers," she reported, then double checked her figures. "Damn, their Mage must have blown his numbers – I bet they were planning on coming out right on top of us."

As if to prove her comment, the heat signature on the new contact flared with a sudden, massive, brightness.

"Boss, if I'm reading this right, she just lit off a fusion rocket at six gees," Jenna said quietly, and David winced.

"Time to missile range?" he asked steadily.

"If they're using the same birds as last time, about an hour," she admitted. "If the turrets hold up, it'll take them just over five hours to match speeds and rendezvous with us to board – that's if we start burning now."

Five hours. That would make it over six hours since Damien had jumped, which meant that, if they could make it, the young Mage would be able to jump them *before* the pirate ship boarded them.

"Sound the emergency acceleration alert," Rice ordered, "and lets burn directly away from them. Let's buy as much time as we can."

A klaxon began ringing through the ship and the bars on his screen showing the rotational speeds of the ribs rapidly shrank.

"All ribs at full stop," Jenna reported. "Initiating emergency burn… now."

The four massive fusion torches at the rear of the ship lit up, and a large man sat down on Rice's chest as his ship began to accelerate at two full gravities.

#

It seemed like Damien had barely closed his eyes when the klaxon woke him up. He certainly didn't have time to wake up or prepare at all before the rib stopped rotating and the motion of his waking up sent him drifting away from the bed beneath him.

Then the engines engaged, and two gravities of force slammed him into the back wall of his cabin, crushing the breath from his body. He struggled against the gravity to regain some measure of breath, and then wove magic around his body to reduce the force to something he could move in.

"Captain, this is Damien," he said as he opened a link to the bridge. "What's happening?"

"We've been ambushed," Rice said shortly, his breath strained. "They missed their jump, though, and we should be able to stand off the missiles until you can jump us again. How long?"

Damien focused for a moment, testing the reserve of energy buried deep inside of him. It had recovered somewhat during his hour-long nap. The gravity spell wasn't a major strain, and from the feel, he could handle anything that wasn't major.

Of course, a teleport spell was the definition of major.

"At least a few more hours," he admitted. "I'm still shot to hell."

There was a long pause, during which Damien pulled on a shirt and grabbed a folded up emergency pressure helmet.

"We're running," Rice said finally. "But he's got four gravities on us, and he'll be in missile range in under an hour. Anything you can do?"

"I can knock down some missiles from the simulacrum chamber," the Mage told him. "Not sure what else…"

"Any little bit helps," the Captain told him.

"Then I'll be in the simulacrum chamber," Damien promised.

#

Blue Jay was not a small ship, and there was no direct route from Damien's quarters in the middle of Rib Four to the simulacrum chamber at the center of the vessel. The two gravity acceleration didn't help, though at least the ship had fold-out stairs and other tools to function with acceleration-driven gravity.

By the time Damien made it to the chamber, struggling up a ladder to the small platform beneath the simulacrum, the pirate ship was just drawing into missile range. He opened a video link to the bridge, as well as several windows that showed him sensor data on the area and the ship.

"There he was," Jenna said suddenly, as a spike showed up in the sensors. "Bastard was sitting a full light-hour out of the jump zone with his drives dead – not even the Martian boys would have picked him up at that distance – but he'd have seen everyone jump in. He IDed our signature as soon as it reached him, took half an hour to be ready, and then jumped us. If their Mage hadn't overshot, we'd have been dead or boarded before we even knew they were there."

Damien replayed the sudden burst of energy and saw her point. Up to that moment, now a full hour ago, there had been no sign of a ship in that bit of space. Then the jump flare appeared, marking the pirate's disappearance.

"Missiles," Jenna reported calmly as four more signatures lit up on the thermal scope. "They look the same as last time – two thousand gravities acceleration, seven and a half minute flight time. I'm taking evasive maneuvers – hold on!"

The missiles were anemic compared to the antimatter driven weapons the Protectorate Navy would use, but they were still a thousand times faster than the *Blue Jay*. Damien focused the sensor screen on them, using it to focus in and zoom on the missiles.

Through the simulacrum, Damien could affect the space around them with his magic, but all it did was let him see as the ship saw. His power and range for his normal spells was almost the same, unlike using the jump spell.

One of the spells he knew, however, was explicitly intended for just this situation. It was draining, but it had a range of forty or so thousand kilometers. Normally, that was utterly useless, but here and now, he could take down a missile in its last six seconds or so of flight.

"Sixty seconds to impact," Jenna announced. "RFLAMs engaging."

The lasers were invisible on the visual screens that surrounded Damien, though they lit up the sensor feeds. Their results weren't. One missile and then another disappeared in fireballs that were clearly visible in the zoomed in screen.

A third missile detonated, and then the last came within Damien's reach. His power flicked out through the simulacrum's matrix and conjured a tiny fireball, not much more than a spark.

Conjured *inside* the missile's fuel cells, it triggered a reaction that blew the missile apart.

#

Even as Damien breathed a sigh of relief, something was bothering him. A niggling thought at the back of his head. The spell he'd cast hadn't felt right. It wasn't a spell he'd cast many times before, but most of the time he had he'd been in deep space, casting through a window or viewscreen on the side of a ship.

This wasn't the first time he'd cast it from the simulacrum chamber of a starship – but it was the first time he'd done so only a short while after casting the jump spell. The feel of the two spells should have been very different to his mind. The jump spell was tied into and amplified by the rune matrix throughout the starship, but the defense spell was only using the simulacrum to allow him to see what he was aiming at.

Both spells had felt *exactly* the same when he'd cast them. His energy had fed into the matrix that ran throughout the ship, and he swore that the defense spell had started the same amplifying feedback loop that the jump spell had... and then it had simply continued on as normal, as if that loop had broken.

He ignored the pursuing ship as he dove into the ship's operating system, looking for something he knew had to be there.

"More missiles incoming," he heard Jenna's voice report. "I think the RFLAMs have their measure now, but keep your eyes open Damien."

The missiles were still two minutes out when he found what he was looking for. The usage level of the main heat converter popped up on his side screen, tracking back in time... to a massive heat spike when he'd cast the spell.

He stared at the spike in shock, understanding what the strange matrices he'd found did at last. There was no difference between a jump matrix and the spell amplifier a warship would carry – except that those seven sub-matrices would break the amplifier loop for any spell *but* the jump spell.

His moment of realization shattered when the *Blue Jay* leapt under his feet. Five megatons of mass jumped like a startled puppy, and then he was in zero-gravity.

#

"What the hell happened?" Rice demanded. The RFLAM turrets had only just started to engage – the missiles had been tens of thousands of kilometers out, nowhere near close enough to actually hit the ship.

"Three of the missiles were decoys," Jenna said grimly. "They were augmenting their radar signatures, and we nailed all three. The fourth was an x-ray laser. It blew up at twenty thousand klicks and hit the engines."

X-ray laser warheads were rare and expensive – so expensive that even the Martian Navy didn't use them normally. A small atomic bomb triggered a lasing reaction in specially treated crystals, providing a deadly and precise stand off weapon.

Rice flipped up a link to engineering. "Kellers, how bad is it?" he demanded.

"We've a giant hole through the main conduits for Two and Three," the engineer snapped back. "The conduit for One got clipped –

that *might* be repairable, but if we fire up Two or Three before a shipyard's been at them, we may as well just set off a nuke back here."

"Get me at least one engine back Kellers," Rice ordered. He turned back to Jenna, and she answered his question before he asked it.

"It's gained them forty minutes," she said quietly. "Maybe as much as a full hour."

An inexperienced Mage jumping with anything less than a six hour wait between jumps risked the same fate that Kenneth McLaughlin had suffered. Rice looked at the link to Damien, knowing that the youth would likely risk it. If they pushed it close enough, it might even work – assuming the pirate didn't open them to air and let them suffocate. The bounty on Rice's head would be paid as happily for a vacuum preserved corpse as for a live prisoner. He met the young Mage's eyes and saw something there he wasn't expecting: hope.

"Captain, I have an idea," Damien told him.

#

He ran for the front of the ship, power flaring through the runes in his palm as he formed his own 'down' in the zero-gravity of the ship. A bag of tools, soldering irons and silver wire, banged against his side as he dodged around Singh, who trying to make his way backwards along the keel. The big Sikh stared at him in surprise, then flashed him a thumbs up.

"Whatever you're doing Montgomery, good luck!" he shouted after Damien, who barely heard him as he caught a support bar and redirected his personal gravity.

With a bruising thump, Damien slammed into the underside of the ship's radiation cap, where the sub-matrix diverted energy away if it wasn't a jump spell. He focused his gaze on it, following the lines of energy and noting where they detoured.

With a deep breath, he pulled the soldering iron and embossing tools out. With a single slash of the iron, he severed a rune. Molten silver followed, new runes taking shape that loop the energy back into the general matrix.

One link done, he slid sideways and repeated the process. Runes were something to carve carefully, with time, precision and detailed calculations. Without time, Damien relied on his sight, on knowing how the energy would flow.

The forward matrix took him fifteen minutes to disconnect, and then he ran again, redirecting gravity to speed him towards Rib One.

He had mere hours to change the entire nature of the rune matrix, and all he could do was pray he was doing it right.

Damien had made it to Rib Four when the ship lurched out from beneath his feet, his spell failing to compensate for the entire kilometer-length of the vessel jerking a full meter sideways. He slammed into the wall, gouging his hands and cracking his jaw.

Carefully feeling his jaw for any major injuries, he opened a link to the bridge.

"What the hell was that?" he demanded.

"They have a laser," Rice said shortly. "And we no longer have a forward turret. You're out of time, Damien. Whenever that thing recharges, we lose the rear turret, and then we either jump or die."

Damien looked at the sub-matrix for Rib Four. Most of the runes were severed, with only one rune chain still linking it. With a deep breath, he focused on the lines of energy, and slashed with the soldering iron. If he'd judged it right, he'd broken the rune without creating a dangerous feedback loop, but at this point he could only hope.

"Computer, connect me to engineering," he ordered his PC as he charged rearwards for the simulacrum chamber.

"Kellers, it's Montgomery," he told the engineer, focusing his gravity spell so that he fell towards the rear of the ship.

"I'm a little busy trying to keep us from blowing the fuck up kid, this better be important," the engineer snapped.

"You know those runes on the main heat exchanger?" Damien asked, grunting as he slammed into the ladder leading to the keel. He hadn't slowed himself enough, but he hadn't broken any bones.

"What? What about them?" Kellers demanded. *"Watch that hydrogen line,"* he bellowed at somebody else. "Do *not* connect that thing to the conduit yet; hold off till I *tell* you to hook it up."

"I need you to break the rune chains connecting them to the rest of the ship's matrix," the Mage told him.

There was silence on the other end of the line as Damien forced his bruised, weary, legs to carry him towards the keel.

"And how the fuck am I supposed to do that?" Kellersfinally demanded.

"It shouldn't matter," Damien told him honestly. He was pretty sure that destroying the other six matrices would render the one in engineering utterly ineffectual – but he couldn't be certain. "Weld it, gouge, burn it – take an ax to it for all I care, but I'll be in the simulacrum chamber in two minutes, and I need those runes disconnected when I get there."

Another pause. "You owe me one hell of an explanation Montgomery, but I'll see what I can do," Kellersfinally said.

"If we live, I'll explain with diagrams," Damien promised, and then redirected his gravity spell towards the simulacrum.

As long as he made it to the simulacrum in time, he didn't care if he broke something anymore.

#

Leaving the door to the simulacrum chamber open had been one of his better ideas. He fell through the door, barely slowing himself at the last minute. With a deep breath and steeling himself against the result, Damien grabbed onto the simulacrum to slow himself.

The simulacrum *couldn't* move. He barely held his grip, and one of his arms was clearly going to make him pay later, but he stopped.

He looked up at the bridge link and met Rice's eyes.

"They have a six minute recharge on the laser," the captain told him. "It's no Navy gun, but it's plenty for their purposes. We are now out of defenses, so I hope your idea works."

"We'll see," he said quietly, opening a link to engineering. "Kellers?"

"It's done," the engineer replied. "You have no idea how scared shitless I am right now."

"Join the club," Damien told him. "Everyone hold on."

With a deep breath, he placed the runes on his palms on the model, and became the ship.

This was the true purpose of the matrix. He knew it the moment he linked in. Before, only trying to cast the jump spell had linked this completely to the ship. Now, just completing the matrix changed everything.

He saw as the ship saw. Felt as it felt. The scars where the turrets had been burned away hurt as badly as his own strained limbs. The broken engines burned as if his own skin had been seared with fire.

And the *Blue Jay*'s eyes were his eyes. He saw in radiation and heat as clearly as day, and saw the pirate ship closing on them, certain now that it had disabled its victim – so certain they hadn't even demanded their surrender.

This time, he had no intention of scaring anyone off. The simple self-defense fire spell every Mage learned leapt to his mind and power leapt from his hands into the runes of the ship. He sensed the power loop through the ship, repeating and building so quickly no one outside the spell would have sensed it.

Fire lit the darkness of deep space as his magic lit a tiny sun and flung it across the void. His senses and power followed it the entire way, waiting for the pirate to try to dodge.

They never even saw it coming. Super-heated plasma ripped through their hull, tearing a hole through the length of the ship, until the fireball reached the antimatter storage that fueled the pirate's engines.

The ship vanished in the searing white flame of annihilating matter.

#

As the *Blue Jay* drifted in space, the senior officers gathered on the bridge. Damien joined Kellers, Jenna and the Captain and found himself the center of attention.

"What did you *do*?" David asked.

"I turned our jump matrix into an amplifier," Damien explained. "There were limiters built into the spell matrix to make it only amplify the jump spell – I removed them."

"That's *possible*?" Jenna exclaimed.

"A week ago, I would have said no," the young Mage said. "We're discouraged from looking too closely at the Jump Matrix – messing with it in flight is illegal. I just had no choice."

"Can we still jump?"

"Yes," Damien replied, unhesitatingly.

"Good enough," Captain Rice replied, turning to Kellers. "What about the engines?"

"We've fixed the conduits for One, but Two and Three are gone until we get to Corinthian."

The Captain nodded, looking around at the officers.

"Then, whenever you're ready Mr. Montgomery, let's be on our way."

###

2

Damien Montgomery floated at the core of the starship, his hands resting on the tiny scale-model of the ship that sat at its exact center. The simulacrum of the ship allowed his magic to stretch to every corner of the immense, kilometer-long, vessel and made the young Mage, in a strange sense, the ship's engine.

Around him, viewscreens showed the stars arrayed around the freighter, and under his hands, the simulacrum reflected the damage the ship had taken in the pirate attack eleven jumps and four days before.

"You may jump when ready, Mage Montgomery," David Rice, Captain of the *Blue Jay,* ordered from the tiny window on the all-surrounding viewscreens that lined the starship's heart.

Damien nodded to the video screen, and focused his magic on the tiny model itself. The ship's rune matrices leaped to life with an eagerness that was still strange to him, born of the changes he'd made to the matrix to allow him to fight off the pirate attack a mere handful of days ago.

It picked up his magic in that eagerness, reflecting it from the bow of the ship to its mighty fusion engines, only one of which was still working, building strength with each reflection.

Then, with a deep breath, the Mage grabbed that power and moved.

The *Blue Jay* jumped into the Corinthian system.

#

With the jump complete, Damien made his way through the ship to join the other ship's officers in the conference room on Rib One, one of the flattened structures that rotated rapidly around the *Blue Jay*'s central steady-state keel to provide a semblance of gravity as the ship coasted.

Entering the tiny conference room, he slid into the last of the five chairs, nodding his thanks to the ship's first officer, Jenna Campbell, as she slid a steaming hot cup of coffee in front of him. He was always exhausted immediately after jumping, but this meeting was important.

The stocky blonde exec smiled at him, gesturing at the carafe in the center of the table to make it clear there was more coffee left.

To the Mage's right sat the ship's First Pilot Narveer Singh, the man in charge of the ship's several heavy lift shuttles. Dark-skinned and wearing a blue turban, the pilot flashed a bright grin, baring stunningly white teeth.

Just past Narveer, looking even darker-skinned than usual next to the dusky Sikh, was the ship's Chief Engineer, James Kellers. The bags under his eyes were almost invisible on his near-black skin, but Damien could see the man's exhaustion regardless. The *Blue Jay* had limped from jump zone to jump zone for four days since they'd been attacked, and only the engineer's skill and determination had kept her together.

At the end of the table drinking his own coffee was the dark-haired and squat figure of their Captain, David Rice, looking surprisingly calm for a man whose ship had nearly been blown out from under him.

"How are we doing James?" the Captain asked once Damien was seated. "Are we going to make it into Corinthian Station?"

"Engine One is fully up and running with no flaws or cracks that I can detect," the engineer replied. "Two and three… we'll need to get fixed at Corinthian. We can make half a gravity without straining anything too hard though, so we'll start decelerating a bit sooner and drift in a bit later – nothing worth worrying about."

Damien let out a breath he hadn't realized he'd been holding, and he wasn't the only one. The laser strike had almost destroyed the ship when it had ripped through the freighter's engines, and it had been entirely possible they wouldn't have any of the main engines. Thankfully, the magic that teleported them across the stars didn't *need* engines, but Damien could only bring them so close to a gravity well.

"That's good to hear James," Rice told him. "Well done." He brought up a picture of the planet on the screen along the wall of the room, a massive silver three-part cylinder hovering in the corner of the picture.

"I think James and I are the only ones here who've visited Corinthian before, so here's the run-down," the Captain continued. "Corinthian is the most heavily industrialized system outside the Core, and Corinthian Prime is, among other things, a first class shipyard that's better than some *in* the Core."

He tapped the cylinder.

"Top part of the cylinder is civilian docks, bottom part is the shipyard, and the middle is a rotating habitat with an artificial eco-system, including parks, trees, and semi-wild animals. It's an impressive station, unique in the Midworlds, and only possible because of Corinthian's industry.

"Our raw materials are for the factories and our luxuries for the factory owners," Rice continued. "We'll trans-ship on the station and get repairs done – there's nowhere better.

"Now, Corinthian is a world to step carefully on," he warned. "The factory workers are better off than most, but they compare themselves to the factory owners, who compare themselves to the even richer magnates. The entire culture is obsessed with moving up that ladder by their bootstraps… and they occasionally run rough-shod over anyone in the way. Corinthian Prime's dock module is home to some *nasty* organized crime, and we are going to stay *far* out of their way, clear?"

All of the ship's officers nodded, Damien feeling a little intimidated. Rice didn't help that feeling by focusing his gaze on Damien.

"Damien, you especially have to tread carefully," he warned. "Corinthian isn't an UnArcana world – magic is legal – but they *don't* like Mages."

"I'll keep that in mind," Damien said quietly. "I should probably stay on the ship regardless – the last thing we want is Guild Mages looking at the rune matrix. I'm… not sure how legal my modifications are."

The rune matrix woven throughout the massive freighter allowed a Mage like Damien to teleport it between the stars – but that was all they were supposed to do. Damien had broken that limitation, though, and used the matrix to amplify a self-defense spell to destroy the pirate who'd attacked them.

"You don't *know*?" Singh asked.

"I know they aren't *legal*," Damien admitted. "But the thing about Mage Law… it's vague, and the punishments aren't spelled out unless you break them. The idea is to keep us from breaking them at all."

"Then let's make sure no one goes poking around the runes unsupervised," Rice ordered. "On top of everything else, the last thing we need is problems with the Guilds!"

#

David Rice sighed in relief when the *Blue Jay* finally approached close enough to Corinthian Prime for the scanners to make out the familiar white pyramid shapes of two destroyers of the Royal Navy of the Mage-King of Mars. While they hadn't seen any sign of the pirates since the attack when they'd left Sherwood, the Protectorate destroyers were always a sign of safety.

He watched carefully over Jenna's shoulder as she gently adjusted the freighter's course, aligning carefully on the immobile docking end of the cylindrical station, and brought up the communications himself.

"Corinthian Prime, this is Captain David Rice of the freighter *Blue Jay* out of the Sherwood system," he informed them. "We are carrying a data download and several cargo contracts, but be advised that we were attacked by pirates and currently only have one functioning main engine."

A few moments later, a traffic controller came on the channel.

"*Blue Jay*, this is Corinthian Control. Message received. What is your maneuvering status – do we need to arrange a tow?"

"Negative, Control," David told them after a long moment of thought and a glance at his XO. "Maneuvering thrusters are fully functional, we should be able to maneuver to dock without issues, but our acceleration is heavily reduced."

"Understood *Blue Jay*, please proceed to Dock Seven," the controller ordered. "It's the most accessible for repair craft," he continued. "Please contact your deliveries as soon as possible to arrange offloading. Welcome to Corinthian, Captain Rice."

"Thank you Control," he replied. "Maneuvering to Dock Seven."

A tiny diamond appeared on his screen, bracketing the indicated dock as Jenna began to adjust the cargo ship's course. Dock Seven, he saw, was designed for the much bigger heavy container ships. A *Venice* class ship like the *Blue Jay* would be surrounded by plenty of empty space on all sides – the best working space for repairs short of slotting her into an actual shipyard. Dock Six, right next to them, was of a similar size and currently contained the large module components of a pre-fabricated colony ship in the process of being assembled.

"The yards must be full," he muttered aloud. A colony ship's components could be assembled easily in a standard dock, but it was faster and easier to slot the cylindrical modules together in a real shipyard.

"See any issues getting us in?" he asked Jenna. "I think the neighbor is the biggest issue," he added, watching the small swarm of repair ships guiding one of the modules in.

"I could get us into that dock blindfolded with just the maneuvering jets," his first officer replied. "We'll be fine."

"All right. I'm going to contact the company receiving our cargo," Rice told her, heading into the office just off of the bridge.

The *Blue Jay* carried three hundred ten thousand ton cargo containers, but a hundred and sixty of them were the 'main cargo' – the contract that covered the fuel, salaries and other operating costs required to get the immense starship from Sherwood to Corinthian. The other hundred and forty containers were filled with over three hundred single and partial container contracts, but those Rice would leave to the ship's three clerks to contact the customers and arrange delivery.

He always handled the main cargo personally. Problems with that contract could easily bankrupt him, so he made a point of knowing who he was dealing with. It was a matter of moments for him to pull up the communications codes for the company receiving their load of raw hardwood and luxury furniture.

A cheerfully redheaded girl who looked barely out of school answered the call.

"Bistro Manufacturing, Jessica speaking, how may I help you?" she spieled off brightly.

"Good morning Jessica," Rice replied, checking the station time on the corner of his screen as he spoke. Like most ships and stations, Corinthian Prime ran on Olympus Mons Time and the twenty-four hour day of Earth and terraformed Mars, but it was always good to check.

"I have a cargo for delivery to Bistro from the Sherwood system," he continued. "My contract says to arrange delivery with Mister John Bistro himself."

"The starship delivery!" the girl squealed, and David barely concealed his wince at the pitch of her voice. She was *very* young. Given that Bistro Manufacturing was easily in the top twenty corporations on Corinthian, David was pretty sure he knew her last name. "Mr. Bistro will want to speak to you straight away, please hold," she finished.

A corporate boilerplate hold screen pulled from a template Rice had seen on at least twelve worlds covered the screen as he waited for the girl to get her boss, the manager and sole owner of a billion-dollar planet-wide enterprise, on the line.

He was considering looking for a book when the hold screen evaporated to show a different room entirely. John Bistro was an iron-haired older man who could have passed for brothers with Mage-Governor McLaughlin, the overlord of Sherwood who'd left Rice with so many troubles.

"Captain Rice, it is an absolute pleasure to hear from you," the industrial magnate announced. "I have to admit, every time I send a few dozen million out-system to purchase a cargo, I never really relax until the cargo makes it back to Corinthian. You had no issues, I trust?"

"Unfortunately, I can't say that," Rice told him dryly. "We were attacked by pirates just outside Sherwood, but I don't believe any of the cargo containers were damaged. I would recommend," he continued after a moment's thought, "that you have your staff check over the cargo as quickly as possible, so we can include any damage in the insurance claim."

Bistro blinked rapidly for a moment. "Pirates?!" he said incredulously. "What were they going to do with a million tons of raw hardwood?"

Rice cut off a chuckle quickly, but he saw the smile on the magnate's face and returned it. The image of the Blue Star Syndicate trying to fence hardwood through channels normally reserved for drugs, guns, and slaves was certainly… interesting. He wasn't going to admit to the other man, though, that the pirate attack had been directed at him personally.

"I imagine they were after some of the smaller, high value, items in the secondary shipment," he told Bistro after a moment. "Thanks to some ingenuity on the part of my Ship's Mage, however, we saw them off with only hull damage."

"That is good news, Captain," Bistro agreed. "I'll have my people co-ordinate offloading our cargo with Prime control. Do you have any time restrictions we should be aware of?"

"Only the standard ones," Rice told him. Basically, that if he wanted to off-load for more than one shift in a row, he'd be responsible for the hotel bills for the *Blue Jay*'s crew. The four ribs that rotated around the starship's keel to provide gravity couldn't do so while offloading, and policy in the merchant fleet was to avoid having people sleeping in zero-gravity.

"Of course," Bistro replied. "I will be shipping up to Prime to audit some of the review of the cargo myself. Would you and your ship's officers be available to meet with myself for a dinner in, say, four days?"

Rice was taken aback. Normally, he was wined and dined by the people looking to hire him, not the people he'd just completed contracts for.

"We can arrange a direct transfer for the payment at the dinner, once we've reviewed the cargo, and I may have another commission for you," Bistro continued when Rice didn't immediately respond.

"My officers and I will be pleased to meet you for dinner, Mr. Bistro," Rice agreed. "Though I will note that the *Blue Jay* will be under repair for some days after the cargo is off-loaded."

Bistro made a throw away gesture with one hand, blinking rapidly again. "This is interstellar shipping, my dear Captain. You should know better than I that nothing moves quickly between the stars!"

#

The description of the central portion of Corinthian Prime's segmented cylinder as 'an artificial eco-system' failed to prepare Damien for the reality of it. He stepped out of the elevator from the motionless docks onto the outer rim of the station and into a glass-roofed atrium in the middle of a forest.

He blinked at the sight, taking a moment to put it into scale. The atrium was, obviously, set into one end of the cylinder, so it was only surrounded by trees on the interior side. The trees themselves were trimmed and maintained, planted in the neat lines typical of a ground-side park... but were very real trees.

A man standing near the elevator cleared his throat, bringing Damien's gaze back down to the room he was standing in. The other five occupants of his elevator had already cleared through the security checkpoint leading into the main segment, and the security guard was gesturing Damien forward.

"Welcome to the Spindle, Mage Montgomery," the guard said after reviewing Damien's ID for a moment. "First time on Corinthian Prime, I see. Is there anything I can do to help?"

"I'm looking for the Jump Mage Guild," Damien told him. The *Blue Jay* had been blacklisted in Sherwood, so they had been unable to register his contract with the ship in his home system. Unlike most things, however, Jump Mage contracts could be registered anywhere. The details would be included in the encrypted download the *Blue Jay* would take with it to any system they jumped to.

"Ah, yes," the guard nodded calmly. "The main path from the atrium meets up with LengthWay Seven about forty meters Yard-wards. From Seven, you'll want CircleWay Twenty-Six." The man looked at Damien's blank expression and chuckled. "It does make more sense if you think about it," he insisted, "but since the Guild is halfway across the Spindle from here, I suggest you grab a cab when you reach the LengthWay. They're pretty common, and decently priced."

"Thank you," Damien told him, agreeing with the assessment of the directions after a second. LengthWays ran the length of the center cylinder – apparently called the Spindle by the locals – and CircleWays ran around the exterior of the cylinder.

If they followed the Protectorate's standard one hundred meter blocks, CircleWay Twenty-Six was over two and a half kilometers away, which was a bit further than he'd been expecting to walk.

Stepping out of the atrium into the open air of the Spindle, however, he found himself considering it. To both sides of him, the artificial world rose gently up in the slope of the cylinder. From where he stood in the trees outside the atrium, he could see the entirety of the segment – there was no horizon, only a slight misting of water vapor in the air as he looked across or down the cylinder and the brilliant light of the central spire made it hard to see directly across the cylinder.

Five kilometers long and fourteen hundred meters in diameter, the Spindle represented more square footage than many cities in the MidWorlds, and much of it was covered in greenery. A neat grid of roads split the surface into blocks, and rarely did he see more than two blocks together of houses or industry. It was so unlike the compressed corridors in the many rotating rings of Sherwood Prime that it took Damien a long minute of standing in the shade of the trees to wrap his head around the sight.

Damien started walking down the LengthWay, looking for signs to tell him the numbers of the CircleWays that crossed it. It took him a few minutes to leave the cultured forest the Corinthians' had chosen to wrap around the entrances from the civilian docks, and that was when he saw the building.

The trees had blocked his view of it before, but now he wasn't sure how he'd missed it. The structure rose in blocks of black iron, softened somewhat by trees growing in terraces atop the blocks, but it remained a sprawling fortress in the middle of one of the more spectacular stations built by man.

A tiny whirring noise caused Damien to turn and spot the promised cab – a low slung vehicle with a cloth cover and two seats behind its driver.

"Can I give you a lift?" the driver asked.

"Sure," he answered. "I need to get to the Jump Mage's Guild."

The driver's gaze flicked down at Damien's collar, then he spat over the side. "Sure," he said flatly. "We don't call it the Guild though, here."

"What?" Damien asked quickly.

The driver pointed at the fortress Damien had been staring at.

"Mages don't trust us lot not to burn their homes down around their ears," he said bluntly. "They built that thing when the Spindle was finished. It's the home of your Guild, but we just call it the Citadel."

#

Security at the Guildhouse Citadel seemed lower than the cab-driver's words and its fortress-like structure suggested. The gates in the artfully concealed fence that surrounded the fortified compound were wide open, and foot traffic passed in and out in a slow but steady stream.

Passing through those gates, though, Damien spotted the two men just inside who were all the security the Guildhouse needed. Both were clad in dark robes over matte-black combat armor, and the gold medallions at their throats bore a single sword, compared to Damien's three stars and a quill. His three stars marked him as a Jump Mage. Their sword marked them as Enforcers, the police officers of the Guilds, and the only fully combat-trained Mages outside of the Mage-King's military.

Those two men could stand off an entire battalion of conventionally armed troops, at least for long enough to close the gates. For all that efforts had clearly been made to soften the appearance of the Citadel with the trees and gardens, they were still being very careful.

The thought was sobering as Damien entered the main hall, looking for the sign to direct him to the Ship Mage's Guild. Corinthian was a major MidWorld, hardly one of the UnArcana worlds where Mages weren't allowed to set foot on the surface, but the Guilds here clearly felt threatened.

With a shake of his head, he stepped into the Ship Mage's Guild office, relaxing slightly in the surroundings of the dozens of plants they'd used to soften the stark angles of the building's walls. A single desk stood in the middle of the room, with no one waiting to see the older woman sitting at the desk.

"Can I help you?" she greeted him bluntly.

"I'm here to register a Jump Contract," he replied, pulling the chip containing the formal contract between himself and Captain David Rice from the pocket of his blazer.

She grunted. "Give it here." He passed her the chip, and she slotted it into the reader on her desk. A holographic screen shimmered into existence at a wave of her hand, displaying the information.

"This says you signed the contract in the Sherwood system almost two weeks ago," she observed. "You should have registered it there."

"It slipped our minds while we were preparing for departure," he told her. In truth, the Mage-Governor of Sherwood had unofficially blacklisted the *Blue Jay* from taking on a Jump Mage, so he and David hadn't believed that they would have been permitted to register the contract in Sherwood.

The woman at the desk grunted, clearly unconvinced, and hit a few more keys on her projected keyboard.

"Well, it's registered now. Charge to your ship?"

"Yes," Damien confirmed, then reeled off the local account number for the *Blue Jay*.

"Done," she said, ejecting the chip and passing it back to him. "Anything else?"

Damien shook his head, but paused as he turned to leave.

"Do you know why the Guildhouse here is so fortified?" he asked. Anything further from the airy, sprawling complex of bungalows in Sherwood City that served his home was hard to imagine.

She sighed. "Corinthian Prime was built fifty years ago," she told him. "Just before that, there was a bombing in Corinth City that killed two Mages and twelve bystanders. Two more Mages were killed in the ensuing riots, and both the Guilds and the Governor agreed that moving the Guilds somewhere more securable and out-of-the-way was a good idea."

The woman, a senior ranked but still mundane employee of the Guild, shrugged. "It's only been ten years or so since it became illegal to bar Mages from a restaurant or store," she told him, some of her earlier gruffness lost in the sad tone of her voice. "If the government didn't think flouting the Charter laws around segregation was going to impede their effort to get the first MidWorlds Fleet Yard, I think you'd still see every second or third restaurant with a 'No Dogs or Mages' sign."

Damien winced.

"That's... different than I'm used to," he admitted. "Thanks for explaining."

She shook her head.

"Wish I didn't have to," she told him. "Step carefully, Mage Montgomery. There's a reason your kind built themselves a fortress here."

#

The first day on station was a blur for David. Bistro had taken them up on the offer for twenty-four hour offloading, so he'd had to arrange hotels for everyone. He'd then touched base with his insurance, a surprisingly un-confrontational appointment where they'd taken his telemetry data and confirmed within twenty minutes that they would cover the repairs under the piracy clause.

He settled into his hotel room, an expensive one in the docking area with magical artificial gravity that allowed him a view of the *Blue Jay* from the window. David watched the ships and robot arms swarm over his ship, detaching the cargo containers and slowly transporting them to the station. From there automated transfer tubes whisked them away to either destinations on the stations, or transfer shuttles to carry them to the sky-tether that would deliver them to the surface.

Each container removed from the *Blue Jay* was a check mark in his mental book, and in many cases, a literal entry in the ship's ledgers. Unless he'd missed his math, even with the repairs from the pirate attack, the revenue from this trip would allow him to make the last payment on the ten billion dollar note he'd taken out to finance acquiring the *Blue Jay* a decade ago. It would take time for the funds, encoded in a deep bank cipher, to make their way back to the Martian banking syndicate that had financed him, but under Protectorate Law, once he sent the money, the *Blue Jay* was completely his.

Now if only people would stop *shooting* at his ship.

#

"Is there any part of the matrix we can let another Mage inspect?" Kellers asked as Damien crawled under the fresh welding in Rib Four.

Damien's 'holiday' had come to an abrupt end as soon as the two days of offloading were complete and the repair crews started swarming over the ship.

"In theory, anywhere not attached to the seven matrixes I highlighted on the chart," Damien told him. Those seven were the matrixes that prevented a jump matrix from acting as a general amplifier for all spells instead of just the jump spell.

"In practice," the young Ship's Mage shrugged, eyeing the glitter of energy along the runes and checking for errors, "I would want to review all of the runes around the work *anyway*, so not wanting someone to see what I did to the matrix just adds to the urgency."

He paused, noting a set of runes where the energy didn't flow quite right. "Pass me the inlayer?" he asked the engineer.

With a bright white grin, the engineer passed the tool over.

"I'll sell it to my guys as professional skepticism, I think," Kellers told him. "I don't think we want to explain to everyone on the ship just what you did."

Damien carefully drew the engraving tool along the line his gift showed him. A tiny laser burned a trench into the steel, and a soldering iron attachment filled the trench with silver inlay. He pulled the inlayer away and looked at the runes again. He wasn't actually sure the runes had been damaged when the repair crew had replaced the conduits, or when they'd originally burnt out from the corona of the pirate laser that had disabled the engines. Either way, it would work now.

"The fact that it's not supposed to be *possible* helps with that," he said dryly, shivering a little at the thought of the entire crew knowing what he'd done to the ship. The *Blue Jay*'s crew of eighty-plus were good people, but spacers weren't exactly known for their tact and discretion.

Kellers laughed sharply.

"I thought ships were supposed to blow up if you jump with a damaged matrix," he continued, his dark face grim for a moment.

"They usually do," Damien admitted, shivering again, and sliding out from under the conduits. "These runes are good. They're still working on the bow cap?"

"The engineering firm said they'd have the new RFLAM turret installed by the end of today, but weren't going to be working on the plating until tomorrow," the engineer told him. Rapid-Fire-Laser-Anti-Missile turrets were mounted on all merchant ships, their first defense against pirates with missiles.

61

"Hold on one moment," Kellers continued as Damien continued to pack up. "What do you mean; ships with a modified matrix usually blow up? How the hell did you know *we* wouldn't?"

Damien sighed and finished packing up the tools he used to maintain the ship's runes.

"To put it as simply as I can," he said slowly, "the runes are like a circuit diagram – they control a flow of energy, right?"

"I follow so far," Kellers agreed with a nod, his eyes dark as he held Damien's gaze.

"Most Mages know the runes we've been taught – think of them as standard circuit diagrams," Damien continued. "Scribes are taught how to combine the runes into new matrices." He touched the quill on his collar – he'd qualified as a base level Rune Scribe along the way to his Jump Mage certification, mostly because runes came very easily to him.

"We have to know the runes and the language around them, because like an electrician, we can't *see* the power that flows through the runes, right?"

"Yeah, but an electrician uses a voltmeter," Kellers objected.

"Yep," Damien agreed. "And we don't have anything like that. So we don't modify existing matrices or runes, because it's dangerous. A damaged jump matrix could leave a ship in pieces across an entire light year."

"So why didn't that happen to us?" the older man demanded.

Damien sighed. "Because I *can* see the flow of energy through the runes," he admitted. "I've never met another Mage who can, but it lets me adjust runes with a far better idea of what I'm doing than any other Mage."

"It's why I could tell that those seven matrices were limiting the matrix to just a jump spell," he said quietly. "And how I knew that jumping wouldn't blow us to hell. I could look at the matrix and *know* it would work."

There was a long moment of silence, and the engineer shook his head at Damien.

"You may be damned crazy, son," he told the Mage, "but I'm glad you were aboard!"

#

On the fourth day in Corinthian, David Rice found Damien under the forward radiation cap on his own, putting the final touches on a re-inlaying of the forward rune matrix. This section had survived the pirate attack relatively intact, but had needed to be cut around when the repair crews had replaced the forward turret.

"You realize we're supposed to be on station meeting Bistro in less than two hours," the Captain observed, slowing his drift through zero-gravity to come to a rest next to the Mage. He glanced over the rune matrix that the young man was working on. Even to his eyes, it looked different than the old version – most notably, there was a blank space where one of the youth's 'seven limiter sub-matrices' had been.

"Hadn't been watching the time," the Ship's Mage said distractedly, carefully connecting a final set of runes with an odd looping line that Rice was sure meant something quite specific to the Mage. The Captain noticed, with a minor pang of envy, that the Mage was standing on the deck to work, in his own magically generated field of gravity.

"I need to get down to the engineering spaces once I'm done here," Damien continued. "The repair crew is working on the main hydrogen feeds for Engine One. I'll need to check for rune damage when they're done."

"I note, Damien, that there *are* no runes on the hydrogen feeds," Rice observed dryly. "We were told to bring the ship's officers, which includes the Ship's Mage."

"There are runes close enough to the feeds that a Mage need to check they're intact," Damien replied. "Those include the runes on the main heat exchanger, which I *really* don't want anyone else taking a look at."

Rice shook his head as his youngest officer. "They're not going to be any more or less damaged tomorrow," he told him. "I appreciate both the concern around strangers looking at our runes now, and your dedication to overseeing the repairs."

"That said," the Captain continued, "I believe I am *ordering* you to take the evening off. Finish up the runes in this section and then get yourself cleaned up. Clear?"

The youth looked at his boss and sighed.

"Clear, Captain," he replied.

"We'll meet in the lobby of the hotel in ninety minutes," Rice concluded. "It'll take you fifteen to get there, so you'd better work quickly."

#

Damien stumbled out of the hotel room shower with about five minutes to spare on Rice's deadline. The hotel Bistro had put the senior officers up in was located next to the docks to allow easy access to the ship and had floors marked with gravity runes throughout to avoid the dock's lack of gravity. Maintaining the spells that allowed artificial gravity required weekly renewing by a trained Mage, which explained much of the cost of the rooms.

To Rice and most other ship's captains and officers, the extra price was worth it to be close to their ships and still not have to sleep in zero-gravity. Damien agreed completely, as the rune work he'd been doing around the new forward turret had taken longer than expected. If they'd been staying at a hotel any further away, he wouldn't have been able to be ready in time for the Captain's deadline.

As it was, he carefully rushed dressing. He slipped into black slacks and the black mock-nocked dress shirt common for Mages. Where a non-Mage's shirt collar would fold down over the tie, Damien locked the warm leather of the rune-inlaid collar that carried his medallion over the half-neck. That gold coin, with its three stars and quill, marked him as a recognized Mage of the Royal Orders and Guilds of the Protectorate of Humanity. Without it, he would feel naked.

In the end, he was two minutes late into the lobby. David, Jenna and Kellers were all waiting, the ship's two senior officers in quiet conversation with the dark-skinned engineer. He joined them wordlessly, exchanging nods with the other officers.

"Where's Narveer?" he asked.

"There was a problem with one of the heavy lift shuttles," Jenna explained. "He didn't make it back to the hotel until after you did, he'll be a few more minutes."

The Captain shook his head with a smile, and was about to say something more when the ship's First Pilot bustled into the lobby, his turban neatly tied, but his dark blue tie flapping loosely around his neck and the jacket of his charcoal suit wide open over it.

"Stop," Rice ordered flatly as the Pilot reached them. "Hold still." The squat Captain swiftly grabbed the loose ends of Singh's tie and knotted them in a blur of motion. "Better. Are we ready?"

Kellers and the Captain wore the same style of charcoal gray suit as Singh, similar enough that Damien suspected they'd all be acquired at the same time. Jenna wore a plain black suit that looked somewhat newer than the men's, though still worn.

All four of the ship's officers, including Damien, nodded their readiness to the Captain.

"Alright," Rice replied. "Let's go collect our paycheck."

The Captain led them out and drifted into a transit pod that would take them to the Spindle. Damien kicked off after him, stepping out of the gravity in the hotel lobby and into the zero-gravity of the docks.

He caught the handle on the side of the pod and swung in, managing not to embarrass himself too badly he thought. The other officers quickly followed, all moving with the practiced ease of professional spacers that Damien had not, quite, picked up yet.

The pod shot away as soon as the five were all aboard, a small acceleration pressing the officers into the back of the cushioned seats.

"How are the repairs proceeding, James?" Rice asked once they were on their way.

"Better than I was figuring," the engineer shrugged. "Forward repairs are basically done, and the repair crew promised to have the engine conduits fixed up tonight. If they manage that, we'll have the new rear turret bolted on and wired in by the end of tomorrow."

"Those turrets are getting expensive to replace," Jenna observed. "That's two sets in as many trips!"

"I'd rather replace them than not have them," Rice told them all grimly. "So we'll be done the major repairs tomorrow then?" he asked, sounding surprised to Damien's ears.

"We'll have dozens of tiny repairs throughout the interior of the ship," Kellers admitted, "but the major work will be done. I'd like a couple of days to test everything too, but technically we could jump out tomorrow evening."

"Let's not," Damien said dryly. "I'd like a couple of days myself to review the entire rune matrix. With all of the repairs, there may still be issues I'd missed."

"I don't expect to be leaving tomorrow," Rice assured them both. "I do want to be able to tell Bistro how quickly we can depart if he does have a cargo for us."

The conversation was interrupted by their arrival at the Spindle. Damien felt a bit better about his own original awe at the sight of the interior of the cylinder when he saw Singh and Kellers both stop and stare in shock.

"Impressive, isn't it?" Jenna told them with a chuckle. "The Captain and I came through here back before we commissioned the *Blue Jay*. It's a bit of a shock to see for the first time."

They could only spare a few moments to look at the impressive view down the rotating cylinder with its parks and towns, though, as the cab Bistro had sent was already waiting for them. Rice gestured them forward, and the freighter officers piled in.

The conversation in the human-driven taxi, Damien noted, was far sparser than it had been on the entirely automated transit pod. Like the others, he kept in mind that there were ears listening, and they talked little in the five minute trip before the cab delivered them to a sprawling mansion, tucked away off a side road from one of the main LengthWays and concealed by a forest that looked to have been planted when the Spindle was built.

A uniformed butler met them as they exited the car, gently directing them into the house. Damien almost took him at face value, until Singh bumped him, directing his gaze with a jab of the chin. As the butler opened the door for them, his suit jacket opened enough to reveal a shoulder holster. Secure Bistro might be here on Spindle, but he clearly took no chances.

#

Bistro was waiting for them in the front hall of the mansion accompanied by another man that David didn't recognize. The stranger was younger than Bistro, tall and slim with dark red hair and piercing green eyes. Dressed in a demure dark gray suit, he fit into the elegant furnishings of the mansion like he belonged.

"Captain Rice, welcome to my home away from home," Bistro greeted him, offering his hand for a firm handshake. "I'd like to introduce you to Mr. Carmichael, a business associate of mine. I am only going to be on Prime for tonight, so I decided to combine two dinners into one. This isn't an issue, I hope?"

Rice shook his head – he was hardly going to object to whoever the billionaire magnate chose to include in the evenings events.

"Mr. Carmichael," he greeted the stranger with a nod and turned to present his crew:

"My first officer, Jenna Campbell," he introduced Jenna. "Then this is my Chief Engineer, James Kellers, my First Pilot Narveer Singh, and my Ship's Mage, Damien Montgomery."

"I have heard of some of your crew before," Carmichael murmured, shaking hands with each officer in turn. "But Mr. Montgomery is new to me. I believe you had a McLaughlin aboard before?"

"Yes," Rice said shortly. "He is sadly no longer with us."

"Of course, my apologies," the stranger murmured. "It is a pleasure to meet you all."

Bistro shook each officer's hand in turn as well and gestured everyone towards a door off of the wood-paneled hall.

"The dining room is through here," he announced. "I believe the cook should have dinner just about ready, if everyone can take a seat."

David waved his crew ahead of him, and eventually ended up seated at the right hand of the head of the table, directly across from Carmichael and next to Bistro. Jenna sat to his right, with Damien opposite her next to Carmichael, the youth looking somewhat out of sorts, though David suspected he had more experience with high society dining than the other three officers put together.

As the food arrived, Bistro slid a small black chip across the table to David, which the Captain took and pocketed with a nod.

"Payment for a successful delivery, Captain Rice – and I hope, only the beginning of our commercial relationship," Bistro told him quietly. "I have managed to confirm some details around that commission we spoke of, but nothing is set in stone yet. You still have some repairs to complete, you said?"

"It will be at least two or three days before we're even ready to begin loading cargo, let alone planning on shipping out," David agreed. "If you're thinking you may have a cargo for me, my ears will be open for a few days more." More than that could put his ability to find a cargo in Corinthian at risk, something he was unwilling to do.

"What is the cargo we're speaking of?" he asked. "I've learned in the past that not asking too many questions can get me in more trouble than I'm prepared to accept."

From the way Carmichael nearly choked on the extremely good clam chowder the cook had served, the other man knew something of the events David was referring to. That was... unexpected.

"It will be a load of machine parts and antimatter," Bistro said calmly. "The only -- complications -- are that it's shipping to Legatus, one of the UnArcana worlds, so there is always more paperwork."

David nodded. Of the just over a hundred known colonies, fourteen had officially banned the practice of Magic on their planetary surfaces, a decision that put them in sharp dispute with the over-arching government of the Mage-King of Mars. They sent their representatives to the Council at Mars like every other world, and jump ships still carried Mages to the worlds and Mage-commanded Martian warships guarded their worlds... but no Mage was allowed to set foot on the surface except on the King's business. Collectively, those fourteen systems were known as the UnArcana worlds, where Mages feared to tread.

"That makes sense," he agreed. "As I said, it will be a few days before we can begin to load cargo, so I can wait and see if your commission comes through."

"It will," Carmichael observed quietly, laying his spoon down on his empty bowl and leaning back. "The right requests have all been filed; it's just making its way to the desk of the man who signs off on these things. Antimatter shipments are especially sensitive, as it's so damned hard to make the stuff without magic."

David nodded silently as the soup plate was removed, and a plate of chicken and vegetables was placed in front of him. From the looks of it, the chicken breast had come from an actual bird, rather than a vat as most 'meat' aboard a space station or starship did. Neither Bistro nor Carmichael, however, acted as if this was unusual.

"What was it you do, Mr. Carmichael?" he asked politely, wondering how this man could speak so authoritatively.

"Ah," the man sighed appreciatively as he swallowed a mouthful of chicken. "This is good, Bistro," he said to the Magnate at the head of the table, then turned back to David. "I am an information broker," he explained. "I deal in being aware of events across as many systems as possible, and providing that knowledge to men like Bistro here for a fee." He glanced down the table, at the mostly silent faces of David's crew, wisely focused on the food.

"In fact, Captain, you may be able to assist me," he continued. Laying down his fork and carefully cleaning his fingers, he removed an archaic paper card from the breast pocket of his suit. "I like to get the first-hand impressions of ship's captains of the systems they've visited – the kind of details that don't make it into the news download. There would be some compensation if you could make time for me."

David shrugged and took the card.

"I'll see what I can do," he said noncommittally. His time for the next few days would be tied up quite tightly. On the other hand, having an information broker owing you a favor was never a bad thing.

"Enough dreary talk of business," Bistro interjected, somewhat boomingly and then directing his attention down the table. "Young Montgomery! I take it Corinthian is the first world you've visited since you left home, correct? What do you think of the Spindle?"

#

The dinner ran late in the night, with large quantities of very good wine. Damien awoke in his hotel room the next morning late and bleary eyed. Unfortunately for him, healing with magic required even more years of training than he already had, so he settled for a solution older than spaceflight: aspirin and a giant glass of water.

That, combined with a shower, left him feeling almost human as he maneuvered his way through the docking cylinder of Corinthian Prime to the *Blue Jay*. If Kellers's comments on their way to the dinner last night were correct, the conduit work should be done and ready for him to check around it for rune damage.

The *Blue Jay*'s corridors were busier than they'd been in days. Between the access port and the main engineering spaces he ran into two teams of four of the freighter's crew, both with panels open as they checked portions of the ship's electrical grid for burnouts caused by the ship's damage.

Busiest of all, though, was the engineering space itself. The massive chamber that contained the reactors, engines and life support of the freighter was a single open space, allowing a small crew to

68

operate on them all in anything from zero-gravity to two gravities of emergency acceleration.

The main fusion reactor quietly hummed away in the center of the space, ringed by a catwalk aligned with the ship's main engines. Up, down and sideways were all arbitrary when the ship wasn't under acceleration, and all parts of the wall and much of the empty space was taken up with hardware and the catwalks for operation under acceleration.

The arbitrary up-down axis of the engineering space was generally agreed to be that 'up' was towards where the RFLAM turret was mounted, and 'down' was towards the massive primary heat exchanger directly opposite. Currently, Kellers and a dozen crew members were pulling spools of fiber optic cable down through a hole in the 'upper' wall – the connectors for the new turret being installed.

Damien was more concerned about the power conduits for Engine Two and Engine Three. They ran on either side of the heat exchanger, which meant they actually passed *over* some of sub-matrixes connecting the jump matrix to the aft hull of the ship. It also meant they were close to the sub-matrix that had been carved into the heat exchanger itself – the matrix that, in an unmodified jumpship, converted any non-jump spell into heat energy and dumped it into space. There was some risk that the engineers would have damaged the runes, so they needed to be checked over by a trained Mage.

Spotting his approach, one of the crew pushed off from the cables and drifted to land close to Damien.

"Mage Montgomery, good morning!" she greeted him cheerfully.

"Good morning Kelly," Damien greeted her. Kelly LaMonte was the most junior of the *Blue Jay*'s three actual engineers. "Did we get the conduit repairs finished up?" he asked her politely, gesturing at the conduit for Engine Three, just behind where the engineer had landed.

"Got them finished up last night," she confirmed. "You don't need to worry about them though – since you weren't around they had their own Mage check the runes."

Damien froze in place, locking his gaze on the junior engineer, who was maybe a year older than him.

"She was working on the colony ship in the next bay over," Kelly said in a rapid-fire blurt of words. "They wanted to be able to sign off completely for the insurance last night, and you were at the dinner with the rest of the officers."

Wordlessly, Damien maneuvered around her, dropping himself to 'stand' where the other Mage would have had to be to check the runes under the conduit. The scar on the heat exchanger where Kellers had cut through the rune matrix with a blowtorch was clearly visible, and served to draw attention to the smooth area around it where Damien

69

and the Chief Engineer had burned away the matrix. Any Mage sufficiently trained to be able to check the rune matrix under the conduit would have known something was wrong as soon as the scar drew their eye.

"It's okay, Kelly," he said quietly, realizing he had been silent for a long time and the redheaded engineer was wilting further by the second. "We were just hoping to get all of the review done by me."

"She wasn't going to charge us," she explained hopefully. "We… you and the Chief had been working like dogs; we wanted to ease your mind a bit."

Damien smiled tightly. The only way his mind would ease now would be when they *left* the system.

"What's the meaning of this?" a voice bellowed, training projecting it to fill the entire vastness of the engineering chamber. Damien and Kelly both turned to see what Kellers was shouting about, and Damien's heart collapsed out of his chest at what he saw.

Two black-robed and black-armored figures stood in the entrance with magnetic boots locking their feet to the hull of the ship - and providing enough stability for the two Mage Enforcers to fire the ugly black battle rifles each carried.

"What the hell are you doing on my ship?" Kellers continued, the Chief Engineer managing to cross engineering to land in front of the Enforcers in a handful of breaths.

"We have a warrant," a voice said coldly, and a third figure stepped out between the two Enforcers. The third Mage also wore magnetic boots that matched his plain gray suit. From halfway across Engineering Damien couldn't make out the symbols on the man's medallion, but he could guess.

"We are here to inspect this ship's Rune Matrix, on the authority of Guildmaster Varren," the suited Mage, almost certainly a senior Rune Scribe, continued. "You *will* stand aside."

Damien was frozen. He just stood there as the three Mages crossed engineering to him. One of the Enforcer's subtly tracked Kellers with his eyes and rifle, but the other locked his gaze on Damien and held the Mage's attention as they approached.

The scribe ignored Damien and Kelly, stepping around the two *Blue Jay* crew members and over the conduit, his gaze on the scar and the space around it where the rune matrix *should* be. It felt like the entire room was holding their breath as the man stepped up to the exchanger and ran his fingers over the warm metal, down to where the rune matrix began.

"So it's true," he said simply, and turned back to the Damien, who realized the Enforcers were now on either side of him.

"Mage Damien Montgomery," the older Mage said quietly, "you are under arrest for a Class A Violation of Mage Law."

Still frozen in shock, Damien did nothing as the Enforcers slapped heavy, rune-inlaid, manacles on his wrists.

#

David Rice had lived aboard ships and space stations for his entire adult life and after twenty years as a spacer, he could count the days he'd spent planet-side on his fingers. Along the way, he'd mastered the complex, somewhat contortionist, art of typing in zero-gravity. He worked through the documents on his screen, signing off on each of the reports on the repairs completed the previous day for the insurance company, with the occasional wince at his part of the price tag.

He was just beginning to go through the documentation around paying off the remaining principal of the note financing the *Blue Jay* when the door to his office was thrown open.

"What is the meaning of this?" he demanded as two men marched through the door on magnetic boots. Both were dressed in the dark blue on black uniform of Corinthian Security, and carried ugly-looking black carbines.

"Sir," the older of the two security men greeted him politely. "Please come with us – this ship is being evacuated."

"This is *my* ship," David snapped back. "No one is evacuating me!" Even docked, the main authority aboard a starship was its captain.

"I'm sorry, sir," the officer told him. "The Ship Wright's Guild has declared the vessel unsafe for use, we've been ordered to remove everyone from the vessel for their own safety."

"What do you mean, *unsafe*?" David demanded. "I am not leaving my ship."

"We don't have any details, sir," the security man told him. "I am sorry, but you will have to come with us." The man's carbine, David noted, carried an under-barrel stungun, which was now, ever-so-subtly, pointing at David.

"I demand to speak to someone who can explain this," he ordered.

"I can do that, sir," the officer agreed quickly, "but you'll have to come with us."

His options appeared to be to either go with the officers, or get shocked into compliance. David sealed his computer, transferring the data to a chip to take with him, and floated away from his desk.

"Take me to whoever is in charge of this," he ordered.

The senior officer nodded calmly, leading the way out of the office. The magnetic boots the two security men wore clanged softly against the freighter's metal floors as they made their way down the corridors to the tube connecting to the station.

The halls and corridors of David's ship were empty. He had expected to run into at least one of the parties he knew were working on the electrical grid, but all he saw was an open set of paneling where one of the teams had been working.

When they exited the ship, he found the docking tube already under guard. Four security officers, each equipped with the same black carbine/stungun combination as David's escorts, manned a barricade blocking entrance or exit from his ship.

He finally began to understand what the hell was going on when he saw the man in charge of the operation. Standing amidst the security guards, keeping David's crew back with nothing more than his black-armored robe and a flat glare was the readily identifiable figure of a Guild Enforcer.

"Sir, we found Captain Rice," the officer who'd been doing all of the talking told the Enforcer. "He insisted on speaking with you."

The Enforcer turned to face Rice, his magnetic boots clicking sharply on the ground. David found himself floating in the zero gee as he met the Mage's gaze, and wished he had magnetic boots of his own. They wouldn't have allowed him to be any more intimidating to the Mage soldier, but they would have let him feel less ridiculous.

"Is everyone off?" the Enforcer asked the security officer, ignoring David.

"We left the Captain to last," the man confirmed. "One last team is sweeping the ship right now, they'll be out shortly."

The Enforcer turned to the four men on the barricade. "As soon as the sweep team returns, lock down the ship under a Security Code," he ordered. "Provide the Code to Guildmaster Varren's office, then maintain security over the docking tube," he met David's gaze levelly, "just in case."

"What is the meaning of this?" David finally demanded, done with being ignored.

"I am Enforcer Evan Santos," the man introduced himself calmly. "Your ship's rune matrix was reviewed by a Rune Scribe this morning, under warrant from Guildmaster Varren," the Enforcer continued. "Based on that review, your matrix was judged unsafe for use. There was also a noted risk of feedback and other issues that render the vessel unsafe for current habitation. Your Ship's Mage has been arrested for illegal experimentation – you are damned lucky no one was hurt!"

"I was aware of the change to the rune matrix," David responded. "There have been *no* issues from it, and it may have saved our lives."

Santos shrugged.

"I am *not* an expert on these things," he replied. "However, we escorted James Marlow, a senior Rune Scribe who *is* an expert, to review the matrix, and that was his judgment."

"So, how, exactly do I get my ship back?" David asked.

"That will be up to Guildmaster Varren," the Enforcer told him. "You will need to make an appointment with him – I was merely charged with evacuating and securing the ship your Mage made a deathtrap."

"What happens to Damien?" David asked.

"If he saved your lives as you say, you might be able to argue some clemency," Santos replied. "But I wouldn't count on it – the Guildmaster cannot risk being seen as weak in disciplining Mages."

#

Six walls, one door, zero-gravity. The walls that surrounded Damien were covered in silver runes that suppressed his gift, locking the nature of reality so that no magic could be done inside the cell. A hammock hung from one corner and the intimidating hoses of a zero-gravity toilet in another.

The cell was somewhere in the core of the Spindle, the cylinder that ran through the heart of the habitation zone of Corinthian Prime. Here, the rotation of the outside station was nonexistent, helping create a high security prison in the heart of the station.

Strangely to Damien, the runes that suppressed his ability to wield magic didn't do anything to his gift for reading the flow of it. He spent the first few minutes after being tossed in the cell floating in shock, but then he'd turned to deciphering the runes to help keep his mind engaged.

Following the lines of energy revealed that the rune matrix binding the cell was surprisingly fragile. If he'd had the tools to do it, there were four connections tying together different components that would break the entire matrix if severed.

If he had the tools to do it.

Given that he was in the cell for illegal experimentation with rune matrices, Damien doubted that his captors were going to casually leave silver inlaying tools floating around the high security cell.

Mage Law was notoriously bad for laying out just what crimes fell under what category. Some were easy to guess – the standard 'example' given for a Class A Mage Law Violation was Pre-meditated Murder by Magic – but for a lot of the more esoteric crimes, the only people who really knew were Judges and Enforcers.

What Damien had been taught, though, was the penalties. The Class A Violation he was charged with carried a minimum sentence of twenty years forced labor. Mages put to forced labor weren't hauling stones or swinging pickaxes, and the living conditions were supposed to be decent – but the work was things like 'conjuring antimatter'. Mage prisoners did some of the most dangerous jobs in the Protectorate. Civilian and military Mages doing the jobs they made prisoners do were extremely well paid. Prisoners… simply had to do them.

That was the minimum sentence. There were rumors about the maximum sentence, rumors Damien wasn't sure he believed. The Protectorate Charter forbade the death penalty for anything except treason… but the rumor was that if you were convicted of a truly heinous Class A crime, they would take away your magic.

And then let you go.

#

"So?" Jenna asked when David entered the hotel bar where his remaining officers were waiting. A bottle of expensive whiskey was set amidst the three of them, and Kellers silently poured David a glass after seeing his face.

"Apparently, this whole situation isn't enough to get anything resembling urgency out of the Guildmaster's staff," he said quietly. "They may have impounded my ship and imprisoned one of my officers in a high security cell, but they can't make time in the Guildmaster's schedule for two days." He sighed.

"I took the appointment, obviously," he continued, "but Guildmaster Varren is in control of both the *Blue Jay's* impoundment, and Damien's imprisonment. No one else can do anything about either."

"What about the system government?" Singh demanded. The turban-wearing pilot gestured energetically with a cup of milky tea – he was the only one not drinking the whiskey being passed around.

David took a slug of the whiskey, letting it burn its way down his throat as if that would help.

"It's Mage Law," he said bluntly. "The Compact says the mundane government can't interfere unless they have evidence of a flawed trial." The Compact was one of the two documents that underlay the legal structure of the Protectorate – the Charter defined the rules and laws that governed everyone, and the Compact defined how Mage and Mundane dealt with each other. Simplest of those rules: Mages tried their own, unless they were clearly abusing the privilege.

The table was silent for a long moment as the whiskey bottle made its way around.

"So what do we do?" Singh finally asked.

"The note on the *Blue Jay* is almost paid off," David said quietly. "If everything falls apart, I pay out the crew, return to Mars and finance a new ship. If you're willing to come, I'd be pleased to have you all with me."

"Fuck that," the pilot said bluntly. "I meant: what do we do about Damien?"

"We wait," David replied. "I'll keep paying the crew until we know for sure what's happened with the ship, and I'm not going *anywhere* until I have a chance to speak for Damien."

"The hell if any of us going anywhere till we can do that," Singh said firmly, and the others nodded.

"I'm not sure we'll make any difference," the captain warned them. "Varren apparently plays hardball with Mages in Corinthian – apparently, he wants to prove that Corinthian has nothing to fear from Mages."

"He certainly isn't showing Mages have nothing to fear from Corinthian," Kellers murmured. "What do we do if they're going to throw away the key? Or worse?"

David didn't answer immediately, looking down at his hands and the glass of whiskey in them. At the end of the day, he could replace his ship – though his other issues would probably continue to pursue him – but was he really willing to abandon the young man who'd saved his life and the lives of all of his crew?

"We'll cross that bridge when we come to it," he eventually said, his voice steady. "But I'd ask you all to remember this: what he's being punished for, he did to save our lives. And he doesn't even know why we were in danger."

#

The Protectorate had stringent rules on keeping prisoners in zero-gravity cells, Damien discovered, as twice each day he was removed from the cell and taken to a gym with magically induced gravity to exercise and eat. The entire time he was outside of his cell, he was accompanied by two Enforcers in their ominous black armor, neither of whom said a word to him that wasn't a direct instruction.

It wasn't until after the fourth exercise session, at the end of the second day of his imprisonment, that Damien saw anyone other than his two guards. Instead of escorting him back to his cell, they escorted him to a small office with gravity runes where a bespectacled and balding man in a plain black suit waited for him.

"Please be seated Mr. Montgomery," the stranger told Damien, gesturing towards one of the two chairs in the room. He was seated in the second, behind a desk that was too plain and empty to be his. "Please leave us," the man then instructed the Enforcers.

"There's a panic button under the desk Mr. Burton," one of the Enforcers responded calmly. "If there are any issues, we'll be back inside in seconds."

The door swung shut behind them, and Burton met Damien's gaze levelly.

"I am Zach Burton, your appointed defender," he said calmly. "I apologize for not being in to speak with you sooner, but I had to research the particulars of the charge levied against you – as you can imagine, it's not a common one."

Damien glanced at the locked door.

"They're acting like I'm dangerous," he said quietly, the words half a complaint.

"Son, from what I'm told, you came within a sunbathing snowflake of scattering everyone aboard your ship in pieces across several light years," Burton said dryly, looking over the tops of his glasses at Damien. "You're facing charges of illegal modification of a Jump Matrix and eighty-six counts of attempted murder."

The words hit Damien like a body blow and he sank in his chair as the full magnitude of the accusations sank in.

"I didn't... I never..."

"I have to admit," Burton continued after he realized Damien wasn't going to be able to say anything coherent, "that I don't believe I've ever seen quite so open and shut a case from this side. The ship itself constitutes an insurmountable degree of evidence."

"No one was hurt!" Damien burst out. "It was completely safe, I could *tell*."

Burton was silent for a moment, and then sighed deeply. "Damien, I've looked up what they've charged you with. They can take away your magic. An insanity plea won't help you."

"I am *not* crazy," Damien told him. "I turned the matrix into an amplifier to save us all – if it hadn't been safe, I *wouldn't have jumped us*."

"The Guildmaster and his experts – you know, the people who *build* those matrices? – disagree with you," Burton said calmly. "They say you all burned up several lifetimes worth of luck surviving so many jumps, and the ship is at risk of coming apart just sitting there at this point. I'm honestly not sure what you can do other than plead the stupidity of youth and throw yourself on the mercy of the court."

"They *might* let you get away with two or three decades of labor if you do that," the lawyer continued, "and you're young enough that you'd still have a few good decades left after that."

Damien sat in the chair in silence for a long time, staring at the lawyer.

"Look, there's not a lot I can do here," Burton finally said. "Unless you want to tell me magic space pixies modified the runes on that ship, they've got the physical evidence to prove the matrix modification charge, which leads inherently to the attempted murder charges. If you want to avoid this, you shouldn't have broken the most complicated spell known to man and Mage!"

"If I hadn't, I and those eighty-six people would be dead," Damien told him quietly. "What do you want of me?"

"Listen, the trial won't be for a few more days," Burton told him. "Think it over, and I'll see if I dig up some grounds for clemency. The guards will call me if you ask – they have to."

The defender stood up, offering his hand to Damien.

"I'll do my best, Mr. Montgomery, but the truth is you're screwed," he said bluntly. "I stand by my recommendation: throw yourself on the mercy of the court and plead ignorance. It's your only way out of here."

Damien shook the man's hand. The man was trying his best. None of the other Mages apparently thought what he'd done was possible, so, from their perspective, they were right. He had tried to kill everyone aboard his ship.

It wasn't their fault that he had done something they *knew* to be impossible.

#

Captain Rice arrived at the Guildmaster's office ten minutes early for his appointment. Two days had passed without any news of his ship or his Mage, and his staff and crew were starting to get impatient for their Captain to fix things. David had no illusions about his ability to fix *this*, but he knew he had to try.

The Guildmaster was almost half an hour late. David sat, surrounded by potted plants, in the waiting room on one of the higher floors of the black metal fortress the Guild called home on Corinthian Prime for forty minutes.

He spent most of the time trying not to take his growing frustration out on the gentleman holding down the massive wooden desk outside Varren's office. There was nothing the assistant could do to hurry Varren up from wherever the man was hiding, and David had learned long ago never to piss off the people who organized the schedules.

When Varren finally showed up he entered through the waiting room himself. He was a large man, on the edge of grossly obese, wearing a perfectly tailored gray suit that tried to hide it. His hair had gone pure white around a growing bald spot on the top of his head, and his eyes were a cheerful bright blue. The gold medallion at his throat was the first David had ever seen to be larger than standard, but the number of symbols etched into it explained the need. Damien was unusual in that his medallion bore the marks of two specialties. Varren bore the three stars of a Jump Mage, the stylized atom of a Transmuter, the quill of a Rune Scribe, and the sword of an Enforcer.

For all of his size, the Guildmaster was light on his feet and approached David immediately.

"I apologize profusely for keeping you waiting, Captain Rice," he told the Captain. "The Inspectors on the *Blue Jay* finished their work a bit earlier than planned, and I wanted to meet with them so I could give you an update on the status of the ship."

"I appreciate that," David replied. *Any* answers would be helpful at this point.

"My office then," Varren instructed, gesturing forward. He turned to the assistant. "Cob, can you re-arrange my schedule for the rest of the day to make sure I have enough time for Captain Rice? The Governor is the only thing we shouldn't be able to change."

"I'll see who I can push off till tomorrow," the assistant promised.

"If someone's willing to meet me after dinner, set that up instead," Varren told him as he opened the door into his office for Rice to precede him.

The Guildmaster's office was not what David had expected. The front room had been expensive furniture and green plants. The furniture of the office was probably expensive, but that was about all the room shared with the outside. Squat bookshelves covered every wall, surrounding an immense desk that might have been real wood, but was hard to identify under the paper that covered it. The shelves were bulging with paper copies of reports. The desk was occupied with four monitors, and two more were set up on the appropriate nearby shelves to provide more real estate for data.

Varren entered, and waved his hand. The monitors all rolled themselves up, shrinking into single bars lying on the desk, half-hidden by paper.

"I apologize for the mess," the Guildmaster told David. "It drives Cob to distraction, but I find that the more data I can lay eyes on at once, the better I'm able to think. I always seem to end up with half the station spread around my office, though," he admitted ruefully as he gestured David to a chair that, mercifully, did not seem to be occupied by paper.

Settling into the indicated seat, David almost jumped as the fabric and frame automatically adjusted itself to an appropriate ergonomic position for his body shape. Moments later, he felt a knot he hadn't quite realized he'd been carrying in his back release, and he glanced down at the chair appreciatively for a moment.

Then he looked up, meeting Varren's gaze across the man's massive and crowded desk.

"My ship," he asked quietly.

"I was hoping to have better news," the Guildmaster answered, the cheerfulness of his voice fading. "The Inspectors have concluded that the damage done to the rune matrix is too pervasive for repair. Even if we could fix it, there's so many changes that the ship would never be truly safe to jump. The *Blue Jay* is being condemned."

Condemned. David had known it was possible – even likely - from the moment he and his crew had been evacuated at gunpoint.

"We jumped that ship *fourteen times* after the modifications were made," he argued. "The *Jay* is perfectly safe!"

"Captain, please!" Varren replied. "You and your crew should be scattered in pieces from here to Sherwood! Just because you have been unbelievably lucky doesn't mean you should keep pushing your luck!"

"The Jump Matrix hasn't been changed since the first Mage-King *wrote* it," he continued, "because no one has *ever* managed to do so and have the ship and Mage survive.

"The *Blue Jay* will be held to serve as evidence in Mage Montgomery's trial, and then scrapped and the parts and scrap sold," Varren concluded. "You will, of course, receive the funds from the sale, less costs and a service fee."

The chair wouldn't let David slump backwards.

"What about Montgomery?" he finally asked.

"Mage Montgomery has been charged with modification of a jump matrix and eighty-six counts of attempted murder," the Guildmaster said gently. "So far as I can tell, he is either utterly ignorant and callous, or completely insane – and only an impossible amount of luck kept him from utterly destroying your ship."

"He *saved our lives*," David replied. At this point, it sounded like Damien's only hope was to tell Varren everything. "He turned the matrix into an amplifier, Guildmaster," he continued quietly. "If he hadn't, the pirates would have killed us. Instead, he destroyed them. I agreed to let him. If someone has to be punished for this, punish *me*."

Varren stood from his chair. It was a slow process – light on his feet or not, the Guildmaster was a massive man – and he was silent as he walked away from David to look out the window.

"If a man orders a doctor to remove his heart because it is broken - and the doctor does it," he said quietly, "do you call it a suicide – or charge the doctor with murder, because he should have the knowledge to say no?"

79

"Even if he managed what you claim," Varren continued, his voice still quiet as he refused to face David, "The Jump Matrix wouldn't have survived intact. Bring what evidence you have to the trial, Captain, and you may manage to argue the Judge down in his sentence, but I have no choice."

"No choice, Guildmaster?"

"Based off of the evidence I have seen, my assessment is that Damien Montgomery is either dangerously unaware of his limits or criminally insane," the old man told David, his gaze on the greenery of the Spindle. "My recommendation to the Judge will be that his magic is taken from him, and we have already requested the presence of a Hand to carry out the sentence."

A Hand. Damien's crime was so severe, they were bringing a Hand of the Mage-King of Mars, the roving warrior-Judges who served as the King's enforcers and wielded his authority outside Sol, to punish him.

"I understand your loyalty to your people," Varren continued. "It says good things about both you and Mage Montgomery, but his crimes are inarguable and the punishment is not mine to set."

The Guildmaster finally looked away from the window. His hands behind his back, his eyes were sad as they met David's across the room. "I am sorry, Captain Rice, but with what Mage Montgomery has done, my hands are tied."

"I understand," David replied. He might not understand the reason, but he understood the reality. He stood. "If you'll excuse me, then, I must inform my crew."

"I appreciate your understanding Captain Rice," Varren replied. "If there is anything I or my office can do to assist you while you remain in Corinthian, let me know. I realize how difficult a situation you are in."

"Thank you," David told him, the words ashes on his tongue.

#

The Citadel had an efficient elevator system, and David was outside, blinking in the light from the glowing core above his head, within a few minutes. He quickly left the main pathway, losing himself in the parks around the Guild's offices until no one could see him.

No ship. No Mage. No crew – for his officers would never forgive him if he couldn't save Damien.

He wouldn't be able to forgive *himself* if he let this happen.

He stared at the trees for a long time, and then pulled a business card from his pocket and plugged a contact number into his personal computer.

A few moments later, a red-haired man with piercing green eyes answered.

"Captain Rice. I wasn't expecting to hear from you at this point," the man told David.

"You said you deal in information, Carmichael," Rice replied. "I need some. We need to meet."

#

Alaura Stealey was not drunk. Given the five now-empty bottles of stupendously expensive, actually-shipped-from-Scotland-on-Earth, whisky sitting on the desk in her office, this would be a surprise to anyone who interrupted her, and was a disappointment to her.

As a Hand of the Mage-King of Mars, Stealey was sent into the worst conflicts that the Protectorate had to offer, and the mess she'd just resolved on Corona was no exception. The original colony had been funded by a corporation out of Tau Ceti, third oldest of the Core Worlds. That corporation had been leaning on the local elected government to allow them mining access in explicitly designated reserves.

A portion of the local populace had responded with violence. After six *weeks* of negotiation, Stealey had finally managed to ram a deal that neither side was satisfied with down everyone's throats. The corporation didn't get to mine in area that was unique in the Protectorate and in *need* of protection, but there were no pardons for the rebels either. Nine of their leaders were going to be spending the next couple of decades as guests of the Coronan prison system, judged and sentenced under *her* authority as Hand of the King.

Unfortunately for Stealey's desire to get very drunk, one of her first operations as a Hand of the King had run her into a similar group of rebels, with less of a point and less of a willingness to negotiate. *That* encounter had resulted in her taking several explosive rounds to the stomach. She'd lived, but every organ in that section of her body had been replaced with cybernetic parts.

Cybernetic parts served the purposes of those replaced organs in the main, but the toxin filters didn't distinguish alcohol from any other poison. Her new and improved guts didn't allow for such minor things as getting drunk. Or pregnant, for that matter, which she hadn't expected to bother her before it happened.

With a sigh, Alaura reached for the sixth bottle -- she *liked* the taste of whisky, and it was theoretically possible she could get drunk if she drank *enough* -- only to be interrupted by a 'New Message' alert on her desk. She stared at the alert as the monitor extended itself up off her desk, noting that it was an interstellar delivery, carried by a courier ship out of Corinthian.

"I stayed in one place too long," she said aloud, and then opened the message with a sigh. She paid almost no attention to the recorded video message from the Corinthian Guildmaster, beyond confirming that they needed her presence, but then started skimming the attached files.

A modified matrix had made *fourteen jumps*?

That was only possible if it had been successfully modified and turned into a true amplifier. As Stealey understood it that was theoretically possible, if you had the full schematics of the jump matrix *and* understood that a jump matrix was a restricted amplifier.

Without those, working with no time and under fire, it should have been impossible.

Alaura hit the intercom, raising the control bridge of her personal ship.

"Harmon," she greeted the ship's first officer. "Is anyone off ship?"

"The last of the crew shuffled aboard about fifteen minutes ago according to the master at arms," the Lieutenant, seconded from the Protectorate Navy to her personal service, replied. "What do you need, ma'am?"

"If everyone is aboard and we're fully fueled, set a course for the Corinthian system," she ordered. "I have business there."

"Yes ma'am," Lieutenant Harmon replied. "Computer gives me an ETA of five days with the Crew Mages working standard shifts," he advised her after a moment's pause.

"Include me in the jump rotation," Stealey ordered. "This may be important."

"Yes ma'am."

Stealey cut the intercom and turned back to the console to see what she could pull up about Damien Montgomery.

There *was* a way that what he'd done could be possible. The young Mage could be the find of the century.

And the Corinthians wanted her to take his magic away.

#

Carmichael met David at his office. Late in the evening by Spindle's time, the immense tube of light down the center of the station dimming towards its programmed night, the discreet three story building tucked on the edge of one Spindle's many small towns was empty.

82

The information broker let David into the building himself, leading the Captain silently through an office of brick and carpet that looked like it belonged in the twentieth century instead of the twenty-fifth. Finally, they reached an office on the top floor with windows looking out over the artificial world of the Spindle.

"Close the door behind you," Carmichael instructed. As David obeyed, he lowered old fashioned blinds across the windows, blocking out the fading light outside.

Hidden panels on the room automatically began to glow to counteract the reduced light, keeping the office at a comfortable level of light as David looked around the room. Everything in the room had been done in Sherwood Oak – the expensive hardwood that he'd just delivered a cargo of himself. The walls were paneled in the smooth wood, likely concealing filing cabinets and bookshelves, as there was no furniture in the room other than chairs and a large desk – also Sherwood Oak.

"This entire building is swept for bugs daily," Carmichael said calmly. "This room, once the door and blinds are closed, functions as a Faraday Cage. If someone can get past *that*, there are white noise generators mounted in each corner to prevent anyone outside listening. I stole the idea for the setup from the Navy," he explained when David looked at him questioningly. "A contact of mine was the electrician they hired when they were expanding the base at Tau Ceti. This is as secure a place to have a conversation as you'll find in this system."

"Now, what did you want from me?"

"You told me you deal in information," David began. "I tend to presume that dealing tends to drag you into the grayer areas of the world. I need... criminal contacts. Preferably organized - with resources. I'm going to need certain materials and equipment that isn't legally available, and I'm hoping to be able to acquire additional manpower."

"I see," Carmichael said aloud, resting his hands on his desk. "You are a ship's captain; you have some idea of the price of what you are asking for. I'd guess that you wouldn't be here if you didn't think you could afford it."

"Your plan, I assume, is to breakout your young Mage and flee the system?"

"Yes," David answered flatly. He wasn't going to give this man everything, but he had to trust him that much if he was going to get anywhere.

The broker sighed, looking down at his hands for a long moment in silence.

"If you were anyone else, Captain, I think I could help you," he said finally. "But the criminals of this station won't deal with you, unless it's to collect the bounty on your head."

"The Blue Star Syndicate isn't even *here*," David argued. Widespread as the Syndicate was, he'd quietly checked to see if they had any presence in Corinthian before he'd taken the contract.

"But they have a long arm," Carmichael said softly. "And even if they didn't, men such as you want to deal with are unenthused with those who turn their kind in to the law!"

David shivered slightly at the words, remembering just how he'd acquired the bounty the Blue Star Syndicate had put on his head. Desperate to make a note payment on the *Blue Jay*, he'd taken a cargo contract without asking questions. Unusual power readings had led them to investigate the containers, which had turned out to contain *hundreds* of kidnapped teenagers in cryo-stasis, destined to be forced into various forms of slavery.

He'd delivered the containers and collected his payment. He'd *also* told the Mage-King's Navy what he'd delivered. The ensuing raid had seen eight hundred and fourteen kidnapped children rescued – and the son of the leader of the Blue Star Syndicate killed in the firefight.

David couldn't bring himself to regret that decision.

"So money won't be enough," he said aloud, meeting Carmichael's eyes. "But Damien is being held in the zero-grav high security cells up there," he pointed up at where the central core ran through the station. "Their people and resources can't break anyone out – they're all known to System Security. I might be able to. Surely at least one of the bosses has to have someone locked in there?"

"You're offering to breakout the kind of man who gets locked in zero-grav confinement?" Carmichael asked dryly.

"I'm already planning to break one man out," David replied. "If that's the price I have to pay, that's the price I have to pay."

The information broker held his gaze for a long moment, and then nodded.

"I think I can get someone to make a deal," he said quietly. "I'll set up a meeting. How much time do you have?"

"They'll scrap my ship after the trial," David told him. "So before then – I'm told it will be in four days."

"I'll contact you once I have a meet," Carmichael instructed.

David left the broker's office with a sense of hope for the first time in days. He didn't want to know what kind of man he'd have to breakout of Corinthian Prime's highest security prison – almost certainly the kind who belonged in there – but he knew something he hadn't told Carmichael and wouldn't tell the crime boss.

Somehow, he didn't think that any escaped criminal still on the station would remain at large once the Hand arrived.

#

If David had had any doubts about the degree of connection that Carmichael had with the underworld on Corinthian Prime, the speed with which the broker organized the meeting would have laid them to rest. The next morning, station time, the broker sent him instructions to come to a specific bar in the zero-gravity docks district that evening – and to only bring one person with him.

He brought Narveer – the pilot had learned to fly in the Martian Marine Corps, which insisted that all of its personnel be capable in hand to hand and rifle combat before they let them learn any other specialty.

They arrived exactly on time, to find Carmichael waiting for them outside the bar with a pair of men David could only describe as 'muscle.' They were big men, dressed in matching cheap suits and wearing matching glowers.

"You made it, good," the broker greeted him. "Let's go," he gestured down the street.

"We're not going in the bar?" David asked. He'd been relying on a somewhat public location to keep the meeting civil.

"Carney don't like crowds," one of the muscle rumbled. "You meet where he says."

"He's promised safe conduct," Carmichael told David. "Carney doesn't give explicit promises very often – because he doesn't break them when he does."

"All right," David agreed uneasily, glancing at Narveer. The pilot's face was blank, his eyes tracking the two thugs.

Carmichael led the way and the two thugs followed up the rear as the five drifted their way through the zero-gravity part of the station. Eventually, they reached what looked like one of the dozens of storage warehouses scattered throughout the docks. Following the information broker into the warehouse, though, David felt himself yanked towards a specific 'floor' – the 'warehouse' had gravity runes.

Inside the unassuming door, walls blocked off most of the space from an entrance that was utterly bland and empty. A metal detector covered the only way further into the warehouse, and a pair of guards, matching to the set following him in, flanked the door.

"Leave any weapons with us," the speaker of the muscle that had accompanied them to the warehouse rumbled.

"I'm not carrying any," David replied, glancing at Singh. "Narveer?"

85

The pilot shrugged and pulled a rocket pistol, designed for minimum recoil in zero-gravity, from his jacket. As the guard took that with a satisfied grunt, Singh proceeded to produce two black-handled, back-curved knives from the small of his back.

"Watch the edge," he said sharply as the guard eyed them. "Honed to a few molecules thick."

The guard took the two kukris *very* respectfully, and then blinked as Singh reached up to his turban and produced a collapsible baton, a small yellow lightning bolt on the black case marked it as electrified.

"That's everything," he announced as the guards piled the weapons by the scanner. "It better not leave without me," he told them fiercely.

"The boss promised," the vocal guard told him. "He don't make promises we can't keep."

This, David considered, was as much a warning as a reassurance.

The interior of the warehouse, once you got past the spartan security checkpoint, looked like any small office complex. There were even potted plants that they were led past until they finally reached a plain-looking door. There was nothing to distinguish this door from any other office door they'd seen coming through.

"You're expected," the guard told them, and then opened the door.

Carmichael led the way and David followed into a neat, perfectly organized, office that wouldn't have looked out of place for any corporate CEO in the Protectorate.

"Have a seat," the man seated behind the heavy metal desk instructed, gesturing to the chairs. The mob boss Carney could almost be mistaken for the muscle outside, until you saw his eyes. For all his size and muscle, Carney's eyes were ice blue, flat and cold.

"Thank you for meeting with me," David told him as he and his fellows took the two seats. Those flat eyes leveled on him.

"I'll confess," the boss said, his voice slow and precise, "that Carmichael's description of your offer intrigued me. I do wonder, though, why you think you can succeed in breaking my people out where I would fail?"

"Unless System Security is more incompetent that any force I've ever met," David replied, "anyone coming in to visit your people will be searched and watched like a hawk. They'll assume anyone meeting convicted mob offenders may have been bought or compromised by their employers."

"My man, on the other hand, has been a model prisoner and we have not caused any trouble on the station. They won't suspect us, so we can get useful gear closer than any of your people," the Captain explained.

"Fair," Carney grunted. "What's your offer?"

"We need a distraction and certain gear – flash-bangs, Nix-Six grenades and stunguns," David told him. "I need security away from the connector between the jail and the dock – we'll head straight for my ship and break *it* free as well once Damien is clear."

"In exchange, we'll free one of your people when we break Damien out, and pay you one million Martian dollars."

"Nix-Six is not an easy item to acquire," Carney observed. Nix-Six was the common name for 'Neutralization Solution Six,' the current standard knockout gas issued to police riot suppression squads.

"Corinthian System Security has it as standard issue," David replied. "Do you expect me to believe that if the CSS has it, you don't?"

The mob boss chuckled, a smile momentarily even reaching his eyes.

"True," he conceded. "But a million dollars..." he shrugged. "A million makes almost no difference to the value of your offer, and one rescue is far too little. No deal."

David started to rise to leave in silence, but the mob boss waved him back to his seat.

"No deal at that rate," he clarified. "I don't want your money Captain. But understand that System Security swept up a cell of my best operators six months ago."

"I'll get you your gear – hell, I'll throw in body armor and I think I can get you the codes to unlock the cells in the Core – but we'll do this on my terms. I have six guys in the cells in the Core. You'll free them all."

David winced. It was a better deal than he'd hoped for, but he knew what kind of 'operators' ended up in the Core – hit men and the most violent of pimps and extortionists. He needed the gear and the backup though.

"We'll do it," he said simply.

"All right then Captain," Carney replied, leaning forward across his desk. "What's your plan?"

#

Jenna and Kellers were waiting in David's room when he and Narveer returned to the hotel. Walking into the room, David dropped the case he'd received from Carney – the first part of the requested gear, mostly the flash-bangs and Nix-Six canisters – next to the door.

"Well?" Jenna asked.

"Is it safe to talk?" David asked, glancing at Kellers.

The engineer nodded, pointing at a small black box sitting on the table by David's bed. "There's only a standard, accessible-by-court-order-only, recording box," the engineer told him. "That's showing an empty room right now. It looks like we haven't attracted enough suspicion to rate special attention."

"Good," the Captain answered, looking around his officers. It would take a warrant for System Security to bug his hotel room, but given that one of his people was in a high security cell, *he* would have given the warrant if he was the judge.

"Carney's in," he continued. "Basic gear is in that case," he gestured, "and we have a drop-off location for a crate of stunguns and SmartDart ammo."

"A crate is a few more stunguns than the four of us can use," Kellers observed, glancing around the room.

"We need manpower," David admitted. "Carney's people have promised to draw the guards away from the *Blue Jay*, but we'll need to get ourselves and Damien from the security cells to the dock – and believe me, CSS is going to *know* what we're doing. Much as I wanted to avoid it, we're going to have to involve the crew."

"Unless you were planning on flying the ship with half a dozen people, we needed to anyway," Jenna reminded him. "We need at least twenty of the spacers aboard if we want to be able to get anywhere without the ship coming apart around us."

"Conveniently, we're getting a crate of twenty stunguns," David said dryly. "I want each of you to approach the people you trust most in your departments and feel them out. Make sure they all know that anyone who stays is being released with two months' pay – it's the least I can do for our crew, this wasn't *their* fault."

"You might want to try bribing them to be *involved*, not to *leave*," Narveer boomed with a laugh. "I don't think we'll have an issue," he continued. "The pilots will be in."

"Don't commit anyone to this until you've talked to them," David warned. "Kellers – I want you to pick up the stunners and ammo. Let's try not to draw attention to ourselves."

"I have a scheduled meeting with Damien tomorrow evening," he continued. "That gives us at least twenty-four hours before the Hand should arrive, based on what the Guildmaster said."

"We only get one shot at this," David reminded his people, glancing around the hotel room, his gaze finally settling on the case of grenades by the door.

"If we mess this up, we join Damien in the High Security cells," he finished quietly.

"Or we can watch the boy who saved our lives swing, and lose our ship," Singh summarized bluntly. "Is anyone here *not* in?" the *Blue Jay's* First Pilot demanded.

Silence answered him.

After the one visit from his lawyer, Damien had seen no one except the pair of Enforcers who came to escort him to the gym to exercise and eat. Time didn't quite blur together, as the day after the lawyer visit they at least gave him a tablet with access to a basic entertainment and education library.

While the library wasn't exactly up to the minute on current news – at a guess, someone had to manually review what articles and events could be included – it did allow him to research the previous cases of Mages attempting to modify their rune matrices.

There weren't that many cases anyone was certain of. There were a dozen or so where observers, with hindsight in place, had managed to reasonably prove that the Mage aboard the ship which had come apart into pieces when jumping had been experimenting.

The only two cases where a Mage had actually been brought to trial, it sounded like they'd got it half right – *some* of the ship had survived the jump, enough that the Mage had been alive to arrest. One had committed suicide before his trial, and the legal case study Damien found on the other ended with the ominous note of 'Turned over to the Hand of the Mage-King for justice.'

There was very little sanctioned experimentation with jump matrices. The rune matrix hadn't been noticeably changed in the two hundred years since the first Mage-King and his people had built the very first jump ships.

The only person who had *ever* done anything with the standard jump matrix, in fact, was the first Mage-King himself. No improvements since. Almost no research since. The few experiments that had occurred had uniformly ended in death and tragedy.

Damien was starting to suspect that he really was crazy when his door slid open, revealing one of his Enforcers, a pair of rune encrusted manacles in his hands.

"You have a visitor Montgomery," the Enforcer told him. "We both know you're not gonna cause trouble, but I've got to put these on you anyway. Gonna make an issue of it?"

Damien shook his head, resignedly holding his wrists out as the mag-booted Enforcer manacled him and gently pulled him out of the cell. There was only one Enforcer today, though Damien saw a few of the uniformed Corinthian System Security officers guarding the cells as well.

They passed by the entrance to the cell block, where Damien couldn't resist sagging against the restraint, glancing over the security desk's metal detector and armed guards. He'd seen it before, and the only thing that stood out was the black case someone had left floating in the waiting area beyond the security gate, latched to one of the hooks set there for just that purpose

The Enforcer yanked a little, pulling Damien a little faster up to a door surprisingly close to the front entrance.

"Gravity in the room is that way," he said kindly, pointing and helping Damien orient himself before opening the door. "Your Captain has twenty minutes," the Enforcer continued. "I'll be back for you then."

Damien drifted through the door and dropped slightly onto the runed steel of the floor. Behind him, he heard the Enforcer's mag-boots clicking against the door as he returned to the front desk.

The room was undecorated beyond the runes on the floor generating gravity, with only a desk and two chairs sitting in the middle. Captain David Rice was sprawled lazily in one of the chairs, and gestured Damien to the other.

"How're you holding up?" the Captain asked quietly once Damien was seated. "This place looks like a precursor to hell."

"They gave me a library," Damien said dryly, "or I'd be going nuts. It's damned weird – I know there are other prisoners in here, but I haven't seen any."

"From what I've been told, that's as much to keep you safe from them as anything else," David told him. "Most people in here killed someone, and the reasons were rarely good."

"It's terrifying," Damien admitted, glancing up at the cameras and audio pickups in the corner. "I... just want this over. However it ends, I just want it over."

"You know how they want it to end," David said flatly.

"It's not set in stone," Damien argued. It was only in the worst cases that he'd lose his magic. More likely was twenty or thirty years at labor – he could *live* through that.

"The Guildmaster's already made up his mind and summoned a Hand," his Captain replied, and Damien felt his stomach drop out beneath him.

A Hand had already been summoned. Without trial or chance to defend himself, he had already been effectively sentenced to the worst punishment the Mages could inflict on their own. Up to that moment, he'd kept some hope for mercy – given the alternative, he'd have *happily* gone to work making antimatter for the rest of his life. Now, with David's words, he had no hope.

"Oh," was all he managed to say.

His Captain looked down at the time on wrist computer.

"I don't think it's fair or just," he said quietly. "They've condemned the *Blue Jay* as well, and I'm honest enough to admit that has pissed me off, but what they're doing to you isn't fair. It isn't justice."

For a moment Damien felt hope, and then his heart fell again. They *couldn't* do anything – he was inside a secured facility in the heart of a main planetary space dock. Between Enforcers and security systems and guards, there was no way they could save him – they'd only drag themselves down with him.

"Please Captain," he said quietly. "Don't try anything stupid – I *beg* you. I couldn't live with myself if anyone else was dragged down with me."

"That's noble of you Damien," David replied, checking the time on his wrist-bound personal computer again, "but, unfortunately, about twenty minutes too late."

Damien had barely opened his mouth to ask what his Captain meant when a series of loud cracking noises echoed through the security door. The young Mage started to turn towards the door and realized that David was not surprised at all.

"Take this," David ordered, passing David a plastic respirator he'd pulled from inside his coat. "There were two gas grenades in with the flash-bangs," he explained. "The entire front section of the jail is going to be full of knockout gas for the next few minutes."

David waited for Damien to put the respirator on, and then opened the door out to the corridor. He gestured for Damien to hang on to his shoulder, and then strode away, his magnetic boots clicking sharply on the metal floor.

They passed the Enforcer who'd escorted Damien to the room, suspended in the strange sagging position of someone passed out in zero-gravity while wearing magnetic boots. Another uniformed CSS officer was just inside the door to the reception, hit by the rapidly expanding cloud of gas.

The four guards in the front security office were out cold, and the metal cylinders of David's grenades spun lazily in the middle of the room.

"Watch yourselves," a voice said gruffly, oddly muffled by the respirator he wore. Singh was standing in the center of the reception area, magnetic boots locked to the ground and a stubby-looking carbine-like weapon in his hands. "CSS is good – they'll have officers in gas masks here before the Nix-Six wears off."

"Wrists," David ordered, carefully settling Damien against the security desk. Still in shock and confused, Damien offered his hands forward. Singh slid a set of cutters across the desk and David went to work. Fifteen seconds later, the mage-manacles fell off.

The potential of the universe flowed back into Damien like a breath of fresh air, and his feet locked to the ground as he conjured his own personal gravity field.

"Told you we didn't need to bring him boots, boss," Singh said cheerfully. "Now, *DUCK!*"

Damien and David obeyed as a uniformed CSS guard wearing a respirator and mag-boots stepped through the corridor. Singh's weapon cracked with the sound of chemical propellants, and a dart appeared on the officer's shoulder.

For a quarter of a second, nothing happened. Then, long before the CSS man could do anything, the stungun SmartDart leapt into action, delivering its carefully calibrated sequence of electric shocks. The security officer went down in a convulsing heap.

"Can we get out of here?" Damien asked.

"One last thing," David told him. "The payment for our help." The Captain slotted a datachip into the security desk and started working.

"Gas is clear," Singh reported. "Anyone hit by it will be down for an hour, but rapid response teams will already be on their way."

"Got it," David replied. "Six cells opened."

"Do we stick around to say hi?" the pilot asked.

"Not a chance," the Captain answered, stepping through the security gate and taking the stungun from Singh, who promptly produced another of the stubby weapons from under his coat. "Let's get out of here!"

#

David had memorized the route back to the dock, so he quickly took the lead. The Spindle's central core was an intentionally confusing mess of corridors and galleries, designed to help frustrate any attempt at boarding the immense station.

Their trip was initially unopposed, though. The Captain quickly realized that he and Singh, in their magnetic boots that required *very* careful walking, were slowing Damien down. The young Mage's personal gravity field would have allowed him to sprint down the path, dodging any attempt to slow him down or stop him.

"Where is the security?" the Mage asked as they made their way rapidly through the core.

"That's what we bought by opening those six cells," David said grimly. "One of the station's major gangs is making a very noisy attempt to rob a bank in one of the Spindle's larger towns. Hopefully by the time anyone realizes it's a distraction, we'll be at the *Blue Jay*."

Shortly afterwards, they ran into the still-manned security checkpoint between the Core and the docks, where four armed CSS officers quickly fanned out to cover the lines of approach when they saw them.

"Stop right there," the leader told them. "We have word of a breakout from the Core cells; we'll need to check your ID."

"Our friend left his personal computer on the ship," David lied desperately, gesturing towards Damien's bare wrist with his chin. Unfortunately, that only drew attention to Damien's hands, and the silver runes inlaid into the youth's skin.

The guard officer's eyes went wide.

"That's the Mage!" he barked, and his men went for their guns.

With his hand halfway to his gun, the officer jerked as if struck, and started to spin around to look behind him. A quarter second later, he convulsed and collapsed as a stungun's SmartDart delivered its calibrated charge.

The other guards had enough time to realize their commander had been shot before half a dozen men in plain gray coveralls swarmed them. The electrified batons they carried weren't as effective or as safe as a stungun's darts, but the officers were outnumbered two to one and swiftly disabled.

Kelly LaMonte, the *Blue Jay*'s junior engineer, emerged from the docks with a bright smile lighting her green eyes at the sight of Damien, and the stubby barrel of a stungun in her hands.

"Thought that if we hid out and waited for a ruckus, it would be you lot," she said cheerfully.

"What's with the clubs?" David demanded. A stungun's SmartDart was almost guaranteed not to kill someone – so much so they could be used as impromptu defibrillators – but the electrified batons were nowhere near as safe. "Kellers should have had a crate of twenty stunguns!"

"He did," Kelly agreed. "But that wasn't enough, and he figured that we'd need more of the guns at the docks if the distraction worked. Come on, let's get going."

"Wasn't enough?" David asked. "How many of the crew joined us?"

One of the coverall-clad spacers smiled gently at the Captain.

"We all did," he explained. "What else did you expect?"

#

Kelly led them through the docks as quickly as was humanly possible. The entire area was quieter than Damien had ever seen a space dock before. They saw no one on their way through what should have been a busy industrial dock.

"Where is everyone?" he finally asked.

"Our distraction seems to have gotten out of hand," David said grimly, glancing down at his personal computer. "I don't think anyone's been killed, but the bank robbery has managed to turn into a mid-scale riot – apparently they covered their escape by dumping about ten million dollars in cash on the street. It hasn't spread, much, but I think people are keeping quiet."

"No lockdown yet?"

"Only in the Spindle," David replied. "It takes a *lot* of paperwork to get through a dock shutdown. I suspect our 'friends' plan is to sneak everyone out on a liner that's scheduled to leave in two hours – it'll take more than that to get a shutdown order in place to stop the ship leaving."

He was cut off by the buzz of his personal computer announcing an incoming call.

"Captain, you got the package?" Kellers's voice demanded once David answered.

"We do," David confirmed.

"Good," the engineer replied. "We have a problem at the door – an Enforcer-type problem."

"We'll deal with it," the Captain replied, cutting the channel before turning to Damien as they jogged through the station. "I think you're up, Ship's Mage."

"An *Enforcer*?" Damien asked, shocked. The Guild's police Mages weren't the war-trained Mages of the Royal Martian Marine Corps, but they still had a lot more combat training than he did. And any Mage who'd qualified to be an Enforcer was probably a stronger Mage than Damien too.

"No one else in the crew can take him," David replied grimly. "He's between us and the ship, and if you can't get him to step aside, all of this has been for nothing."

For worse than nothing, Damien realized. If they couldn't escape, then every member of the *Blue Jay*'s crew was going to go down with him now.

He was silent for the last few minutes it took them to approach the *Blue Jay*'s berthing dock, where they met Kellers. The black-skinned man looked uncharacteristically grim, while behind him Jenna was busy organizing and co-ordinating the growing mob of *Jay* crew members.

"What do we do?" the engineer asked bluntly. "There's a station-wide alert out to security – we were hoping the Enforcer would answer the call. Instead he sent the CSS officers and settled in here himself – he's watching the only way in like a hawk."

"Do we have any gas grenades left?" David asked.

"Won't work," Damien told him, cutting into the conversation. "You took the Mages at the cells by surprise – forewarned to expect trouble, that wouldn't even work on me." The young Mage considered the access to the dock. It was a single wide corridor leading to the hatch, big enough for small cargo and completely lacking in cover or gravity.

"They're only guarding the personnel lock," Singh interjected. "I can steal a shuttle and take everyone over."

"That would work for twenty of us, but the rest would be arrested before we could come back for them," Damien told the pilot, still distracted and thinking.

"Gas grenades won't work," he repeated. "But do we have any flash-bangs left?"

#

There was no point in trying to sneak up on the Enforcer, so Damien simply came around the corner, slowly approaching the man while keeping his hands visible.

"Damien Montgomery," the Enforcer greeted him. The black-armored man was helmetless with short-cropped black hair that accented the face of an older officer, his face carved with the laugh lines and slight ruddiness of a man who lived happily and well.

"Enforcer," Damien greeted him, inclining his head slightly as he stopped, about two meters away from the man. The Enforcer had a stungun to hand, but made no move to aim it.

"I somehow doubt you've returned to the scene of the crime to surrender," the older Mage said quietly, "though it would make life easier and less painful for everyone – including you."

"No," Damien admitted. "I don't suppose I could talk you into stepping aside?"

"Why in the stars would I do that?" the Enforcer asked, clearly surprised by the thought.

"Either that ship is the deathtrap that the Guildmaster thinks it is, or it's safe to jump," the Ship's Mage said bluntly. "Letting me and those who *want* to risk it aboard the ship doesn't hurt anyone except us if we're wrong. It might even save you time! And if the ship still works... has there really been a crime?"

The Enforcer shook his head, finally starting to lift the stungun. "You're crazy, you know that right?" he said conversationally. "If you jump that ship, you and everyone crazy enough to go with you dies. Some might call that evolution in action – *I* call it something I'm supposed to stop."

95

"What's your name?" Damien asked, his eyes riveted on the stungun. He honestly wanted to know.

"Mallory," the Enforcer told him, the gun rising to point at Damien's chest but still unfired. "James Mallory. Why?"

"Because you're a good man, James Mallory," Damien told him quietly. "And I'm sorry for this."

He flipped the two flash-bangs that he'd been dragging along behind him up and over his head, closing his eyes and shielding his ears with magic as they went off next to his head – and barely two meters from the unprepared Enforcer.

Mallory lurched backwards in shock, raising his hands to paw at his suddenly blind eyes. Damien dove forwards, augmenting his lunge with a little extra gravity, and grabbed the stungun from the Enforcer's suddenly limp hands.

The guard hadn't even begun to recover from the grenades before the SmartDart slammed into his neck and disabled him in a spasm of electricity.

#

Hands of the Mage-King of Mars did not, as a rule, help jump their own ships. When Alaura had 'borrowed' the latest-model destroyer from the Royal Navy, they'd lent her the crew too – with a reasonable degree of grace even!

Something about the situation in Corinthian, though, made her want to rush. Adding herself to the cycle took them from two Mages making four jumps a day to three Mages, which let the warship make twelve light years a day.

She'd insisted that the last jump would be hers as well. There was a reason for that, which was glowingly clear to the handful of crew, includes both other Mages, standing in the simulacrum chamber of His Majesty's Starship *Tides of Justice*. Where most Mages only had silver runes inlaid into their palms, allowing them to interface with rune matrices, Alaura had a series of runes wrapping around her left arm back to the elbow, carved into her flesh by the Mage-King himself.

Those runes glowed with a brilliant white fire as she jumped the ship with a greater degree of accuracy, and *far* closer to the planet of Corinthian, than any of her crew could have managed. The *Tides of Justice* erupted into normal space less than half a million kilometers from Corinthian Prime.

Traffic Control, understandably, panicked.

"Unidentified vessel, identify yourself immediately!" a voice barked from the radio, and Alaura took personal control of the communications.

"This is the Hand of the Mage-King Alaura Stealey," she said flatly. "I am arriving by request of the Guildmaster to take over a Mage Law case."

Silence answered her, then a sigh of relief.

"Thank the Gods you're here," the voice replied. "We're having a situation – there's been a riot and a prison breakout, no one has any idea what's going on!"

That was obvious.

"Prison breakout? Who escaped?" Alaura demanded.

"I don't know!" the anonymous traffic controller replied.

The Hand sighed.

"Transmit the Dockmaster's office's co-ordinates to my ship," she ordered. "Tell him to have the details of the breakout ready for me; I will be meeting with him in five minutes."

"You can't possibly dock and get here in five minutes!" the bureaucrat replied.

"Ma'am, look!" one of the sensor technicians in the simulacrum chamber exclaimed, pointing at a sudden flare of light on the screens surrounding them. The stereotypical four-keeled shape of a freighter had released itself from the station, flipped up ninety degrees to clear the station, and then brought its drives up at maximum emergency acceleration.

"That's a *Venice* class freighter," the tech reported. "She's making just over three gees – her crew is in one *hell* of a rush."

Alaura eyed the ship for a second, and then turned back to the video. "I am a Hand of the King," she said bluntly. "Never tell me what I cannot do. Tell the Guildmaster to be ready."

Cutting the channel she glanced around the simulacrum chamber, the rune encrusted room at the heart of every ship, covered in screens and technology to allow the Mage to understand everything happening around her. On a Navy ship like the *Tides of Justice*, the simulacrum chamber doubled as the bridge – there was no point in doing anything else, as the ship's main weapon was the amplifier that increased power of the Mage at its center a hundredfold.

"Watch everything," she ordered Harmon. "Locate every ship that's moving, and every ship that's not and keep me in the loop. Do *not* take any action without specific orders – this whole situation stinks."

"Understood, Ma'am," the Lieutenant confirmed. He didn't even look at his people; both Alaura and he knew they'd already be on it.

She nodded to him, and then funneled magic through the Rune of Power on her arm and *stepped* across half a million kilometers, to the Dockmaster's office.

Damien hung onto the simulacrum at the heart of the *Blue Jay* with both hands. Even with the freighter's jump matrix turned into an amplifier, there was little he could do against the crushing acceleration of her engines at full power.

All around him, viewscreens showed the space around them, overlaid with icons from the ship's sensors. Linked into the amplifier, he barely needed them, as the freighter's sensors were his eyes and ears.

He saw the destroyer erupt into normal space terrifyingly close to the station and couldn't help himself from staring at it. The sharp lines of the white warship were clean, and terrifying. If things went wrong, that warship could easily shoot them down, no matter how hard they ran.

The advantage to the punishing acceleration they were under was that *only* a Navy destroyer could catch them. If nothing intervened, they would reach a region of space flat enough for him to jump the ship in just over a day.

#

"How the hell did you get here?" the Dockmaster demanded rudely as Alaura overrode the security on his door and strode in. "This is a private…" his voice trailed off as she removed the golden chain from around her neck and dropped the tiny golden open-palmed hand symbol of her office on his desk.

"The station is in a state of emergency," she told him flatly. "I came here to judge a case, and I find a hornet's nest. What happened?"

"There was a bank robbery," the Dockmaster replied, after swallowing hard. Hands were terrifying to anyone sane, and Alaura wasn't exactly trying to set him at ease. "It turned into a riot, and while System Security was dealing with that, seven prisoners broke free from the Core Zero-gravity Cells."

"Only seven?" she asked. She would expect somewhere like Corinthian to have more prisoners in the station-side high security cells than that.

"Just the Mage they had locked up in there and half a dozen mob hit men," the Dockmaster confirmed. "No one's been reported dead yet, but they're only getting back into the Cells now."

"Have any ships left since then?" she demanded.

"The *Blue Jay* launched without permission," the Dockmaster replied, sounding affronted. "I was *told* she was locked down – why the hell didn't they at least unfuel her?!"

Alaura held the man's gaze coldly. The Dockmaster of a station the size of Corinthian Prime had to know the answer to that question – *she* knew that un-fuelling a freighter of the *Blue Jay*'s size was an exercise of days, so he should. That answered one question, at least. Damien Montgomery was gone, and he'd taken his ship with him.

"Any other ships?"

"No," the Dockmaster pulled up a list on his computer. "There's a liner scheduled to launch in an hour, we're trying to get permission to seal the docks."

"Why haven't you?" she demanded, shocked.

"The docks are the lifeblood of this system!" the Dockmaster insisted proudly, his back straight as he looked her in the eyes. He then deflated slightly. "So, only the Governor can order them sealed, and he's tied up in meetings."

"Right," Alaura said slowly. She tapped the golden hand on its chain on the man's desk. "Seal the docks," she told him. "My authority."

The Dockmaster stared at the golden icon on his desk, the symbol of authority of a woman authorized to do anything short of shoot him at a whim. Shooting him, Alaura reflected, would require her to actually hold a trial, however short, and record the evidence in favor.

After a moment's hesitation, however, the man quickly got to work, typing messages into his computer and talking on the com.

Turning away from him now that he was working, Alaura's earpiece buzzed.

"Stealey," she answered quickly. "What is it, Harmon?"

"You wanted to know what was going on," the Mage-Lieutenant told her. "Well, we just noticed something you may want to intervene in."

"Which is?" she asked. Normally she had more patience with Harmon – he was extremely competent, just a little fussy.

"There are two Navy destroyers in the system other than the *Tides*," he told her. "They both just vectored after the *Blue Jay* – a request coming from the Corinthian Guildmaster. Given that there's an escaped Class One Fugitive aboard…"

"They will shoot to kill," Alaura finished for him, grimly. "Thank you, Harmon. I'll deal with it. Prep the *Tides*' Marine detachment for crowd control and search work," she added. "It looks like we have some scum we'll need to find on station."

Turning back to the Dockmaster, she smiled grimly at him.

"Where would I find the Navy System Command Center?"

#

There were few things in the universe David hated more than full emergency acceleration. He was strapped into his Captain's chair, with his crew around him, but he couldn't focus on much more than the fact that he felt like he weighed over two hundred kilos.

The computer was programmed for twenty-four hours of this, which was going to leave the entire crew *very* cranky –but alive and free. Alive was important – and free was even more so.

"Hey boss," Jenna announced, her voice showing almost none of the strain of the acceleration. "Got a com channel inbound for you – looks like its Carmichael."

"Put him on," David told her; and a moment later the image of the red-haired information broker appeared on the screen of his captain's chair.

"Captain Rice," Carmichael greeted him. "You look uncomfortable."

"Emergency acceleration is quite bracing," David replied. "You should try it sometime."

"I *like* my home system," the businessman replied. "I have no intention of pissing off enough people to need to run. I'm surprised you ran as fast as you did though," he admitted. "Carney and I were planning on the three hours it was going to take to get the Governor to authorize the lockdown – and the fact that the liner in dock has a notoriously stubborn captain."

"You were right, though," Carmichael continued. "The dock just went into lockdown, which means Carney's men are stuck on station, instead of being snuck off until the heat dies down. I can't help but suspect you knew something was coming."

"Everything I told you was true," David replied.

"Indeed, you are a man of your word," the broker agreed. "Also, a man with more morals than most in our business, so I was surprised when you agreed to free six of the worst men in those cells – I doubt you didn't look up their resumes."

"So tell me, Captain, what speeds up the lockdown by three hours and makes you unafraid of those released thugs?"

David considered it for a moment, eyeing the plot of the system showing the destroyer he was quite certain had delivered the Hand to the station, and shrugged.

"The Guildmaster was planning to burn Damien out," he said simply, "and summoned the only Judge who could. The same kind of Judge who could order a lockdown without the Governor."

"You have a Hand on your station, Mr. Carmichael," David continued, "and if you will not run, I would strongly suggest that you hide."

Carmichael's face was frozen, and he was silent for a good minute.

"You played us all," he finally said, and his voice was admiring. "I appreciate the warning, Captain Rice, and I do believe I will follow your advice." He paused. "I wouldn't return to this system if I were you."

"I know," Rice agreed.

"That said, if you find yourself in Legatus, look up a man named Bryan Ricket," the broker continued. "Tell him I sent you. He'll find you work that stays under the radar."

"Thank you," David answered. "I might just do that. Keep your head down."

"And the same to you, Captain Rice."

The channel broke off, and David looked up at a choking sound from Jenna. Her face had gone pale, and she met his gaze wordlessly, throwing up a wider chart of the system.

On it, glowing in a bright green that mocked the reality of the situation, was the pair of Martian Navy destroyers he'd noted when they arrived in the system. They would intercept the *Blue Jay* well short of jump range. Not that it mattered. With what they'd done, the Navy would settle for putting a missile into them.

#

Two uniformed Marines guarded the entrance to System Command. Armed with black battle rifles and clad in digitally camouflaged armor, they were a barrier to any random and most non-random intruders - a barrier that melted away instantly at the sight of the golden hand hung around Alaura's neck.

Inside, glowing wall-screens surrounded a massive holographic display that displayed the location of every ship, structure, and rock ever identified in the Corinthian system. Arrows showing vectors and paths criss-crossed the display, but three were glowing brightly as the system focused on the *Blue Jay* and the two destroyers chasing it down.

"Understand me Mage-Captain," a voice was saying into a communicator, "Damien Montgomery is a Class One Fugitive and the crew aboard the *Blue Jay* accomplices in his escape. We have no idea what that ship might be capable of – you are to destroy it from maximum range."

"Belay that," Alaura interrupted, stepping up next to the Commodore, who was clearly taking his orders from the Guildmaster standing on the other side of him.

"Break off the pursuit and return to the station," she ordered.

"Who the hell are you?" the Commodore demanded, turning to face her. "No one has the authority…"

He trailed off as he saw the chain around her neck.

"*I* have the authority," she said bluntly, looking past the Commodore to the Guildmaster.

"Look at it this way, gentlemen," she continued calmly. "If you're right, it won't matter – the *Blue Jay* will tear itself apart when Montgomery jumps her."

"And if you're *wrong*, Montgomery has achieved something unique. I *need* to know which it is, do you understand me?"

Both men glanced away, cowed by the golden hand she wore, and she leaned into the communicator.

"Confirm receipt of your orders, Captains," she said calmly. "You will return to the station and prepare your Marines to assist Corinthian System Security in tracking down the escaped criminals. Understood?"

#

Damien looked at the two deadly pyramids showing up on the scanners, feeling them through the amplifier and studying them.

He was reasonably sure he had the same capabilities as either ship in terms of magic, though the Ship Mage's aboard the warships would be better trained. The catch was that he – and the destroyers' Mages – could only reach out about six light seconds with their magic. He wasn't sure of the exact capabilities of the missiles the destroyers carried, but his understanding was that their range was on the order of ten times that.

Destroyers had been *built* to take down ships like the *Blue Jay* – stolen amplifiers and obsolete weapons, retrofitted onto freighters that couldn't outrun the warships, or outrange their devastating antimatter missiles.

Anything they could do with magic, he could do. But they had better technology, and the anti-missile turrets mounted on the freighter would never suffice against *real* missiles.

But he could do anything they could do with magic. Realization sunk in, as he looked back at Corinthian Prime, and the destroyer that had erupted right next to the station.

He reached out through the amplifier and the *Blue Jay*'s sensors, studying the gravity and space around the freighter. His training said it wasn't flat enough to jump, but now he studied it with open eyes. It... might be possible.

"Captain," he said into the communicator. "How far are you willing to trust me?"

Rice gave a surprised bark of laughter.

"Far enough to save us from two destroyers?"

"Cut the acceleration," Damien told him. "Cut the acceleration – and prepare to jump!"

The only sound in the Command Center was the soft whir of computers and the slight, almost unnoticeable buzz of the holographic display.

"Any debris?" Alaura finally asked.

"No ma'am," a Navy sensor tech replied, refusing to look at her as he answered her question.

She glanced over at the Commodore and the Guildmaster, both staring at the simple blue icon of a jump flare exit on the display.

"You were wrong," she said simply. "It appears that Montgomery has given the *Blue Jay* a fully functional amplifier."

"Now... let's see what he does with it."

###

3

For a heavy cargo hauler, the shuttle was surprisingly maneuverable in deep space. Basically a metal box with a rocket pod attached to each side by a gimbal mount, it was controlled by a pair of joysticks, one on either side of the pilot's seat.

Damien Montgomery, Ship's Mage of the interstellar freighter *Blue Jay*, gently pushed the left stick forward while pulling the right stick back, keeping both in the center of their side range. His thumb pulled the toggles on the side of each joystick down, reducing the amount of hydrogen being fed to the fusion rockets to slow the force of the spin to something he and the older man in the copilot's seat could take.

"Not bad," Narveer Singh told the youth, reaching back to scratch under the white turban he wore even while dressed in a flight suit. "I guess you really did qualify on these birds."

"I qualified on the *Hawk* type," Damien admitted. "They're a few decades older than these, but the controls are much the same."

"What else can you fly?" the *Blue Jay*'s senior pilot asked.

The slim young man paused, checking the screens to be sure that the shuttle was clear of its mother freighter. Alone in deep space, they were light years from anything *else* that could pose an obstacle.

"I qualified on light shuttles, heavy cargo shuttles, heavy personnel shuttles and sub-light spacecraft up to fifteen megatons," he reeled off quickly. "I'm also qualified for light aircraft, but anything beyond that wasn't necessary."

Narveer blinked.

"You, you are a pilot!" he exclaimed. "My three boys aren't qualified for all of the shuttles, and even I couldn't fly the *Jay* herself."

"I qualified on a *Dealer* type," Damien told him. "She was basically a *Venice* like the *Jay* without the jump matrix."

The First Pilot shook his head, checking the screens in front of him. "Why?"

"Every Jump Mage trained in Sherwood had to," Damien explained. "The theory was that, since you couldn't make it home at all without the Jump Mage, they'd train us so that we could get the ship home on our own."

Singh plugged a sequence of way points into the computer as he shook his head in response. "Follow those through," he instructed. "Gives us a bit of time away from the ship, but then we'll have to head back. You'll need to jump us again soon."

Damien nodded silently. He was the only Mage amongst the *Blue Jay*'s eighty crew members, which meant he was the only one able to cast the spell that would catapult the three million ton ship across the stars.

"Any idea where we're jumping?" he asked Narveer as he carefully curved the shuttle over their ship. The *Blue Jay* was built to be functional, not pretty, and looked as much as an egg-beater as anything else. Four massive curved ribs extended from her central keel, rotating to provide gravity for the crew to eat and sleep.

"The Captain, he'll have a plan," Singh stated confidently. "He got you out, didn't he?"

Two days earlier, the crew had pulled Damien from a jail cell, saving him from being stripped of his magic. Now, the Protectorate was hunting them, which was why they were in deep space, waiting for the Captain to pick somewhere for them to hide.

#

David Rice, Captain of the interstellar freighter *Blue Jay*, watched his First Officer walk across the ship's bridge towards him with far more attention to the pot of coffee she carried than the heavily built blond woman herself.

"You, XO, are a life saver," he told her as she poured him a cup.

Jenna glanced around the empty bridge. "From your many and varied enemies on a ship in deep space in the middle of the night?"

Rice shrugged his broad shoulders and grinned.

"At this point, 'many and varied' is a good description of our enemies," he reminded her. They'd made enemies of one of the Protectorate's largest criminal syndicates years ago, and now the government of the Protectorate wanted them arrested – something to do with stealing a Mage prisoner out from under the nose of a Hand of the Mage-King of Mars.

"How are the flying lessons going?" he asked her after a moment's silence, nodding towards the main screen, which had one of the *Jay*'s many exterior cameras zoomed in on the shuttle Damien was flying. "I thought you were in Flight Control?"

"After about five minutes, I looked up Damien's flight qualifications and realized I was redundant," Jenna told him dryly. "Why didn't you mention that to Singh?"

"I honestly assumed that Singh knew Jump Mage flight qualifications from the Navy," David admitted. "Once I realized he didn't," the Captain shrugged. "I figured letting him run with it might loosen some of the tension around here."

"Telling the crew where we're going might do that too," Jenna told him. The Captain shrugged, and with a flick of his fingers across the screen on his chair, threw the contents onto the main screen to replace the view of Damien's shuttle.

A three dimensional model of the star systems that made up the Protectorate of the Mage-King of Mars filled the screen. One hundred and eleven stars were lit up in several colors, forming a rough sphere centered on the single gold star of Sol. Scattered through the colored stars were almost four times as many gray stars, indicating systems no one had colonized.

Twelve stars were silver, showing the oldest, most industrialized and most populated systems known as the Core.

Thirty-three were green, systems with solid industry, fleet presences and economies – the MidWorlds.

Fifty, scattered around the edge of the sphere, were blue. These were the latest wave of colonies, systems still struggling to find their feet and desperate for any shipping they could get – the Fringe.

Lastly, a wedge of fifteen red stars, starting at one of the silver stars which had a red band around it, cut out towards the edge of the sphere from the center. These were worlds where magic was outlawed outside the ships that delivered cargos and news – the UnArcana Worlds.

"The Core all have RTAs except Legatus," David said calmly, a flick of his hand causing all of the silver stars except the one banded in red to turn dull. A Runic Transceiver Array was an immense construct of runes and magic that allowed a Mage to communicate verbally with a Mage in another RTA, no matter how far away. "Corinthian *didn't*, but as soon as they get a ship to Sherwood, every system with an RTA is going to have us on a watch list," he concluded. "That takes these systems out."

Over half of the green lights and a single blue light turned dull.

"Anywhere that will have been reached by ship from Corinthian before we get there will also be looking for us," David continued, overlaying a new layer which turned most of the remaining MidWorlds dull in a sphere around Corinthian.

"So we go to the Fringe," Jenna answered, gesturing at the massive swathes of blue stars. "This ship has the fuel bunkers and food storage for the long Fringe runs – she was built for it. We both have contacts out there – so does James, I think."

The Captain nodded. "He does, though he's been busy making sure there's nothing in our data download that incriminates us." James Kellers was the ship's engineer, and he'd been face-down in the normally sealed portion of the ship's computer that carried downloads of all news and financial transaction data between systems since they'd left Corinthian.

"He can *do* that?" Jenna asked, shocked.

"Can't get into the bank data, but he can open up the news and law enforcement downloads and modify them – undetectably, he insists."

The First Officer whistled. The RTAs only allowed verbal communication. The 'mailbox' present on every starship carried the large-scale electronic data transfers required to keep a modern economy and integrated society functioning. Supposedly, only the Royal Post offices in each system could upload and download from them, which meant that, for example, the *Blue Jay*'s mailbox carried the most up-to-date listing of her crew's own finances – data that local banks would use to authorize withdrawals and spending.

"Contacts or not, though, we can't go straight to the Fringe," David finally concluded, touching a control that made the blue stars flash gently. "Fringe shipping is speculative – we'd have to pick up a cargo we know they'll buy and take it in, with no contracts or guarantees. That means we need the capital to *buy* said cargo, and we don't have it."

Jenna looked at him sharply, and David shrugged. "I can cover operating expenses for two years, but even if I put *all* of that in, it wouldn't cover a tenth of a full cargo for this ship. Three million tons of *anything* is expensive."

"So what?" she asked.

The red-banded silver world, on the edge of the Core, flashed on the screen.

"Legatus," David answered. "The first UnArcana world. No Mages, so no transceiver array. Shipping is rarer than in the rest of the Core, and the Navy leaves system security to the Legatus Self Defense Force. We get a contract there; build up our cash reserves as we head outwards. Use the cash to pick up a cargo of survey satellites and combine harvesters in the MidWorlds somewhere, then do the long sweep of the Fringe."

"Once we've done an eighteen month sweep of the Fringe, we won't be on the top of everyone's list," he concluded. "We'll be able to pop back into the MidWorlds for a new cargo, so long as we don't draw attention to ourselves."

"What makes you think we'll find work in Legatus?" Jenna demanded. "I thought most of the shipping through there was locked up by big lines willing to play their games."

"Carmichael gave me a name," David admitted.

"We *played* Carmichael and left him to face the music when a Hand arrived," Jenna pointed out. Carmichael hadn't got anything he'd been supposed to out of the deal he'd brokered between David and a mob boss.

"The name was in trade for warning him about the Hand in time," David replied. "I think the man will help us."

His First Officer crossed her arms and looked at him crossly.

"If you've already made up your mind, why are we still chatting instead of letting the crew know?" she asked.

"Because until I said this all aloud, I hadn't made up my mind," David told her. "I can still change it if you have a better idea?"

Jenna shook her head slowly.

"Fine boss," she conceded. "The belly of the beast it is!"

#

Rice was waiting for Damien when he and Singh exited the shuttle, carefully, into the zero-gravity of the *Blue Jay*'s shuttle bay. As the final test of his skill, the old Sikh pilot had made Damien slot the cargo shuttle into its bay, one of the seven on the 'roof' of the bay. Like everything else Singh had asked, Damien did it slowly, carefully, and without a single mistake.

"I'll hook up the fuel lines and check her over," the pilot told Damien as they spotted the Captain waiting for them. "Looks like the Captain wants you."

"Thanks," Damien told Singh and then, gently, launched himself across the shuttle bay to the freighter's commander.

"We have a destination?" he asked Rice.

"We do," Rice confirmed. "Let's go to your lab, I want to pull some data up for you."

Damien's lab slash office was situated at the heart of the ship, just behind the simulacrum chamber that occupied the jumpship's exact center and allowed him to teleport her through space. Unlike the rest of the ship's core, though, his office had gravity due to a set of runes the previous Ship's Mage had carved into the floor.

Entering the tiny space, which combined the best and worst aspects of an office, a chemistry lab, and a jeweler's workshop, Rice dropped himself into the chair next to the workstation. Three screens were set up on the desk, creating a pseudo-three-dimensional image of the space the freighter was suspended in.

That space was unusually empty. They'd made six basically random jumps after leaving Corinthian minutes ahead of a pair of Navy destroyers, and now sat in the dead black space between stars, light years away from even the normal jump zones.

"Carmichael gave us a contact who can probably get us work, regardless of our questionable legal status," Rice finally told Damien, the heavyset Captain looking over the screens at the Mage. "There's two problems – first, we're talking a long way away, and second, he's in Legatus."

Damien watched carefully as Rice manipulated the controls on the workstation, zooming in on the star in question. The Captain was faster with the software than *he* was, though even now most of his experience with it had been in school. He leaned in over Rice's shoulder, and read the course projection the computer was providing.

A computer's projection of the course a Mage could take was always slightly off, but it would give him a starting point to work from.

"That's forty-two light years away," he observed quietly. "Two weeks in transit. Can we risk it?"

Damien was trained and qualified to perform a one light year jump of a ship like the *Blue Jay* every eight hours. In practice, he could probably cut that down to six hours, and he'd known Mages who could jump after as little as three hours – but those paces weren't sustainable. To travel halfway across the Protectorate, he'd stick to the safe pace.

"They don't have a transceiver in Legatus," Rice replied, "and they don't get as much shipping as you would think. I think we'll still have a few days' leeway before the news gets there."

"Legatus is a Core World, isn't it?" the Mage asked.

"It's also the first UnArcana world," Rice told him grimly. "One of the first colony ships after the Mage-King revealed that the Mages could take humanity to the stars – the colonists got to Legatus, got off the ships, and told the Mages who'd brought them to go to hell."

"You've never been a real UnArcana world," the Captain continued, "so I wanted to warn you where we were going. You won't be allowed on planet. Use of magic off of the ship is grounds for imprisonment – I suggest you stay aboard."

Damien swallowed, looking at the innocent looking yellow star again.

"Do we have a choice?" he asked finally. Heading to a system where he'd be hated just for breathing sounded unappealing.

"We need to make a big payday, fast," David admitted. "If we do, we can pick up a bunch of high tech gear the Fringe worlds won't *care* who delivers on our way out, but without enough capital, we're trapped trying to find contracts. Anywhere we can get a contract for; the Protectorate will find us sooner or later."

And then they would strip Damien's magic. *That* had been made very clear on Corinthian.

"I'll start plotting the jumps."

#

Two days and six jumps later found Damien back in his lab, slumped in the chair by his monitors as they projected the calculations for the next days' worth of jumps. A cold bulb of coffee rested on the

110

corner of the desk, long ignored when the sound of the admittance buzzer jerked him awake.

"Hey Damien, are you in here?" the soft voice of Kelly LaMonte, the junior-most of the ship's engineering officers, asked.

"Yeah," he answered blearily, checking the time stamp on the screens to be sure he hadn't slept right up to his next jump. This wasn't the gap between jumps he'd scheduled for sleep – that was after the jump that was coming up in four hours now. "Come in."

The door slid open and the dark-haired engineer lithely grabbed the top of the door, swinging gently through the transition from the keel's zero-gravity to the lab's magical gravity zone and landing softly to smile brightly at Damien.

"Is something up in Engineering?" he asked, wondering what had brought the young engineer down to the center of the ship.

"I wanted to check up on you," she answered, her gaze flicking around the empty coffee bulbs and the most recent cold one. "I haven't seen you since we started jumping towards Legatus."

Damien shrugged, glancing at the calculations on the screen and the starscape they were overlaid on.

"Keeping an eye on things here," he told her. "I don't want to risk any mistakes."

"You joined us for lunch most days on the way to Corinthian," she reminded him, stepping closer and perching on the edge of the desk, looking down at him.

He didn't respond immediately. She was right, though he hadn't realized it until she'd pointed it out. On the trip from his home system to Corinthian, his only previous jump route with the *Blue Jay*, he'd made the time to eat with the junior engineers and pilots regularly – they were the only people aboard his own age. He worked with Kellers, Rice and Campbell, but those three were all ten years or more his senior.

The girl sitting on his desk looking concernedly at him was the same age as him, with a degree in starship engineering to his degree in thaumaturgy.

"I wanted to apologize for what happened," Kelly finally said into the silence, and Damien winced. His own age and pretty or not, Kelly was also the one who'd allowed a strange Mage onto the ship to discover the modifications he'd made – which had directly resulted in his arrest.

"They were going to take my magic away," he finally replied, looking away from her and the computers to stare at the bare metal walls. That was the fate that Rice and the crew of the *Blue Jay* had saved him from, at the cost of them all becoming fugitives from Protectorate Law.

"Singh told me," she admitted. "I am so sorry, Damien – I didn't know."

Damien looked directly back at her, meeting her eyes and noticing for the first time how brilliantly blue they were.

"You didn't know," he repeated back to her. "We didn't tell anyone what I'd done to the matrix. Even if we had, it's not like you know Mage Law."

"The whole mess was the exact opposite of what I was trying to do," she said with a sigh. "I was trying to make your life *easier*, not get you arrested!"

"I'd say the thought was appreciated, but, well, arrested," Damien replied dryly.

"Let me make it up to you by buying you dinner," Kelly told him suddenly, a bright smile returning to her face.

Damien glanced from her to the starscape behind his calculations.

"We're roughly five and a half light years from *any* star system," he pointed out. "Seven from anywhere with a restaurant, and still almost two weeks from Legatus – a system where I shouldn't leave the ship. Where are you planning on this dinner?"

"Anywhere *not* your lab, and any meal *not* made of cold coffee. Deal?"

The reference to the forgotten coffee bulb made Damien wince again.

"Okay," he agreed. "Deal."

\#

Every jump from deep space to deep space was very much the same, even to Damien. Memorize a set of calculations, focus on the small, impossibly perfect, replica of the *Blue Jay* at the heart of the ship and channel energy into it to move the vessel and all of its contents across a full light year of space.

It was exhausting, incredible, and done three times a day, became surprisingly routine.

After the first jump of the day, Damien would review the calculations for the next jump, and then have lunch with Kelly and the other junior officers. He would then carry out the second jump of the day, review the calculations for the last jump, and spend part of the day wandering the ship, studying the ship's rune matrix and making tiny modifications where his ability to see the flow of magic through the runes revealed inefficiencies in the centuries-old design.

To his knowledge, no one had ever successfully modified the jump matrix of runes carved into the hull of every civilian starship – not since the first Mage-King of Mars had drawn up the design in the twenty third century. Removing the limiters that prevented the matrix being used for any spell except jumping was the first step, but given the time to go over the runes closely he realized it was improvable in dozens of small ways. Many of the changes were, he suspected, tied directly to his own use of magic.

He couldn't make the ship jump further – that seemed tied unavoidably into his own ability to channel power – but he could make the jumps take a little bit less energy from him.

The routine consumed almost two weeks, until the night before they arrived in Legatus, when Rice invited the ships' senior officers to dinner.

#

Rice normally found the fact that the designer of the *Venice* type freighters like the *Blue Jay* had included a dining room in the Captain's Suite vaguely ridiculous. The room wasn't large enough to host a meal for all of the freighter's dozen or so officers, but was really too large for the Captain to eat alone.

The round table was sized for six, barely enough for a business meeting or a gathering of the ship's senior officers – him, the First Officer, the First Pilot, the Chief Engineer and the Ship's Mage.

He greeted each of his officers as they arrived and poured them drinks himself from the small set of vacuum-sealable carafes on a side counter. Jenna, as always, went at his right hand, and he sat Damien, the youngest and newest of the senior officers, at his left.

When he served the dinner himself, Damien looked at the plates in surprise.

"You cooked this, Captain?" the youth asked.

"Welcome to my culinary experiments club, Damien," David told him with a smile. "I like to cook, but I don't normally have time. I foist my creations on my senior officers occasionally."

He smiled to himself as the young Mage silently took the food, clearly not quite sure what to make of having a Captain who cooked. David continued to serve up the plates, an old recipe he'd found involving potato dumplings and diced ham.

The quiet sound of enthusiastic chewing proved that he'd done well, again. The room was quiet until the food was mostly devoured, and then James and Narveer, opposite David, began to talk over some of the repairs to the shuttles.

David turned to Damien, who was looking uncomfortable at the social setting.

"This is just a quiet get-together," he told the youth. "We're going to be stuck together on this ship for a while now, if we can't socialize with each other, we'll all go mad."

"That makes sense," the Mage admitted. "I hadn't thought things through that far." He paused. "How long are we really going to be stuck together?"

Rice considered sugar-coating the situation for a moment, but decided against it. They'd all volunteered to take on this burden to save Damien, they owed him the truth.

"If we get into Legatus, get a working contract, and get out to the Fringe with a cargo, the usual Fringe run is twelve to sixteen months," David told him. "After that, we should be able to sneak back into the MidWorlds to restock and pick up a cargo, but we won't be able to stay – we'll have to head back out to the Fringe."

"It could easily be five or six years before things die down enough for us to really return to the MidWorlds," the Captain admitted. "None of us," he gestured around at the officers, "will ever be able to return to the Core. We're marked now, and you don't enter a Core system without that showing up. The MidWorlds… don't care quite as much."

"Five or six years," the young Mage repeated. "I hadn't realized saving me could cost so much."

Rice shrugged. "Crew is crew," he said simply. "We don't abandon our own."

Damien was silent for a while, staring at his food. Feeling guilty, Rice tried to change the subject.

"Speaking of socializing, James tells me that you and Miss LaMonte have been seeing a lot of each other," he said. To his surprise, Damien jerked like he'd been stung.

"It's not like that," the Mage answered hurriedly. "We've just been eating lunch together – she dragged me out of my lab."

The Captain, much older and wiser than Damien, decided to mostly hold his peace in response to that.

"This isn't a military ship," he pointed out. "There'd be nothing wrong if there *was* anything going on."

The faint blush on Damien's cheeks reminded Rice that, however vital the Mage was to the functioning of the ship and however much the entire crew owed him their lives, he was still in his early twenties and one of the youngest people aboard. He decided to spare the youth any more harassment, and glanced across the table to Narveer.

"Narveer, there's something I need you to do while we're in Legatus," he said softly. The First Pilot recognized his tone, and sat up sharply, his dark eyes attentive to his Captain. "Right now, the only weapons we have aboard are half a dozen pistols and a case of stunguns. While I'm tracking down Carmichael's contact, I need you to track down a gunrunner and pick us up some real hardware. We're heading Fringe-ward; I want us to be packing."

"Will we find that many guns on Legatus?" Kellers asked, sounding curious.

"They're the biggest arms manufacturer after Sol itself," Singh told him. "We can find anything we need there – I might even be able to track down an exosuit if I look hard enough."

"Nobody else aboard is 'suit-qualified,'" Rice reminded the ex-military man. Exosuits were powered body armor designed for use in vacuum and microgravity, but also used by elite Protectorate soldiers.

"Then I'll only pick up one," Singh replied calmly, and David couldn't help but laugh.

"If you find a suit of body armor designed for the Mage-King's shock troops, I suppose you can buy one," he allowed.

#

"What the hell is *that*?" Damien asked, staring in surprise as the data being fed to the screens covering the walls of the simulacrum chamber by the *Blue Jay's* computers.

'That' was a massive metal ring around Legatus's fifth planet, a gas giant roughly the size of Jupiter. Damien had jumped them into the system inside the fifth planet's orbit and they were heading towards the third planet, Legatus itself, but the mega-structure wrapped around the outer world stuck out like a sore thumb on their sensors.

"That's the Centurion Accelerator Ring," David replied over the link from the bridge. "It's a million kilometer long series of particle accelerators they use to produce antimatter – the answer of a society that hates Mages to the modern need for antimatter."

"That must have been… expensive," Damien said quietly, looking at the distance measure. The *Blue Jay* wouldn't detect a ship of her own size at that distance, even under full acceleration. The immense structure wrapped around Centurion was impossible to miss.

"Forty years, a million workers, and more money than I think Legatus has ever admitted to anyone," the Captain confirmed. "They maintain a one light minute no-fly zone around it and no Mage, not even those working for the King, gets inside that no-fly zone."

Damien continued to eye the structure for a long moment. He had only minimal training in transmutation, but even he could transmute a few dozen kilograms of antimatter a day. Most systems ran production facilities, with a mix of well-paid volunteer Mages and carefully supervised convicted felon Mages, that churned out thousands of tons of the high energy fuel a year. Legatus, of course, wouldn't accept that option.

And the system needed the fuel. That was obvious as he turned his attention to the scanners and cameras tracking the *Jay*'s destination. The world they were heading to *glowed* on every spectrum the freighter could detect – heat, light and every other form of electromagnetic radiation.

Damien had grown up on a MidWorld and he'd *never* seen a system this busy before. The ship's computer was tagging ships with numbers as it identified them, and it was already into the dozens of vessels transiting between Legatus, Centurion, and the fourth world – Princeps. Princeps wasn't even habitable, but it had acquired its own collection of orbital structures supporting what looking like massive mining operations on the surface.

"I didn't realize a Core System was this busy," he admitted aloud, checking for ships that would approach the freighter out of habit.

"Legatus is the second most industrialized system in human space after Sol itself," Jenna answered. A glance at the bridge link showed David was busy reviewing their course in-system. "Most of the other Core Worlds would use Mages for a lot of things Legatus uses tech for, so Legatus needs to build and fuel that tech."

"The Legatus Self Defense Force is also a much more serious force than most Core security forces," she continued. "There are *hundreds* of sub-light gunships in this system, keeping the peace and being paranoid about Mages."

"Speak of the Devil," David interrupted, haloing a closing heat signature on everyone's screens. "That *Crucifix* just went squid-mode, and is heading our way fast. Damien..." he trailed off, looking at Damien's screen.

"Yes, Captain?"

"I'd rather we not incinerate a police ship, but if they try to arrest us, I know we need more space to jump," the Captain answered grimly. "Try to disable it if you can, but you are our only defense."

"Understood," Damien answered. The amplifier centered on the simulacrum would allow him to use any of his regular self-defense spells at the ship's scale, more than enough to deal with a single gunship – but not enough to take on the entire star system!

He saw almost instantly why Rice had referred to the ship as in 'squid mode.' The ship's main hull was a deep hemisphere, with four pods locked behind it on outriggers, likely providing a magnetic channel to increase the efficiency of the antimatter flare. A quick check of the *Jay*'s database showed that, normally, the four outriggers were extended around the ship in a cross shape – hence the name of the ship – and rotated to provide artificial gravity to the crew.

"I'm copying you in our channel," Jenna told Damien. "They won't see or hear you, but you'll see both of us."

116

A second screen popped open next to the bridge link, blank for a long moment.

"We're receiving a transmission," the First Officer announced. "Aligning our com array, and throwing them on-screen."

The new screen on Damien's display lit up, standing out even more sharply against the starscape and sensor data around it. The screen rapidly resolved into a utilitarian command center, six uniformed men and women belted into chairs clearly designed to function as acceleration couches.

Centered in the camera was a seated woman in a dark blue jumpsuit uniform, gold cuffs and a gold oak leaf on her collar presumably marking her as being in command.

"I am Lieutenant Commander Hunts of the LSDFS *Broadsword*," she stated sharply. "You have performed an unscheduled jump into the Legatus System, identify yourself immediately or be fired upon."

The database entry that Damien had pulled up on the *Crucifix* class gunships happily informed him that the gunship carried a load out of antimatter missiles rated similarly to the Martian Navy – which Hunts was already in range to use.

"I am Captain David Rice of the independent freighter *Blue Jay*," Rice responded immediately. "We are transmitting our credentials now."

Seconds ticked by in silence as the crew of the *Jay* waited for the signal to cross the distance between them, and for the return to reach them as well.

Hunts relaxed, slightly, from her iron-locked position when they received the transmission and one of her officers gave her a thumbs-up. She made an almost concealed hand gesture, and the *Broadsword*'s acceleration cut by three quarters - back to a more reasonable single gravity, but still heading towards the *Jay*.

"We don't see a lot of unscheduled jumpships, Captain," Hunts finally said. "You're a long way from your last port of call, too – what brings you all the way here from Corinthian?"

"I was asked to come directly here as a favor for a friend," David told him. "He told me that a contact of his needed a jumpship transport as soon as possible."

Seconds ticked by, and the gunship commander nodded slowly.

"Understandable," she answered. "You'll forgive me, I hope, if I require you to tell me who you were supposed to meet?"

Her tone suggested that whether or not they forgave her was utterly irrelevant.

"I was asked to meet a man named Bryan Ricket," David replied.

This time, Damien recognized the *exact* moment when Commander Hunts received David's reply. The Legatan officer physically twitched when she heard the name. Damien wasn't sure anyone else saw it, but the woman clearly recognized the name.

"Mr. Ricket may indeed be able to use your services," Hunts answered, leaning back slightly in her chair. "You are aware, Captain Rice, of the regulations in this system with regards to Mages and runic artifacts?"

"Yes, Commander."

"An updated version of the regulations is being sent to you regardless," she continued. "Make certain your crew – and *especially* your Mages – obeys it."

The tone of voice in which the officer said the words 'Mages' made Damien very glad he wasn't openly on the call.

#

Legatus' orbit was busy. Of the almost two thousand thermal contacts that the *Blue Jay* had picked up in the inner system, each representing a spaceship under engine power, almost eight hundred were in orbit around the system's main habitable planet.

The ships were the least of it, though. The sheer scale of the orbital infrastructure dwarfed the surrounding vessels. No less than fifty space stations, each a rival for Sherwood's Prime station or the Corinthian Spindle, were scattered in various orbits, servicing the ships that filled the system. The two largest, originally captured asteroids, anchored the immense tethers of two space elevators.

David had seen bigger and more impressive infrastructure twice in his life – around Earth, and around Mars. Each of the Sol system's two main worlds outclassed Legatus, and combined the system out-produced almost the entire rest of the Protectorate combined.

"Wait; are those what I think they are?" Jenna asked out loud, distracted for a moment from the delicate process of inserting the *Blue Jay* into the whirling maelstrom of a Core World's orbital traffic.

David followed her questioning gaze and swallowed at the sight she pointed out. Orbiting in neat ranks, just above one of the two massive counterweight stations, was over *sixty* gunships similar to the one they'd encountered in the outer system.

"I see," he paused, checking the system count, "sixty four gunships. Looks like the other Counterweight has a similar flotilla playing guard dog too."

Jenna whistled. "That's a *lot* of gunships, boss."

"Mars has almost as many Navy *destroyers* in orbit," David pointed out. "Plus the only full squadron of battleships in the galaxy."

"But that's *Mars*."

118

"And to these people, Legatus is just as important," the Captain said quietly. "Do we have docking clearance yet?"

Jenna checked her instruments.

"We just received a course from the automated traffic system – we're cleared through to Interface Station," the stocky officer adjusted some of the controls on her screen and David felt a slight pull as the ship re-directed. "It looks like we're staying well above most of the traffic and stations."

"Makes sense," David replied. "From what I've heard, they don't like letting jumpships close to the planet – something about not trusting Mages."

"You're not making me feel better about this," his First Officer replied. "Have you seen what they want me to dock with?"

A slip of his finger across the touch controls brought Interface Station up on the screen. Suspended in a high orbit, further out from Legatus than Luna was from Earth, the station was a simple ring, roughly five kilometers across, which continually rotated to provide gravity.

"There's no steady docking section," she pointed out. "I have to match the rotational velocity."

"It's five kilometers across," David told her calmly. "It's barely rotating once every three minutes. Should I get Narveer up here to fly us?" he asked dryly.

"The only other people qualified to fly this heap are you and Damien," she retorted. "And he's barely out of school, and you haven't touched the controls for something this complex in a decade. I'll get us in."

"Of course you will," David agreed. "It's why I hired you."

"Great. Now shut up," his First Officer ordered. "This is *not* as easy as you want to make it seem."

#

One impeccably executed docking later; David Rice climbed a ladder against the centripetal acceleration now providing pseudo-gravity into Interface Station. The hallway he entered, a personnel access way never intended to hold cargo or supplies, appeared to be little more than an ordinary station corridor, with a series of arrows marking where people boarding the station should go.

As David set off down the corridor towards customs, he realized that someone had taken the time to actually decorate the plain metal of the corridor. It was small things, a few curving lines not part of the directions here, a subtle mural worked into the metal on the wall there, but it was more than he'd usually seen outside of the luxury docking points reserved to passenger liners and yachts.

The corridor passed by another seven hatches, marking docking tunnels like the one he'd entered from, before he emerged into Legatus Customs Five. The corridor widened into a large room, blocked by a series of security gates watched over by the re-hinged bones of a Legatus Megarex.

The fact that the room was tall enough to *fit* the bones of the five meter tall predator should have been a shock on its own, but the looming bones were something he'd never expected to see aboard a space station. Named for its resemblance to Earth's pre-historic Tyrannosaurus Rex, the Megarex was Legatus's top predator before man arrived – and like most planets' apex predators, it was near extinction now. The bones were likely a century or more old, and easily worth millions.

"Captain Rice?" a voice interrupted his shocked gaze at the dead lizard, and he turned to his gaze to a young, dark-skinned, gentleman in a plain gray working uniform. "I am Customs Officer Ryan Shallot," the man introduced himself. "I see that Maggie Five has made her usual impression."

"Maggie Five?" David couldn't help asking.

"Somehow, the first one of them they brought up was nicknamed Maggie," Shallot shrugged. "Since we ended up with one in each customs section, they ended up just being numbered by the section they watch over."

David nodded his understanding as he gestured for the young officer to precede him. Shallot led him to a small cubicle next to one of the security gates. Each gate had a cubicle, though six of the eight gates were closed.

As they approached the cubicle, a second figure appeared out of a semi-hidden alcove next to it. The woman was tall, towering over David's stocky solidity and Shallot's slim averageness alike, and moved with a grace that belied the heavy black armor she wore locked over her limbs and torso.

The guard wore only one piece of insignia: a golden cog with a lightning bolt carved into it pinned to her collar.

"Hold out your arms," she ordered flatly. David looked into her eyes as he did so, and blinked as he saw her square pupils and the tiny blinking red light behind them as she looked him over. The woman hadn't used any kind of scanner to check him for weapons. She *was* the scanner.

"Captain Rice, this is Augment Talia," Shallot introduced the cyborg.

"He's clean," she reported sharply, ignoring the introduction. "No weapons, no unauthorized thaumic signatures."

David dropped his arms and inclined his head. "Greetings, Augment Talia."

Reputation said the Augments were trained Mage-killers, born, raised and cybernetically *modified* to identify, track and destroy Mages who tried to operate in Legatus. Reputation also declared them soulless robots, but David swore he saw a spark of appreciation for him and Shallot treating her as a person in Talia's strange eyes as she returned his nod.

Entering the office, Shallot opened a drawer and removed a chip tray, lowering a mass data interface over the chips as he interfaced the personal computer wrapped around his arm with the cubicle's systems.

"What is your business on Legatus, Captain Rice?"

"I'm looking for cargo," David explained calmly. "I was given a man to make contact with who I was told was looking for reliable carriers."

"Not a lot of jumpships come to Legatus on spec, Captain," the Customs Officer observed, making entries on his computer.

"It's a favor to the man recommending it as much as anything else," David lied smoothly. "He said it would be worth going this far out of my way."

"I never tell a man how to run his business," Shallot replied cheerfully. "Now, I can run a pass for just you, or any member of your crew you wish. What is your plan?"

"I'm planning on allowing my crew to take a day or two of shore leave while I track down my contact," David told him. He slid a chip containing the data on his crew over. "If we can get passes for everyone to Interface Station, and myself and my First Officer down to the planet, that would be best."

"Of course. You wish a pass for your Mage?" the youth asked, looking questioningly at David. "Those are quite expensive, and come with a large number of conditions."

"I and Mr. Montgomery are aware of them," the Captain replied firmly.

Shallot nodded wordlessly, hitting a command on his computer that beeped at him. The data transfer array over the chip tray starting blinking a progress light.

"Passes will be ready in a moment," the young man told David, then blinked as he glanced at something on his personal computer. "We have a physical package for you," he continued, sounding surprised. "Give me a moment."

The Legatan returned a minute or so later with an archaic paper envelope, just as the chip tray beeped its completion. He pulled the tray from the writer and passed it and the letter to David.

"Each chip is marked with the name of the individual it's a pass for," he explained. "They will all allow access through the security gates here after a basic security scan. Only the ones for yourself and Miss Campbell will allow you aboard shuttles away from Interface Station, but we have most amenities aboard the station itself." He glanced down at the letter in David's hand. "I'm honestly not sure what the letter is for," he admitted. "It arrived shortly before you docked."

"Thank you Officer Shallot," David told him. "I'll be back shortly once I've turned the passes over to my crew."

He shook hands with the Legatan and walked away, aware of the eerie eyes of the Augment guardian on him until he'd made it around the corner.

Curious and concerned, he juggled the tray carefully to allow him to open the envelope and remove the single sheet of paper inside it. The text was very short.

Captain Rice.
Meet me at the Silver Lion Restaurant at 19: 00 tonight. Come alone.
BR

It seemed he didn't have to go hunting for Bryan Ricket after all.

#

Damien was in his lab, working on a course plan that would take them through about half of the Fringe worlds, hitting the five that the Captain had said they had to visit, when his armband computer chirped with an incoming call.

"Damien," he answered absently, hitting the button while looking over the demographic data of yet another world that exported only food.

"It's Singh. Want to get on station?" the ship's senior pilot asked.

"I figured that wasn't the best of plans," the Mage observed.

"On your own, sure," Singh agreed. "But you come with me, you'll be perfectly safe! Plus, I have a meet for the guns, and I don't trust this man – but I just *bet* he's scared of Mages."

"I can't *do* anything on station, not without being thrown in jail," Damien pointed out, but he was shutting down his workstation and digging out the station-pass the Captain had given him.

122

"You are allowed to act in self-defense," Singh reminded him. "And I don't expect a firefight anyway, it's just business. Meet in the flight bay in ten?"

"Okay," Damien replied, standing up and slowly shaking his head. The pilot did tend to run rough-shod over anyone who wasn't entirely compliant with his plans.

He stepped out of his lab, swinging carefully from the magical gravity he maintained there into centrifugal pseudo-gravity Interface Station's spin imparted to the rest of the ship. The normally zero-gravity keel had a series of panels that folded out to turn the large, cylindrical, corridor into a giant spiral staircase running down the middle of the ship.

Heading 'down' towards the flight bay at the stern of the ship, he ran into Kelly LaMonte coming 'up' from Engineering.

"Hi Damien," she greeted him with a bright smile. "I was just coming up to find you. Can I steal you for that dinner station-side?"

Damien returned her smile, warmed as always by her greetings, but shook his head.

"Can't – I'm heading up to the shuttle bay to meet Singh. We're going shopping," he finished dryly.

"Shopping?" she asked, turning around to walk with him towards the shuttle bay.

"The Captain asked Singh to line up some weapons," Damien told her quietly, glancing around the 'stairwell' to be sure no one else was in hearing. LaMonte was at least an officer, but he wasn't sure how far the Captain wanted the knowledge that they were bringing weapons aboard spread. "He apparently has a contact, and figures that having a Mage around in an UnArcana system should be respect-inducing."

"Guess that makes sense," Kelly said quietly. "Be careful, will you? I feel bad enough over what happened in Corinthian without you ending up in trouble again!"

"We'll be fine," Damien assured her. "Singh scares me a lot more than any Legatan arms smuggler is going to!"

The engineer smiled at him, slightly less brightly than when she'd arrived, and shook her head as they reached the access to the flight bay.

"Just come back, okay?" she asked. "You still owe me dinner!"

"I'll remember that," he promised, and headed into the flight bay. The cavernous expanse holding the *Blue Jay*'s shuttles echoed with his footsteps. All of the freighter's small craft were locked carefully into their individual bays, secured against the gravity this part of the ship rarely felt outside of acceleration.

"Damien, over here!" Singh boomed. The dark-skinned and turbaned First Pilot was standing by a set of lockers that Damien had never noticed before, one of them open as Singh was taking objects out.

"Here," the pilot continued as the younger man arrived, shoving a vest, belt, jacket and gun at him.

"What's all this?" Damien asked.

"Model Twenty-Four Forty Hyper-Kevlar," Singh began, pointing at the vest. "Absorbs most small arms fire, once or twice." He passed over the gun. "Macy-Six – that's Martian Armaments - Caseless 6 millimeter. Twenty rounds in the grip, fully automatic. Belt to hold the gun. Jacket to cover it." The pilot eyed him for a moment. "Can you cover your medallion with that shirt?" he asked.

Wordlessly folding his collar over the gold coin declaring him a Mage and shrugging on the ballistic vest, Damien looked over the pilot. He was wearing the same vest, with the same sleek black pistol mounted under his shoulder he'd handed Damien. The young Mage copied the arrangement of the shoulder holster he'd mistaken for a belt, and then checked the slide and safety of the MA-C 6, carefully keeping the weapon aimed at the blank wall next to the lockers he now realized were the *Blue Jay*'s armory.

"Good, you do have a clue," Singh said approvingly as Damien holstered the weapon. He went over the youth's holster belt quickly, tightening and tucking it to fit under the jacket. "I know Navy Mages are pistol-certified, you?"

"I lived in the Sherwood countryside," Damien told him. "There were still creatures in those woods that hadn't worked out that humans were dangerous, so we had to go armed. That said," he glanced down at the weapon nervously, "I haven't fired a pistol since I started school, and I've never fired a full automatic."

"You shouldn't have to," Singh replied calmly. "If anything happens, well," the big man shrugged, "you spray bullets in the bad guys' direction to keep their heads down, and I'll take care of any that don't."

#

The Silver Lion Restaurant's entrance occupied the center of one side of a raised courtyard around a decorative pond. Five restaurants, all of which looked out of David Rice's normal budgets, had clearly combined their water rations and financial budgets to build the water feature, which had lilies and fish he was sure had to be robotic. Between the pond, a dropped ceiling, and careful paintings of the walls, it was hard to tell you were on a space station.

At the far end of the pond, across a bridge that might actually have been wooden, a pair of silver-painted lions flanked an entrance covered by a deep red silk curtain. A dark-haired and -skinned woman in a black silk dress stood behind a podium next to the entrance, watching all prospective guests approach.

"Do you have a reservation, sir?" she asked, her voice smooth as silk. "We do not have tables for unexpected guests, I'm afraid."

"I believe so," he told her. "I am here to meet a Bryan Ricket."

The woman nodded calmly, her fingers tapping out commands on a holo-screen that was being projected directly to her eyes by the podium.

"Captain Rice?" she asked after a moment, and David nodded. "Vice-Director Ricket is waiting." She conjured a younger version of herself, in a matching black silk dress. "Saffron will lead you to him."

Vice-Director was not a title that David had been expecting to hear associated with the man Carmichael had sent him to meet. He swallowed his questions and followed the young waitress into the restaurant.

Starship Captains were not poor men. David had personally signed for a credit note worth almost two hundred million Martian Dollars when he purchased the *Blue Jay*, and had paid back every penny of it before rescuing Damien.

The restaurant behind the curtain was entirely outside of his experience. Each table was at a slightly different level, separated from the others by burbling artificial brooks and real, growing, trees. He'd seen something similar planet-side once, but to encounter this extravagant a use of space and water on a *space station* was a level of wealth beyond his experience.

The gorgeous waitress led him across two brooks and around one perfectly trimmed hedge to an archway formed of living trees. The table beyond was sized for six, but only held one man. Another man stood just beside the entrance, and stopped David as he entered the booth.

"Hold still, Captain Rice," the man ordered. He slowly looked David up and down, reminding him vividly of the Augment in customs. Somehow, he was not surprised to see the tiny pin of a golden cog with a lightning bolt cut out of the middle on the man's collar when he looked.

"He's clear, Mr. Ricket," the Augment reported.

"Apologies for the security, Captain Rice," the man at the table said calmly. "Please, take a seat."

Feel utterly out of his depth, David took the offered seat directly across from Ricket. The Vice-Director, whatever that was, was a slim man with a shaved head, clad in a plain gray business suit.

"I took the liberty of ordering for us all," Ricket continued. "I suspect you have not encountered true Old Chinese cuisine in your travels?"

"I have heard of the country," Rice admitted, "but I haven't encountered the food, no."

"You will be pleasantly surprised then," Ricket said calmly. "Like I was, a few hours ago, when my fellows in System Security passed a report on from one of our sterling Gunship Commanders telling me that a jumpship Captain was in system, looking for me. Tell me, Captain Rice, why exactly are you here?"

The last sentence was delivered softly, gently, and so utterly flatly that David *knew* that the wrong answer would have the Augment behind him disposing of a body very quickly.

"I worked in Corinthian with an information broker named Carmichael," David answered slowly, picking his words carefully. "We ran into some trouble with Protectorate authority, and in exchange for a warning to him, he suggested that I look you up. He said that you would be able to find us a cargo that was under Martian radar."

"And Travis told you nothing of what I do, I take it?" Ricket asked.

"Nothing, sir," David replied.

"Your honesty does you credit, Captain. What trouble did you encounter with our erstwhile Martian friends?"

Rice took a deep breath.

"One of my crewmen was arrested on charges I didn't agree with," he explained. "It looked like it wouldn't be a fair trial, so we... liberated him."

The conversation was interrupted at that point by the return of the waitress, who silently poured tea and wine for each man before stepping back out, making subtle eyes at the sharply carved physique of the cyborg guarding the table.

Ricket picked up his glass and offered a toast to Rice. "To loyalty to one's subordinates, and to you Captain Rice. This was Mage Montgomery, I presume? I have heard... some of what occurred with him."

David sipped his wine, trying to cover his surprise. From the other man's smile, he suspected he failed.

"I think introductions are in order, Captain Rice," Ricket continued. "I am the Vice-Director in charge of UnArcana Affairs for the Legatus Military Intelligence Directorate. I should say that, if your young Mage has achieved what some of our analysts think he has..." the Vice-Director shook his head. "You have the most valuable civilian ship in the Protectorate, Captain," he said quietly. "To anyone, that is, who was not opposed to any but the most necessary use of magic."

David couldn't help himself from sighing in relief.

"Carmichael did not tell me that he was sending me to the Legatus government," he replied. "I'm not sure he and I have the same idea of 'under the radar.'"

"Oh, I believe you do, Captain," Ricket told him with a smile. "LMID," he pronounced it el-mid, "tries to keep a *very* low profile with Protectorate authorities. And you are in luck," he continued, "in that I do need a jumpship, and your *Blue Jay* will fit my needs perfectly."

"What do you need, Mr. Ricket?" David asked. The Legatan held up his hand, though, as the food arrived at just that moment. Bowls of rice, meat, and veggies covered in steaming sauces were laid out in front of each man, and a third place for the Augment.

Once the waitress had left without violently attacking anyone, the cyborg bodyguard joined David and Ricket wordlessly and dug in to the food himself.

"What is your personnel transport capacity, Captain?" Ricket asked as he dug into his food with the provided chopsticks.

"We can carry eighty or so comfortably," David said carefully. The food was spicier than he expected, but extraordinarily good. "Depending on how comfortable they are crowding, we could easily double that."

"Excellent. And you're rated for three megatons of mass, correct?"

"We're a *Venice* class, so yes. Three hundred cargo containers."

"This won't be cargo containers, Captain," Ricket told him. "As it happens, a *Crucifix*-class gunship masses three hundred thousand tons unloaded, and is of a size that will fit inside your ships rotating ribs. I need four gunships, cadre crew of twenty per ship, and a thirty man security team transported from Legatus to the Mercedes system. Under the radar, as you say."

"That's a bit different from our usual cargo," David said slowly, trying to buy himself time to think. "And riskier."

"That's why I think your ship is perfect," the Legatan spy told him. "Also, the security team are Augments. I would recommend that you simply let any pirates board, and allow them to deal with the issue."

"We are also prepared to pay handsomely for this delivery," Ricket continued. "Would five times your normal delivery fee be reasonable for the risk?"

David almost choked on his dumpling. He'd been hoping for a high risk-reward job to provide the seed capital they would need for a Fringe run. Twice his normal delivery fee, plus the existing reserves he had, would have done.

"I keep the Augments the hell away from my Mage," he tried to insist calmly.

"Of course," the Legatan agreed. "That's only sensible."

"All right. We'll do it."

#

Where David's appointment took him into the luxury of Interface Station's wealthy sections, Damien and Singh's took them into the dingy corridors of the Station's cheaper warehousing section. When the Station had been built, a significant chunk of the outer arc had been left hollow. Standard ten-thousand cubic meter cargo containers had been brought in, welded into place, and turned into row upon row of dingy, cheap, warehousing space.

"Row seventeen, level K, box nine is where we'll find our man," Singh told Damien, leading the way to a rickety-looking elevator. It clanked and chugged its way up seven layers of the cargo containers and disgorged them onto a catwalk that looked only slightly safer.

"Is this place safe?" Damien asked, following Singh along the catwalk and looking for the haphazard mix of pre-fabricated signs and glorified graffiti that marked the various sections of the warehousing section.

"Not a chance," Singh said cheerfully. "That's why we're carrying guns."

Something about the cheerfully deadly Sikh pilot, however, got them through the sparse crowds and darkened catwalks without incident. They reached the box they'd been told to go to, and a youth with most of his hair shaved away, leaving a row of spikes down the center of his skull, popped the door open for them.

Two more spiked-hair youths, a man and a woman, were waiting inside with blocky but effective looking carbines.

"Leave the guns here," the woman ordered in a hoarse voice. "Nobody sees the boss armed."

Damien followed Singh's lead in unslinging the shoulder holster and leaving it on the table the ganger pointed at.

"This way," she instructed hoarsely, leading the pair of officers from the *Blue Jay* into the next room. There, sitting cross-legged on a table surrounded by black metal cases, waited the tiniest adult man that Damien had ever seen.

The wrinkles and lines on the face showed the man's true age, as did his head, out of scale with his body. The small man wore his black hair, streaked with iron gray, shoulder length – and he leveled his gaze on Damien and Singh like a gun turret.

"Narveer," he said flatly. "I really didn't believe you'd have the balls to try to deal with me after the last time we parted."

"That was duty, never personal," Singh replied calmly. "And this is business – not personal."

Before Damien could react, the man was off the table and pointing an immense pistol directly at Singh. The gun was almost comically mis-matched to the man's size, but the barrel didn't waver or tremble in the slightest.

"You're unarmed. What's to stop me blowing you away as a down payment for that cargo?"

"Damien, roll down your collar," Singh instructed calmly. Damien reached up, slowly so as not to disturb the dwarf, and rolled down his collar – revealing the gold coin declaring him a Mage. "Even here, he can use magic in self-defense," the ex-soldier reminded the smuggler.

The gun remained trained on Singh's head for a long moment, and then was tossed aside with a massive guffaw.

"Damn Singh, you got me," the dwarf announced, and turned to offer his hand to Damien. "Victor Rotha, gunrunner, smuggler, and former pilot for the Protectorate Navy. Until this lunk turned me in for the whole gun-running thing."

"You got sloppy," Singh told him sharply. "I couldn't turn that much of a blind eye!"

"Nah, and you gave me enough of a heads up that I could get out," Rotha allowed, turning back to the tables with the gun cases. "So, you need guns. What are you after?"

"Sidearms, body armor and carbines for sixty," Singh said immediately. "Decent stuff, not any of that MidWorlds manufactured crap."

"Ha, you think I can get away with selling Amber or Corinthian guns in Legatus orbit?" Rotha replied, digging through the cases. He opened one and passed the box over to Singh.

"Legatus Arms 71 Model 2445 heavy pistol," he announced. "Fires a seven point one millimeter, high muzzle velocity, solid round. The LSDF discontinued their use earlier this year as they lack the penetration to get through the level of body armor they wanted from their side-arm. They traded up for the Model 2450, which uses a sabot penetrator round, but is less effective against unarmoured targets."

The case held ten of the guns. As soon as Singh took it, Rotha dived back into the pile of cases.

"Got racks of the twenty-four-forty Hyper-Kevlars," he said over his shoulder. "Lauren, grab me four standard cases of those, and seven more of the twenty-four-forty-fives."

The spiky-haired woman promptly leapt to obey, clearly more aware of how the cases were organized than her boss.

"This is what you want," Rotha finally announced, returning with longer black metal case. He popped it open to reveal four matte-black carbines.

"This is *just* going into service with the LSDF shipboard marines," he continued. "Legatus Arms SC-5 battle carbine, Model 2454. Caseless rounds, electronic firing, electromagnetic round advancement. It's a block of metal and molecular circuitry – not a single moving part. Takes two fifty round magazines of a five millimeter bullet – standard load is one frangible, one armor-piercing. Box of a hundred of 'em just fell out of a shuttle as I was walking by, and I just couldn't leave 'em lying there!"

"Sounds good," Singh replied. "We'll sixty each of the pistols, the armor, and the carbines."

"Oh ho ho!" Rotha replied, his gaze settling on an unrelated box, the height of a man. "And you'll take this too, if you know what you need!"

The small man ran over to the casket and popped the lid, swinging it open to reveal a man-sized suit of full body armor.

"Martian Armaments Mark Seventeen Combat Exosuit," he announced proudly. "The Legatans just switched over to a home-grown combat suit, so a bunch of these were being destroyed. I saved a few for better fates. Still qualified on this monster, Singh?"

Damien looked from the Exosuit to the Pilot, and back to the Exosuit. He sighed. Whatever Captain Rice had given them as a budget had to cover it, because from Singh's expression, they weren't leaving without the suit.

#

"Is Narveer back aboard with those guns?" David asked Jenna as he re-entered the bridge.

"Not quite," his First Officer responded, checking her console and the radar. "He took Damien with him and they checked in about ten minutes ago – their contact is delivering them, along with the goods, in his own shuttle. Their ETA is about another twenty minutes."

"That'll work," the Captain accepted, settling into the acceleration couch next to his console as he brought up the navigation software. "Is anyone else off-ship?"

"Kellers and his engineers are out for dinner," Jenna replied. "I got the impression LaMonte tried to go out alone with Damien, but Singh had already grabbed him for gun-shopping. Why?"

"We have cargo inbound that's self-mobile," David explained. "We need to be clear of the station and in a steady orbit in about ninety minutes. Have you heard from Kellers?"

"I'll check in with him. Make sure they won't have to pour Kelly back onto the ship."

David shook his head with a chuckle. "Is Damien holding a grudge over her getting him arrested?" he asked. "For that matter, is our high school love fest being a problem at all?"

"Nah, the rest of the crew just thinks they're being idiots," his XO replied calmly. "Which they are – Damien isn't holding a grudge. He's just oblivious. Self-mobile cargo?" she finished.

"We'll be carrying four gunships, plus skeleton crew, to the Mercedes system," David told her. "We'll also be taking on a security platoon of Augments. Can you get someone to check through the quarters on Ribs Three and Four to make sure they're presentable for a hundred and ten strangers?"

"We can double up some of the cabins and fit them in," Jenna confirmed. "How long do we have?"

"About two hours," David told her. "Ricket moves quickly. And pays well," he added. "It'll be worth it."

#

With the *Blue Jay* separated from the spinning wheel of Interface Station and floating in its new assigned high orbit, Damien floated in the middle of the simulacrum chamber in zero-gravity. The screens surrounding him showed the busy space around the ship.

The freighter's external ribs, usually in motion while the ship was orbiting, were frozen in place. Beyond them, five sets of engines flared as the Legatan ships approached. Damien gestured on his control panel, zooming in on the squadron.

Four *Crucifix* gunships, all in what the Captain had referred to as 'Squid Mode', decelerated carefully towards the freighter. In the midst, a single shuttle shaped its own, slightly different, course. The *Blue Jay*'s computer told Damien it was an assault shuttle, of a class unique to the Legatus Self Defense Force.

The assault shuttle, probably chock full of the Augments assigned to guard the tiny but deadly squadron the *Blue Jay* had been hired to transport, hung back as the gunships slowly approached the freighter.

They approached closer than any full size ship had ever come to the *Blue Jay*, the pinpricks of their engines cutting out as they expanded into the hulls fully visibly from Damien's cameras and sensors. Each gunship was a hemisphere, forty meters deep and as many around, to which four twenty meter cubes were linked by sixty meter long cylinders. With the modules swept behind them, the ships were sixty meters across at their widest, and a hundred and twenty meters long.

The ships were tiny next to the *Blue Jay*. As the first slowly slid between Rib One and Rib Two and fired small thrusters to arrest its motion and bring into the freighter's hull, Damien realized that four gunships was nothing against the normal volume of cargo they carried. The plan was to lock a single ship in each quarter of the hull, but they could just as easily have locked all four ships nose to tail along one side of the ship, and carried sixteen of the gunships all told. Of course, the *Blue Jay* could only have carried the mass of eight of the ships.

The lower mass was a factor in some of his jump calculations. He was starting to update the course he'd been plotting when the buzzer sounded for entry to the simulacrum chamber.

"Come in," he instructed.

The door slid aside, temporarily blocking off part of the view of the outside universe as Kelly LaMonte drifted in.

"Figured I'd find you here," she said softly. "Do you know how to not work, Damien?"

"That shuttle," Damien said quietly, pointing at the small spaceship now shaping a gentle arc towards the *Blue Jay*'s shuttle bay, "carries twenty-eight men and woman who voluntarily submitted to life-altering surgery to allow them to hunt and arrest Mages like me. It's a little sobering."

The engineer caught herself on the platform next to where Damien floated and settled onto it.

"We get this job done, we get out of UnArcana space, and we never deal with these crazies again," she told him. "Why get hung up on their issues?"

"It's nerve-wracking to realize that anyone hates you that much," Damien shrugged.

Kelly carefully laid her hand on his shoulder, balancing perfectly in zero-gravity.

"Not your problem," she said forcefully. "You didn't break their laws, didn't use magic on the station. Besides, if they cause problems on the ship, the Captain will throw them out the airlock."

He looked 'up' at her, somewhat disbelievingly.

"He won't stand for his officers being harassed, you'll see," she promised.

"Fair," he allowed. After a moment, he reached up to cover her hand with his own. Her skin was warm against him. They floated there in zero-gravity in silence for a long moment.

"I was starting to wonder," she said quietly, "if you were still mad at me for getting you arrested. James told me it was nothing of the sort. *He* said you were just young and oblivious." Kelly took advantage of her better leverage to turn Damien around to face her. "So, Damien, let

132

me be as obvious as I can. Want to come back to my quarters and I will *cook* you dinner?"

Even he wasn't that oblivious.

#

David was waiting in the shuttle bay with Narveer and Kellers when the Legatan shuttle came aboard. The three officers floated behind a safety shield, watching the pilot neatly slow the ship to a halt in the exact center of the bay, and then gently connect her to the deck with a tiny burst from the top-side maneuvering thrusters.

The shuttle was a thick, dark-painted wedge, designed to be equally at home in space or in atmosphere. Each side of the wedge bore the golden cog with the lightning bolt cut out that was the symbol of Legatus's Augment Corps. Hatches on the front likely covered weapons systems designed to clear the way for the platoon of soldiers aboard. A larger hatch, roughly halfway back the port angle of the wedge, opened shortly after the shuttle settled onto the deck.

An eerily skinny man with iron gray hair, clad in a blue-trimmed black uniform with the Augments golden cog at his collar, exited the ship first. He saw David and his officers and kicked off from the shuttle, neatly directing himself to grab the blast shield and efficiently orient himself to face them.

"Major James Niska, commanding Security Team Alpha-Seventeen," he reported crisply, giving a credible zero-gravity salute.

"Welcome aboard the *Blue Jay*, Major Niska," David greeted him. Behind the Major, more black uniformed men and women spilled out of the ship. Each carried a duffel bag and a slung rifle, and they quickly aligned themselves in neat lines behind their commander. "How was your flight?"

"Utterly boring. It was perfect," the Augment replied cheerfully. "All of the gunships looked to have hitched on correctly. Are their crews aboard?"

"They are coming in through the maintenance outriggers," David confirmed. "My First Officer is checking up on them. If you want to meet up with them, I can have my First Pilot," he gestured carefully to Narveer, "show your men to their quarters."

"That would be perfect," Niska agreed, gesturing for one of his team to approach him. "Karl, take the platoon and get them settled in. Follow Mr...?"

"Singh," Narveer replied, shifting forward to face the platoon. "Narveer Singh."

"Follow Mr. Singh," Niska finished. "We'll sort out the rotation and guard schedules once I've had a chance to sit down with Captain Rice."

"Understood, sir," the non-com replied sharply before turning to the team behind them.

"This way, Major," David told the Augment officer, leading him into the central core of the ship. Behind them, the Legatan non-commissioned officer started snapping sharp orders to get the troops into line.

"We'll be putting your men and the gunship cadre up in Ribs Three and Four," the Captain told Niska as the shuttle bay doors closed behind them. "I assume you'll want to split your platoon between the two Ribs, to keep an eye on the crews?"

"Of course," Niska agreed. "We will also need unfettered access to the ship. The layout of the *Venice* class is not entirely consistent from vessel to vessel, so we will need to review all of the *Blue Jay*'s own peculiarities. I will also want to post guards on the bridge, Engineering, and, preferably, the simulacrum chamber."

David winced at the thought of Augments guarding the chamber where Damien worked.

"Believe me when I say the men I would select to guard your Mage are very specifically chosen," Niska continued, clearly catching both David's reaction and the reason for it. "In the case of any attack on this ship, however, the simulacrum chamber is one of the three areas that will be the focus of a boarding attempt."

"All right," the Captain agreed with a sigh. "But if your men cause *any* issues – especially with Montgomery – that access will start restricting itself *extremely* quickly."

"I will do my best to make sure we have no such issues," Niska said calmly. "If there are, you must, of course, do what you feel is necessary."

The conversation was interrupted as they emerged into the cross-chamber that linked in the rear set of airlocks and maintenance outriggers. An open cross-section of the *Jay*'s keel, the room was large enough to be difficult to crowd, but with everyone floating free in zero-gravity, the gunship cadre crews were managing it.

"Major Niska," one of the officers greeted the Augment as he and David entered the room. "Captain Rice," she added after a moment, nodding to the man who was merely here to transport her several dozen light years. "Group Commander Harriet Mons. If you have quarters ready for us, I think it's best if we break up this incipient clusterfuck."

"Where's Jenna?" David asked before noticing his First Officer tied up with several of the blue-uniformed officers.

"She's dealing with some of my prima-donnas who are worried about scratching their paint," Mons replied. "Let me shut them up and we can get some order in place here."

Moments later, Mons arrived, forcefully, in the middle of the conversation Jenna was having with the gunship crew. David couldn't hear the conversation, but it looked rather like she was telling them to listen to Jenna.

"All right," he bellowed, years of practice projecting his voice across the echoing compartment. "Everyone, look to Officer Campbell," he pointed at Jenna. "She is responsible for getting you to your quarters. Cause her any more trouble, and your quarters will be in the smelliest latrine we can find on the ship. Am I clear?!"

The silence that answered was only broken by Mons' chuckling. Finally clear of the previously un-relenting set of officers, now looking thoroughly cowed by the Group Commander, Jenna promptly had the crews moving with her usual efficiency.

Five minutes later, Mons, Niska, and David were alone on the *Jay*'s bridge.

"What is our ETA at Mercedes?" Mons asked.

"I'll have to confirm with my Ship's Mage," David admitted. "Once Jenna has your crews settled, we'll be clearing to accelerate out-system. Mercedes is forty light years from here, one of the furthest MidWorlds, so it'll be eleven to twelve days."

"That's about what I expected," the Group Commander accepted with a nod. "I'm impressed so far, Captain Rice. If there is anything you need me for – and especially of any of my pack of super-intelligent monkeys give your crew any trouble – feel free to contact me."

She turned to Niska. "Once you've discussed your security plans with the Captain, please meet me in my quarters, Major. We have some matters to discuss."

Mons shook David's hand and left the bridge, leaving him alone with the Augment Major once more.

#

Damien was eating breakfast the next morning when Major Niska found him. With the ship under acceleration out towards space flat enough for him to jump them, the mess was oriented ninety degrees from normal. It at least had a definite down that it had lacked while they'd been waiting for the gunships to lock on.

"Mage Montgomery, I am Major James Niska," the Augment introduced himself, sliding into the empty seat opposite from Damien with a tray of food. The crew Damien normally ate with, including Kelly, were on shift so he was eating alone.

135

"I know who you are," Damien responded, looking up and taking in the Augment's strange square-pupiled eyes. "And what you are. What do you want from me?"

"I wanted to have a chance to talk to you before any misunderstandings occurred," Niska said softly. "I see I may be a little too late."

"What is there to misunderstand?" the Mage asked crossly. "I am about as happy to have you aboard as you are to be relying on a Mage to ferry you around."

"I don't get the impression that you are calmly content and glad to have the option to have us available," the Augment replied. "In the absence of a technological solution, men like you are the only tool we have to tie humanity together. I admire and appreciate Jump Mages like you."

"Working as a Mage-killer is a great way to show that appreciation."

Niska shook his head. "It is not my job to kill Mages," he said sharply. "My job is to arrest Mages who break the laws of the Legatus system."

"Which is basically breathing on the surface, so far as I can tell," Damien replied.

"To an extent," the cop admitted. "Don't make the mistake of assuming that we hate Mages, though. I won't deny that prejudice exists, but it's not the reason for those laws."

Damien sighed and leaned back, looking at the Augment who seemed determined to convince him of something.

"And why, exactly, would my setting foot on Legatus be a crime then?" he asked after a moment. Partly, he was humoring the man. But part of him was curious too – he'd always wondered how exactly the UnArcana worlds had come into being.

"Because if you set foot on Legatus, you are not subject to our laws," Niska explained. "We were not allowed to opt out of the Compact, so any crime you commit on Legatus has to be tried by Mages. You have separate rights and privileges from anyone else."

"Our ancestors weren't prepared to allow the master race the Eugenicists had built to rule over them," he continued. "The Mage-King told them that they had to accept the Compact, or the jumpships wouldn't carry cargo to Legatus. They agreed – but then barred Mages from their worlds to render the Compact meaningless."

Damien shivered at the mention of the Eugenicists. The group had taken control of the Mars colony centuries before, and then subjected the population to strict breeding controls and restrictions. Earth had tried and failed to stop them for decades.

"I'm a Mage by Right, not by Blood," he pointed out. "My ancestors didn't come out of the Olympus Project."

"There's been a lot of research on the Mages by Right that suggests that the vast majority of them can trace their ancestry back to the lucky rejects of the Project," Niska replied.

The 'Olympus Project' had been a massive, bloody-handed, forced-breeding program of individuals who tested as 'gifted' to a number of tests the Eugenicists had developed. It took them eighty years, but they succeeded in creating the modern Mage. Along the way, they'd dumped a few tens of thousands of 'lucky rejects' into the general population – and were estimated to have murdered almost a *hundred thousand* older subjects once they'd been bred.

In the end, the Eugenicists had been destroyed by their own creations, led by the man who became the first Mage-King of Mars. He had, in turn, imposed the Compact to protect the other Mages from those who feared the Eugenicists' creation. In exchange for that protection, the Mages had agreed to serve – most importantly as the Jump Mages that carried man's colonies to the stars.

"So we are all to be tarred with the brush of the Eugenicists then?" Damien asked. "Even those descended from those who, arguably, suffered worst?"

"When Legatus was founded, it was seen that placing the Mages as a ruling caste over us would be allowing the Eugenicists to win – accepting the master race they'd built. Now," Niska shrugged. "Now it's about not wanting to have a separate privileged caste imposed on us from outside. And a certain degree of stubborn pride in doing things our way."

"As one of the people caught in the gears of your 'stubborn pride,' I can't say I'm enthused," Damien pointed out. "Seems to be more about prejudice than anything else."

"I already said I don't deny that," Niska replied, shrugging uncomfortably. "I don't *like* it – personally, I think there would be grounds for compromise with the Compact and the Mage-King at this point. The Legatus Legislature wouldn't stand for it now, though, and too many worlds have followed our example."

"Regardless of that, though," the Augment continued, "I'm supposed to be providing security for this ship, which means I need to work with you. I wanted to clear the air between us, as I know the reputation Augments have with Mages. Are you okay with us assigning a sentry to the simulacrum chamber?"

Damien sighed. "I see the logic," he admitted. "If they cause trouble though…"

"If they cause you trouble, let me know, and you won't see that agent again," Niska said flatly. "You are under our protection, and I will not stand for my people being rude. We clear?"

The youth nodded, taken aback at the fierceness of the soldier's declaration.

"We're clear."

#

Mikhail Azure watched the bounty hunter pass through the outer office of his establishment with the security cameras. The man was one of Azure's favored mercenaries, though he had twice turned down membership in the Blue Star Syndicate.

If he succeeded at the mission he was currently set upon, Azure would offer again. If he declined again, more permanent measures would have to be taken. Azure appreciated the man's skill, but could also not allow that skill to be used against the Syndicate.

After five minutes of back and forth with the secretary, she reached down under her desk and hit a button that didn't appear to be connected to her phone.

"Sir, there is a Mr. Able here to see you," she said through the intercom. "His pass-phrases are valid."

"Thank you Meryl," Azure replied. "Please send him back."

Azure leaned back in his unprepossessing chair and glanced at the door to his office. It was an unassuming office – officially that of a small, utterly average, trading house – tucked away in a secondary orbital station above a moderately advanced MidWorld. Nothing about it stood out, but the Protectorate's law enforcement would collectively trade their right hand for its location.

From this plain office, Mikhail Azure – not the name he'd been born with – ran the largest criminal syndicate in the Protectorate. He'd once planned to pass that enterprise onto his son, but David Rice of the *Blue Jay* had changed that.

He hoped Able had good news.

The bounty hunter, a slim man of average height, with average brown hair and calm blue eyes, entered the office with his eyes tracking around for any possible threat. None of the defenses were visible, and the deadliest sat behind the desk.

"I do not see the *Blue Jay* docked at my station," Azure said calmly. "You have brought neither a prisoner nor a corpse before me. If you are not delivering David Rice to me, Able, why are you here?"

"It seemed an appropriate time to check in," the bounty hunter replied, his voice equally calm. "I know where the *Jay* will be next and I had a question I needed answered."

"And what, Able, do you know that no other who was in the same system as them wouldn't?"

The hunter laughed.

"I know that the *Blue Jay* was hired by Bryan Ricket, of LMID," he answered. "That means whatever flight path they filed is exactly where the Captain thinks he's going – and nowhere near where they actually are headed. Ricket couldn't think in a straight line if his life depended on it. So I asked the right people, and now I know what even Rice doesn't: where he's going. They've only got the one Mage," Able concluded, "so I will beat them there."

Azure held the mercenary's gaze flatly. He knew from long experience that his own ice-cold blue eyes, the only part of him he never changed when he modified his face and body to hide from the law, could intimidate the strongest of men.

"I see," he acknowledged. "But I do not see why you are here?"

Able shrugged. "The job was for Rice," he said. "But with what rumor says was done to his ship, I have to ask – do you want it too?"

Azure considered.

"What rumors have you heard?" he asked. Many different stories had made their way to him from Sherwood and Corinthian. He knew that Rice's new Mage had been charged with illegally modifying a jump matrix, but that the ship continued to jump without issue.

"Rumor says that the *Blue Jay* took out a pirate near Sherwood," Able answered. "Says that it was an amplified attack spell – something a freighter shouldn't be able to do. And then Montgomery was charged with modifying the jump matrix – but the ship can still jump."

"I think he gave the *Jay* an amplifier," Able concluded. "And I think that's worth even more to you than Rice."

"You dare much, if you plan on telling me what I think," Azure snapped. It was almost automatic though, as he thought over Able's words. If the hunter was right – and it fit with what he knew – the *Blue Jay* now represented the prize of the century.

"I don't think it's a stretch that the ability to turn any freighter you get your hands on into a raider to give the Navy nightmares is of value to you," Able replied. "But if it's not," he shrugged, "I'll go back to the old plan of blowing the ship apart from the longest range I can and extracting Rice's flash-frozen corpse from the wreckage."

The bounty hunter turned to go, but Azure froze him in place with a gesture and a flick of power. The criminal overlord rose from behind his desk and crossed to the mercenary, walking around to face the man he'd frozen in place before releasing him.

"You are correct, so you will do nothing of the sort," he told Able, watching as the bounty hunter quailed away from him. "Bring me Rice – dead or alive. Bring me Montgomery - alive. Bring me their ship -

intact. Do this, and I will pay you ten times what you were promised for Rice. Deal?"

Able swallowed, slowly straightening to face his employer. "Deal."

"What's your plan?" Azure demanded. The hunter seemed to consider refusing for a moment, then shrugged.

"Ricket is having them deliver gunships to Chrysanthemum," he explained. "I have friends in their security apparatus, and they'll *leap* at the chance to bring in a Mage the Protectorate wants arrested. While they're on planet dealing with that, I'll seize the ship. If I tell the Chrysanthemumites I'm delivering them to the Protectorate, they'll turn Montgomery and Rice over, and I'll hop, skip and jump right back here."

"Easy money for you then," Azure observed. "Don't fuck it up." He gestured to the door.

Able stumbled from the room, and the Blue Star crime lord watched him go. Once the bounty hunter had left the office, he re-activated the intercom to Meryl.

"Meryl, contact Captain Shepard," he instructed calmly. "He is to prepare my yacht for an immediate trip."

"Then arrange for a runic transceiver message to be sent to Echelon, to our Mr. Wong. He is to have his people prepare the *Azure Gauntlet* for action."

"You expect Able to fail." It wasn't a question.

"I do not place great faith in his success, no," Azure confirmed. "And if he fails, no lesser force than my *Gauntlet* will succeed."

#

"Jump complete, Captain," Damien reported over the intercom. David glanced at the screens on the *Blue Jay*'s bridge slowly resolving their new location.

"Everything is looking clear up here Damien, we're bang on target," he told the young Mage. "Next jump on schedule?"

"I need a nap," Damien replied, yawning. "After that, I think so. Will let you know if I need a delay. I'm out."

The com channel to the simulacrum chamber closed, and David turned back to checking their course. They were four days – two of flight inside Legatus and two of jumping - and six jumps out from Legatus. Like most stopping points along the way for interstellar travel, there was absolutely nothing around them for light years in any direction.

"The jump is complete?" Niska asked, the Augment entering the room behind David. "How far out are we now?"

"I've never met a Mage trained to jump anything other than a light year, Major Niska," David pointed out, turning back to face the cyborg. "I imagine you are perfectly capable of doing the math."

The iron-haired soldier smiled tightly, and then turned to his men outside the bridge.

"Seal the bridge," he ordered flatly. "Miller will see Montgomery up here. No one else enters or leaves till I give the all clear."

The bridge door slid shut behind him as he stepped in, to David and Jenna's stares of shock. For the first time since he'd boarded the ship, the Augment Major was visibly armed, with a massive black block of a pistol slung on his hip.

"What's going on?" David demanded, starting to rise.

"Please stay seated, Captain," Niska instructed. "No harm will come to you, but certain matters should be discussed in confidence. I will explain once Mage Montgomery arrives."

The Major leaned against the wall next to the door, watching David and Jenna with his strange eyes. The bridge was silent for a long few minutes, until the door slid open again and Damien walked in.

"What's going on, Captain?" he asked. "One of the Augments said you wanted to see me? Why are *they* passing on your messages?"

"I apologize for the deception," Niska answered, stepping in behind Damien and closing the door. "I needed to speak to you three alone, with the rest of the ship in the dark for the moment."

"Now that Damien is here, can you please explain why the hell you've locked me on my own bridge?" David demanded. On his console, he'd brought up a series of commands that would lock the Legatan crews in their quarters, slam down barricades to split up the Augments, and order Singh to break out the Exosuit and the guns.

"Vice-Director Ricket did not explain all the details of this contract with complete honesty," Niska replied calmly. "We are not making this delivery to Mercedes."

"Are you hijacking my ship?" David asked, his hand hovering over the activate command.

"No," the Augment replied cheerfully. He tossed a datachip to Jenna. "You'll find the details of your new course on there. You will also find, if you review your contract, that you are subject to non-discretionary revisions such as this on the authority of an appropriately authorized officer of the Directorate – in this case, me."

David released the activate command, sighing as he faced the soldier.

"And just *where* do you want us to take these ships?"

"Chrysanthemum," Niska answered.

"No," the Captain replied flatly. Chrysanthemum was one of the worst of the UnArcana worlds – a Fringe system notorious for finding any fault they could with the Mages coming through, and for running a military junta as a government. "I agreed to deliver to a civilized planet, not a Fringe hell-hole."

"Your contract allows..."

"That clause is unenforceable, and we both know it," David interrupted.

"Yes," Niska agreed. "However, you would have to take us to court in a Protectorate system – a place that you have even less interest than us in ending up."

"So if we deliver to Mercedes, you won't honor the contract?"

"As the contract has now changed, we would not feel obligated to reimburse you for delivering to the incorrect system," the LMID soldier replied. "That said, I am authorized to expand your remuneration if you do deliver to Chrysanthemum. As you pointed out so eloquently, the risk profile is significantly different."

David cursed himself for ever taking a job from a Military Intelligence unit. Throwing the whole lot out of the airlock was tempting, but he wasn't entirely sure that being vented into deep space would actually kill Niska and the other Augments.

"How much?" he grated out.

"I am authorized to double your compensation," Niska offered.

Doubling their compensation would bring this job to ten times their normal rate for a delivery of this scale. It would easily set them up for the Fringe run that would keep them safe.

"That's... almost worth it," he said bluntly. "If this contract had been openly presented as such, I would likely have accepted it. Why the cloak and dagger?"

Niska seemed to relax slightly.

"Among Chrysanthemum's longest-standing issues is a conflict with one of the large interstellar corporations from the Core," he explained. "They worry, not entirely without precedent, that the corporation will use mercenaries – or possibly even outright Navy pressure – to force them to change their stance in certain negotiations."

"In exchange for certain contracts, promises, and domestic reforms, my government is providing them Group Commander Mons' ships and crews at a token price. But we want to keep both that Chrysanthemum is arming, and that we are engaging in such a charity case, very quiet. Mercedes *could* buy the gunships, so we officially declare they are being shipped there. We re-direct now, light years from anywhere, and no one is the wiser."

"And if someone *does* try and force Chrysanthemum, they run into a gunship squadron that shouldn't be there," Damien observed quietly.

"Yes," Niska confirmed. "And since the core crew is Legatan, there is also an increased pressure on the Chrysanthemum government

142

to keep their promises of internal reform. They've been giving the UnArcana worlds a bad name recently."

"No one is going to argue with that," David agreed. He sighed, and turned to Damien. "Once you've had a chance to rest, start plotting a new course. It looks like we're visiting Chrysanthemum."

#

"Welcome to Chrysanthemum, left butt cheek of the universe," Jenna announced as the system resolved around them. Two weeks of jumping with the gunship crews and augments had started to grate on the *Blue Jay*'s crew – the ship wasn't *that* big, and an extra hundred and ten bodies filled up the space on the Ribs more than anyone was used to.

Chrysanthemum was a six planet system wrapped around an old but unchanging K-class red dwarf. The outer three planets were gas giants, with the second planet easily habitable with a workable biosphere.

"I'm reading one station orbiting the fourth planet," Jenna reported. "Maybe a dozen in-system ships shuttling back and forth between the station and Chrysanthemum, nothing over a couple hundred thousand tons and some change."

"There's no station over Chrysanthemum?" David asked.

"Yes there is," Niska told them. The Augment had arrived on the bridge shortly before their arrival in-system. "May I?" he asked, stepping up to an empty console. David gestured for him to go ahead, and he manipulated the controls, zooming in on the habitable world.

"They pulled an asteroid into orbit when they colonized the planet," he explained, highlighting the captured rock. "The plan was to eventually use it as a counterweight for an orbital elevator, but right now they've set up some fuelling infrastructure and a few micro-gee factories on the Rock."

"Send a note to the planet," David instructed Jenna. "And then set our course for the Rock." He turned to Niska. "I suggest you and Mons' people start going over the ships," he continued. "I don't really plan on staying here for long. When do I get paid?"

"Once the ships have been delivered and we've had a chance to inspect them," Niska told him. "Give me a day or two once we're in place – should let you find some kind of cargo on Chrysanthemum."

"And just what does this place export?" David asked, eyeing the planet on the screen.

"Paranoia. Surveillance satellites. Tanks. Some really good fish."

#

An hour passed in quiet. Niska eventually left the bridge as the *Blue Jay* slowly made its way towards Chrysanthemum. David sent Jenna to get some rest, as they were easily thirty six hours from the planet still. He was alone on the bridge when the transmission from the planet finally arrived.

"Chrysanthemum System Control to freighter *Blue Jay*. We have received your identifiers and cargo description. Please confirm that you can establish an encrypted link with the Group Commander of the LSDF contingent and stand by."

David flipped open an intercom channel to Group Commander Mons quarters.

"Commander Mons, I have a request for an encrypted channel for you from the surface," he informed her. With a four and a half minute delay on all communications, he had the time to check with her before replying.

"Thank you Captain," she replied, sounding brightly awake. "I'll link in and provide you with a code set to use to link them directly to me."

A few keystrokes later, David had set up a connecting channel for Mons that even he couldn't eavesdrop on, and then recorded his response to CSC.

"System Control, this is Captain Rice aboard the *Blue Jay*," he introduced himself. "Channel 77-15-AC has been set up for an encrypted channel. Group Commanders Mons advises you to use encryption group Gamma-Five."

He sent the message, and settled back into watching the ships move around the system. Five minutes for each transmission to travel one way made for long conversations.

Ten minutes later, his console advised him that an encrypted recording had come in on the channel he'd provided. A few minutes later, Mons used the *Jay*'s transmitter to send a response.

By the time several exchanges had passed along the encrypted channel, an hour had passed, and then he finally received a transmission directed at him.

"Captain Rice, welcome to the Chrysanthemum system," the uniformed traffic controller told him. "Unfortunately, we have no ability to provide docking for a vessel of your size – any attempt to land a vessel of your size on the Rock would likely cause structural damage. I am transmitting an orbit that will allow Commander Mons's teams to land the gunships without issue. Once that is complete, we will be able to send a tanker out to fuel your ship up – consider it our part of your fee."

The man glanced over to one side, reading a message that must have come up on a screen that was off-camera, and then glanced back to David with a surprised look on his face.

"The President has also personally asked me to invite you and your senior officers to join us for the celebration of the Midsummer Festival," he continued, slowly. "Your arrival is timely – the summer solstice for our northern hemisphere falls tomorrow night, so you should be able to enter orbit, offload the gunships, and make it down with time to spare. We should be able to get your ship fuelled while you're on the surface."

David waited for a long moment, trying to make sense of the man's reaction. He wasn't sure how comfortable he was with the tanker docking with the *Jay* while he was on the surface, but it would allow them to head out quickly if he found – or clearly wouldn't find – a cargo. With a shrug, he switched the recorder on and smiled at the traffic controller.

"Thank you for the welcome," he began. "Inform your President that my officers and I will be glad to attend."

The best way to avoid a trap, in his experience, was to walk into it with your eyes wide open.

#

Damien had spent almost the entire trip either in his lab, the simulacrum chamber, or hiding in Rib A with Kelly, where none of the passengers had quarters. After his one meal with Niska, the only members of their Legatan passengers he'd seen had been the four Augments assigned to guarding the simulacrum. Those four young men had been unfailingly polite, if skittish around the Mage.

He was in his lab, ignoring the guards outside and looking forward to a planned dinner with LaMonte, when the Captain buzzed him.

"Captain," he answered the intercom, flipping the feed from the bridge up onto his work-screen.

"Damien, how is everything looking on your end?" Rice asked, his eyes focused on his own screens, away from the camera.

"We've no issues," Damien answered, somewhat confused. "All of the runes are clean, the amplifier is fully functional."

"The locals have invited the ship's senior officers to the surface to join them in a local festival," David told him.

"You need me to mind the ship while you're gone?" Damien asked. If the remainder of the ship's senior officers were ground-side, he would technically be in charge. He wouldn't leave the simulacrum chamber, but the console there would allow him to fly the ship – and the amplifier he controlled from there was the *Jay*'s only real weapon.

"That's the odd part," David replied, shaking his head. "They didn't exclude you, and every other time I've been invited surface-side on these kinds of planets, they usually make that point very clear. I'm not sure they're saying what they mean, and I want you to keep your eyes open."

"You think the Legatans are plotting something?" Damien asked, thinking back over his limited encounters.

"No," the Captain answered, sounding a little surprised himself. "I think Niska and Mons and their people are as level with us as they're going to be, outside of the diversion. The locals though... I don't trust them. I want you with us on the surface – *without* your medallion, Damien."

Damien touched the gold medal he wore on a leather collar around his neck. The three stars and quill carved into it marked him as a fully trained Jump Mage. He'd earned those carvings, and technically Protectorate law made it a misdemeanor for him not to wear the medallion itself. Without it, though, there was no way to identify him, even for another Mage.

"I can do that," he said softly. "Who are we leaving behind?" Unless they wanted to put his medallion on someone else, they could only claim four senior officers – Captain, First Officer, Chief Engineer and First Pilot.

"I'm leaving Narveer aboard, with that war-suit of his," Rice explained. "They'll be sending that fuel tanker over while we're on the surface. The whole thing stinks, but I don't see a way out without risking offending Niska – who still has our money. So we play nice, and take precautions."

"Understood, Captain," Damien replied, his fingers on his medallion. "We're flying down when?"

"Late afternoon local time, about noon tomorrow Martian Standard," Rice told him.

Before Damien could respond, a buzzer announced someone at the door to the Chamber. "I have a visitor," he told his boss. "I'll be there tomorrow."

As he cut the video feed, the door to the room slid open and Niska stepped in. Damien turned on the platform suspended in the center of the ovoid room to face the Augment, who calmly stood on the screens that made up the walls.

"What are you after, Major?" Damien asked.

The Legatan soldier shrugged, hitting the button to slide the door shut behind him before he said a word.

"I'm here to warn you," he said bluntly. "I heard about Chrysanthemum's invitation – I'm sure your Captain is wise enough to see the trick in them not explicitly excluding you, but I wanted to make sure."

"Most UnArcana worlds make the *use* of magic illegal," he explained. "On Chrysanthemum, *being* a Mage is illegal. I don't think they'll risk pissing of Legatus by causing issues with your crew, but they've been known to use any excuse to arrest Mages and seize ships."

"We weren't planning on it," Damien told him dryly. "I've been arrested, Major; I don't care to repeat the experience."

Niska shook his head. "Be careful, Damien," he asked. "I know *you* don't like me, but you're one of the most humble Mages I've ever met. If all your kind were like you, the Protectorate might be a better place."

"Chrysanthemum is run by a paranoid military junta," he continued. "In exchange for the gunships, they're supposed to be running elections in the next six months. Until then, though, the place is run by scum I wouldn't trust to polish my boots, and they're my *allies*."

"Whatever you do, Damien, don't go to the surface."

#

Damien watched the gunships leave early the next morning from the simulacrum chamber, with Kelly LaMonte, one of the other junior engineers, two of the pilots, and a bottle of champagne. With the *Blue Jay* in orbit, the room at the center of the ship had no gravity, making pouring difficult, but the small celebration was worth the effort.

Each gunship detached from the cargo pylons on the side of the keel in turn. A few, carefully timed, jets of the maneuvering thrusters flung the small warship through the gap in the freighter's rotating ribs. Once clear, the characteristic white flare of an antimatter rocket flashed into existence, and the ships headed towards the Rock, the captured asteroid fifty thousand kilometers ahead of the *Jay*.

"That went a lot better than I was afraid it was, even with their cloak and dagger bullshit," the older of the two pilots, a buzz-cut young man named Kelzin, announced. "Can't imagine it was comfortable for Damien here," he nodded to the Ship's Mage, "but they were polite to the rest of us."

"The ones Niska let deal with me were polite," Damien admitted. "I think if he or Mons had any people they weren't sure could play nice, they kept them under wraps."

"It is going to be so nice to have half the ship back," Kelly observed. It was hard to cuddle in zero-gravity, but she was doing her best to stay snuggled up to Damien's side – with his enthusiastic assistance.

"We've still got some time on station here," Damien replied. "The Captain's going to try to find a cargo – we may end up carrying passengers out, too."

The pretty young engineer made a face.

"We'll see what comes out of the party," Kelzin told the others. "Singh says I have to pretend Damien is my boss."

"What?" Kelly asked, turning to look concernedly at Damien. "Chrysanthemum is an UnArcana world, you can't be planning on going down?!"

"There's a lot going on the Captain isn't comfortable with," Damien told her quietly. "He's hedging his bets by keeping the only one of us trained in boarding and counter-boarding up here, and taking the heaviest firepower we have – me – down to the surface."

"I'm leaving my medallion behind, and pretending to be the *Jay*'s First Pilot," he explained. "I'll be fine."

"Singh says the whole setup stinks," Kelzin agreed. "We're sticking a whole bunch of those carbines Singh found us aboard the shuttle."

"I don't think the Captain really thinks anything is going to go down," Damien reassured Kelly. "But if it does, between the Captain, Kelzin and me, they don't have a big enough army to take us down."

He felt her shiver against him regardless.

"Be careful, Damien," she asked. "You'll be in more danger than us – the only thing the rest of us will be up to is hooking tubes into receptacles."

"Yep – and you have lots of practice with that recently," Kelzin told her innocently.

Kelly promptly emptied her champagne bulb into the pilot's face, causing him to spin back, messily wiping bubbling liquid from his face, to the general laughter of the *Blue Jay*'s younger officers.

#

The shuttle landed gently on a floating landing pad, mounted on pontoons a hundred meters away from the shore. As the sound of the craft's thrusters faded away, Kelzin stuck his head back into the passenger cabin.

Damien and the other three officers were all plain gray suits. Damien's was worn over a shirt borrowed from Kellers, the dark-skinned engineer being the only person on the ship even close to the Mage's short and slight frame.

"We are landed and locked in on docking pad five at Chrysanthemum City," the pilot informed them all. As he spoke, he made his way to a locker and pulled out one of the Legatan Arms SC-5 carbines, sliding and locking both magazines in.

"Your PC's are running coms through the shuttle relay," Kelzin continued. "That'll provide encrypted channels for about fifteen klicks out. I checked the map on the way down, the 'Festival Hall' is seven klicks from here, you should be fine."

"Check in via radio often, and don't stay out too late," the pilot concluded. "If you're out past midnight, my little friend and I will come and enforce your curfew." He patted the carbine.

"Let's try not to start a war if we don't have to," David observed dryly. "That said," he glanced around the officers, his gaze settling on Damien, "I don't trust these people at all. Let's make nice, see if we can get a cargo – but don't go anywhere alone!"

The safety lecture done, Kelzin hit the door latch, opening the shuttle ramp onto the cooling pad.

"It is a balmy twenty six degrees Celsius," he informed them, "and the wind is from the south, so you get to dodge the smell of the fisheries to the north. Enjoy yourselves. I'll keep the lights on."

Kellers led the way out, with Damien and Jenna following out onto the gently bobbing platform. The smell of the salt air hit Damien like a brick wall. He'd lived near the coast on Sherwood, but the smell was different here. There was a slight edge of something he couldn't identify to the smell of sea and waves, something completely different.

The smell of a new world. For the first time in his life, Damien was walking on the surface of a strange world. At Corinthian and Legatus, he hadn't gone to the surface, which made Chrysanthemum his first 'alien' world.

The water was a different shade: a deep purplish blue that lack the slightly iridescent tinge of his homeworld's waves. The sky was darker than Sherwood's, with a dimmer sun shining through a thicker atmosphere. The floating landing pad wasn't something Sherwood would have used, as his home had significant areas of granite to hold landing facilities near most of the inhabited zones.

A blonde-haired man clad in a dark blue suit was standing at the edge of the platform, where transparent barriers protected beds of bright pink flowers. He gestured for the *Blue Jay's* officers to approach, and stepped out to greet them with a bright smile that made Damien think of oil.

"Welcome to Chrysanthemum City, Captain Rice," he greeted David. "I am James Margrave, Aide to President Holsen. And these are your officers?"

"They are," Rice confirmed, stepping past Damien to face the aide and give quick introductions. Damien found it odd to be introduced as 'Damien Montgomery, my First Pilot,' but nodded along regardless.

"I have a car waiting for us on the shore to take us to the Festival Hall," Margrave told them. "President Holsen is looking forward to meeting you. If you'll follow me?"

#

The trip to the Festival Hall took the *Blue Jay*'s officers through a neighborhood of neatly trimmed hedges, public flower gardens of dozens of varieties of chrysanthemums, and large houses set well back from the road in treed surroundings.

The impression of peace and luxury was spoiled somewhat by the view of the massive industrial complex, fisheries, factories and warehouses mixed together, that David could see to the north. He also could see the omnipresent cameras and security men that he suspected his officers missed.

He doubted even Damien missed the two patrols of uniformed, face-masked, police in black armored personnel carriers that they saw sweeping the streets. They'd been directed to the shuttle pad for the system's dignitaries and industry leaders, so the path ran through a showcase neighborhood. Those same dignitaries required round the clock armed security on Chrysanthemum.

The Festival Hall was the clear centerpiece of the neighborhood, and of Chrysanthemum's attempts to show off to anyone they felt they needed to. It was a massive structure, built of local stone and painted a brilliant white. Two wings swept away from a central structure that looked like an immense white clam.

The entire bottom section of the 'clam' apparently slid up, providing a semi-open air central chamber that open out onto a front green lined in carefully nurtured flower beds and containing a small, somewhat tasteful stone water fountain carved in the shape of a giant chrysanthemum – in case anyone had forgotten the name of the planet.

Margrave stopped the massive, open-topped black ground car he'd delivered them in, and gracefully opened the doors for them.

"Welcome to the Solstice Festival gentlemen, lady," he told them. "The food is inside, to the left. Waiters are circulating with drinks and appetizers." He turned to David. "Captain Rice, the staff will take excellent care of your officers. If you'll come with me, the President wishes to speak with you."

David nodded wordlessly and turned to his officers.

"Stick together," he told them quietly as Margrave started away. "No booze."

"I'll keep the boys under control," Jenna promised him. "Go see what the President wants – it's not every day a planetary head of state wants to see you!"

With a firm nod, David followed Margrave towards the fountain. Crossing the green lawn he saw that a number of men and women at the party wore gold-trimmed black military uniforms. He had no idea what insignia Chrysanthemum used for its military, but he suspected that the officers with multiple gold leaves on their collars were high ranking.

"There's a lot of soldiers here," he observed to Margrave as they paused, allowing a team of waiters to make their way past with a trolley of hot food.

"The military is important to Chrysanthemum," the aide replied. "Many of our politicians are retired soldiers, and they have the right to still wear the uniform."

"Most Fringe worlds don't have much of a military," David observed as they set off again. "What happened here?"

Margrave stopped, looking at David with sharp eyes. "You don't know?"

"I've heard rumors," he said politely. Most of those rumors were related to the fact that a military junta controlled the government, not how there'd been enough of a military to take over in the first place.

"Chrysanthemum was founded as a corporate colony," Margrave explained as they headed into the clamshell of the main Festival Hall. "Our parents and grandparents came here for the promise of a good life. When they arrived, they discovered they were effectively indentured servants."

"In the end, we revolted, and drove the corporation out," he continued. "After ten years of war, we'd formed a true formal military, and one we owed our freedom to." He glanced back at David. "And since the only Mages we'd known had worn the boots of tyrants, we barred them from our world and began to deal with Legatus."

David let that pass in silence. There'd been a number of worlds where Core world corporations had abused the colonists they'd imported. Most, sooner or later, came to the attention of the Hands. The corporations involved tended to cease to exist once the Mage-King's wandering Judges got involved, but it seemed the law of the Protectorate had missed Chrysanthemum.

"Ah, President Larson, sir," the aide greeted his boss as they finally reached a large, white-clothed, table in the center of the main hall. "May I present Captain Rice – he is the master of the ship that brought us Group Commander Mons' squadron."

The man Margrave had led him to wore the same gold on black military uniform as most of the men at the party, but where they had various rank insignias with numbers and material marking their rank, President Larson wore an exquisitely worked rose gold chrysanthemum on a chain around his neck.

Otherwise, the President of Chrysanthemum was an utterly unimposing man. He was short, barely taller than Damien, and rotund with a receding hairline and a double chin. Something in his ice blue eyes, though, suggested that while the Generals might run the planet, this man was still not to be taken lightly.

"President Larson," David greeted the man. He realized that Group Commander Mons was standing at the President's right shoulder. The Legatan officer's plain blue uniform had blended in with the crowd around them, and he hadn't known she was going to be here. He'd need to keep her away from Damien – she would recognize the young Mage and know he wasn't supposed to be here.

"I want to thank you in person, Captain Rice," the President told him. His voice was soft and highly pitched, almost that of a child. "Your ship should be receiving a more tangible token of said thanks soon. You are welcome to our world."

Almost on cue, David's personal computer beeped an incoming communication.

"Excuse me, Mr. President," he said politely as he stepped away from the crowd and raised the wrist-computer to his lips.

"Rice here," he answered, as quietly as he could.

"It's Singh," the First Pilot's voice said sharply. "Our fuel tanker has arrived. Everything is hooked up; and the gas is flowing."

"That's good," Rice told him. He paused, considering the ex-Navy officer's likelihood of calling him for nothing. "What's wrong?"

"I'm not sure," the Pilot replied. "They docked further back than I was expecting – close enough that they could reach the shuttle bay. It's making me nervous."

"Are you armed?"

"Strapping the suit on now," Singh replied grimly. "I'm getting twitchy." In the background, David heard someone shouting, and then Singh was speaking urgently. "Shit! They've fired a boarding tube at us – we've got…"

The signal dissolved in distorted static. A type of distorted static that David hadn't heard since he'd left the Navy – *jamming*.

#

Damien had followed Jenna and Kellers to the buffet table, but was spending his time watching the crowd, not eating the food. It had been years since he'd gone anywhere in public without the gold medallion proclaiming him a Mage, and it was odd to realize just how much extra personal space and minor courtesy the coin gave him.

The noticeable decrease in his personal 'bubble,' despite the relatively sparse crowd at the Festival Hall, put him on edge and alert. The first thing he noticed was Group Commander Mons, standing by a rotund man of Damien's own height. Carefully, he turned away from her, looking first at the buffet table, and then past it.

The back wall of the Festival Hall had been covered in curtains painted in a mural of an agrarian landscape entirely out of sorts with the buzzing industry and paranoid security of the city so far. He was looking to see if the artist had hidden any hint of the reality of life on Chrysanthemum when the breeze from an opening door flipped aside the curtains, revealing who was coming through that door.

Three black armored soldiers with face-covering helmets, armed with familiar looking stunguns, were now hiding behind the curtain. Where there were three, there were likely more.

He slipped over next to Jenna, grabbing a glass of champagne to cover his approach.

"We have a problem," he told her while pretending to sip. "Soldiers behind the curtains. I doubt they're here to seize the Legatans."

The XO didn't seem to hear him for a moment, and then sighed. "Let's make for the Captain."

"He's got Group Commander Mons with him," Damien replied, noting as David stepped away from the President.

"She's not a squad of soldiers looking to shoot us," Jenna pointed out, putting her glass on the buffet table and gesturing for Kellers to join them.

As the three made their way over to David, Damien saw the Captain jerk in surprise, and pull his PC away from his face, as if the noise it was making was painful. Out of the corner of his eye, though, he saw the soldiers stop trying to hide as they saw the *Blue Jay*'s officers moving away.

A dozen soldiers, armored in faceless black unmarked except for a gold chrysanthemum emblazoned on their chest, cut through the crowd like sharks through water. Even the officers and other soldiers in the crowd parted ways, clearing a rapidly growing space around them as they reached David. The Captain looked up at the arrival of his officers, and then beyond them.

Before any of the *Blue Jay*'s officers could speak, however, Group Commander Mons stepped forward, between them and the soldiers, and turned to Larson.

"What is the meaning of this?" she demanded. "These people are under the protection of the Directorate!"

"I apologize, Group Commander," Larson told her. The President's voice was oddly childlike, and yet utterly flat. "These people are wanted by the Protectorate for major crimes. I would be remiss in my duties as the leader of a Protectorate world if I allowed them to go free."

Mons glanced at David, who shrugged back at her.

"Did you think Ricket hired a perfectly clean crew for his illegal delivery?" the Captain asked.

The Legatan glanced past David and met Damien's own gaze. Her eyes widened at the sight of the Mage, and Damien inclined his head slightly. He was already preparing his body and magic, and thankful that the crowd around the police squad had cleared.

"They are under the protection of the Directorate," Mons repeated. "I do not care what crimes they committed before they entered our service – they are protected."

Larson shrugged. "The Directorate is welcome to fund their legal defense," he said coldly. "Please stand aside, Group Commander. I have no desire for my men to injure you."

Mons paused and looked back at Damien again. On meeting the young Mage's eyes, she nodded sharply and stepped aside.

"Do what you must," she ordered.

She wasn't speaking to Larson.

"Seize them!" the President snapped, but Damien was already acting. Power flowed through his body as he spun to face the soldiers, his hands splayed out palms down.

A wave of pure force blasted out from his hands at knee-height. The Chrysanthemumite soldiers went down in a tumble, the snapping noises of breaking bones and shattering kneecaps suggesting none of them were getting up quickly.

The buffet table shared their fate, as did many of the decorations, but none of the guests were injured. That didn't stop them panicking and bolting for the exits at the sight of an angry Mage. Damien gestured again, and the stunguns tore themselves from the hands of the flattened soldiers to land at his feet.

David picked one up with a calm nod to Damien, and then turned to the frozen in shock Larson and Mons. The non-lethal weapon barked twice and two of the calibrated electro-shock SmartDarts slammed into the planet's President. Mons caught him as he fell and gently laid him down before looking back up the *Blue Jay*'s crew.

"They'll mobilize quickly, and I doubt they left your ship alone," she told them. "I'm being jammed – I can't reach Niska on the Rock. Get to your shuttle – I certainly won't be stopping you!"

Damien shook his head at the thought of being helped by an UnArcana military officer to escape a trap set by an UnArcana government. Wordlessly, he followed David out of the Festival Hall.

#

Margrave had abandoned the long open-topped car he'd driven them from the landing pad in. Damien kept watch as the others piled in, Jenna grabbing the wheel while Kellers settled into 'shotgun' with a stolen stungun at the ready.

The only soldiers actually at the Festival Hall, it seemed, had been the squad now lying whimpering on the floor, nursing their shattered limbs. Some of them might be crippled for life, but so far as Damien could tell they would all live.

He followed David into the backseat of the car, and Jenna gunned the engine, heading towards the shore.

"I can't raise Kelzin or the ship," Kellers reported, fiddling with the personal computer strapped around his wrist. "They must have slammed a jamming field on us just as the soldiers moved. What did they expect the *Jay* to do from orbit?!"

"The *Jay* is under attack as well," David informed them all grimly. "Singh told me they'd launched a boarding tube into the shuttle bay. We could easily escape to our ship and land directly in a trap."

"You've *met* Singh, right?" Jenna said drily, swerving the car around a speed bump and ignoring a set of traffic signals. "Strap him into that exosuit, and it would take an army to get to the ship."

"From the size of the tanker, they could have *brought* an army," David reminded her. "Or some Augments or exosuits of their own."

The car was silent for a moment - a silence suddenly interrupted by gunfire as Jenna whipped around a corner into the face of a blockade of black armored vehicles. Three of the black armored personnel carriers they'd seen while driving through the neighborhood had been parked in a row, blocking the road to the landing pad.

"Turn us around!" Kellers shouted, and they all lurched to one side as the car swerved in a dangerously tight turn.

"Hold me down," Damien told David sharply, rising to his feet in the back of the car and facing the APCs. The other man grabbed onto his waist, and Damien stretched out his hands. He felt for the core of power within him, throwing it out in front of him.

The second burst of gunfire from the APCs was more on target than the first. For a moment, even Damien thought the heavy bullets were going to rip through the car – then they slammed into the shield he'd raised with a force that shoved him backwards. Without David's grip, the Mage would have fallen out of the car.

155

Grimly, Damien held the shield as the car turned around and Jenna slammed on the accelerator. Bullets continued to splash off for a few moments, and then they were clear. The young Mage slumped, leaning on David for a second as they screamed around another corner, turning onto a different route to the landing pad.

"Damien!" Kellers shouted. "Up ahead!"

Blocking the way to the road and rumbling towards them was a tank. Damien barely got his shield forward in time, and was slammed back into his seat when the first shot from its main gun slammed into his defense.

He took a deep breath as the world seemed to slow down around him. The soldiers in the Hall had brought stunguns – they hadn't been trying to kill him and his friends, so he'd tried not to kill them. Now he was being shot at, and he was out of patience.

Surging back to his feet, Damien thrust his right hand out in a clenched fist. Bright light flashed around him as he moved, a field of super-hot plasma coalescing around him without touching his skin, and then blasting forwards with the motion of his fist.

The bolt met the tank shell coming the other way and incinerated it before slamming into the tank's turret. Molten metal exploded away from the top of the armored vehicle, and then Damien slammed a second plasma bolt into the main chassis.

This one went clean through the tank, and hit the ammunition on the way. From sixty meters away, the explosion rocked the car the *Blue Jay*'s crew had stolen, the heat blasting against Damien's face.

Exhaustion collapsed him back into the seat and it felt like his head was exploding as a vicious migraine stabbed into his skull. Blinking against the pain, he put his hands to his face – and at a warm wet feeling, pulled them away to see them spattered in his own blood.

"Damn it Damien, you're bleeding from everywhere but your eyeballs," David hissed, tossing him a package of gauze from somewhere in his suit. "I saw Kenneth after he overdid it, I *won't* bury two Mages!"

Wincing at the fierceness of David's speech and the migraine, Damien shook his head. "Not likely," he half-whimpered.

"I've got something!" Kellers suddenly snapped, turning the volume up on his personal computer.

Most of what they heard was static, but a few words came through: "Pad... attack... took off... your way."

"That's Kelzin," Jenna exclaimed. "Where is he?"

"Not close enough," Kellers replied grimly, as they reached the end of the road with the burning tank, and a second light battle tank emerged from the greenery at the side of the road. Another APC and a dozen infantry had dug in behind a temporary barrier to block the road behind the tank.

"Shoot them!" David ordered, suiting actions to words and opening fire with the stungun. The weapon's range was impressive, but the SmartDarts couldn't penetrate military body armor. The Captain ducked back down next to Damien as more bullets rattled off the hull.

Damien tried to rise; to see if he could shield them again, but David easily forced him back down as the migraine stole his balance.

"What do we…" Kellers' voice was cut off by the roaring of rockets as their shuttle came screaming overhead. Down-facing thrusters sent the soldiers scattering as the shuttle set itself down, its back ramp opening.

The tank started to train its gun on the shuttle, and then a new sound ripped the sky. Modern armor-piercing rounds ripped through its armor like tissue paper, each bullet carrying only the tiniest of explosive charges – but the accumulation of a hundred rounds enough to shatter the tank's armor and leave it a burning mess.

"Get over here!" Kelzin shouted, stepping around the shuttle as he loaded another pair of magazines into the carbine. "These guys are *not* playing nice!" Fitting actions to his words, a hail of gunfire landed around the pilot, who ducked behind his shuttle before returning fire.

Jenna slammed the car into a screeching stop, throwing her door open and leaping out. Kellers followed her, but paused to look back at David and Damien.

"Can you walk?" David asked as Damien struggled to his feet. Gunfire echoed around them, and before Damien could work up the energy to reply, the Captain looked at Kellers. "Grab him," he ordered.

Strong arms grabbed each of his shoulders and dragged him forward. He stumbled, struggling against the migraine and the exhaustion wracking his body.

"I can't do this," he muttered to David. "I'm not an Enforcer."

"Cover us!" David shouted forwards, continuing to drag Damien forward. "You're my Ship's Mage," he said harshly. "I don't *need* you to be a soldier!"

They rounded the shuttle to discover there was no cover between them and the Chrysanthemum soldiers now except the second burning tank. Jenna had made it into the shuttle, and was returning fire with a carbine she'd grabbed from inside.

Kelzin was next to them, pumping careful bursts at the locals.

"Go first, I'll cover you," the pilot ordered.

Damien felt more than saw David nod, but managed to struggle enough to his feet that he wouldn't be completely useless when they ran.

"Go!" Kelzin snapped.

David and Kellers took off, half-supporting, half-carrying Damien as he ran with them. For a moment, gunfire echoed around them, but then it diverted. A few steps behind them, Kelzin followed, spraying bullets with abandon to keep the soldiers' heads down.

Damien slumped into a seat on the side of the shuttle as David and Kellers released him, breathing a sigh of relief as Kelzin followed them in and slammed the button to close the hatch.

The young pilot opened his mouth to say something, but stopped with an expression of shock on his face as blood exploded from his stomach. A heavy sniper round slammed into the shuttle wall next to Damien as Kelzin collapsed to the ground.

Jenna dropped her carbine and was at the pilot's side in a moment.

"Toss me the medkit," she ordered. Kellers was quick to obey, passing over the white box with the green cross.

"Can you fly this thing, boss?" the engineer asked David.

Damien forced himself to a sitting position, knowing the answer the Captain was going to give. David shook his head, and met Damien's eyes.

"Can you fly?" he asked.

"I can fly anything," Damien replied, as confidently as he could with his face covered in his own blood and a migraine eating at his skull.

"That wasn't the question."

"It's fly or die," the Mage replied. "Someone's going to have to carry me to the cockpit."

#

The heavy cargo hauler had been built tough. Even as Damien was hauled into the cockpit and strapped in, the soldiers continued to spray it with rifle and machine gun fire, but it lifted smoothly into the air when he engaged the thrusters.

That was the cue for the remaining soldiers to scatter, hiding behind their APCs as the shuttles thruster fused hydrogen to blast the street with masses of ionized particles as the ship blasted for orbit.

Damien quickly brought up the various displays, checking their height, velocity, and acceleration. Three gravities of acceleration pressed them into the chairs, and he prayed silently that the pressure wasn't making Kelzin's wounds worse.

"We're clear?" David asked, and Damien shook himself, focusing on the displays again.

"We have enough fuel to make it to the *Blue Jay*," he reported. "Can we com her yet?"

The Captain was in the copilots seat and checked the communications panels for a moment before shaking his head.

"We're clear of the jamming, but I'm getting nothing from the ship," he told Damien. "Most likely they're being jammed too."

Damien nodded, blinking against his migraine, and then blinking again as a set of indicators began flashing on the console. It took him a minute to remember what they meant and bring up the radar display.

"We have a problem," he told the Captain quietly. Before David could ask, the Mage pointed at the screen he'd just opened, which showed two atmospheric interceptor jets at the maximum range of the shuttles sensors.

"Can you evade them?"

Damien checked his fuel gage, and then the computer's estimate of the jets closing speed.

"I have barely enough fuel to reach the *Blue Jay*," he said grimly. "If I push hard enough to evade them, I won't be able to slow down for rendezvous. I can evade if they fire on us, but I can't escape them."

He flipped two timers up on the screen. "Left is time to orbit – these guys can't follow us that high," Damien told David. That timer showed just over ten minutes. "Right is time to when they'll range on us."

That timer showed seven minutes.

"You're done for magic," David told him flatly. "This ship has no weapons. All we can do is hold on tight, and hope you're good enough to dodge missiles."

"No pressure, I see," the Mage replied, gently massaging his temples. "Let's see what happens."

The next minutes passed in a terrifying silence as Damien watched his fuel gage, his height, and the distance to the jets. After five, Jenna clambered in against the acceleration and dropped into the last seat.

"Kelzin will live," she said flatly. "The round pierced his intestines, and he'll need serious medical care once we get him aboard, but the bullet went through cleanly otherwise. Patched up what I could and have compresses on it. He won't die before we make it home."

"Unless the rest of us do," Damien muttered. "Have any ideas about evading atmospheric interceptors?"

"Be somewhere else?"

"Working on it," the Mage replied, running through a series of menus, trying to see if he could eke any more acceleration out of the ship without spending more fuel than he could afford.

"Watch it!" David snapped. "Incoming!"

Damien snapped his gaze back to the main screen, wincing against the sharp movement. It looked like he'd underestimated the interceptors range. With four minutes before they passed beyond the region of the atmosphere where the air-breathing craft could follow them, the fighters had each launched two missiles.

A moment later, he had a timer to impact up, and kept an eye on it as he twisted the ship slightly, arcing their course away from the missiles.

"What do we do?" Jenna asked, her voice very small.

"Pray," David told her grimly, his eyes on the radar as the missiles came screaming in, far faster than the shuttle could fly.

"That might not hurt," Damien told them absently, his mind on the missiles, the shuttle... and the shuttles ridiculously overpowered engines, designed to lift it from a planetary surface into orbit.

"I'd also recommend hanging on," he finished, grabbing onto the manual controls as the missiles entered final acquisition. "This is going to suck."

The shuttle had no ECM, no defenses and wasn't maneuvering. Presented with an easy target, the smart missiles had clustered together, sweeping in from one vector, with no more than a hundred meters between each of them. As they screamed in on the shuttle at several thousand miles an hour, Damien jerked the ship about, pointing her nose up and away from the missiles before hitting the engines at maximum power.

For a moment, half a dozen beefy men sat on the Mage's already bruised chest. Then the engines cut back to normal strength, and the shuttle stabilized.

The impact counter had gone negative. David reached over and shut it off, looking at Damien in surprise.

"What was *that*?"

"That was running air-breathing missiles into the blast of four fusion rockets at maximum power. They're designed for atmosphere – not the equivalent of a point blank solar flare," Damien explained.

"We're clear of atmo," he continued. "They're breaking off."

The Captain breathed a deep sigh.

"Alright, Damien. Get us home," he instructed.

#

Chrysanthemum orbit was quiet. After everything they'd seen on the surface, Damien was expecting *some* kind of resistance as they shot towards the *Blue Jay*, decelerating to make rendezvous now.

"Can you see anything?" David asked.

"The tanker is still attached," Damien replied. "There's nothing else moving that I can pick up, but the shuttle isn't big enough for decent heat sensors, and the radar is stupidly short-ranged."

"We'll see if we can fix that," the Captain replied. He touched a command on the screen again, and then twitched in surprise as it actually turned green. "We have a connection," he told Damien, before leaning forward.

"*Blue Jay*, come in, this is Captain Rice," he said over the channel. "Singh, please come in. Someone tell me what's going on over there."

"Oh thank gods," a female voice – *Kelly's* voice, Damien realized in relief – answered. "Captain, it's good to hear from you."

"What the hell happened? Where's Singh?" Rice demanded.

"They tried to board us through the shuttle bay," LaMonte told them, her voice weary. "Singh took that suit and half a dozen of the crew with carbines to stop them – he said they were mercs of some kind, not local troops."

"The locals certainly had a hand," the Captain told her grimly. "Where's Singh?"

"I don't know," the young engineer replied. "I'm in touch with engineering via the hardline, but the jamming cut off all contact with him and his team – the last I heard they were fighting in the shuttle bay, but twenty minutes ago a bunch of shuttles fucked off from the tanker. Looks like they were meeting up with someone – scanners show a jump-yacht running for the jump zone at crazy speed."

"The jammer must be on one of the shuttles," Jenna murmured. "They took it with them when they ran. Why would they run?"

"We would have been visible to decent sensors twenty minutes ago," Damien told her.

"Kelly, can you send us the sensor telemetry?" Rice asked. "We're coming in through the shuttle bay, we'll check up on Singh on our way in."

"Okay," she replied. After a moment's pause, she asked softly, "Is Damien okay?"

"He's the only reason any of us are," the Captain said bluntly. "Get us that telemetry – we need to get the hell out of this star system before those gunships launch."

Damien blanched as the *Blue Jay's* sensor data started to come up on his screen. He hadn't even thought of the four gunships they'd delivered. If he managed to rest and make it to the *Jay's* simulacrum, he could take them, but if he tried in his current state, he likely wouldn't survive to jump them out.

"They know what you did to the ship," David said quietly. Damien glanced over to the screen the Captain was working on. He'd pulled together a projection of the shuttles' and the jump-yacht's courses. "The Navy – and most people – treat two million klicks as the maximum range of an amplifier – and their course will pull them out of that range before we can get aboard. They wanted to make sure they were clear before you could take them out."

"How would they know that?" Damien asked.

"I don't know," David admitted. "But if one set of mercenaries does, others do. That makes us a target."

"I don't know about you guys, but I think we were *already* a target," Jenna interrupted. "Let's see if we can get out of this trap before we start worrying about the next one, okay?"

Damien nodded in agreement, his attention suddenly consumed by the final maneuvers as the *Blue Jay* rapidly expanded in the screen ahead of them.

#

The *Blue Jay*'s shuttle bay was a mess. The bay the shuttle normally belonged in was filled with the burning wreckage of the end of the boarding tube, while the main length of the tube was occupying a third of the door.

Bodies, weapons, and debris floated in the zero-gravity, all coated and obscured by a faint pink haze of loose blood. Damien swallowed down a moment of nausea as he oriented the shuttle on a spare rack and slowly locked the ship into place.

"We're down," he told the Captain. "There's almost no atmosphere outside – the main door won't be able to close until we remove that tube."

"I saw," Rice replied grimly. "There are breathers and coveralls in the shuttle. We need to get into the ship."

"I didn't see Singh," Damien said quietly. "Just his handiwork."

David nodded grimly and set off for the back of the shuttle. Carefully, wary of his still-fragile balance, Damien followed. Kellers had already pulled out five sets of coveralls and, wearing one himself, begun the careful process of sliding Kelzin's unconscious body into one.

The emergency coveralls were designed to be quick to put on, and had decent enough gloves that Damien was able to take one of the carbines and be confident he could use it. The suits weren't designed for long term duration – they lacked plumbing connections, if nothing else – but would do to cross the bay and deal with any mercenaries left behind.

"Watch out for hostiles," Rice told the others. "Just because we know some of them fled doesn't mean they didn't leave anyone behind."

Damien nodded, carefully controlling his movements in the shuttle's zero-gravity. The magic he'd normally use to provide his own personal gravity field would be too much for him in his current state, so he'd have to move through the microgravity like everyone else.

Kellers slammed the button to open the ramp, and then scooped up Kelzin carefully. Jenna and Rice kicked off first, launching themselves into the blood-soaked bay, carbines moving in gentle patterns to track potential targets without throwing themselves off-course.

Damien followed, relying on them to have kept the room clear as he lacked the training to track targets without sending himself spinning. He landed gently next to the emergency airlock leading forwards into the ship.

Six men in ship's clothes with the Hyper-Kevlar vests he and Singh had picked up were collapsed around it. The body armor was pocked with marks where they'd stopped dozens of rounds, but in the end they'd been too little. From the almost twenty bodies floating in the shuttle bay, they'd given a good account of themselves with the carbines in their hands, but the professional boarders had taken them down.

Rice joined him, and tapped a quick code into the airlock door. It slid open, admitting them all and allowing Kellers to bring Kelzin over.

"Ready?" Rice asked after a moment after they were all inside. Damien joined the others in bracing himself against the wall and outer door, ready to fire into the ship, and then nodded.

The airlock filled with breathable air, and then the inner door opened into the antechamber of hell.

As many men as had died in the shuttle bay had died in the corridor at the core of the *Jay*, and there was less space for the bodies to separate. To make it worse, these had been shot down with explosive rounds and micro-grenades. The air was filled with blood and parts of bodies. Damien choked back more nausea, and was glad he'd left his coveralls on.

"Forward," Rice ordered, suiting actions to words and pushing through the mess.

Cringing against the *wet* pressure against his suit, Damien followed behind – so he was the one close enough to watch the Captain drop his rifle, grab a wall and launch forward like a rocket.

A moment later, Damien saw what Rice had seen and followed his Captain. He landed by the shattered combat exosuit only moments after Rice, who'd already lost his breather helmet and was floating in air next to Singh's head.

"Narveer!" Rice snapped, reaching out to check for a pulse. Damien was about to say it was a waste, no one with *that* many holes in him was still alive, when Singh's eyes popped open.

"Sorry Captain," he groaned. "I tried."

163

"Tried, hell," Rice told him fiercely. "You drove them off Narveer – they left running. You saved the whole damn ship."

"Ah," Singh exhaled a sigh, blood bubbling from his lips as he did. Damien watched in horror as the pilot struggled to breathe. Armor-piercing rounds had gone clean through the suit, and his left leg had been blown off by a grenade. None of the wounds were bleeding much – the suit had to be doing something to stop it – but he had *so many.*

"You are *not* permitted to die," the Captain ordered, his voice choked. "This was *my* mistake."

"Never," Singh coughed, more blood interrupting his words, "give an order you know can't be obeyed."

An armored hand reached up and grabbed at Damien. Wordlessly, Damien reached out and grabbed the older pilot's hand in his own. Rice grabbed Singh's other hand and the old Sikh warrior looked from one of them to the other.

"Stay strong boy," he ordered Damien. "Both of you," he glanced at Rice, and then back down the hall at the mess he'd created holding the corridor.

"Not a bad way to go, I gue…" he trailed off, and was gone.

Damien gently, carefully, folded Singh's hand back onto his chest. He looked over at Rice, the Captain was frozen, covered in other men's blood, and holding the armored gauntlet of his friend.

"Captain, you've got to get to the bridge," he said quietly. "I need to get to the simulacrum. If we can't save the ship, Singh died for nothing."

Rice met his gaze, swallowing hard and slowly releasing Singh's hand. He looked back at Jenna and Kellers.

"Get him and Kelzin and the others to the infirmary," he ordered. "I need to go make sure our former passengers don't blow us to hell."

#

Kelly looked up in obvious relief as David entered the bridge, snagging his chair as he drifted by and strapping himself in.

"Thank gods you're here, sir," she told him. "I have no idea what to do!"

"You're doing okay so far," David replied, spotting that the *Jay's* two anti-missile turrets had been spun up, ready to intercept any missiles launched from the running shuttles or the ship they'd run to. "Any word from the Rock?"

"Not a peep," Kelly answered. "It's like they haven't even noticed what's going on."

"With the jamming, it's possible. But it's not likely," David said grimly. "How are the engines?"

164

"Everything's green – the boarders seemed to be heading for the bridge and the simulacrum chamber," she explained.

"Makes sense," David realized aloud. "They thought Damien was on board – they were trying to eliminate him before he could return the favor. They'd brought enough men they could deal with him – and not enough to deal with Singh."

"You found Singh? He's okay?" Kelly asked quickly, only to whiten as David shook his head silently.

"You're the best engineer on this ship bar Kellers himself," the Captain said gently, trying to get her to focus. "Can we burn the engines with that tanker still attached?"

"She's latched onto our cargo points," LaMonte answered. "We're a bit unbalanced, but the computer can adapt for that automatically."

Turning away from the only crew-member currently on his bridge, David hit a series of commands on the screen mounted on his chair, opening a ship wide channel.

"All hands, hear this, hear this," he said into. "Cruise acceleration in thirty seconds. Secure for acceleration. I repeat, cruise acceleration in twenty-four seconds."

He ran the toggle bar up on his screen, and hit a command that activated 'automatic mass balancing.' It had been a while since he'd flown the freighter himself, but it was a lot less complex than flying a shuttle. His full weight pressed him down into his chair, and he breathed slowly, beginning to relax.

The other jump ship in the system was a shining beacon on his scanners as they continued to scream out-system at an ungodly acceleration. Every person aboard had to be strapped in and half-crushed, but the push had put them outside any range at which Damien could reach them with the amplifier, even if the Mage wasn't half-dead *anyway*.

"Sir, we're receiving a transmission from the Rock," Kelly, who was covering every task on the bridge that David wasn't – thankfully! – announced.

David flipped a few controls and brought the video transmission up on his screen. He was unsurprised to see the strangely-pupilled eyes of Major Niska, though the Augment looked oddly relaxed given that a battle had just taken place on the planet beneath him.

"Captain Rice," Niska greeted him cheerfully.

"Major Niska," Rice answered carefully, somewhat put off. "What can I do for you?"

"I want to inform you that we've completed our inspections of the gunships, and we've found no issues related to their transport," the Legatan officer said. "Your contract is fully fulfilled, and we have no complaints."

David opened his mouth, about to ask what was going on – they'd just escaped the local army and a space-borne boarding attack, and Niska was talking about the *delivery contract*? – but the Augment slightly, almost imperceptibly, shook his head.

"We did run into some issues with the ships' engines," the Augment continued, "but my techs have them stripped down and assure me that it's a manufacturing defect – they'll have all four ships running in a few days."

The *Blue Jay*'s Captain stared at his former passenger in shock for a moment. The gunships, which he'd been worried were going to chase his ship down, had their engines stripped down? The Augment had *disabled them*?

From the cheerful smile on Niska's face, he was *perfectly* aware of what he'd done, but was mugging for the inevitable Chrysanthemum interception of the communication.

"I've just transmitted your funds now," the LMID soldier continued. "I've included a small bonus for your patience with us and with the locals. I hope you've come out of this with a positive impression of the Directorate, at least."

David ever so slowly nodded to the camera.

"I think I have," he admitted. "And thank you, Major Niska. Thank you."

He didn't say what he was thanking the cyborg for. From the bright grin the other man flashed him, he didn't need to.

The bridge was silent for a moment as the channel cut out and he met Kelly's shocked gaze, and then Damien's voice cut in as the Mage brought up the intercom screen from the simulacrum chamber.

"Did he just do what I think he did?" the young man asked, his voice incredibly tired.

"I think he did," Rice confirmed, and glanced back at the screen. "You go get some rest Damien. We're going to burn for the outer system as fast as we can – and as soon as you can, jump us out of here, I want to brush this planet's dirt from my heels!"

###

4

The deep voice of the recorded words of the Sikh *Kirtan Sohila*, strange to Damien's ears, echoed through the shuttle bay of the jump-freighter *Blue Jay*. He figured no one left aboard the ship understood the ancient words of the Sikh prayer for the end of the day, they only knew it was appropriate to mark the passing of the man they owed their lives to.

Seven bodies floated in the bay's lack of gravity, and the remaining eighty members of the freighter's crew floated with them, listing to the old words of the recording. Only Narveer Singh of the seven dead had been a Sikh, but Damien knew none of the others would have objected to the words.

As the prayer faded, Captain David Rice drifted out in front of his crew, standing next to the black bags containing the members of the crew who'd died fighting off a boarding action by bounty hunters before he or Damien, the Ship's Mage, were able to return aboard to intervene. The Captain's normally stocky and solid presence seemed subdued, small next to the weight of the bodies.

"As our ancestors before us did to the sea, so we commit our honored dead to the depths of space," Rice said formally. "All things began from the stars, and so we return the bodies of our friends to those same stars."

"Narveer Singh, Leonard Champion, Li Hu Wong, Michael Reeves, Kyle Lawrence, Raphael Santiago and Karla Hammond died protecting us," he continued softly. "We will not forget them."

Damien stood as straight as he could in zero-gravity. The slight Mage tried not to look at the body bags. If he'd been aboard instead of Narveer, he likely would have died, and the ship would have been taken. They'd switched places to fool the government of Chrysanthemum, and so Narveer had died and Damien had lived. Where Damien would have failed, though, Narveer had saved the ship.

Dozens of the mercenaries had died. Their bodies had been dumped into space without ceremony a day earlier when they'd flushed out the bay and corridors of the ship where their boarding attempt had been launched.

A moment of silence passed, and then Rice gestured a command to a crewwoman floating by a control console. A clear barrier descended between the mourners and the floating bodies, and then the massive outer shutters of the *Blue Jay*'s shuttle bay slid open.

The bodies floated in zero-gravity for a moment, and then the air in the shuttle bay rushed into space, taking the *Blue Jay*'s fallen crew and friends with it.

The shuttle bay was silent. Damien felt a hand slip into his, and carefully turned his head to smile at the girl beside him. Kelly LaMonte was the ship's junior engineer, and he and the dark-haired brunette had grown close in recent weeks.

"It always hurts to lose friends," Captain Rice said into the quiet. "There are no words I can say to soften that blow. Narveer and the others died to protect us from the bounty hunters after us."

"We have to be careful," he reminded them. "Our next destination is in the MidWorlds, and there will be people there who know who we are, and why we are hunted. From now on, no one goes off-ship alone, and no one goes off-ship unarmed."

"There are very few friends of ours left, it seems. We have to rely on each other."

#

With Narveer gone, there was a spark missing from the meetings of the *Blue Jay*'s senior staff. His replacement as First Pilot was Mike Kelzin. The young pilot's face was deathly pale under his buzz-cut, and he moved carefully around the bandage that still wrapped his stomach.

Jenna Campbell, the ship's executive officer, sat next to Kelzin keeping a careful eye on him. She was the closest thing the ship had to a human doctor, though she had to rely heavily on the auto-doc to deal with wounds as bad as the pilot's stomach injury.

Damien sat across from her, watching Kelzin almost as carefully as the XO. He lacked her medical skill, but he owed Kelzin his life. Without the pilot's intervention on Chrysanthemum, he'd have died trying to protect the others.

Next to him sat the ship's Chief Engineer, James Kellers. The dark-skinned man responsible for keeping the ship running looked exhausted – much of the work of cleaning up the mess the mercenaries had made of the *Blue Jay*'s rear corridors had been directed by him.

The only person who looked more tired than Kellers was the Captain. David Rice sat at the end of the table, watching his staff, and Damien couldn't help but worry at the slump in the burly man's posture. He'd been keeping things close to his chest – he'd told Damien where they were heading, but had asked the Mage not to tell even the other officers.

"All right," the Captain finally said once everyone was settled, with beverages of choice to hand. "It's good to see Mike on his feet and joining us," he continued. "How do you feel?"

"Like someone shot me in the stomach," the new First Pilot replied. "But I'll live. Playing it up might keep the other pilots in check, too. Being in charge is going to be a new experience for me."

"Remind them that *they* picked *you*," Rice told him. "Any issues on the first day on the job?"

"None," Kelzin confirmed. "I'm just thoroughly aware of what kind of jokers they all are."

"Good," the Captain said, then turned to Kellers. "What's the status of the ship, James?"

"We got the... debris from the boarding attempt cleared away," Kellers replied quietly. Damien shivered slightly at the memory of the gore-filled corridors they'd returned to the ship through. "We suffered some minor damage to the shuttle bay, which has been repaired already. I had LaMonte take a work team over to the fuel tanker yesterday as well. There was some damage from when we blew the boarding tube out of the bay, but nothing we can't fix in short order."

"Can anyone *fly* it?" Rice asked.

"None of the pilots," Kelzin admitted sheepishly. "Narveer might have been able to, but the rest of us are only qualified on shuttles."

"I can," Damien reminded the Captain.

"As can I," Jenna said as well. "Do you have any thoughts on using her?"

"Did they do any special work to her for that boarding attempt?"

"No," Kellers told them. "The boarding tube was an extra module, probably brought along by the mercenaries. The ship itself must have been running on automatic – there's no crew aboard, and if there had been, they probably would have detached before we jumped out-system."

"I don't see a lot of use for her," the Captain admitted, "but get her repaired up – worst case, we can probably find a buyer for a slightly used in-system tanker somewhere along the way."

"The way being...?" Jenna asked pointedly.

"Damien has drawn up a thirteen month route through the Fringe systems," David told them. "We hit nine systems along the way, though we dog-leg around Nia Kriti and the Navy Base there. All nine systems are in various stages of development and they need everything from weather satellites to farming equipment to planes and cars.

"The first few systems are lower-end, but then we hit Theogeny, where we'll be able to trade food and raw materials for some of the higher tech items the later systems will want," David continued. "It's a good, solid, Fringe trade route that will both make us a lot of money and keep us out of the Protectorate's eye for over a year."

"First we need a cargo though, boss," Jenna said pointedly. "Given that everywhere in the Core and MidWorlds is going to know who we are now, where exactly are we planning on getting that?"

"Somewhere where they just don't care," David told her. "We're going to Amber."

Damien was the only one in the room not shocked into silence, though his reaction on being told had been much the same. Even on Sherwood, people had heard of Amber.

"Isn't that place, well... a hive?" Kelzin finally asked.

"I was going to go with 'lawless hellhole,'" Jenna agreed.

"It's not *that* bad," Kellers pointed out. "I grew up there. It's certainly... different from the rest of the Protectorate."

Amber had been founded by Libertarians from old Earth's North American continent. They'd looked at the Charter that defined the rights and responsibilities of a member government – and had set up a government that *only* carried out the handful of services the Charter required, run as a co-operative paid for by a transaction fee at the system's banks.

Amber's laws were limited in both text and application, leaving many things that were illegal in the rest of the Protectorate perfectly legal under Amber law. Based on Damien's research over the last few days, something like ninety percent of the pirate ships ever captured and traced by the Navy had undergone their conversion to predators in the yards around Amber.

But since the Co-operatives that served as Ambers 'government' didn't violate the Charter, all the Protectorate would ever do was shut down the specific yard involved, and make ominous threats to the rest. They weren't even permitted to station warships in the system, as the Charter guaranteed each system the right to provide their own protection if they chose.

"Amber's a mess, and we'll have to walk carefully," David confirmed. "But we can find everything we'll need there – *everything* transships through Amber – and the Defense Co-op won't care that we're in system."

"There will be Hunters," Kellers warned. "There's a standing deal for bounties on people wanted for crimes by the Protectorate. But you're right," the engineer sighed. "The ADC won't stop us docking or leaving, so long as we pay the associated fees."

"We can deal with Hunters," the Captain replied. "A real planetwide police force would worry me, but a few independent contractors shouldn't be a problem if we keep together. James and I have contacts there, too, so we should be able to buy up what we need quickly."

"I'll be staying aboard ship," Damien assured the others. "Even if everything goes to hell, we can run as soon as everyone gets aboard – and I *know* I can jump out from closer in then they expect."

"We won't be allowing shore leave," David concluded. "James and I will go ashore, armed. We'll meet our contact, and then we'll get the hell out of here for the Fringe.

"Amber is as safe as a MidWorld will get for us for a while," he reminded them, "but they have a transceiver, and *someone* is going to smell cash in telling the Protectorate where we are."

#

Deep space didn't have many virtues in the grand scheme of things. To Damien's mind, it had two main ones: it was astonishingly beautiful to see the stars with no light from a local sun to interfere, and it was safe. Outside some of the busy trade lanes in the Core or an ambush, you would almost never run into another ship between the stars – and you were almost impossible to track, too.

He floated at the center of the *Blue Jay*, in the ovoid room covered in viewscreens that showed him the outside of the ship, and ran his fingers over the silver form of the magical simulacrum at the exact center of the starship. Runes spiraled away from that silver artifact, linking to the matrix throughout the ship that would amplify his magic a million-fold.

Energy flickered eagerly at him from the construct that both represented and, in a strange way, *was* the ship. It was far stronger on the *Jay* than on any of the ships he'd trained on, a side-effect of the changes he'd made to the runes. Unlike any other Mage he'd ever known, he saw the energy flows that underlay the runes, which had allowed him to remove the 'extra' runes that prevented the jump matrix of a freighter like the *Jay* being used as a full-scale amplifier.

Damien suspected that the knowledge of how to do that was what the mercenaries had been seeking when they boarded the *Blue Jay* at Chrysanthemum. The ability to turn any jumpship, anywhere, into a concealed warship capable of destroying anything the onboard Mage could reach was a terrifying weapon.

Out here, in deep space, they were safe. Even a single light year away from Amber, it was unlikely anyone would ever stumble upon them. Of course, they could never *do* anything from here, either.

With a small sigh, Damien activated his intercom to the bridge.

"I am ready to jump," he reported to Captain Rice. "On your word."

"The ship is prepared to jump," Rice replied. "You may jump at will."

Damien nodded and placed his hands on the silver simulacrum of the starship. Runes etched into his palms with silver glowed with his power, and channeled that power into the model at the heart of the *Blue Jay*.

With a deep breath, Damien threw his magic into his link with the ship and *stepped*.

A fleeting moment no artifice of man or magic had ever been able to measure passed, and then the jump-freighter was *here* instead of *there*, materializing one hundred and seventy million kilometers – roughly ten light minutes – from the planet, and about seventeen light minutes from the star.

"We have arrived in Amber," Damien told the bridge after a long moment. The teleportation spell took a *lot* out of him, though he'd been making minor tweaks here and there throughout the amplifier matrix to make it a bit easier.

"Running scans," Jenna announced.

The screens of Damien's simulacrum Chamber showed a visual view of the space around the *Blue Jay*, but he could also bring up any other function of the ship's computers. The Chamber's interior was the largest computer screen on the ship. Bringing a copy of the the XO's sensor data and translations up was easy.

"Is that a Navy destroyer?" he asked, his gaze picking out a data code he remembered from their *last* encounter with the Royal Navy of the Mage-King of Mars.

"It's *a* destroyer," Kellers told them over the intercom from engineering. "That's the *Osiris*, the flagship of the Amber Defense Co-operative – and their only functioning jumpship. They also have a couple dozen home-built corvettes that don't have amplifiers or jump matrixes, just some godawful lasers."

The engineer's voice was bitter.

"They'll hail us in about a day as we approach," he explained. "There are docking fees to be paid to both the ADC and the station owners. Refresh of oxygen or fuel will cost extra, as will entering the station. This is Amber – *everything* has a price."

The intercom was silent for a moment.

"If anyone needs me," Kellers finally said, "I'll be in the bar on Rib A. Trying to forget why I *left* this place."

"Welcome home, huh?" Jenna said a minute later, the scans throwing more detail up of the orbitals of Amber. Warned what he was looking for, Damien picked out seven corvettes, larger and blockier than the gunships they'd transported for Legatus, but similarly dangerous for their size against a ship without an amplifier.

He was helping Jenna collate data on the orbiting stations – eight fragile looking collections of gantries and work modules that were what passed for shipyards in Amber, and one very functional and ordinary looking spinning wheel orbital station that operated as a space dock – when LaMonte drifted into the Chamber.

"Hey Damien, Kellers is inviting everyone up to the Rib A bar," his girlfriend told him. "He apparently has some special liquor he had saved up for if he ever came back to Amber."

"Is it poisonous?" Damien asked dryly. Given Kellers' apparent enthusiasm for his homeworld, he wasn't sure anything the Chief Engineer had saved up for this occasion would be safe to drink.

"Well, it's *from* Amber, so I'm not sure it's *safe*, but he seems determined to drink it," the younger engineer told him.

"We can finish this later," Jenna told him over the intercom. "From the sounds of it, I should check up on Kellers myself. Amber liquor is harder than hard, to put it mildly."

Saving and dismissing the data with a swipe of his hand, Damien turned to Kelly and smiled.

"It looks like you've found a hidden override on our ship protocols," he told her. "My time is yours, my dear, what's the plan?"

#

Agreeing to share Kellers' Amber Fire Liqueur ranked as one of David's worst decisions in recent years. It had seemed fine at the time, but the next morning his pounding headache happily reminded him that Amber Fire Liqueur was *illegal* in a good half of the Protectorate.

The bridge of the *Blue Jay* was quiet. Jenna was at her station, watching the sensors and maneuvering controls, but the only words they'd exchanged so far today had been grunts and a vague mention of 'Kellers' liqueur.'

"Heads up sir," Jenna told him, her voice quiet. "Incoming contact – she's on an unpowered orbit, but she'll pass within a million klicks of us in about an hour."

"Show me," David ordered, also pitching his voice low to avoid making both of their headaches worse.

Jenna swiped a command on her console, and a view from one of the *Blue Jay*'s many exterior cameras appeared on the main screen, and then zoomed in.

A few billion times magnification later and it was clear the contact was the boxy hundred meter length of an Amber Defense Co-operative corvette.

"Looks like she saw us," his executive officer told him. "Incoming video channel."

He nodded to her and she threw the image on the main screen, replacing the grainy image of the ship.

173

The image was of a small but neatly organized bridge, similar in many ways to *Blue Jay*'s own, with four working consoles arranged in three dimensions around a command chair. A man with silver hair and a young face was strapped into the center command chair against the ship's microgravity.

"This is Commander Antonov of the Amber Defense Co-operative corvette *Williamson*," he said calmly. "Please identify yourself and transmit your cargo manifest.

"Note that if we are forced to pursue you, you or your heirs will be required to compensate the ADC for fuel and munitions expended."

David tapped a few commands on the control screen built into his command chair, transmitted the *Blue Jay*'s registry and manifest information before opening a video channel back to the *Williamson*.

"Commander Antonov, this is Captain David Rice of the *Blue Jay*," he told the Amberite. "We are bound in-system to pick up a cargo in preparation for a Fringe shipping run. Our pylons are currently empty, though we do have an in-system fuelling vessel we may sell in-system."

Seconds ticked by as the transmission shot across the intervening empty space, and then Antonov nodded in response.

"I appreciate your prompt response, Captain," he told David. "You are clear through to Heinlein Station. Be aware that there are fees for being assigned an entry vector, docking, fuelling and access to Heinlein Station that will need to be paid promptly upon arrival."

"I appreciate the heads up, Commander," David replied. "This is our first time in the Amber system."

"Well, then let me be the first to welcome you to the only truly free system in the Protectorate," Antonov replied with a broad smile. "Enjoy your time in Amber, Captain. I am sure you will find all you need in terms of cargo."

The transmission ended and the screen defaulted back to showing the small warship continuing along its long, fuel-conserving, orbit around the system's sun.

"Is there anything we're not going to be charged for in this system?" Jenna asked after a long moment.

"Based off Kellers' reaction to coming home, no."

#

Leaving Jenna to dock the ship – Heinlein Station had a well-designed central hub that remained stationary while the outer wheel spun to provide gravity, rendering docking straightforward – Rice headed towards the shuttle bay to meet Kellers for their sojourn onto the station.

He found the engineer in the corner of the shuttle bay that had once contained a handful of armored lockers, and now contained row upon row of neatly strapped down cases and crates containing enough guns and body armor to arm and protect every member of the *Blue Jay*'s crew.

Rice stopped in surprise when he did spot the engineer, though. Normally, he saw Kellers either in a suit when the senior officers of the ship had to meet clients, or wearing a set of coveralls covered in enough muck to be as dark as his skin.

Today the black-skinned man was wearing a pair of camouflage fatigue pants and a black tank top that clearly emphasized the sharp-cut muscles of a man who worked with his hands and heavy, dangerous, equipment every day.

The sparse outfit did absolutely nothing to conceal the holster strapped to Kellers' hip containing a Martian Armaments Caseless Six Millimeter automatic – and even less to conceal the stungun carbine in a quick release strap over his torso.

"Are we expecting a war?" David asked finally, standing at the edge of the new armory area and eyeing his Chief Engineer warily.

"We're in Amber space," Kellers replied. "It's considered rude to go unarmed – and only slightly less rude to use lethal force first." He gestured towards the solitary bench in the middle of the crates of weapons, where he'd laid out a similar set of harness and weapons for Rice.

"Is *everyone* going to be armed?"

"Yes," the Amber native said flatly. "Most Amber children begin firearms training between six and eight years old and regularly carry an automatic like this from the age of ten."

That took David a moment to process. Protectorate gun laws were up to the judgment of the individual planets, but generally boiled down to 'you can get a permit for that if you have a reason for it.' The thought of everyone going armed all the time on a planet without immediately dangerous wildlife was strange to him.

Nonetheless, he was wise enough to listen to a native guide and started strapping on the harness.

"What about the Hunters? They're a kind of police, right?"

"Sanctioned Hunters aren't police," James told him. "They're the folk charged with bringing in people who refuse to voluntarily appear in front of a court, or charged with Protectorate crimes. Since they're basically bounty hunters, though, your right to self-defense still applies."

"It is," he continued after a moment, "considered rude to use lethal force against Hunters – and is likely to result in them delivering you to the Judicial Co-op's courts in pieces."

"Wonderful," David replied dryly, double checking the quick release strap on the stungun. "And this contact of yours? Is he going to sell us to these 'Hunters'??"

"Keiko owes me," his engineer replied. "We went to school together, and she's already agreed to the meet. She runs a shipping company now, so she should be able to get us what we need."

David nodded and re-strapped the stungun to his torso. Two magazines of the stunguns SmartDarts and four of the clips for the MAC6 went on the harness as well, and then Kellers carefully checked his gear.

"I'm not as good a shot as Narveer was," Kellers said quietly. "I'd really prefer to avoid trouble, boss."

"You and me both," David told him. "This is Amber, though. How likely is that?"

Kellers shrugged.

"Even if we hadn't pissed off the Protectorate, the Blue Star Syndicate has a bounty on us," he admitted. "Those Sanctioned Hunters aren't averse to collecting un-sanctioned bounties."

"And we're in the system responsible for building almost every pirate ship in existence," David Rice said wryly. "Why did I think this was a good plan?"

"You didn't," Kellers replied. "None of us did. It was just the least *bad* plan."

#

The access to the station from the *Blue Jay* was close to the shuttle bay. The two officers, both experienced in zero-gravity maneuvering, made it there as the docking connections completed and a personnel tube extended from Heinlein Station locked onto the airlock.

"We're all connected up, sir," Jenna reported over David's wrist personal computer. "You don't *want* to know what regular docking cost us."

"Tell me," he ordered. He winced at the figure she told him in response. It was roughly twice what he'd expect to pay at a MidWorld orbital station. "Understood Jenna. Keep the lights on; we should only be on station for five or six hours this time."

"I'm guessing no shore leave?" she asked.

"If anyone wants to pay the entry fee themselves, they're welcome to," David replied. "No more than twenty percent of the crew at once, no more than eight hours at a time. Everyone stays in contact with the ship at all times, stays armed, and moves in pairs."

Kellers looked almost offended as Jenna acknowledged and sign off. "Boss, for all my bitching, Amber is a civilized world. No one is going to get rolled in a back corridor. It would be bad for business."

"I'm worried *because* it's a civilized world," David admitted, opening the airlock and breathing in the air of Heinlein Station for the first time. "A *lot* of people want us dead, and the Protectorate wants to arrest us all."

His Chief Engineer didn't reply, and David led the way down the tube. It connected to a circular corridor that could have belonged on any station in any system, with signs directing disembarking spacers to the left.

At the end of the corridor, though, warning signs advised that the next area had 'thaumaturgically induced gravity.' Most stations that David had been on didn't bother with the expense of having Mages set up and maintain the runes necessary to create an artificial gravity zone – the weekly renewals ended up costing a *lot* of money.

The two spacers carefully oriented themselves according to the sign, and then 'dropped' onto the floor as they entered the main processing area of Heinlein Station.

The floor was, as promised, covered in the swirling silver markings of artificial gravity runes. The walls were plain steel, stretching up to the roof of the double-height compartment. Along each side of the compartment, half-height windowed cubicles marked the offices where spacers would meet with the officers of Heinlein Station. At the far end of the room, to make sure no one entered the station without paying all the correct tolls and fees, four men in matte black body armor carried assault rifles and grim expressions.

In contrast to the implicit threat at the other end of the hallway, a perky redhead in jeans and a blue tank top was waiting at the entrance for them. Her bright smile almost distracted David from the rocket pistol she wore strapped to her hip.

"Welcome to Heinlein Station, gentlemen," she greeted them. "Your docking fees are paid up, but you'll need to discuss station access fees and visitor's insurance with one of our Intake Specialists." She checked her wrist PC quickly, and then gestured towards one of the cubicles. "Specialist Wan is available in office five. Please speak with her so we can get you into Heinlein as soon as possible."

Wan was a dark-skinned tiny woman with an unusually pronounced epicanthic fold for a child of the twenty-fifth century. As they entered, she waved them to the seats in front of her desk.

"Welcome to Heinlein Station," she repeated the girl outside. "Which of our station's many services are you intending to make use of while you're aboard? Passes to the station are separate for each external quadrant."

David glanced at James, and gestured for the engineer to answer the question.

"We're meeting someone in Quadrant Gamma," Kellers told the woman. "We will also need access to the Promenade in Quadrant Beta. Several members of our crew will also be coming aboard who will need Promenade access for shore leave, so we will want a group rate for that."

Wan nodded calmly. "You have a crew of eighty, correct?" David nodded. "I will give you the group rate for forty Quadrant Beta passes. If your crew use more, all individuals will be refunded the difference for the higher group rate – if you use less, your ship will be billed for the difference. Acceptable?"

With a quick glance at Kellers, who nodded, David agreed.

Wan touched a command, and both of their wrist PCs blinked receipt of a message.

"Your passes are loaded to your PCs," she explained. "If you are found by Heinlein Security aboard station without having paid for access and oxygen, you will be required to pay for the unauthorized use at a punitive damages rate. If you cannot pay, you will be required to work off your debt.

"We strongly recommend that you purchase Amber Medical Co-operative and Amber Judicial Co-operative temporary insurance," she continued. "Without these, you will have minimal access to the Co-operatives' medical or judicial services."

"I have standing memberships in both," Kellers told her, tapping his PC to a reader on her desk. "Have Captain Rice added as my temporary auxiliary."

"Ah, a Citizen," she said approvingly, glancing at the profile that the engineer had transferred to her screen. "Of course. The requests have been sent," she finished after a moment. "Is there anything else I can set up for you?"

"Not at the moment," David confirmed. "If we wish to travel to the surface, do we need to discuss that with you?"

"We are only concerned that the Heinlein Station Corporation is properly reimbursed for use of our facilities and oxygen," she told him calmly. "You can book transport to the surface or any of the shipyards with any available in-system transport companies."

Thanking Specialist Wan, David and James headed to the back of the room, where the grim-faced Heinlein Station Security soldiers waved them through with the slightest hints of smiles.

Outside the processing area, only a single pathway was marked out with gravity runes, leading towards the set of elevators that accessed the outer rim with its centrifugal gravity.

"What's the rest of the core?" David asked Kellers, noting that there were doors and corridors leading away, most sealed with a three letter symbol – ADC.

"The Spire is the main dock for the Amber Defense Co-operative as well as civilians," James told him. "They keep the munitions for their corvettes here, under tight lock and key. As an ADC member, I approve of their security," he added dryly.

"I thought you'd left Amber years ago?" David asked in response to that.

"I did," James confirmed. "But on Amber, you're not a true Citizen unless you contribute to the three Co-operatives – Medical, Judicial, and Defense. *Officially*, there's no benefits for being a Citizen beyond those of being a member of the Co-ops – but it opens a lot of doors I didn't want to see closed if I ever came home."

The elevators were clearly marked where each one led, so the two men clambered into one for Quadrant Gamma. There were none of the warning signs that most worlds would have, but the lack of gravity and belts on the seats made the need to strap in obvious.

A few minutes of dizzying acceleration and twisting later, the pod settled into the outer ring. Feeling somewhat motion-sick, David unstrapped himself and stumbled out into the upper access way of Heinlein Station's Quadrant Gamma.

The central corridor of the Quadrant was an immense, six storied, gallery. They stood on the top level and looked down a thirty meter drop to the bottom of the gallery. Each level was marked by advertisements and signs. People bustled around, all of them dressed in bright colors and carrying various varieties of personal weaponry.

David had seen busier stations in his life, but it wasn't quite what he'd been expecting of Amber, the notorious semi-outlaw of the galaxy. He glanced over at Kellers, and the muscular black man grinned at him, clearly enjoying his discomfiture.

"Amber was built to an ideal, Captain," he said quietly. "You and I don't really agree with that ideal – and for all that I left, I probably agree with it more than a Mars native like yourself – but enough people do that this world is a Mecca for them. They come here to be free from the bureaucracy of the other Protectorate worlds." His smile faded. "Many get squished in the gears, exploited, or just lost, but that is the darker side of the dream they come here to find. Come on," he concluded. "Keiko is on level one. We need to get downstairs."

#

The omnipresent nature of weapons on Heinlein Station threw David's fine-tuned paranoia for a loop. Everywhere he looked, everybody was openly carrying a weapon. It made it difficult to identify what might qualify as a threat – especially as no one around him was reacting as if this was particularly unusual.

The culture shock was enough that he missed the *actual* threat until it was almost too late. The six men and two women converging on him and Kellers were dressed the same as everyone else, other than that each wore a long black cloak closed at the neck with a golden insignia of some kind.

When eight people wearing a pseudo-uniform start closing in on you, it's generally time to get out of the way. David had been following James through the station up to this point, as the other man had a clue where they were going and David didn't.

Now he grabbed his engineer's shoulder and began to duck away through the crowd.

The response from the cloaked pursuers was instant. The two in the direction that David dodged produced weapons from underneath the cloaks – larger ones than the usual sidearms being worn around them.

"David Rice, halt where you are!" one of the women bellowed as the other produced weapons. "We are Sanctioned Hunters, you will surrender."

For all of his intellectual understanding that he'd become a criminal when he'd broken Damien out of the jail in Corinthian, part of David rebelled at drawing and firing on police officers *again*.

James Kellers had no such hesitation. Even before the cloaked hunters in front of them had cleared their weapons, the short but muscled engineer had yanked his stungun clear of the quick release harness he wore and opened fire.

The loud announcement from the Hunters had at least had the effect of clearing the immediate area, as the locals scattered for cover. The SmartDarts from Kellers' weapon slammed into both of the Hunters in front of them, pausing for a moment to assess their targets' health, and then delivering calibrated incapacitating electric shocks.

Both of them went down in convulsing heaps, and David dived past them. He skidded past a cart selling hot dogs; in time to watch a tangleweb shell from one of the Hunters shotguns splatter itself all over the ground next to the cart – the goo instantly hardening into foam that would immobilize a target.

David found himself staring into the barrel of the hot dog vendor's pistol. He met the woman's eyes carefully, and she jerked her head sideways. He realized after a second that she was pointing towards a hatchway leading off of the main gallery. With a grateful nod, he dived for that hatchway, barely missing a second tangleweb shell.

Breaking into a run down the corridor, he realized he'd lost James along the way. He turned back to check for the engineer, only to see two of the cloaked Hunters follow him through the hatchway. His hesitation about shooting police was gone now, and he opened fire with the stungun.

One of the Hunters went down, convulsing from the SmartDarts' electric shock. The other dodged back around the corner, firing a round from her shotgun at David.

David dodged around the corner and managed to avoid *most* of the impact when the flashbang round went off in mid-air. He blinked against what spots he hadn't dodged and a passing inability to hear, and then took off down the hallway again.

He turned another corner, moments later, and ran into *another* Hunter. The other man spun his cloak in a carefully practiced gesture, catching the SmartDarts David fired in the non-conductive fabric of the garment.

Before the Hunter had his weapon targeted, David had closed into his personal space. He knocked aside the barrel of the shotgun, brushed aside an attempt to slam him with the butt of the weapon, and then redirected the Hunter's momentum into the wall.

Spin-induced gravity and inertia handled the rest, and the bulky bounty hunter went down. Before he could get back up, David grabbed the other man's weapon, checked the digital display to see what shell was up, and blasted him with a tangleweb shell.

He spared just enough time to be sure the solidifying foam wasn't threatening the Hunter's ability to breathe, and then took off again. He was moving a bit slower this time, pulling up a map of Gamma Quadrant to find Kellers.

The engineer was heading towards him, and he changed his course towards James. They finally met up in a dimmer back corridor, each checking behind the other for Hunters.

"How much trouble are we in now?" David asked, breathing heavily. He wasn't used to running this much.

"No more than we were before, unless you killed one," Kellers replied. The engineer didn't seem to have even worked up a sweat. "Amber respects the right to self-defense, even against Hunters. It's rude to kill one though."

Both tensed up when they heard voices coming from behind Kellers, and the engineer gestured for David to lead the way away. They weren't fast enough, however, and an emergency bulkhead suddenly slammed shut ahead of them.

David swore. "Can you open this?"

"Not a chance," Kellers replied grimly, turning back to face their pursuers. "There can't be many of them upright at this point, though."

"Surrender now, Captain Rice," a voice shouted from up the corridor – the same woman who'd ordered them to lay down weapons before. "You aren't going to change how this ends."

"I can bloody well try," David muttered, checking the ammunition count on his stolen shotgun before tucking himself next to the wall, covering himself as much as possible. Kellers did the same with his stungun – he hadn't lost his, unlike David.

"Flashbang," Kellers muttered, closing his eyes as a small metallic object bounced down the corridors. David followed suit, opening his eyes as soon as the flash and noise had faded. He was disoriented, but not as badly as he could be – and he saw the Hunters coming.

Four of them now, all with their black cloaks wrapped completely around their bodies to protect them from SmartDarts, marched down the corridor, their weapons seeking any movement or sign of David or Kellers.

David had three of the tangleweb shells left, and he opened up with them immediately. The automatic shotgun cycled smoothly as he blasted the bounty hunters with the non-lethal shells. Two went down, wrapped in the rapidly hardening foam, but the other pair took cover against the wall, blasting back with similar shells.

Neither hit, and Kellers fired back with his stungun. The SmartDarts didn't penetrate the black cloaks, however, and the engineer grimly dropped the non-lethal weapon to draw his pistol.

The shotgun had one flashbang round left, and then the remainder were notoriously unreliably non-lethal 'beanbag' rounds. Wincing against the impact, David fired the flashbang at the roof in front of the Hunters.

The bright lights flashed, hurting his eyes, and the sounds pounded his ears. When the chaos faded, he loaded the beanbag rounds and stepped around his tiny corner.

All of the hunters were down, the last two tanglewebbed to the floor from behind. Standing over them, holding an automatic shotgun very similar to the one David had stolen from the Hunters, was a dark-skinned youth with a bright grin.

"Keiko sent me," he said cheerfully. "She wanted to be sure you didn't get into trouble on the way down – though I think she underestimated how much trouble even *you* could get in."

James shook his head as he approached and dragged the youth into an embrace, rendering the familiar resemblance unmistakeable – their rescuer was lighter-skinned than the engineer, but clearly related.

"Let's get to Keiko's," James told David. "These guys are likely to have friends, and we don't want to be here when they arrive."

#

182

Damien was lost in his work when the door slid open, so Kelly's voice interrupting his thoughts was a complete surprise. He jerked, turned to face her, and slashed the line of silver fire he'd conjured across a third of the wall of his workshop before he cut the spell.

The acrid smell of burning steel filled the room and he coughed slightly, blinking at the shocked face of his girlfriend.

"Sorry, I missed you opening the door," he said quickly. Embarrassed, he walked over to the wall his spell had scorched. He'd been practicing against a backdrop he'd enspelled to resist the force of the spells he'd been testing, but his shock had almost caused him to take out the computer screens showing a series of verbal instructions and diagrams.

"You were supposed to meet me for dinner half an hour ago," Kelly told him quietly. "What's up, Damien?" She walked over to him, seemingly unbothered by his slicing up his office. She looked at the screen, with its meticulous instructions. "What's this?"

Damien shrugged.

"This is Amber, and they say everything is for sale," he repeated to her. "So I decided to test the theory – this is the first of the four combat training manuals the Guild uses to train their Enforcers. I found them all."

"Enforcers are like cops, right?" she asked.

"And private soldiers," Damien admitted. "They're the deadliest Mages the Guild can recruit after the Navy and Marines are done hiring the very best. If the Captain had an Enforcer with him on Chrysanthemum instead of me, one of them could have saved everyone."

"Like you did?" Kelly reminded him. "Nobody down on Chrysanthemum with you died, David. You *did* save everyone. I don't care how good these Enforcers are, they couldn't have saved Narveer from half a world away!"

Damien glanced away, but nodded his admittance.

"An Enforcer wouldn't have collapsed and needed to be carried," he said, very quietly. "Kelzin almost died because I was weak."

"So, what, you read these books and you're better?" she asked.

"No," he admitted, his voice still quiet. "I can learn a lot from these, but training isn't everything – it's also raw power. I have unique gifts," the very nature of their ship – and their problems – proved that, "but I am barely even middle of the range in power."

"Learning these spells, using power more efficiently, that's the only way I can hope to face the Enforcers and Navy Mages who *will* come after us, sooner or later. Even with these, though, I don't know if I'll be strong enough to protect everyone," Damien admitted.

That was the fear running under all of his studying, in the back of his mind since Corinthian. *His* actions and *his* gift had made the *Blue Jay* and her crew targets. His presence had made his *friends* targets – and he wasn't sure he was strong enough to protect them.

"You took out an Enforcer on Corinthian, didn't you?" Kelly asked after a moment, pulling a chair up next to him and taking his hands.

"That was luck and trickery," the young Mage told her. "If he'd had a chance to act, he'd have disabled or killed me in moments."

"So we rely on trickery," the engineer replied fiercely. "Your magic saved us at Sherwood and Chrysanthemum – trickery and tricks saved you at Corinthian. The Captain's no slouch at this game, and you're stronger than you think."

She kissed him fiercely.

"I'm not going to tell you not to study these books," she told him. "You *are* our best protection, and the stronger you are, the safer we all are. But our problems are *not* your fault and you are *not* protecting us alone. We're hardly helpless – who saved *you* on Corinthian, after all?"

"You all did," Damien admitted, resting his head against her shoulder. "And we're all on the run for that. I owe you all more than I can ever repay."

"No you don't," Kelly told him. "That's what we do for crew, Damien – that's what *any* of us do for our friends."

"When push comes to shove, there are eighty damned determined people on this ship – and we're not going to let *anyone* push us around. When you do your wizardly duty to protect us, remember that we are *right* behind you – and we are not defenseless. You get me?"

"I get you," Damien replied, giving her a small smile, still worried but regaining some balance.

"Good. Now, you owe me dinner."

#

David followed James and their 'escort' into the office on the bottom floor of the gallery of Heinlein Station's Quadrant Gamma. The entrance was a discreet door tucked between a gun store and a flower shop that the Captain almost missed. Through the door, they followed a plain corridor back about twenty feet, where another door opened into a pristinely decorated reception area.

Plants lined the walls, bringing a sense of freshness to the air that he wasn't used to on space stations. A small number of comfortable looking chairs were tucked in one corner for people waiting, and a petite, dark-skinned young woman with short-cropped hair sat behind a desk.

"James, you found them," she exclaimed. It took David a moment to realize she was speaking to their escort, not his Chief Engineer. "Any issues?"

"They were being picked on by some Sanctioned Hunters," the younger James replied. "Is Keiko in?"

"Conference B," the receptionist told him. "She's waiting for you."

"Right this way," their guide instructed David and Kellers. He led the way through a door concealed behind a large potted tree and into a mid-sized conference room.

The room continued the theme of plants. Plant trays ran along both sides of the room, supporting what David believed to be strawberry plants, of all things. Two smallish trees flanked a professional holographic display podium at one end, and a massive black table filled the room.

Leaning against the end of the table closest to them was a tall, pale woman with flaming red hair and bright green eyes. When they entered, she wordlessly dragged James Kellers into a tight embrace.

She released him after a moment and inspected him carefully.

"You're alright?" she asked sharply.

"We're fine, Keiko," Kellers told her. "I didn't realize James was working for you," he continued, nodding towards the younger man.

David glanced from the younger James, to his James, to Keiko, and saw the familial resemblance all around.

"I thought you said Keiko was a friend from school," he said dryly, nodding towards James. "Did I misread how friendly you were?"

Keiko and both Jameses looked at him strangely for a minute, and then Keiko laughed.

"I'm sorry, Captain," she told him. "James Junior here is my *brother's* son – with James's sister. I didn't think of how it would look."

"And I didn't realize that Brian's kids were both working for you," the older James admitted. "James helped save our asses, though. A bunch of Sanctioned Hunters jumped us in the gallery."

Keiko nodded, her face suddenly grimmer. She turned to the younger James.

"James, can you go and tell your sister to close up?" she asked. "I've no more appointments today, so you two can shut things down and take off." She glanced over at the older James. "Tell your parents that I'll be bringing James and his Captain over for dinner later."

"Will do," the youth confirmed and disappeared from the conference room, carefully closing the door behind him.

"Take a seat," Keiko instructed, gesturing towards the table. "I apologize for the trouble," she continued. "If I'd been expecting anything, I'd have sent more men than just James to escort you."

"We *are* wanted fugitives, Miss Keiko," David reminded her quietly. "I presume James told you that."

"Well, that's the thing," she told him. "According to the Protectorate, you're not. If there'd been a Sanctioned Bounty on you, I'd have known regardless of whether or not James here had told me when he set up this meet."

Keiko touched a spot on the black conference table with a long pale finger. A section of table around it lit up with touch controls, which she promptly manipulated to bring up a page of text on the holographic display.

"They must have been after the Blue Star bounty," she admitted. "I knew it existed, but it looks like it's been expanded recently. Azure has doubled the bounty on you, Captain Rice, and added specific bounties for your ship and your Mage Montgomery. Montgomery is specified alive."

"No such consideration for me, I presume," David said quietly. The lack of a Protectorate arrest order was strange. Even ignoring Damien's modifications to the *Blue Jay*, they'd staged a *mass jailbreak* to get him out.

"No, Azure still wants you dead," Keiko said calmly. "Which is a recommendation in my books," she added. On the holo-display, data continued to flow as she searched through databases. "Huh," she said suddenly, "that's strange."

"What is?" Kellers asked.

"There's no Protectorate *warrant* for you," she explained, "but there *is* a request to inform the Navy if you are in-system and to hold your ship." She shrugged. "It's a mass-mailing to every MidWorlds system."

"So we're going to be trapped here?" David asked.

"Hardly," the woman replied with a laugh. "For warrants, there's a standing agreement for payment to the Co-ops for delivering prisoners, but for a one-off like this, there's no money attached. Which means that the ADC won't do shit – they're a business, after all."

The operation of law enforcement and defense in Amber confused David, but he was willing to take her word for it for the moment.

"So, we're safe then?"

"For the moment," she confirmed. "At least, from Sanctioned Hunters who want to keep their Sanction – the idiots who went after you in the Gallery will be unemployed by morning. The Defense Cooperative does *not* like their Hunters freelancing – and doing so as publicly and messily as that is a big no-no."

With a sweep of her hand, she cleared the data.

"Sooner or later, someone will look at that request, and *ask* whoever the notification is supposed to go to for money," she admitted. "Then, the Protectorate will pay up, and your ship will be locked down. So we'd better get to your business quickly. What do you need, Captain Rice?"

"We're heading out on a Fringe run," David told her. He slid a datachip across the table to her. "I need a pretty standard speculative cargo; the details are on the chip. We'll be paying cash by electronic transfer."

"Let me see," Keiko told him. As she began to review the data, she began to wrap one curl of her red hair around her left hand, distracting David enough that he almost missed Kellers' sigh beside him.

"I can get this, but about a third isn't manufactured here," she admitted. "The price will be higher, and we'll need to convince some people to re-direct cargos in mid-transhipment – that's money *and* favors."

David took his gaze off of her hair and blinked himself back to reality.

"What do you need?" he said finally.

"Smart man," she said approvingly. "Favors make the world go around – if I'm going to call in favors I'm owed to help you, then I'll need a favor myself. A big one."

David simply gestured for her to continue.

"I am involved with several organizations in the Fringe," Keiko said slowly. "Groups resisting the influence and control of the Core World Mega-Corps."

"Rebels," Kellers clarified next to David.

"Not against the Protectorate, in general," the woman told them. "But, generally the Protectorate's attention doesn't get drawn to abuses before things start coming apart. I have a blockade runner slated to take supplies to their destination, but he can't even make it into Amber without getting jumped – your bounty from the Blue Star Syndicate is *nothing* compared to what the Mega-Corps have on Seule."

"So you need us to deliver these 'supplies' to Seule," David said. "What kind of supplies are we talking?"

"Twenty standard shipping containers," she replied. "They run the full gamut of the needs of fighting a war – guns, ammunition, artillery, tanks, aerospace fighters, a handful of surface-to-space missiles."

Twenty interstellar shipping containers was *two hundred thousand tons* of weapons.

"That's not a small war," David said with a soft exhalation.

"When you're talking a planetwide revolution, that's barely enough to get started," Keiko told him. "If you'll deliver that to my rendezvous point, I can get your list for the two hundred and eighty containers on your ship."

"Just two hundred, unfortunately," David told her. "Unless you've heard of someone looking to buy a slightly used in-system re-fuelling ship?"

"Even in Amber, you can't sell spaceships without more paperwork than I think you want to deal with," the merchant told him with a smile. "I can get you skimming gear for the tanker though," she said after a moment. "If you can use the tanker to skim giants and re-fuel, that will save you money – and make a Fringe run easier."

"That would help," Kellers interjected. "I'm pretty sure Kelly and I can rig it up for remote control, too."

"Done and done," David finally said. "We'll transport your revolution-in-a-box for you, Keiko. How quickly can you get the rest?"

"I'll need three days to track it all down and get it loaded onto your ship," she told him. "First things first, though, I promised James's brother dinner with the three of us. I keep my promises."

David hesitated. He'd been hoping to get started on loading as soon as possible – and the earlier incident didn't make him any happier about wandering around Heinlein Station more than they needed to.

"It'll be fun, Captain," Keiko told him when he didn't answer, winking at him. "Trust me; I'll make sure of it."

Next to him, he heard Kellers sigh again – much louder this time.

#

By the time midnight Olympus Mons Time rolled around, Kelzin and Kelly had managed to drag Damien at least partially out of his moping. The trio, the youngest of the dozen officers aboard the *Blue Jay*, had found their way to the shuttle bay with a case of beer.

With the ship docked with the zero-gravity hub of Heinlein Station, only the rotating ribs had gravity. They'd discovered that the beer was not, as they'd assumed, in zero-gravity bulbs but in regular cans.

"You can magic up gravity, can't you?" Kelzin asked Damien.

"If you ask nicely," the Mage replied, already feeling relaxed from earlier drinks with Kelly.

"Let *him* float," Kelly told him, taking his hand and settling into the field of gravity rolling out around Damien.

"Hey," Kelzin objected. "I'm the one who bought the beer!"

"Fine," Damien told him, and gestured with his free hand. The pilot dropped the last few inches from where he was free-floating to the deck with an audible thud.

188

The field of gravity Damien had woven around the three included the edge of the array of crates that now functioned as the *Blue Jay*'s armory, allowing the three to take seats on the crates before cracking open the beers.

There was a moment of silence as they all tasted the Amber craft beer.

"That's *good*," Kelly finally said aloud. "I guess Amber produces more than guns and pirate ships, huh?"

Neither of the men answered her, both enjoying the complex favor of the beer.

"How's being in charge of the shuttles?" Damien finally asked Kelzin after a long moment.

The pilot shrugged, wincing slightly as he pulled at the bandages over his stomach.

"It's different, that's for sure," he admitted. "I'm still friends with the others, but we can't really hang out as much as we did before – now I'm in charge, so I can't get drunk and horse around with them like I used to."

"So *that's* why you're drinking with us," Kelly told him. "We're your substitute buddies!"

"Well, I don't normally *volunteer* to be the third wheel," Kelzin told her with a grin, gesturing at where she had wrapped her leg around Damien's on the crate.

Kelly made a tossing gesture, and accidentally threw beer at the pilot. The liquid passed out of the tiny area of gravity Damien was maintaining and continued its arc over to splatter against the wall – about a quarter-meter to the right of where James Kellers had just entered the bay.

"Sorry boss!" Kelly immediately apologized, but Kellers just carefully waved, as if to dismiss the sticky mess.

"I'll forgive you if you've got more of that beer," the Chief Engineer told them.

Damien wasn't always certain that Kelzin was the sharpest tool in the shed – he had, after all, got himself *shot* – but the pilot was definitely capable of translating that hint. By the time Kellers joined him, he had a fourth beer open and ready for the dark-skinned senior officer.

"Where's Captain Rice?" Damien asked as Kellers joined them, pulling up a crate of his own as the Mage expanded the gravity field to cover the other man.

"Our contact is an old high school friend of mine," James told them as he took a swig of the beer. "They hit it off even better than I expected – David's spending the night on the station."

"Wait, the Captain is doing *what*?" Kelzin exclaimed. "That old dog – I didn't expect that!"

"If he hears you call him 'old' *or* a 'dog,' you might find yourself looking for a new ship to sign on to," Kellers warned the pilot. "David's been divorced for over two years, and so far as I know Keiko is the first woman to do more than catch his eye in all that time. Even if I thought she was dangerous, I don't think I'd have warned him off."

"So she's harmless?" Kelly asked, her voice sharp.

Kellers laughed aloud, and then took a careful sip of his beer.

"Keiko has had her fingers in at least four violent revolutions I'm aware of," he told them calmly. "She outright owns four ships like the *Blue Jay*, and runs a financing syndicate that has helped folks like David buy at least fifteen more. She is wealthy, powerful, politically involved, and anything *but* harmless."

"She also seems quite taken with David, and has to be careful about who she spends her time with," Kellers concluded. "Amber isn't a world where anyone else watches out for you. She's been burned a few times by lovers out to rob her or use her."

He shrugged, with a sad smile on his face as he drank more of his beer.

"They both have that in common," he admitted. "They'll be good for each other."

#

There was only so much time Damien could spend reading over and practicing the many offensive and defensive spells contained in the Enforcer textbooks. One of the limitations that he faced versus the type of Mage who would be accepted as an Enforcer was a limit in how much magic he was able to wield over time, as well as how much he could command at once. Some, though not many, of the spells in the books were completely beyond him. Those that weren't still wore him out quickly, leaving him drained and exhausted.

He preferred runes. His ability to see and trace the flows of power through the silver etchings Humanity's Mages used to guide and control larger spells was unmatched by any Mage he'd ever worked with. One of his classmates had once complained that he felt like he was reading a circuit diagram, where Damien could tell *exactly* what the current was doing without even reading the script.

That was the gift that had allowed him to turn the *Blue Jay* into a full, unlimited, amplifier – something normally restricted to the destroyers and cruisers of the Royal Navy of Mars.

His ability to *see* the flows instead of having to actually read the runes made going over the rune matrices that tied together the

190

freighter's amplifier a task of a day or so, rather than the weeks that a Mage without his unique talent would have taken.

He studied the Enforcer handbooks and reviewed the ship's rune matrix, looking for the tiny efficiencies he could find that no other Mage even saw, while the rest of the crew loaded the cargo aboard or worked on the tanker, installing hardware that Kelly's explanations of went right over his head.

At the end of the third day, he drifted onto the bridge to join Jenna. The ship's First Officer was sprawled in the Captain's chair, data flowing across the screens on the chair while the main viewscreen showed a three-dimensional representation of the system.

"Still holding down the fort?" he asked her.

"Yup," Jenna confirmed cheerfully. "You think I'd get in the way of the boss's only tryst in three years to dodge standing a watch or two? Not a chance in hell."

Damien leant against the console that was normally Jenna's station with David in command. The *Jay*'s bridge was on Rib One, and with the loading basically complete the ship had spun up for gravity again.

"So how many guns are we carrying?" he asked after a moment, eyeing the cameras showing the over two hundred ten thousand ton containers latched to the *Blue Jay*'s cargo pylons.

"I didn't think we'd told you about those yet," Jenna replied, turning to eye him. "How did you know?"

"Kellers mentioned that his contact had her hands in a bunch of revolutions, and we're heading to the Fringe," Damien shrugged. "Putting two and two together with Amber's reputation for manufacturing weapons, it made sense. Not to mention that the Excelsior system wasn't on my original plan for the Fringe run."

Jenna shook her head.

"You have too much time on your hands, Ship's Mage," she told him dryly. "Yes, we're carrying weapons – but I don't think the Captain wants to spread that about until we're out-system, clear?"

"I figured that too," the young Mage told her dryly, and she shook her head again.

"Shouldn't you and your pretty engineer be imitating the Captain?" she asked.

"Kelly's busy leading half of our techs all over the tanker," Damien admitted. "Something to do with an 'artificial stupid intelligence'?"

"Artificial Sequential Intelligence," Jenna corrected. "Though I've heard engineers call them artificial stupids before." Damien directed his best confused look at the ship's exec, who laughed. "It's the closest thing to artificial intelligence that isn't the size of the *Blue Jay*," she told him. "But, at the end of the day, it's a massive list of if-then commands, so it requires a hunk of computer to run through them quickly and needs to be custom-written for whatever you want it to do. I think Kellers said your girlfriend was the only person on the ship qualified to code for it."

"And now I understand why my eyes glaze over when she talks shop," Damien told Jenna.

"Don't worry, you can do that to any of us aboard the ship at will," Jenna reminded him. "I know nothing about 'Thaumaturgical differential quotients' or whatever it was you were trying to even out in Rib Four yesterday."

The young Mage opened his mouth to try and explain, and then turned to study the main viewscreen when he realized that even the *simplified* explanation was a mouthful of jargon.

"That's a lot more detail than we usually have," he realized aloud, his now-practiced eye reading the symbols and text showing the region of space around Amber and Heinlein Station – easily out to several light minutes.

"Yeah, it turns out the Amber Defense Co-operative sub-contracted building and running the planetary sensor arrays," Jenna told him. "Since they then had information everyone wanted, and this is Amber, that company provides subscription access to what would be military grade arrays anywhere else in the Protectorate."

Damien nodded his understanding – and bemusement at the way Amber ran its defenses. He paused as a new icon appeared on the screen.

"Jump flare," he said quietly, eyeing the icon and wondering how much data the link into the planetary arrays would give them.

"Oh shit, shit, *shit*," Jenna starting cursing behind him as the icon stabilized, and the sensor arrays calmly populated the transponder signal of the Royal Navy of Mars destroyer *Golden Sword of Freedom*.

The Protectorate was here.

#

David was finding it surprisingly hard to say goodbye to Keiko. They'd had barely three days together, and neither had pretended that it was anything but a friendly fling between two people of a shared age and attitude towards the world, but as they watched the last of the loading gear retract from the *Blue Jay* from an observation lounge, he found himself mentally making excuses to put off the moment.

The observation lounge was a quiet, elegant place. The sort of spot where wealthy merchants and starship captains made deals and watched their ships through the walls of steel made transparent through magic. Runes swirled across the floor, creating a gravity field that held

192

everyone and everything down, and discreet human staff delivered drinks to the widely scattered quiet tables.

"I guess that's it then," he finally said, watching the *Blue Jay*'s ribs spin up. If Jenna had spun up the ribs for gravity, then the last of the cargo was loaded. "Your special cargo came aboard with the rest. I'm impressed you found it all," he admitted.

"I am the best at what I do," Keiko told him cheerfully, her gaze meeting his. "This has been nice, David, but I'm not one for teary goodbyes. I hope you weren't expecting one."

"Hardly," he said with a snort of laughter. "It would clash with your 'hardened revolutionary' vibe."

She put a finger to her lips. "Shush," she replied, laughing herself. "That's not part of my reputation here. On Amber, I'm known as wealthy, ruthless, and perfectly willing to bury people in lawsuits if they get in my way."

"Guess that's how business is done here," David admitted, eyeing his ship. "I was surprised by how good the safety gear was, to be honest. I was expecting…"

"You were expecting slaves driven with whips?" Keiko asked dryly. "Which do you think is going to motivate a business to do better at safety: a government standard that, once they meet, they're no longer liable – or the knowledge that a death will see them sued out of business? Our companies have the best safety gear around – they know they won't survive a death liability case."

David figured much of that to be exaggeration – the gear wasn't as *bad* as he'd feared, but he'd definitely seen better and safer work crews, too. That was also, he understood, at least partially the choice of the crews – and that was how Amber worked. He kept his peace, though. Keiko was a native of Amber, and a fervent believer in its unique system.

"I should get to my ship," he said finally. "We need to leave by morning if we're going to make the rendezvous at Excelsior."

Keiko's eyes were suddenly softer, and she laid her hand on top of his.

"Seule won't disappear if you're late," she told him. "You can spend the night on the station if you want."

"I thought you weren't one for long goodbyes?" he asked.

"I'm not planning *goodbyes*," she told him with a wicked wink. "I'll twist some arms; make sure you're clear all the way out in the morning. What's the point of influence if I can't spend some of it to get laid?"

David laughed, and was about to agree when his wrist computer buzzed. The tone was an urgent message, not something that Jenna would use unless it was an emergency. He flipped the message up on the screen, and the laughter died.

Protectorate destroyer in system. Return to ship ASAP – it's time to go boss.

"I have to go," he said quietly, meeting Keiko's eyes. "There's a Protectorate ship in system. I don't think even the ADC will ignore a direct request from a warship to hold us – not once the destroyer realizes we're here."

Wordlessly, Keiko dragged him into a surprisingly fierce embrace.

"I understand," she told him, then kissed him thoroughly. "If you're ever back in Amber, look me up," she ordered. "I won't make promises, but we can always see what happens."

"I will try," David said, cautiously, and she laughed.

"Go, my dear Captain," she told him after one final kiss. "Tell Seule I say 'hi' – and remember, the *Luciole* in the Excelsior Three trailing Trojan cluster."

"The Graveyard," he said softly. "I remember."

David paused on the edge of the lounge for one long moment, looking back at the tall, thin, Amberite – his opposite in many ways – and gave her one last wave.

Then the Captain of the *Blue Jay* left, heading for his ship.

#

David found himself envying Damien's ability to generate his own gravity with magic as he made his way down the zero-gravity keel of the *Blue Jay*. The personnel tube, which had retracted behind him as he came aboard, connected at the rear of the ship. The *Blue Jay*'s bridge was on Rib One, at the front of the ship.

It was noticeably *faster* to make the long dive along the keel and around the simulacrum chamber from the shuttle bay to the forward elevators than it was to run along the Ribs themselves with their centrifugal gravity. What it wasn't, David considered as he plummeted towards the front of his ship, was *safer*.

Practice allowed him to catch one of the handholds by the elevators with his stronger hand, and swing himself to a halt. The effort almost wrenched his arm out of its socket. He oriented himself towards the elevators gingerly, wincing at the now-vicious pain in his shoulder.

As he reached the elevator, he felt a familiar vibration run through the ship, followed by a faint but definable sense of 'down' – the ship was moving. He spared a moment to be grateful that the engines hadn't engaged *while* he was making his one handed landing from his reckless zero-gravity jump.

Moments later, the elevator delivered him to the outside of his bridge and he carefully walked in, trying not to let the pain in his twisted shoulder throw him off too badly.

"Where are we at?" he asked Jenna, settling into his command chair with a concealed wince.

His XO was at her usual station at navigation, her fingers flying across the screen as she brought the *Blue Jay* away from the immense-yet-vulnerable bulk of Heinlein Station on their maneuvering thrusters.

"To no one's surprise, I'm sure, Heinlein Station will bump you to the head of the clearance queue if you pay an extra fee," Jenna told him. "We're pulling clear on thrusters and should be ready to engage main engines in about five minutes."

"How's our Martian friend?"

Jenna gestured towards the main viewscreen, which was zoomed in on the single icon and showing a series of numbers around it.

"They came out roughly the standard one hundred sixty million kilometers out," she told him. "I don't think they've noticed us yet – they're burning in at three gravities, but that's pretty standard for a Navy ship."

"We're heading in the opposite direction, I presume?"

"Of course!" she confirmed. "As soon as I'm clear, I'll push us up to about one and a half gravities."

David nodded and turned to the channel to the simulacrum, where Damien was patiently waiting.

"What's your status, Damien? When can we jump?"

"The matrix is clean and functioning," the Ship's Mage told him. "I can jump closer in than most with the amplifier as well – at a gee and a half, we'll probably be clear in six hours."

David nodded appreciatively. He kept being surprised by the capabilities that Damien squeezed out of the amplifier he'd turned the jump matrix into. A Navy destroyer could jump at three million kilometers from a planet if they needed to, but it wasn't fun for anyone.

"Keep an eye on things," he ordered his Mage. "I don't want to pick a *fight* with a destroyer, but I'm not sure I want to surrender either."

"They can't catch us in time," Jenna asserted. "We'll be heading in the opposite direction at half of their acceleration, and we have a lot less distance to cover."

"I hope you're right," Damien said quietly. "Because they have more Mages aboard, and theirs are trained in the use of an amplifier in combat. I couldn't face them. And *that's* assuming they don't just blow us up with missiles."

David didn't respond aloud. He simply nodded his acceptance of the Mage's comments, and settled in, watching the viewscreen's data on the million-ton warship carefully.

#

The next several hours passed quietly. With the course plugged into the computer, David sent Jenna to rest while he and Damien continued to watch the *Golden Sword* and their own location.

It was obvious when the destroyer's crew finished running the beacons of all the ships through their databases and identified the *Blue Jay*. The destroyer's arc shifted, moving away from a direct course to Heinlein Station and instead shaping an intercept for the *Blue Jay* – and she sped up, her acceleration increasing from three gravities to ten.

A number of warning signs starting flashing on David's screen a few moments later, as the Protectorate warship painted the *Blue Jay* with directional radar and lidar – both lightspeed sensors being targeted on the *Blue Jay* from several light minutes away.

The *Jay*'s sensors warned about the laser and radar hits for several seconds, and then the warnings were silent. Standard procedure, David knew from his own long-ago days in the Martian Navy, would be to scan the ship flying a flagged identification beacon to both confirm that it was the right ship and identify any unknown dangers.

From eight light minutes away, it took almost twenty minutes for the sensor reflection to reach the *Golden Sword of Freedom*, the bridge crew to review it and decide that yes, this was the ship in their database, the commander to record a transmission, and for that transmission to wing its way across space back to the *Blue Jay*.

When he received the transmission, David threw it up on the screen after checking that Damien was in the communication loop. He preferred the Mage to know what was going on – after all, if things came apart, it would fall to Damien and his amplifier to try and save them.

The image in the transmission turned out to be a tall, slim, black woman with a shaved head and the dark blue uniform of a senior officer in the Royal Navy of the Mage-King of Mars. Behind and around the woman was visible the room-encompassing viewscreens and silver runes of the destroyer's simulacrum Chamber – since the main weapon of a Protectorate warship was its amplifier, the simulacrum Chamber at the heart of the ship doubled as the vessel's bridge.

Unlike the simulacrum Chamber aboard the *Blue Jay* or any other civilian ship, however, the *Golden Sword*'s had magically controlled gravity. Despite the ten gravities of acceleration the other ship was pushing, the Captain showed no sign of being under force except a normal gravity.

"Captain David Rice of the *Blue Jay*," the woman said calmly. "I am Mage-Captain Amelia Okoro of His Majesty's destroyer *Golden Sword of Freedom*." She paused, seeming to consider her words carefully.

"I know you are running," she finally continued. "I am ordering you to heave to, and prepare for a rendezvous."

"I promise you, upon the honor of His Majesty's Navy, no harm will come to you or your crew if you surrender, but you *must* surrender. I will range upon you before you reach jump distance. Do not force me to act hastily."

David ran the geometry through his computer, and then glanced up at Damien on the screen to his own simulacrum Chamber.

"When can you jump, Damien?" he asked.

"I could jump now," the young Mage told him. "I'd be useless for at least twenty-four hours afterwards, though. If we wait three hours to when I originally estimated, I'll be fine. Can they intercept us short of that?"

"No," David told him. "She *could* intercept us well short of the nine light minute mark though, even if she maneuvered to board and we did our best to escape. We'll jump on schedule, Damien."

He glanced back at the main viewscreen, then shrugged and activated his own recorder. He leant forwards slightly and focused his gaze on the camera.

"Mage-Captain Okoro," he said calmly, "I am afraid that I have no intention of surrendering this ship to His Majesty's forces. I will not allow a member of my crew to have his magic stripped from him to calm the fears of the foolish."

Another twenty minutes passed while his short message reached the *Golden Sword*, and Okoro's response came back. He played it when it arrived.

The black-skinned Captain had acquired an odd quirk to her mouth, as if she was trying not to smile.

"Your loyalty to your crew does you credit, Captain," she told him. "To my knowledge, Mr. Montgomery is in no danger of that anymore – but I am required to deliver him, yourself, and your crew to the Lady Hand Stealey."

David smiled, and activated the recorder again.

"If you wish to deliver us to the Hand, you will hardly be able to fire into my ship, Mage-Captain," he told her dryly. "I have no intention of surrendering or being intercepted. You may as well let us go."

Time passed. Every exchange burned more time until the *Blue Jay* could escape, but the destroyer continued to blaze towards them on a pillar of antimatter flame.

This time, when the transmission arrived, Okoro was clearly smiling.

"You may be correct, Captain, in that I cannot fire into your ship," she said. "It is even possible, given the data I have from Corinthian, that you can escape. Understand this, Captain Rice. I may not be able track your jumps. I may not be able to chase you from star to star. The Hand can – and the Hand *will*."

"These are her orders from Mars. She will not fail. If you run, you will be run to ground. If you hide, you will be found. If you surrender now, you will be safe. You have my word, and the honor of his Majesty's Navy on that."

A chill of fear ran down David's spine, and he met Damien's eyes through the intercom video.

"No one can track a jump," the Mage reminded him. "Hand or no Hand, she does not know where we're going – and she *cannot* follow us."

David suspected that the younger man was speaking as much to reassure himself as his Captain, but it made him feel better. He turned the recorder on and faced it one last time.

"I am sorry, Mage-Captain," he said quietly. "But the fact remains that I can no longer trust the Protectorate. I will guard my crew from you with all that is in my power. By the time you receive this message, I will be less than an hour from leaving this system. You cannot catch us. You cannot pursue us."

David Rice sat in his command chair for a long time after that, watching the Protectorate destroyer draw ever closer, until, finally, Damien wrapped him and his ship in a sphere of magic and whisked them away to safety.

#

"We found them."

The words were quiet, but Alaura Stealey, Hand of the Mage-King of Mars, hadn't missed the door to her private office opening. She heard Mage-Lieutenant Harmon, the executive officer of the destroyer *Tides of Justice*, perfectly clearly.

With a small sigh of satisfaction, she closed down the screen she was reviewing, filled with the latest in a series of reports from agents across the Protectorate. While the Mage-King's instructions with regards to Montgomery had been clear, she couldn't ignore the rest of her duties. There were too many trouble spots, here and there across the sphere of human space, which would eventually require the touch of a Hand.

"Who found them, and where?" she asked. There was no question as to who had been found.

"The destroyer *Golden Sword of Freedom* was making one of our irregular 'you're not building pirate ships, promise?' stopovers in Amber. They detected the *Blue Jay* making a run for it. Mage-Captain Okoro challenged them, but Rice refused to surrender. The Mage at the transceiver provided a transcript of the conversation."

Alaura nodded, quickly taking the sheet of hardcopy from the Navy officer and skimming through it. She grimaced at Rice's words about trusting the Protectorate, and sighed aloud.

"I guess it was too much to hope that dropping all of the charges would get them to talk to us," she said quietly. If only she could talk to them herself! The limitations of the use of transceiver arrays made that impossible unless she could actually convince the *Blue Jay* to stay somewhere until she arrived – and Rice had his opinion on that clear to Okono.

"After Corinthian made it clear they intended to strip Montgomery's magic, I'm not surprised," she continued." But, why Amber?"

Amber was a problem child for the Protectorate. While Alaura found herself somewhat in sympathy with the basic *philosophy* behind the planet, the fact that the world's lax law enforcement tended to be abused by scum to do things like arm pirate ships gave her a headache.

"They were probably looking for a cargo, Ma'am," Harmon told her. "From Amber, they'll likely sweep out to the Fringe – carry cargos between worlds that see maybe three ships a year, and possibly three Protectorate ship a *decade*. They could make a lot of money, and avoid any attention from us."

"Which will make tracking them almost impossible," Alaura said aloud. She cursed, glancing around the tiny office. Her officer gave her command of any resource the Protectorate had to offer, and she had runic tools most didn't even think were *possible*, but even she couldn't track a starship once it had jumped. There were rumors that some people had managed it, but if they had, the Navy had never worked out how.

"Someone on Amber has to know where they're going, though, don't they Ma'am?" Harmon asked.

"It's not a certainty," the Hand told him. "If they're smart, they wouldn't have trusted anyone on Heinlein Station as far as they could throw them." She shrugged. "With that said, it's our only lead."

"Send a message back through the Runic Transceiver Array," she ordered. "Our agents on Amber are to try and track down who Captain

Rice dealt with. Once you've transmitted that, get us underway. Time is of the essence if we are to find young Montgomery."

"Understood Ma'am," Harmon replied crisply. "I'll inform the Captain, we should be able to break orbit within the hour."

#

Mikhail Azure, leader of the Blue Star Syndicate, crime lord and master of the underworlds of a dozen systems, floated in zero-gravity in a perfect meditation pose. His eyes closed, he felt the world around him through the tiny twitches of energy and matter carried to him by his magic.

Through his magic he felt the pulsing energy of the *Azure Gauntlet*, his personal warship. Stolen from the Martian Navy years ago, she represented the ultimate iron fist of his organization. It had been some time since he had been aboard her, and the sense of sheer power the stolen cruiser represented was... calming.

The door to his private zero-gravity meditation room opening should have been a surprise – only one person on the ship would dare interrupt his meditation and only if it was important – and yet, he had known it was coming.

Azure would never claim to any man or woman that he could see the future. Neither magic nor science, for all their many gifts to mankind, had ever managed to peel back the veil of time. He often found, however, that he had flashes of insight into the future. He had known he would be interrupted this time, and it would be good news.

"Mister Wong," he said softly, without opening his eyes. "What news?"

"The bounty hunter has found Rice's ship," the man who commanded the *Azure Gauntlet* for Mikhail told him calmly as he walked into the room. The scuff of the soft slippers Wong wore aboard the ship was loud in Azure's ears, revealing the other man was using magic to keep his feet on the floor of the chamber.

"But has not captured him," the crime lord said softly.

"They are at Amber, and he lacks the courage to challenge even that world's lax defenses," Wong replied.

"Do not be fooled by their single aged destroyer, Mister Wong," Azure replied. "The Amber Defense Co-operative is a stronger force than they pretend– no lesser threat than your *Gauntlet* would suffice to overwhelm Amber." He slowly rotated to face his servant, magic rotating his body without visible motion.

"Is Able prepared to pursue them?" he asked. He found Wong's refusal to use the name of anyone who was not a senior member of the Syndicate or a worthy enemy a... tolerable foible, most of the time.

Nonetheless, there were enough bounty hunters in the universe that names helped.

"Once he had access to the transceiver array, they had already fled the system before a Navy destroyer," Wong told him.

"Able is a Tracker," Azure said flatly. "He's almost as good as you are."

He felt Wong's self-effacing half-bow, and snorted to himself. To his knowledge, fifteen men and women in all of human space had managed to master the trick of tracking a jump. For all that the jump itself was magic; the key to tracking it seemed to be technology – and an entirely intuitive art of reading the sensor readings of the jump.

Wong was the best at it, and it had made him utterly terrifying as Azure's main enforcer for years. No enemy would evade him by running away in a jumpship. He claimed to be able to track where a ship had gone for days after it had left.

Able wasn't that good. But he *could* track a jump and he'd been *in* the system when the *Jay* had left.

"They are shaping a course for the Excelsior system," Wong said simply. "Able intends to ambush them in the asteroids there."

Azure opened his eyes and lowered himself to the ground. He stretched, towering over the small form of the cruiser's commander with the lanky height of those born and raised in low gravity, artificial environments.

"He will fail," the leader of the Blue Star Syndicate said calmly.

"I agree," Wong said simply.

"Able has underestimated Rice and Montgomery before – at Chrysanthemum," Azure continued, ignoring his ship's captain. "He will do so again, and I do not believe he will survive repeating the mistake."

"Make your course for Excelsior, Mister Wong. If I am wrong, then we will need to make Mr. Able an offer he cannot refuse."

"If I am right, we will have to clean up his mess."

#

Stealey stalked through Heinlein station like a thunderstorm. The locals who didn't get out of her way at the ominous cloud hovering over her head tended to clear out when they saw the golden hand icon of her station hanging around her neck.

The people who lived on Amber had little respect for authority, but what little they had tended to be for the Mage-King and his Hands. Stealey and her fellows had shed sweat, tears, and blood to prove themselves the champions of justice and compassion throughout the

Protectorate – despite being the only men and women who could act as judge, jury and executioner.

Protectorate agents on Heinlein Station had identified the merchant Rice had dealt with before she arrived. Stealey knew Keiko Alabaster by reputation, and the woman should have known better.

Entering the office hidden away on the bottom floor of the gallery of Heinlein's Quadrant Gamma, Stealey fixed an agate gaze on the young, mocha-skinned, woman sitting behind the reception desk.

"I need to speak with Miss Alabaster," she said calmly. "Please inform her that Alaura Stealey is here to see me – she knows who I am."

"Miss Alabaster is not in today." The girl was both smart enough to at least not deny whose offices these were, and loyal enough to shield her boss.

Alaura sighed.

"Miss Jenna Alabaster," she said calmly. "I am aware that your aunt entered this office at seven forty five Olympus Mons Time this morning. Despite this office having three separate concealed exits, she has not left since. Please tell her I am here."

"It's all right Jenna," a voice interjected. "Though I would think a Hand would have better things to do than try to intimidate my staff."

Alaura turned an assessing gaze on Keiko Alabaster, who returned the favor frankly. Where the merchant was tall and slim, Alaura was short and stocky. Where Alabaster was as pale as her name, the Hand was swarthy, her skin worn by years under the sun of space. Where Keiko was young and red-haired, Stealey was aged and graying.

Stealey sighed, nodding acceptance of the rebuke.

"I did not mean to intimidate anyone," she said calmly. "I am in a hurry, however, and both lives and the security of the Protectorate are at stake."

"I do not know what assistance I may be to a Hand of the Mage-King, but please, step into my office," Keiko instructed.

Alaura followed the younger woman into her office. It was a surprisingly cramped space for the mistress of a billion-dollar trade empire. A massive desk filled much of the space, with a single holographic screen that Keiko closed with a wave of her hand as she sat behind the desk, gesturing the Hand to the single seat in front of the desk.

She had to move a stack of papers from the seat. If the dream of a paperless office had died anywhere, it was in Keiko Alabaster's office. Every surface, from the desk to the bookshelves to the guest chair, was covered in paper. Alaura recognized many of the cover pages as belonging to finance and political think-tanks across the Protectorate. In that, at least, the office was what she expected of Keiko Alabaster.

"How may I assist the Protectorate, Lady Hand?" Keiko finally asked, her helpful words at odds with a body language that accentuated her height and position behind the desk.

"I need to know where you sent the *Blue Jay*," Alaura said bluntly.

"I don't believe I own or contract with a ship by that name," the merchant princess replied. Her eyes were level and her voice didn't waver – this woman was *good*, the Hand reflected.

Unfortunately for her, Alaura had done her research before she'd ever stepped into the office.

"No, you don't," she agreed calmly. "You did, however, act as agent for Captain Rice to acquire a cargo of two *million* tons of aerospace craft and maintenance supplies, ground and aerial terraformers, and advanced farming equipment. Given that the *Jay* is capable of hauling *three* million tons of cargo, I can't help but feel that you and the good Captain came to an agreement on what to do with that other million tons of cargo. A load of weapons, for example."

"Such a contract would not be illegal on Amber," Keiko pointed out. "I would have no reason to conceal such a transaction."

"Please, Miss Alabaster," Stealey said quietly. "I have spent the last ten years resolving rebellions in the Fringe. I know where the guns for the more moral ones are coming from. If you were less picky, you and I would have had a discussion a long time ago."

That, finally, pierced the other woman's armor of perfect calm. She obviously hadn't realized the Protectorate knew about her little sideline.

"That is neither here nor there," Keiko said slowly. "I did not engage the *Blue Jay* to haul a million tons of weapons, if that is what you're asking."

"I honestly don't care if you engaged them to fight a fucking war for you," Stealey snapped. "I care if you know where they went, and I know that you damned well know."

Keiko's hand smacked her desk with a resounding clap.

"This is Amber, my Lady Hand," she said coldly. "Your authority here is not unlimited, and I will not be bullied. This interview is over."

"Do not push me, Keiko Alabaster," Alaura warned, her voice equally cold. "Amberites tend to believe their lack of laws limits the power of a Hand here – but this is a matter of *Protectorate* Law. In that, I am the highest authority outside of Sol. Did Rice even tell you why the Protectorate might be looking for them?"

"They broke his Mage out of one of your prisons that he'd been jailed in on trumped up charges," Keiko said. "He was surprised there was no warrant for his arrest."

It was an improvement, Alaura reflected, that the merchant was no longer denying she'd met Captain Rice.

"There are no warrants because I canceled them all," she told the other woman. "The local Guildmaster didn't understand what was going on, and handled it completely wrong. I've spent the last few months trying to *fix* that."

"If the charges *were* trumped up, then just let them go," Keiko snapped, and Alaura noted the flush in the Amberite's cheeks. There was more going on here than just the usual stubbornness of Amber merchants or protecting a contract. This was… personal for Alabaster.

"I can't, Miss Alabaster," the Hand said finally, after a long silence. "The *Blue Jay* has been modified – her jump matrix has been turned into an amplifier."

"That isn't *possible.*"

"It is," Alaura told her. "And those with the knowledge to judge such things tell me that the *Jay* could be used as a template to do that to *any* jumpship."

"In the hands of a pirate, that ship would allow them to produce an entire *fleet* of covert raiders, utterly indistinguishable from regular merchant ships until they unleashed magic on their unsuspecting prey. Can you imagine how bad our piracy problem would grow then?"

Alabaster's face had grown even paler than before, and Alaura knew the merchant was imagining it just fine.

"The Blue Star Syndicate already wanted Rice dead," she continued. "Now they know what the *Blue Jay* can do. They will hunt the *Jay* to the ends of the Protectorate – you can't save them. I can't protect them – not if I can't *find* them."

"They won't be harmed?" Keiko demanded, suddenly and incongruously a young woman concerned for her friends. "Any of the crew?"

"I swear to you, upon the honor of Mars, none of the *Blue Jay*'s crew will be harmed," Alaura told her. The Hands voice was firm as she made a commitment that bound not merely herself, but her King, and, in a sense, the *entire Protectorate.*

From Keiko Alabaster's face, the other woman knew what it meant for a Hand to swear upon the honor of Mars.

"Excelsior, Lady Hand," she finally admitted. "I sent them to the Graveyard at Excelsior."

#

The *Blue Jay* jumped into Excelsior in the middle of the night Olympus Mons Time. Kelly had joined Damien in the simulacrum Chamber and was looking around wide-eyed as they emerged into the new system. The screens all around them began to fill with images as the *Jay*'s many cameras began to record the universe around them again.

"Well, we're here," Damien said quietly to the screen showing David on the bridge. The Captain nodded, checking something on his own screen.

"We're about eight hours from the Trojan cluster we're supposed to meet this Captain Seule at," he told the Mage. "Keep an eye on things, this system has a *lot* of rocks floating about."

The entire system looked odd, Damien realized. There were only four planets, for one thing – one tiny ball of fire-kissed rock tucked in right next to the star, one ball of ice light-hours out, and two mid-sized gas giants. Where orbital dynamics said there should be two more planets between the fire-seared inner planet and the innermost gas giant was two massive asteroid belts.

Both belts were clumped up, with most of the rocks concentrated in a single massive cluster for each. A navigation beacon announced the presence of a number of mining platforms on the outer of the two clusters.

"This place is weird," Kelly said next to Damien. "Those asteroid belts make no sense."

"That's about what the first explorers who surveyed the system said," David told the two youths. "A lot about the system didn't add up, so they pulled some of the historical astronomical data for this region of space. Some oddities showed up in the late twentieth century data – which just gave them more questions!"

"Doesn't look like this system has a lot of answers," Damien said quietly, eyeing the local radar data also being fed to his screens. With the amount of debris in this system, it would be up to him and the *Jay*'s laser turrets to keep the ship safe.

"It doesn't," the Captain admitted. "But the Corporation that had purchased the mining rights wanted to make sure that if something had happened to create the strange asteroid belts, it wouldn't repeat. They funded an expedition to go into deep space and capture the old light from Excelsior."

"They went almost two light centuries outside explored space," he continued. "Dodging systems to avoid tempting fate, they went hunting what they figured was the death of a world."

"Jumping from deep space to deep space, looking backwards the whole time?" Kelly said softly. "Sounds romantic."

Damien was reminded that his girlfriend, as an engineer, had a strange definition of romantic.

"What they found wasn't," David said grimly. "It turns out that about six hundred years ago, a small black hole – a couple of earth masses, nothing more – ripped through the Excelsior system and tore the two middle world to shreds.

"They also discovered what no one had guessed before that – that Excelsior had been inhabited before that. A technic civilization, the only one we know of, had died when that black hole hit. They'd been a couple of centuries ahead of us – early twenty-second century in our nineteenth century – but without magic, they were unable to escape the death of their worlds."

That got Damien's attention. Humanity had discovered a total of five non-human intelligences. So far as the xeno-anthropologists could determine, all had lacked critical biological or mineral resources to achieve anything resembling civilization – all of them were still at the hunter-gatherer level. Now that David mentioned it, though, he vaguely remembered something about a dead technological alien race.

"A couple of space stations survived. Once we knew to look for them, we found them. One of the biggest had survived for almost a hundred years after the black hole before they finally died out from the inability to replace critical tech," David finished. "No one has any idea what pathogens may be aboard, so even the archeologists are only allowed to study it with robots, and only for limited amounts of time. It's under a quarantine order."

Damien glanced at their course, towards the trailing Trojan cluster of the outer gas giant. He noticed, now, that there was a second navigation beacon there. One warning everyone away.

"That's where we're going," he said quietly.

"Yeah," David confirmed. "To the Graveyard of the only other technic civilization we've known." He shrugged. "I'm prepared to bet any ghosts will like me though."

"Why's that?" Kelly asked, sneaking her hand into Damien's. He squeezed, hopefully reassuringly, as he needed the reassurance himself.

"When they identified what had happened, the ship I was serving on in the Navy was part of a task group testing a theoretical way to break up a singularity threatening one of our systems. We took it as a sign of a good test subject."

He smiled sadly.

"We know almost nothing about Excelsior's inhabitants even now – but in a strange way, we avenged them."

#

David was alone on the bridge for most of the approach to the trailing Trojan cluster of the third of Excelsior's remaining planets. The cluster of asteroids followed the massive gas giant in the lull of gravity in the orbit, what was often called the Lagrange points after the eighteenth century mathematician who'd first theorized them.

After the first hour or so proved non-eventful, with the handful of rocks that had come their way readily handled by the *Blue Jay*'s defensive turrets, he'd even sent Damien to bed – though, from the way Kelly had dragged him from the simulacrum Chamber, he wasn't sure the young Mage had got much *sleep*.

As they crept closer to the cluster of asteroids, thankfully, the ship slowly came awake around him and Jenna joined him on the bridge. For all of his brave words to Damien, David found the thought of entering the Graveyard discomfiting.

Part of the reason that the Protectorate had managed to swing putting the Graveyard off-limits was that the final desperate struggle to survive of Excelsior's inhabitants had stripped the Trojan cluster of any useable resources – most specifically, potable water. Most of the rocks that followed Excelsior Three in its orbit were just plain rock now, where a cluster like this should have had ice asteroids and a few captured comets.

"There it is," Jenna said quietly as they finished slowing to a crawl and began drifting into the cluster. In the center of the Lagrange point was the immense structure of the space station that had been the last, doomed, hope of an entire species.

It was possible, sort of, to identify the original mining platform at its center. Welded onto that pitted and ancient heart, though, were the remnants of transport ships, cargo containers, and even entire hollowed-out asteroids. It was dead and silent now, a monument in black iron and meteor pitted rock.

"There is a *lot* of debris out there," Jenna said quietly. "It's full of iron and heavy metals – pretty much every sensor we have is picking up nothing but static."

"No one else can find *us* either," David reminded her. "That's why we're here."

"So, any idea where the *Luciole* is?"

"Keiko gave us a specific set of co-ordinates," he said, typing them into the computer. A flashing sphere appeared on the main screen. "We're to decelerate to zero relative to the Graveyard Station there, and wait for Seule to contact us."

"I keep expecting ghosts to come jumping out of the shadows," Jenna complained. "Why the hell are we meeting here?"

"Because nobody comes here except archeologists, and the latest expedition isn't due in for eleven months," David replied. "It's a perfect place to hand over enough guns to conquer a world."

Jenna shivered visibly. "Yeah, because *that* thought makes me more comfortable."

The Captain shrugged as the *Blue Jay* entered the agreed co-ordinates, and the maneuvering thrusters brought the massive freighter to a halt relative to the ancient alien station. There wasn't much he could say to Jenna beyond that he trusted Keiko, and he wasn't even certain that was wise.

"Do you see anything?" he finally asked.

"Nothing," his XO replied. "Damien?"

The Mage on the video link shrugged. "I can't see anything the ship can't," he said dryly. "So right now, I'm feeling a bit blind."

The *Blue Jay*'s bridge was silent, the two officers and the linked-in Mage all straining their own senses and the ship's, trying to see *something* - anything.

"There! What's that?" Damien asked.

David followed the icon that the Mage threw up on the screen. It was blinking on one of the larger asteroids, a ten kilometer long hunk of iron and rock that a long-ago mining ship had cut a massive gorge into to extract whatever the aliens had needed to sustain a few more years of life.

Inside that massive gorge, a light was flickering. After a few moments, the light rose out of the gorge and revealed itself to be the fusion maneuvering thrusters of a starship. The ship was smaller than the *Blue Jay*, only three hundred meters and narrow for most of its length with a sizeable 'mushroom head' radiation cap shield at the front and hefty engines at the back.

"That's a Navy High Priority Courier," David recognized it aloud. The Navy had built them fifty or so years ago to carry small cargos at extremely high speed speeds – the ships had been fitted with antimatter engines and carried a warship's complement of Mages.

"Those were all decommissioned, weren't they?" Jenna asked, and David nodded.

"Mars decided that mounting antimatter engines on full-size freighters was more valuable in an emergency, and that they could use normal freighters the rest of the time," he confirmed. "The last one was supposed to be scrapped five years ago, but it looks like our Captain Seule saved one from the breakers."

Antimatter was expensive, and most civilian ships didn't use it. Somehow, though, David was sure that the *Luciole* still used antimatter in her main engines – she was, after all, a blockade runner. Corporations would hire and use private warships, but they rarely mounted military grade engines on them.

Once the spindly blockade runner was clear of the gorge and directed towards the *Blue Jay*, the computer informed them of an incoming transmission. With a swipe across the command pad on his chair, David threw the image up on his main screen.

"You're our drop-off, I presume?" the dark-haired man in the dark red shirt on the screen asked him. "I can't see someone randomly stopping in exactly the right spot, not in this place," he gestured at the space around them."

"If you are Captain Nathan Seule, then yes, I'm your delivery," Rice confirmed. "Captain David Rice, of the *Blue Jay*."

"I am indeed Captain Seule of the *Luciole*, Captain Rice. I see that Miss Alabaster delivered as always. How are you set up for cargo transfer?"

"I have four heavy lift shuttles," David told him. "I think we should be able to transfer the cargo quickly, depending on your own resources."

"Good to hear, Captain," Seule told him. "We only have two shuttles ourselves, so it would take a while if we're left to just my resources. Shall we be about it? I aim to not be around if the miners in-system start asking questions, if you catch my drift."

"I'll have my pilots start loading containers," David said. "Have your pilots contact my First Pilot Kelzin as they approach, he'll guide them in."

#

The entire process of deep space cargo transfer, without the many and varied tools and resources of a space dock, was a new one for Damien. The *Luciole* matched vectors with the *Blue Jay* at about twenty kilometers distance, just far enough that both ships would be safe to light off their main drives, and then dispatched their two shuttles over.

By the time the *Luciole* shuttles arrived, Kelzin and his three pilots had their shuttles out as well. Once the transport shuttles, each minuscule compared to their parent vessels but still forty meters long apiece, were in place, Jenna released the catches holding six of the cargo containers of weapons to the *Blue Jay*'s cargo pylons.

The ten thousand cubic meter containers, each rated for ten thousand tons of cargo, drifted away from the *Jay*. The shuttles, already positioned above each container, swept in and latched onto the containers. Once the connection was secure, they flew over to the *Luciole*, where they repeated the process in reverse.

Both Kelzin's and Seule's pilots clearly knew the drill. The first transfer of six containers went without a hitch, and Damien started to relax – at least with regards to the transfer. There was a lot of small debris drifting through the Lagrange point, and every minute or two, the laser turrets of one vessel or the other would take out a good-sized rock.

"Keep an eye over there," Damien told the pilots, flicking a warning icon over to all eight ships. "We've got a good sized chunk of rock heading our way. The lasers won't be able to blast it, but its big enough and moving slow enough that you should be able to maneuver around it."

As the shuttles continued with the second load of cargo, Damien kept an eye on the rock. It was a mid-sized asteroid, roughly a kilometer long and three hundred meters across at its widest point. With the futz of minor debris in the area, he couldn't tell more about it than that it was primarily iron, and that it was going to pass pretty much exactly between the two freighters.

He figured he could break it up if it turned out to be a threat to either ship, but he also had no reason to expose the presence of *Blue Jay*'s amplifier to the crew of the *Luciole*. They knew nothing about the smugglers they were supplying cargo to, after all.

The second transfer of cargo went as smoothly as the first, and the third as well. As the six shuttles headed back towards the *Jay*, Captain Seule opened communications again.

"I think my shuttles can grab the last two containers," he told Captain Rice. "It's been a pleasure doing business with a competent crew, Captain Rice. If we're ever together in more civilized space, look me up. I think I owe you dinner."

"I'll take you up on that," Rice replied. "For now, I think we'd both like to be a *long* way away from this place. It gives me the creeps."

"I hear you," Seule replied with a laugh.

The last two containers were loaded onto the shuttles. They then paused, orbiting the *Blue Jay* for a few moments as the asteroid Damien had picked up on passed through the space between the two ships.

"That's strange," the senior *Luciole* pilot, a gruff-faced man named, of all things, Vera, said over the channel. "I'm getting an energy reflection off that rock."

Damien took a look at the rock on the scanners and blinked. It wasn't a reflection – all along the dead rock, fusion thrusters were blasting to life.

Without thinking, he grabbed the *Jay*'s simulacrum and merged with the ship. The power of the amplifier, the runes woven throughout the ship, sank into him and he breathed out, focusing his gaze on the asteroid as the ships that had been hiding on the asteroid.

He didn't recognize them – they were small and narrow, almost missile shaped but significantly larger. Before he could say more, though, all fifteen of them fired off main engines – and blasted for the *Blue Jay* at eight gravities.

"*Boarding torpedoes!*" David shouted, and Damien finally recognized the threat.

He had only seconds before the tiny attack ships reached the *Blue Jay*, but he was linked into the amplifier. Time slowed as he shifted his consciousness into the runes, slowing reality *just* enough to let him channel his magic.

A whip of fire, the deadly close-range attack spell he'd been practicing from the Enforcer manuals, appeared in deep space and slashed across the ships. His magic and the deadly fire danced from torpedo to torpedo, shattering hulls, detonating engines – and ending lives. He didn't know how many men each of the fifteen boarding torpedoes carried. Even one might carry enough men to take the *Blue Jay* if he let them board.

The last boarding torpedo died a hundred and twenty meters from the hull of the *Jay*, as Damien unleashed the fury of a fully functioning amplifier on his ship's enemies.

#

"What the *fuck?*" Seule exclaimed over the comms channel.

"Those were boarding torpedoes, old Navy issue," David said grimly. "Someone was trying to sneak up on us – if Damien hadn't been practicing, I think at least some would have made it through."

Unlike his Mage, David knew that each of those torpedoes was rated to carry eighteen soldiers, and that Damien had probably just killed almost three hundred people.

"I meant, what the *fuck* did your ship just *do?!*"

"You're alive, Captain Seule," Rice told him flatly. "I suggest you stop asking questions you don't want to know the answer to and collect your shuttles."

The red-shirted man on the other ship threw up his hands.

"Fine, keep your secrets Captain – they ain't no business of mine, you're right," he told Rice. "But what the hell gets someone to launch that kind of op to try and catch you?"

"Money and revenge," Rice said grimly. "We hurt a bounty hunter bad a few weeks back – if he could find us, he'd throw that at us."

He didn't need to explain the value of the *Jay*'s amplifier. If the other man guessed what Damien had just done, he could guess why the Syndicate would want David's ship.

Seule sighed.

"Listen, Captain – you need to get out of everyone's sight it seems," he told Rice. "Head to Darkport – you should be able to bury yourself in the mess there, maybe upgrade your ship and find some extra cargo to take wherever you're going."

"Darkport is a myth," David pointed out. Rumor mentioned a place by that name – an asteroid complex in an otherwise uninhabited system, where no authority ran. Amber was Libertarian – but Darkport was an anarchic hellhole, if it even existed.

"It exists," Seule told him. "More importantly for your little problem, it's a neutral zone for bounty hunters – if they try and claim a bounty on the station, they're banned for life. Assuming they survive to leave at all."

"Sounds like somewhere we could begin to recharge," David admitted. "But since I didn't even believe it existed, I don't have the co-ordinates."

"Sending them over," Seule told him with a grin. "Tell 'em Seule sent you, that'll get you a docking berth if nothing more."

"David, the Graveyard!" Jenna suddenly interrupted, shouting and pointing at the screen in a moment of panic.

Graveyard Station was just over eight light seconds from where they'd rendezvoused – almost two and a half million kilometers. Emerging over the shadow of the stations massive, sensor-blocking bulk was the characteristic white flare of antimatter thrusters.

A familiar looking jump yacht came around the alien station, the same ovoid vessel that had picked up the shuttles from the failed boarding attempt in Chrysanthemum. This time, however, the other ship clearly wasn't planning on running. As soon as the bounty hunter ship was clear of her cover, she opened fire.

Whatever the ship had originally been built as, she'd clearly been heavily upgraded since. No less than twelve missiles shot forward from the front of the 'yacht,' already carrying a significant velocity before more antimatter thrusters flickered into existence.

These weren't the normal, dirt-cheap, fusion thruster rockets of an ordinary pirate. The missiles blazing towards the *Blue Jay* were the missiles the Martian Navy had used during David's own service twenty years before – and would cross the eight light-second gap in under three minutes.

"Clear the RFLAMs," he ordered Jenna. "Get us a course directly away from that asshole. Damien – the RFLAMs are *not* rated for military grade missiles. Can you do what you did to the boarding torps?"

Damien lifted his gaze to meet David's through the camera, and the Captain was shocked to see that the youth's eyes were bloodshot and exhausted, like he'd just finished an all-night bender.

"I don't know," he whispered, barely loud enough for David to hear. "I don't think I'm strong enough."

"Do what you can," David told him. "You've already saved us all once today."

The young man nodded slowly, and returned his hands to the silver miniature of the *Blue Jay*.

David returned his own gaze to the sensors showing the space around him. Acceleration was pressing him back into his chair now, as Jenna pointed his freighter away from the pursuing bounty hunter. The *Blue Jay*'s three gravities of emergency acceleration was *nothing* compared to the pursuing missiles.

"Entering laser range," Jenna said grimly, her fingers dancing across her console as she opened fire. The ship's computer superimposed the invisible laser beams on their screen, and a pair of missiles disappeared as she scored direct hits.

Then the entire region of space around the missiles dissolved into gray static on the screen as the missiles, real military weapons, engaged their electronic counter measures and turned the *Blue Jay*'s sensor beams to hash.

"I can't get a bead," Jenna exclaimed. "I can't even estimate time to impact."

David hit a button on his controls that took over direct control of the turrets from her, and then brought up a program he'd 'borrowed' from the Martian Navy years before. The turrets started to fire again, sweeping cuts designed to try and cover as much space as possible.

He glanced at the link to Damien. The Mage could see slightly better through the *Jay*'s sensors than they could. What the laser pattern missed, the Mage *might* be able to stop – but David wasn't sure he'd like the price.

The static cloud of the missiles grew ever closer to the *Blue Jay*. There was a flash that might have been the lasers hitting a missile. A couple more. Even in the best case, he couldn't stop the remaining missiles before they reached his ship.

For a long moment, David Rice knew, once again, that he and his crew were going to die.

Then an immense explosion erupted in space where the missiles had been. Antimatter flared and died as *dozens* of sub-munitions swept through the bounty hunters salvo. The static flashed and disappeared, revealing a single surviving missile, still running desperately towards the *Blue Jay*.

The *Luciole* swept past it, a military grade missile defense turret swatting it from space contemptuously as her *own* missile launchers spat fire back at the bounty hunter, and the image of Captain Seule appeared on Rice's screen.

"I was starting to feel hurt that everybody had forgot us," he said cheerfully. "Get out of here, Captain. I aim to teach a lesson here - one that *fils a putain de lignage déloyal* won't forget!"

#

"Do you have the co-ordinates Seule sent us?" David asked over the bridge link as Damien gently massaged his temples.

"I've got them," he replied, slowly. "I'll need at least an hour to run the calculations and recover from the attack before I can jump."

On his screens, Damien watched the running battle between the *Luciole* and the bounty hunter. Recognizing the greater immediate threat, the bounty hunter had launched a second salvo of missiles at the blockade runner – which had responded by demonstrating that it mounted four military grade battle-lasers concealed under its radiation cap.

They'd scored at least one hit, and then the bounty hunter ship had turned and run. Blazing away at a full ten gravities – the ship *had* to have magical gravity – the bounty hunter had ducked behind Graveyard Station even as Seule had used a second multi-warhead missile to wipe away the missiles aimed at his ship.

Then Damien felt the strange, almost indescribable to a non-Mage, sensation of a nearby jump. The hunter was gone.

Resting his head in his hands against the *Blue Jay*'s own acceleration, he checked that his computer was running the new jump details for the first jump of their course to Darkport. A glance at the co-ordinates themselves revealed why Seule had suggested they head to the outlaw port. Darkport was in a system less than ten light years from Excelsior.

That system was supposedly completely uninhabited. It had no habitable worlds, and lacked the extra appeal of multiple exposed planetary cores that had brought a dedicated mining operation to Excelsior. It held just a single gas giant, a sparse asteroid belt, and a couple of heat-seared rock balls orbiting a bloated and radiation-spewing giant red star.

Seule's ship was quickly lost in the debris field of the Lagrange point as the *Blue Jay* flew outwards, towards the spaces clear of debris that Damien could jump from. He needed the time to recover from defending the ship against the first attack more than anything else.

He wondered how many people he'd just killed. He knew nothing about boarding torpedoes, and he knew that looking them up right now was probably a bad idea. His defense had cut so close that he suspected if he *hadn't* been spending his time studying the more advanced Enforcer combat spells he wouldn't have been able to stop them all.

If someone had been judging what a Mage with Damien's formal training and an amplifier could do, and based their attack plan on that... they'd planned exceedingly well. He would have failed, and his friends would have been captured or killed.

The spell had taken a lot out of him though. Not as much as a jump – he would be ready to jump before the calculations were complete – but more than any defense spell he'd known before. He couldn't repeat that kind of attack.

Sighing, Damien starting reviewing the complete parts of his jump calculation. Stopping the boarding torpedoes had proven one thing to him – he wasn't strong enough. An Enforcer or a Navy Mage would have been able to do what he did and then carry on and take out the missiles too. A Navy Mage might be better trained for it, but a lot of it was also sheer power.

If they ever had to face a true warship, with a functioning amplifier and trained Navy Mages, there was nothing Damien would be able to do to save the *Blue Jay*.

#

Deep space jump layovers were the safest place Damien knew of. Exhausted and battered from defending the ship and jumping, he passed out almost as soon as he made it back to his quarters. He barely registered Kelly joining him several hours later, waking up barely enough to shift over for the engineer to join him.

They were both violently awoken by a sudden burst of emergency acceleration that threw them from the bed as the clanging acceleration alarm began to ring throughout the ship.

Damien, half-naked, stumbled to his intercom and triggered it.

"What's happening?" he demanded.

"The hunter is *here*," Jenna told him. "Get to the simulacrum Chamber – *fuck he just launched missiles.*"

Damien was already moving by the time the XO had stopped swearing. He didn't even bother with a shirt, directing his personal field of gravity to sling him out of his quarters and along the corridor of Rib Four. Whatever damage Seule's *Luciole* had done to the bounty hunter's ship clearly hadn't been enough.

In the back of his mind, he was counting seconds as he charged through the ship. Everyone else aboard was crushed to the side by the three gravities of acceleration, but he burned magic recklessly to pull himself through the ship.

With thirty seconds to spare, he saw the simulacrum Chamber at the end of the hallway. Breathing deeply, he kicked off and added his magic *to* the three gravities of acceleration the *Blue Jay* was pulling. A

215

flick of power popped the door open before he hit it, and then he was in the Chamber, heading for the simulacrum and the platform under it for when the ship was under acceleration.

He missed the simulacrum.

His right leg hit the platform and *snapped*, the heart-wrenching noise echoing through the oval chamber at the heart of the ship as the pain slammed into him.

Damien didn't check to see where the missiles were. He didn't look to see how close he'd cut it. He *somehow* drove the pain down, and slapped his bare palms onto the silver simulacrum.

He looked up to see the missiles screaming towards him, in final acquisition, and *jumped*.

#

He realized when he woke up in the ship's infirmary that he'd passed out from the pain. His leg was numb and stiff, and when Damien glanced downwards, he saw it was wrapped in the dark blue extruded plastic casts that the ships auto-doc robot applied to broken limbs.

Standing next to him, putting away a hypodermic, was Jenna. Kelly hovered behind her, he realized, and David was on the intercom screen from the bridge.

"The auto-doc is screaming at me that this is irresponsible and dangerous," Jenna said quietly, "but we needed you awake. We jumped an hour ago – about five seconds before those missiles were about to split all four Ribs in half."

"Split the Ribs?" Damien asked, blinking away the fuzz as the amphetamine the XO had injected him with began to course through his bloodstream.

"Yeah – the missiles had split into four groups and were making kinetic attack runs on the ribs," Jenna explained. "Given their velocity, they'd have snapped the ribs in half but left the keel intact. I have no idea why."

Damien winced at her use of the word 'snapped,' then paused as he thought about it.

"If they severed the Ribs, it would break the amplifier matrix," he said quietly. "The matrix might work with one of the Ribs broken – two would be a stretch, and I wouldn't want to even *touch* the simulacrum if we'd lost three or four."

"He was trying to cripple us, so we couldn't run or fight," David said grimly from the intercom. "That makes sense, even if I have *no* idea how he found us."

"It's supposedly sort of possible to make out a vector in an outgoing jump flare," Damien said quietly. "You need *really* good sensors to even start to get a ghost, and supposedly you can't narrow it down more than twenty or thirty degree arc."

"I'm guessing this prick is a bit better than that," Jenna said drily.

Kelly snuck up next to Damien's bed and took his hand. He gave her a pained grin, and then turned back to the Captain and XO.

"Any sign of him yet?"

"Nothing," David told them. "But if he could follow us from the Graveyard..."

"He can follow us again," Damien agreed, sighing and wincing as the motion moved his leg. "My guess is that he's got two Mages aboard, and is waiting until both can jump. That way, even if I pull a Kenneth and can jump away when he gets here, he can follow us. And with only *one* Mage aboard..."

Everyone in the room winced at the mention of Kenneth McLaughlin, the *Blue Jay*'s previous Ship's Mage who had died saving them from a pirate attack before they arrived at Damien's home world of Sherwood.

"What's your guess?" David asked.

"If I've been out an hour, maybe four hours," Damien replied. "Given what they were prepared to sacrifice in that boarding attempt, I just bet they're willing to risk a Mage jumping a little too early – that isn't fatal. Just very painful."

"So what do we do?" Jenna said quietly. "Our turrets can't stop military missiles. Damien can't jump us away. Do we just sit here and *die*?"

"If he's following us, where will he jump in?" Kelly asked, interjecting herself into the conversation and squeezing Damien's hand.

"At a guess, he'll try for about the same position as last time," Damien replied. "They can probably jump the same exactly one light year as I can, so they'll come out almost exactly where they were before relative to us."

"So we know where he'll come out," Kelly said aloud, and everyone in the room, including Damien looked at the young engineer. "I have an idea, sir," she told David.

#

Freighters were not, by their nature, stealthy creatures. Nonetheless, that was what David was aiming for five hours later. They'd shut down the engines. Halted the spinning of the Ribs. Turned

217

off every exterior light. He'd even, over Kellers' protests, ordered the engineer to shut down the main heat exchanger.

They couldn't do the last for very long – an hour at most – or they'd start to cook in their own skins. But it made them, for a little while, as invisible as they could be.

Kelly had joined him and Jenna on the bridge to help execute her plan. She was having trouble not watching the screen showing the simulacrum Chamber where Damien was floating next to the simulacrum, doing his best to ignore his broken leg.

Exactly five hours, almost to the second, after Damien had jumped them away their sensors reported a new jump flare. Erupting into deep space just over three million kilometers away, the familiar sight of the bounty hunter's modified yacht appeared from nothingness. The *Blue Jay*'s cameras had just enough resolution to show the black and twisted scar along the surface of the ovoid hull where Seule's lasers had hit – but also enough to show the still functional gunports of the hunter's dozen missile launchers.

"Arrogant asshole," David heard Jenna muttered, and shook his head. He couldn't disagree. If the *Blue Jay* had had anything resembling real weapons, they could have opened fire immediately. A battle laser couldn't normally score reliable hits at this range, but it would take thirty seconds or so for the ship to start moving. A Martian destroyer could have shredded the yacht before it even reacted.

To be fair, if the hunter was going up against a Martian destroyer, he was utterly out-gunned and out-massed to begin with. The ship was clearly built to hunt ordinary pirate ships – similar in hull type to the bounty hunter vessel, but with weaker engines and inferior weapons.

"Does he see us?" Kelly asked.

"Not yet," Jenna told her. "He will, though."

A blinking green sphere appeared on the screen – the target zone that the bounty hunter *had* to move through for Kelly's plan to work.

"Come on," David muttered. "You know we're here, and you know where we'd have emerged. Come into my parlor."

"I'm not feeling overly spider-esque here boss," Jenna told him with a laugh. "Here he comes!"

The hunter's ship had lit off its antimatter drives, heading in the *Blue Jay*'s direction. It was impossible to tell if he was simply heading for the logical point, or had picked up residual heat on the *Jay*'s hull. The lack of weapons fire did suggest the former, but they would only know if he'd missed them if he passed the two million kilometer mark.

In none of their previous encounters had the ship come that close – the bounty hunter clearly knew a *lot* about amplifiers.

"Come on, come on," Kelly said quietly, echoing David's words of a moment earlier. The bounty hunter was headed directly for the center of her sphere. Her hands were flying over her console, setting up adjustments and fallback plans.

"Shit! He's gone active!" Jenna snapped. A blinking alert noted that the bounty hunter had fired off a high energy radar pulse, sweeping the area around him. "He's got us – and the tanker!"

Floating in deep space, most of the way towards the bounty hunter's ship was the in-system fuelling tanker they'd stolen from Chrysanthemum. It was abandoned with no crew, running on a simple program fed into the Artificial Sequential Intelligence they'd loaded into its computers.

"Let's give him a target," David ordered. "Kellers, fire up the heat exchangers and give me engines. It's time to play bait."

"He's got to see it," Kelly said quietly.

"It's not whether he *sees* it that matters," David told her. "It's if he *understands* – so let's make him think we ditched it to save mass."

Seconds later, the *Blue Jay*'s mighty engines flared to life. On the link to the simulacrum Chamber, Damien cried out in pain as the acceleration drove his broken leg into the platform, but shook his head sharply when everyone on the bridge looked to him.

"*Look*," he snapped, gesturing to the main screen.

Despite detecting the tanker, the hunter had ignored it – driving directly towards the *Jay* and increased its acceleration. He was in the green sphere now, drawing closer to its center as his speed increase.

"Make the call, Kelly," David told her. The engineer had done the math, programmed the intelligence. She had the numbers on her console to know when to activate her program.

The hunter was only a thousand kilometers away from the tanker when the young woman hit the command. It grew closer as the message flew across the light seconds.

Then the tankers oversized engines, designed to carry a heavy load of super-dense compressed hydrogen, flared to life at full power – throwing the half empty spacecraft through space at almost fifteen gravities.

The bounty hunter had less than ten seconds to react, and their engines had only just started to flare sideways, trying desperately to change their course, when a quarter million tons of starship and fuel slammed into them at over a hundred kilometers a second.

The fireball when the hunter ship's antimatter met the tanker's fuel tanks rivaled a small sun.

#

Azure had heard that most humans who looked at the Graveyard found it depressing – a warning sign of the fate that humanity might

219

share. Staring at the ancient alien station from the bridge of the *Azure Gauntlet*, however, he saw something different. He saw a fate that could *never* befall humanity – thanks to Mages like him and those who had come before him, a single cosmic accident like the one that had befallen Excelsior could not destroy humanity.

Most humans, he reflected, were not nearly appreciative enough for all that Mages did for them.

Behind where the crime-lord stood, his hands crossed behind his back, Wong's bridge bustled as the cruiser's crew pulled together the many tiny pieces of data their commander needed to establish his course.

"Well, Mr. Wong?" he asked after examining Graveyard Station for a few minutes. "What do you have?"

"There was a battle," Wong said calmly. "Your hunter tried to ambush the *Blue Jay* with small craft of some kind. They failed, destroyed by the amplifier. He then tried a direct missile attack, but was intercepted by Navy-grade anti-missile munitions fired by a third vessel. The *Blue Jay* fled. So did your hunter. The Navy ship disappeared as well."

"So Able failed. I am not entirely surprised."

Wong shrugged. "The hunter is aware of the consequences of failure at this point," he pointed out delicately. "I imagine he followed the *Jay* further."

Azure made a throw-away gesture with one hand, his gaze returned to the ominous bulk of Graveyard Station.

"At this point, it no longer matters," he told Wong. "Can you track Rice's ship?"

"I'll need some more time," the tracker answered. "Twenty minutes or so."

"Take thirty," the crime lord ordered. "We cannot afford to fail when we are this close – I *must* have either that ship or Montgomery. We will do whatever is necessary to achieve this; do you understand me Mister Wong?"

There was a long silence behind him, and then he felt the ship captain bow.

"I understand completely, Lord Azure."

#

The stolen cruiser orbited the Lagrange point for another forty minutes, and then vanished in the energy burst of a jump.

Alaura Stealey, Hand of the Mage-King of Mars, watched it for the entire time it was in the Excelsior system. The *Tides of Justice* had arrived barely twenty minutes before the unidentified ship, and they'd gone completely dark the moment she'd realized the cruiser wasn't flying a Navy beacon – apparently, quickly enough they'd gone unnoticed.

"She's a *Minotaur* class armored cruiser, ma'am," Mage-Lieutenant Harmon told her. She'd joined him and the ship's Captain on the bridge for this approach, hoping they would find the *Blue Jay* in Excelsior. "Her hull number's been scrubbed, but we're running her drive harmonics now. We *may* be able to identify her if they haven't changed the engines too much."

"Lieutenant, '*Minotaur* class' doesn't mean much to me," the Hand admitted. "Details?"

"An older class of cruisers," he explained. "First built forty years ago, there are twelve left in the Navy but most have been retired and broken up for scrap."

"But not this one."

"I presume, Lady Hand," Mage-Captain Judy Barnett interjected calmly, "that this one is listed as having been scrapped. That's why I want to identify her if at all possible. We need to understand how one of our cruisers ended up in the hands of pirates."

"It appears that the Blue Star Syndicate may be more dangerous than we feared," Alaura agreed.

"How do you know it's the Blue Star?" Barnett asked. The Mage-Captain had never quite seemed reconciled to being a glorified chauffeur to the Hand, but the sudden appearance of a rogue Navy cruiser had brought about quite the transformation.

"The Blue Star Syndicate has been pursuing Captain Rice for some years," Alaura explained. "No other organization would be willing to commit such a vessel, if they had one, to such a wild goose chase."

"Ma'ams!" one of the sensor techs suddenly interrupted. "There's another ship in the cluster."

"Where?" Barnett demanded. "Show me."

The sensor tech highlighted a region of the asteroid cluster, almost half-way across the clump of rocks from where the pirate cruiser had been.

"She's hiding hard, tucked up right next to an asteroid the inhabitants of Graveyard had mined out," the tech reported. "Without our sensor upgrades, we'd have missed her completely!"

The *Tides of Justice*, Alaura reflected, was the newest and most advanced destroyer the Navy had. She remembered something in her briefing on the ship about her being equipped with the latest breakthroughs in sensors and scanners from Legatus – something to do with magnetic field resolutions.

"Hail her," she instructed sharply. Barnett threw her a cross look, but the Captain held her tongue.

"Recording now," a communications tech told her, and Alaura faced the recorders.

"Unidentified vessel, this is Alaura Stealey, Hand of the Mage-King of Mars," she said sharply. "Please identify yourself and explain your business in a quarantine zone."

There was no response for a moment, and then the tech threw a video channel on screen. A young handsome man in a deep red shirt faced the camera with a twisted smile on his face.

"Lady Hand," he greeted her. "I am Captain Nathan Seule of the *Luciole*. You are known to me by reputation, and I assure you that I am simply passing through."

Seule. Of all the ships and all the captains to show up here, it had to be Nathan Seule.

"You are known to me as well," she said bluntly. What rebellions in the Fringe that Stealey had dealt with that *hadn't* involved Keiko Alabaster had involved Nathan Seule – and many had involved both. "But honestly, today I don't care if you were shipping guns or native art – did you see what happened here?"

The smuggler was hesitant for a long moment, and then nodded sharply.

"I don't normally aim to co-operate with the Protectorate, begging your pardon ma'am," he said quietly. "But jes' this once, I think I can make an exception. I met another ship here for a cargo transfer, but then we got jumped by a bounty hunter. We drove them off, but I figured here was as safe a place as any to fix up the scratching they gave my paint job... and then, well, that cruiser shows up a day later."

"A day ago," Stealey said calmly. "Was the ship you met the *Blue Jay* under Captain Rice?"

She could almost watch Seule desire to help Rice war with his desire to keep secrets, until the Captain sighed again.

"A man doesn't have a choice when faced with this, does he?" he asked her.

"I don't think so," she agreed.

"It was the *Blue Jay*," he confirmed. "And that cruiser – it's after Captain Rice too, right?"

"Most likely," she said. "And if it's commanded by who I fear, they may be able to track the *Blue Jay* into jump. I need to know where they went, Captain Seule."

"Ma'am, there are some secrets that are not mine to reveal, however pretty I think you are or friendly Captain Rice was," Seule said calmly.

"Captain Seule – that cruiser is going to follow the *Blue Jay* wherever they went," Alaura Stealey told him quietly. "Whoever shelters him, whoever aids him, is going to face the wrath of Mikhail Azure. Whoever you're protecting may already be doomed."

The dark-haired Captain nodded once, and sighed again.

"I sent them to Darkport, Lady Hand," he said calmly. "I'll send you the co-ordinates. But if you'll excuse me, I think I need to find a new region of space to frequent."

Darkport.

About the only place in the galaxy Alaura would call a worse hive of scum and villainy than Amber.

The video channel was cut off, and Alaura watched the *Luciole* break away from its hiding spot and flare its engines – heading away from the *Tides*.

"Captain Barnett," she said quietly. "Set your course for Nia Kriti."

"Ma'am?" the Mage-Captain replied. "We have the co-ordinates for Darkport."

"This ship is extremely modern and extremely well-crewed," the Hand told her ship's captain softly. "But she cannot face a cruiser alone."

"There is a Navy base at Nia Kriti. We need more ships."

###

5

Alaura Stealey was a Hand of the Mage-King of Mars, the King's voice and his sword in the worlds beyond the Sol System – a Judge and warrior; the representative of the executive branch of the government that ruled humanity.

She was not used to being kept waiting.

The gray-haired woman stood impatiently in the outer office of Mage-Admiral Lillian Castello, commander of the Royal Martian Navy's Seventh Cruiser Squadron, and the station commander of the Nia Kriti Naval Base.

Stealey had arrived in the system nine hours before and her personal transport had set new speed records closing the distance to the Naval Base. After that rush, however, she'd now been left cooling her heels in the Admiral's office for forty minutes.

She turned back towards the door with its Marine sentry, about to order the neatly turned out young man to stand aside, when it *finally* slid open. A middle aged woman in the dark blue uniform of a Navy Captain exited the office, presumably the commanding officer of the cruiser they were aboard, the *Rising Sun of Gallantry.*

Alaura was through the door into Castello's office before the ship's captain had half-completed her salute. The Admiral sat on the other side of a massive desk of dark black wood, polished to a fine sheen, her mouth half-open in an unvoiced protest as the Hand crossed the space to her desk and stood, facing her in silence.

The two women regarded each other for a long moment. Alaura knew that what Castello saw was unimpressive. The Hand wore an unmarked, black, version of the Navy's uniform, from which hung the open-palmed golden hand of her symbol of office. She was short, stocky, and graying – unbothered by her appearance, she'd declined the many and varied treatments available to a citizen of the Protectorate to reverse the look of age.

Castello, on the other hand, was a lithe red-headed woman who looked in her early thirties – and was closer, Alaura knew, to seventy.

"How may I… assist you?" the Admiral said after a long pregnant pause.

"You were sent a brief of the situation and the forces I requested," Alaura told her calmly. "I presume you have reviewed it?"

"Frankly, Lady Hand, I have not had time," Castello replied, her tone icy. "I am responsible for a security area of fourteen star systems. I cannot drop everything every time a self-important flunky from Mars arrives."

Alaura regarded the other woman with a degree of calm she didn't feel.

"I am sorry," she said calmly. "Did you just tell me you intentionally disregarded a Priority Alpha-One Communique from a *Hand of the Mage-King?*"

"Everyone who comes to this system thinks their needs are Alpha-One, Lady Stealey," Castello replied. "It is my job to decide whose needs actually *are.*"

"Who is your second-in-command?" Alaura asked.

"What?" Castello replied, startled.

"Who is your second-in-command?" Alaura repeated. "Since you are so busy, I will do you the courtesy of not imposing further on your time."

"Mage-Commodore James Medici of the Fifteenth Destroyers," the Admiral said slowly.

"Very well. Pack your things," Alaura ordered. "Mage-*Admiral* Medici will be assuming command of the Seventh Cruisers, as well as the Fifteenth Destroyers, to accompany me on my mission."

"You don't have that authority!" Castello bellowed, surging to her feet.

"I am His Majesty's *Hand*, Admiral," Stealey said flatly. "Be grateful I do not relieve you of your *commission.* You will transfer your flag to one of the ships remaining – I will be taking your cruisers and Medici's destroyers."

"If I were you," she continued, "I would *pray* that your delay does not result in the failure of my mission. His Majesty will be... *displeased* if that's the case."

Alaura turned on her heel and strode from the Admiral's office, leaving the woman whose career she'd just shattered staring after her in shock.

#

James Medici was waiting for Alaura once she returned to the *Tides of Justice*, the destroyer she used as her personal transport. The newly-promoted Mage-Admiral was a tiny man with skin as black as night and the slanted eyes of a Martian native.

"Lady Hand," he greeted her calmly.

"You'll need to get new insignia, Admiral Medici," Stealey told him calmly. He still wore the single star of a Navy Commodore, not the two stars of an Admiral.

"I believed reviewing your brief and meeting with you were a higher priority," he told her dryly. "I did not wish to raise your ire as Lillian has done."

"That would be difficult," the Hand replied. "My office," she ordered curtly, allowing Mage-Lieutenant Harmon, her personal aide and 'Navy Liaison' to lead the way. Medici was silent until they reached her office and Harmon had left them in private.

"Admiral Castello is a capable officer with a lot on her plate," he said quietly. "Your arrival was unexpected, and this region has more than a few priority concerns."

"That is my presumption, Admiral Medici," Alaura told him. "That is why the Admiral is still employed. That said, I need her ships – and I *don't* trust her to command them in action. Don't disappoint me."

He nodded sharply, standing calmly at attention as she took a seat behind her desk. She gestured Medici to a chair, but he shrugged and remained standing.

"You have reviewed the brief," Alaura reminded him. "Your opinion?"

"The cruiser represents a significant threat to the security of the Fringe," Medici agreed. "She is insufficient to present a major threat to the MidWorlds or the Core, of course, but her presence in the hands of the Blue Star Syndicate is a concern.

"That said, the force level you are requesting seems excessive," he continued. "A squadron of cruisers, a squadron of destroyers and three Marine battalion transports? I've seen planetwide rebellions suppressed with one cruiser, let alone eight with as many destroyers."

"You have professional blinders, Admiral," Alaura told him calmly. Unlike with Castello, at least he'd *read* the briefing and seemed prepared to listen. "You're focusing on the rogue warship and not the other factors in play."

"Ma'am?"

"The destruction of the Syndicate's cruiser is a priority," she told him, "but it is one of *two* Alpha-One priorities at play here. The second is the capture of the *Blue Jay* and Ship's Mage Damien Montgomery – and Montgomery *must* be captured alive. That requires numbers, to make sure he doesn't run."

"I also wish to minimize casualties when bringing the Syndicate cruiser down," Alaura continued, "for which overwhelming force seems wise. Could you guarantee the destruction of the ship with no casualties with a lesser force?"

Medici shrugged, still standing at a slightly relaxed form of attention as he faced her, his hands clasped behind his back.

"There are no guarantees in combat, ma'am," he reminded her. "Even outnumbered seventeen to one and out-massed nine to one, the Syndicate ship may still inflict damage."

"The ships are available," Alaura concluded, "so we will use them. They will also come in handy in exploiting the opportunity we have been handed – the opportunity I want those Marine transports for."

"I'll admit to being unclear on that, ma'am," the Admiral said. "My understanding is that we are pursuing the *Blue Jay*, as we know her destination and that the Blue Star ship is also chasing her. Why are we bringing enough Marines to fight a mid-sized war?"

"I take it you didn't note *where* we know *Blue Jay* is going, Admiral," the Hand replied. "My information is that the *Jay* is headed to Darkport to take on supplies and make repairs. I have the co-ordinates."

"If we can bring our various prey to bay there, so much the better. But I see no reason to pass up the opportunity to wipe out the center of the Protectorate's slave trade when it is handed to me on a silver platter!"

The little Admiral considered for a long moment, and then nodded.

"Darkport," he said quietly. "That's a pockmark on the universe I'll be glad to burn out."

#

"I guess that answers that question," Mikhail Azure said drily, watching the footage on the main viewscreen of the Blue Star Syndicate cruiser *Azure Gauntlet*. His cruiser.

The screen was showing the now six days old light from when the deadliest bounty hunter he'd ever known had finally caught up with the *Blue Jay* and its ever-frustrating Captain. For several moments, the crime lord had begun to believe that his pursuit of the hunter and the freighter had been unnecessary.

Then the *Jay*'s 'discarded' fuel tanker had lit up its engines and rammed the bounty hunter ship, removing the most useful contractor Azure had known in recent years from the galaxy in an explosion that put stars to shame.

He crossed over to where Wong, the Captain of the *Gauntlet*, was reviewing the information from the sensors.

"Well, Mister Wong?" he said calmly. "Can you track them now?"

"Now that I can identify the source of the interference, yes," the other man replied. Wong was one of the few in the Protectorate who had mastered the complex art of tracking a jumpship through its jump. "That explosion threw out a massive amount of energy," he continued. "There was no way we could track the *Blue Jay* through its aftermath."

Azure nodded grimly. If he'd had even the slightest doubts in Wong's ability, the Tracker's insistence that he was unable to pick jump signatures out of the hash of radiation in this quiet corner of deep space would have resulted in the *Gauntlet* having a new Captain. As it was, the four day exercise of jumping ever-further out, trying to get ahead of the light and radiation from the 'battle' had strained his patience to the limit.

"Able did not survive?" he asked.

"Only one jump signature, and there was no ship left when we were there," Wong answered with a shrug. "Your Hunter is dead."

Wong did not sound displeased that the *second*-best Tracker in the Protectorate was dead.

"Then find me the *Blue Jay*," Azure told him. "We better not need to repeat this," he added, gesturing at the old light scans on the screen.

"We won't," Wong confirmed. "We will gain on them quickly now. Five days at most – they have only Montgomery to jump them, after all."

Azure himself had never learned to jump a starship, but Wong had three Mages serving on his ship. They would jump three times as fast as the *Blue Jay*. Unless Wong was somehow unable to track the *Jay* again, they would soon bring their prey to heel.

The *Blue Jay* and its Mage would make Azure even more powerful than he was now – and the capture of the freighter's Captain would finally allow him to avenge his son's death.

He settled back into his chair as Wong began to co-ordinate the jump. He would wait. Impatient as he was, for this prize, Mikhail Azure could wait.

#

The system looked empty. Dead. The ugly bloated red giant of a star recently out of its transition from a smaller sun illuminated the shattered wreck of the system it had eaten. A single gas giant, half again the size of Sol's Jupiter, orbited well outside the sparse remnants of what had likely been a dense asteroid belt once. Inside the asteroid belt, two rocky balls of worlds orbited, both seared clean of any atmosphere when their star had begun to burn helium.

The ship that had surveyed the system, almost a hundred years ago now, had written the entire place off as useless, even going so far as to name the system Nani Mo Nashi. According to the survey database the *Blue Jay* had provided Damien, the name meant roughly 'there's nothing here.'

"I've seen colleges after exams are over with more life than this place," the young Ship's Mage announced over the intercom to the bridge. "There's really supposed to be something here?"

"You're seeing what they want you to see," Captain David Rice replied. The ship's stocky Captain tapped a command on the panel on his chair, zooming in the main viewscreen – and the screen in Damien's simulacrum chamber at the center of the ship that was currently mirroring it –on the gas giant.

"Most of the system is dead, but Nashi Three has a massive moon, four times the size of Earth," Rice explained. "This gives it gas giant sized Lagrange points here, here, and here."

Three spheres were defined on the screen in transparent blinking white light. 'Nashi Three' was the gas giant, which had never earned a name other than that of its system. Who would name worlds in a system they never expected humanity to visit?

"From the co-ordinates Seule gave us, Darkport is at this one," Jenna told the two men, zooming in the view on the Lagrange point directly ahead of the immense moon. Zoomed in that far, even the *Blue Jay*'s powerful telescopes could only reveal so much, but they showed that the low gravity zone had accumulated a small collection of good-sized asteroids, including one easily eighty kilometers across.

"I have thermals in that cluster that aren't natural," Damien told the two bridge officers softly. He floated at the heart of the ship, one of his hands on the magical Simulacrum that allowed him to cast magic through the ship itself. The walls of the simulacrum chamber were coated in screens showing the stars and space around the *Jay*, and Damien had begun to master the techniques of adding the more esoteric sensors the starship commanded to that view.

"Looks like at least a dozen ships," he concluded. "If they're careful, they can jump in and out a lot closer than we did – and if they have any kind of sensor network, anyone leaving can use the giant as a shield to hide their jump flare."

"It's a clever set up," David agreed. "Jenna, set us a course for the cluster. We'll see how well this 'bounty hunter truce' holds up once we show up."

Captain Seule, the man who'd sent them here, had assured them that no bounty hunter would try and take them on Darkport. Apparently, the Family that ran the station disapproved of trouble.

Of course, given the... enthusiasm the *Blue Jay*'s pursuers had shown so far, Damien wasn't entirely sure that the threat of such disapproval would be enough.

#

It took the *Blue Jay* twenty-one hours to attract the attention of Darkport's equivalent of Traffic Control. David figured that emerging three light minutes away, easily halfway to the bloated sun at the center of Nani Mo Nashi, had kept them from being noticed. As soon as they made turnover on a Darkport-bound course, however, the station noticed them.

The audio-only transmission, when it arrived, was short and to the point:

"I don't know who the fuck you think you are, but if you don't explain yourself damn-sweet, you're going to be eating missiles up the exhaust port, *capiche?*"

"They're not kidding, boss," Jenna told him. The ship's husky first officer focused in on a new pair of infrared signatures that had materialized in the Lagrange point they were heading to. The telescope showed them as regular looking shuttles, only slightly larger than the four heavy fusion missiles strapped to them. "Missile boats. No idea how good the missiles are, but it doesn't take much for eight birds to ruin our day."

"I was planning on playing nice anyway," David reminded her. He turned to the small camera installed on his captain's chair and hit record.

"This is David Rice of the *Blue Jay*," he told the station. "Captain Nathan Seule sent me. We're looking for somewhere to rest and refit, away from prying Protectorate eyes."

Three minutes later, the audio transmission was replaced by a video transmission, and David knew he'd said the right things. A young, swarthy-looking man with dark hair dressed in an extremely old fashioned suit faced the camera in an extremely ordinary looking traffic control center.

"Darkport is not a resort, Captain," he told David. "That said, if you have trade goods or physical transfer chips, you can do business here."

"Looks like Seule's name does open the door," David muttered to Jenna, but the traffic controller was still speaking.

"You may continue to approach the station, but be advised we will acquire weapons lock at seven million kilometers – just to discourage any ideas, you understand," he said calmly.

"The rules of Darkport are simple. This station is run by the Falcone Family. You fuck with Falcone affairs, we kill you. You risk the atmo integrity of the station, we kill you. You break the bounty ban, we kill you."

"Your safety and the safety of your goods are your problem," he concluded. "The Family are neither cops nor courts. Cause too much trouble, though, and we kill you."

"Your docking fees are payable upon arrival in goods or physical transfer chips, as assessed by the Family *Capo* on hand when you arrive."

"If you've any issues, you can fuck on off right out of our system. *Capiche?*"

David waited for a moment to be sure the Mafia made man was done talking before turning on his recorder again.

"I get it," he said flatly. "We'll be docking in," he checked the system, "twenty hours and thirty-one minutes. We'll negotiate trade good value when we arrive."

He ended the recording and turned to his XO.

"They sound wonderfully welcoming, don't they?" he asked dryly.

"They just want our money," she replied. "Speaking of which…?"

"We have physical transfer chips," David confirmed. The small black chips contained a specific amount recorded into it by a bank, and were registered 'to the bearer.' The Protectorate Council made noises every few years about banning the last form of cash currency, but an anonymous form of interstellar payment was too useful to too many people for that to happen.

"I didn't want to let the Family know that right off the bat though," he continued. "I suspect that hunter ship came from here, and those missile boats make me nervous. I don't want to give them ideas about taking the ship."

"So you're assuming they haven't heard of us, then?" Jenna asked, and David winced.

He hadn't exactly *forgotten* that the bounty hunters seemed to know that Damien had transformed the *Blue Jay*'s jump matrix into a fully functional unrestricted amplifier for magic, but it hadn't occurred to him as a factor.

"If they've heard about us, they'll want the ship anyway, won't they?" he admitted aloud. "There's not much we can do about that, except hope that the bounty ban works in our favor."

"Keep guards on the doors and guards on anyone who goes on-station?" she suggested.

"Given the rules and the threat level, I think I need to take Damien," David said grimly. "His magic is the deadliest short-range weapon we have, and he won't rip a hole in the hull."

Jenna looked at the asteroid on the screens and grimaced. "Is this place as bad as I think it's going to be, boss?" she asked quietly. "Do you *really* want Damien to see that?"

"Even here, they won't pick a fight with a Mage," the Captain told her. "It'll be an unfortunate wake-up for him, but I don't think we have a choice."

#

Damien watched their missile boat escorts carefully as the *Blue Jay* began their final approach to Darkport. The two heavily armed shuttles had met them well away from the asteroid and accompanied them in, as if they expected the unarmed freighter to cause trouble.

With Damien standing at the simulacrum at the center of the ship, his gloves off and the silver runes inlaid into his palms ready to complete the freighter's amplifier matrix, the ship was hardly unarmed. He hoped that Darkport's masters didn't know that.

"Those look familiar," Jenna said over the bridge link, and Damien looked up at that screen to see what she was pointing at.

Floating gently in space was a pair of familiar looking jump-yachts. A quick query of *Blue Jay*'s computers proved them to be the exact same model as had pursued them at Chrysanthemum and Excelsior.

Despite a momentary panic, Damien was quickly able to confirm they were, at least, different *ships*. With the scanners focused in on the two vessels, he was able to tell they had different armaments from the first hunter ship – but were both definitely armed.

"Hunter ships," David confirmed. "There's another docked with the asteroid," the Captain pointed out. "We're putting our lives in the Falcone family's hands here – if any of those guys want to break the bounty ban, this could get messy fast."

"They're criminals. Can we trust them?" Damien asked softly. The *Blue Jay*'s computer was now identifying missile installations on the surface of the asteroids – easily half a destroyer squadron's worth of launchers.

"The Falcone trace their origins back to Sicily on Earth – in the nineteenth century," David explained. "They've been criminals since before we had spaceflight – and they've survived because they have a code, and they *mean* it. You won't get a Falcone to sign a contract or make a vow lightly, but the keep their word."

"So when they say they'll kill anyone who breaks the bounty ban…" Jenna asked.

"They will," David confirmed. "The problem is what those rules *don't* say. There's nothing about the *Falcones* collecting bounties in there. We'll need to watch our backs."

"Damien, you're with me," he ordered. "I don't want to carry military-grade weaponry on that station, but we can't afford to appear weak. Meet me in the shuttle bay in ten."

On the screens that covered the walls of the *Blue Jay*'s simulacrum chamber, a massive hangar was now visible, carved into the asteroid beneath them. They were almost on top of the asteroid, moving at a handful of meters per second. If anyone was going to attack them, they'd have done it by now.

"All right, Captain," Damien agreed. "Let's be about it."

#

Damien didn't know what he'd expected of the central marketplace of a pirate station, but the Grand Bazaar of Darkport was not it. The docks and the tunnels away from them had lived down to his expectations – dark and dreary holes blasted out of the asteroid rock with cheap explosives. The ventilation ducting and power piping had simply been bolted into arbitrarily selected walls of the zero-gravity passages. There were no safety warnings, no hazard labels – just neatly lettered signs providing directions to the various chambers of the pirate asteroid.

They'd followed the signs to the Grand Bazaar, and came out into brightly lit and brightly colored chaos. Someone had either taken a natural cavern, or one that had been blasted out while extracting ore to build the station, and installed a massive cylinder a hundred meters across and five hundred meters long.

That cylinder was now spinning at an eye-tearing three times a minute, producing a full half-gravity on its outside edge. That outside edge, all sixteen hectares or so of it, was covered in a garishly colored mess of tents, shacks, and stalls.

"How many people are in here?" Damien asked aloud.

"Thousands," David responded quietly as they stood on the edge of the tunnel that led into the center of the cylinder. "There's a lot more people here than I expected – they've got to see a lot more business than even my worst fears."

With a sigh and a shrug, the burly Captain gestured Damien onto one of several platforms, clearly large enough for significant amounts of cargo but also the only way to the 'floor' of the Bazaar. The controls blinked at them until David sighed again and fed it a small black chip. The system ground for a moment, and then allowed them to descend.

Damien looked at the chip in interest. In all of his twenty-six years, he'd never actually had to use a physical bank transfer chip. The presumably-small-denomination one his Captain had just paid for an elevator ride with was the first one he'd ever seen. Charging for an elevator-ride seemed petty to him, but he wasn't the one running a black market on the edge of nowhere.

The ride was surprisingly slow, and the young Mage took advantage of the opportunity to look around. He and David were both dressed in casual clothes over body armor. The Captain wore a black leather jacket that covered the armor neatly. Damien wore the armor under a mock-necked turtleneck, clearing showing the black leather collar around his neck with the gold medallion marking him as a Mage.

Even here, he was sure that medallion would buy him a bit more respect and security.

"Do we know where we're going?" he asked David as they reached the ground and they stepped out into the pseudo-gravity.

"Not really," his Captain admitted. "From what I saw from the center, it's pretty disorganized. I thought I saw a collection of starship parts that way," he continued, gesturing along the cylinder, "and I'm hoping they have a missile launcher or two we can mount on the *Jay*."

Damien nodded, and the pair set off through the crowds. Many of the stalls and structures were open-roofed, taking advantage of the lack of weather in a cylinder like this. Even the open-roofed structures, though, had fully-enclosed storage areas, often with complex looking locking mechanisms and *always* under the eye of someone carrying a weapon.

The area right next to the elevators seemed to be mostly personal items. Clothes, food, and an array of illegal weaponry beckoned the eye of the newcomer to Bazaar. Jewelry, likely stolen in pirate raids in Damien's opinion, glittered from behind glass display cases under the eyes of heavily armed guards.

A massive banner hung over the way forward, two simple Latin words that Damien had learned in school: *Caveat Emptor.*

Buyer beware.

#

The Bazaar was a cacophony of sights, sounds, and smells. Every fourth or fifth stall was cooking food – and *every* stall keeper was shouting out their wares at Damien and David as they passed by. They were offered medications, guns, jewels, and mercenaries in the first five minutes.

The pair was halfway to the starship parts section David had spotted when Damien clearly made out one of the offers directed at him and nearly stopped on the spot in shock.

"Hey young man, want a girl? We got all kinds, all sizes – rent by the hour, or buy 'em to keep! Guaranteed docile and well-behaved."

Damien spun around at the voice and found himself staring at an older man in one of the roofed stalls. The area behind him had been set up as a pseudo-lounge, with red leather couches and thick carpeting. A trio of young women reclined on the divans, clad in flimsy negligees that barely managed to leave anything to the imagination. All three also wore dainty silver collars locked around their necks, each connected to a solid looking chain attached to the couch.

David's hand locked, hard, on Damien's shoulder and pulled him away even as the young Mage's mouth opened to say something intemperate in response.

"Not here, not now," the Captain hissed. His grip was hard enough to hurt as he yanked Damien along with him.

"But those girls are…"

"Slaves," David said bluntly. "Kidnapped and forced into slavery, yes. Darkport is the center of the slave trade, and that trade *is* Falcone business. If we do what both of us would like to do, they will kill us."

Looking around now, Damien spotted several groups of men and women with metal collars. Often, the entire group was linked together with small chains tied to the waist of the men or women around them. Elsewhere, single collared individuals were scattered around. Some had chains linked to the wrists or waists of their companions, others were on their own, their body language meek and defeated.

"What hell-hole *is* this place?" Damien demanded.

"Darkport," his Captain said flatly. "The darkest underbelly the Protectorate has. I'm sorry you have to see this – I knew what it would be like, but I needed you with me as security. This place is not safe."

The shock of the slave girls broke Damien's distraction by the exotic and gaudy nature of the bazaar. Now he kept his gaze sharp, looking past even the obvious guards and weaponry for the even darker layer hidden underneath.

There were no children here. A marketplace like this, he would have expected to see them running everywhere – the children of the stall-keepers if no others – but no one would bring a child to this place. Alongside the medications being offered was a full suite of illegal drugs, from the mundane he'd heard of like Hyper-X, to something called Dreamy White he didn't *want* to hear of.

As they approached the parts store, they came across the remnants of a firefight. It wasn't clear who had started it, but three men lay on the ground. One was still whimpering in pain as they approached, until a single gunshot silenced him to allow the killers to loot the bodies uninterrupted.

Finally, after an eye-opening fifteen minutes through the twisting mess of the alleys and stalls, they arrived in a small open space in front of the junkyard they'd spotted. The pile of starship parts was easily eighty meters across and as many deep, and the owners had cleared a space around the only entrance.

A terrifying-looking black weapons turret sat beside that entrance, a massive man with milk-white skin watching the crowd with cold eyes.

"Whatcha business?" he asked as David and Damien approached.

"We're looking for starship weapons," David told the guard. "Willing to deal in trade or currency chips."

The big pale man nodded and tapped something on a screen in his turret, invisible from the courtyard.

"Just Captain," he said after moment. "Mage stays. Safety promise." He patted the big black turret affectionately as he said the last.

"Stay here," David told Damien. "Keep your head down, don't go too far, and don't cause trouble." After a moment's thought, he slipped Damien a handful of the black chips. "Your PC can tell you how much is on each," he told the Mage. "If you see anything useful to you, check it out – just stay in sight of this gentleman," he nodded towards the pale guard.

The guard drew himself up sharply at the gesture. "Will watch Mage, no trouble, promise!"

With this apparently agreed, David approached the gate next to the guard's turret. The door swung open, and the Captain passed through.

Behind him, Damien exchanged glances with the guard, who gave him as reassuring a smile as the massive beast of a man was capable of.

"Anyplace decent for food near here?" the young Mage asked after glancing around the courtyard. After considering for a moment, the guard pointed at a specific stall, about thirty yards away and still easily in sight of the turret.

"Angie's. Good steak!" he said enthusiastically.

Damien accepted the recommendation with a nod, and set off down the courtyard.

#

After an expensive but surprisingly good steak, Damien found himself wandering the edge of the courtyard, checking out the various stores. Few of them had any items of interest, until he reached what looked like an almost stereotypical 'gypsy seer' stall.

The owner had assembled a cloth ceiling to bring the stall into murky shadow, and then covered the furniture in brightly colored cloth that stood out even in the shadow. The inventory seemed haphazardly scattered about the tables, but Damien's trained eye picked out the patterns that would show any missing item clearly.

Most of said inventory was crap, the usual pseudo-mystic forgeries and frauds inherited from the old 'New Age' movement, given new life by the discovery of real magic. At the back of the store, under a gentle white light mostly concealed from the main courtyard, was a single table of *other* items. The shopkeeper, wrapped in so many layers of gaudily colored fabrics their gender was unidentifiable, watched Damien carefully as the Mage reviewed the items.

Runic artifacts generally required a Mage to charge them, and none of these had been charged. To Damien, though, their runes were as clear as day. He traced the tiny remnants of power woven into the runes of a silver and green hand-made bracelet that would, if recently empowered by a Mage, actually stop bullets.

Next to that bracelet was another whose runes took more interpreting for him. After several moments, he realized that the runes on the jade arrowhead necklace were medical in nature – a field of magic he was extremely unfamiliar with – and, he was quite certain, would duplicate the effects of virility drugs.

"What do you seek, young Mage?" the store owner asked as he ran his fingers over the items. "You are trained and wise, what brings you to the shadowy corners of Erena's store?"

"Spending time while the ship is docked," Damien replied. It had the virtue of being both true and saying absolutely nothing.

"Ah yes, the new ship. The one here for safe haven from the bounty hunters," Erena, said in a voice pitched so as to conceal the user's accent and gender. "So, young Mage, do you seek to hide then? Or to flee?"

Damien looked up at the garishly clad storekeeper. "Nothing you have here is of any use to me," he told them. That wasn't *entirely* true – he was tempted by the shield bracelet, if only to make Kelly wear it – but there was nothing here he couldn't easily make if he had the time and energy.

"Ah," Erena said triumphantly. "So you seek *power* do you, little Mage?"

Something in the fake gypsy's tone and voice caused Damien to narrow his eyes.

"What are you after?" he asked bluntly.

"I have... an item," the shopkeeper said slowly, as if trying to draw out the anticipation. "A rune, to call it what it is. This rune was taken from the arm of one of the Mage-King's Hands – and I have seen with mine own eyes the wonders and terrors that the Hands can invoke in His name!"

"And you think this rune is what allows that?"

"I know this to be true, young Mage," Erena replied with a flash of bright teeth under the shawls. A box materialized from behind the shopkeeper's desk, and Erena opened it carefully. A scanner demanded finger- and thumb-prints before the case finally opened, revealing its contents.

The strip of material inside was thirty centimeters long and ten wide. It took Damien a good ten seconds to realize it was actually tanned human skin – the skin of the man they'd taken the rune from.

Silver had been inlaid into the previous owner's skin, a weave of power unlike anything Damien had ever seen in his entire life. Every other rune he had ever seen had been written in the Martian Runic Script, with its multitude of characters and connectors that *almost* met the true lines and flows of power only Damien saw.

This rune had never been written in a Runic Script. Where the Script had defined characters and connectors, this had been shaped as the power flowed – an *exact* match for the truth of magic, not the Script's re-usable approximations.

Damien turned his gaze on the silver in the dead man's flesh and *looked* at the power that had once flowed through it. The rune had been tied into the man's own magic, reflecting and re-doubling it. It was everything the shopkeeper said it was.

And it was utterly useless to anyone.

His Sight, his ability to see the flow of magic, told him the truth – this rune had been *intimately* tied into the magic of the man who'd worn it. If Damien were to carve this rune into his own flesh, it would *kill* him.

"I have a man who can carve the rune for you," Erena offered breathlessly. "He is careful, his hands steady. Think of it – immense power, and it is yours!"

"How many of those you've carved it upon have died?" Damien asked flatly, and the shopkeeper jerked back in surprise. "This rune was tied to the life and power of the man who wielded it – upon any other Mage; it would be a death sentence."

"How do you... how did you?" Erena was thrown completely off, and then was silent for a long moment as both of them stared at the tanned skin before them. "Well, that explains that, doesn't it?" the shopkeeper said finally. "Thought it was just bad luck."

"This thing *is* bad luck," Damien told Erena. "Just think what a Hand would do if they learned you had this." He considered. "I'll take it off your hands – before anyone comes back looking for revenge."

The shopkeeper drew up to an impressive height. "I give nothing for free!"

Damien sighed, and quoted a figure. It was less than the shield bracelet had been labeled for, and Erena winced – only to wilt as he looked back at the human skin with its inlaid silver.

"Done. Take it and be gone."

The box scanners re-keyed, Damien paid Erena and left. Under his arm was the last remnant of a man who had died for the Protectorate and part of him was grimly determined to see it returned home.

The rest of him wondered if he could do what Erena couldn't –
and somehow make use of the rune.

#

"Lord Azure."

"Yes, Mister Wong," Mikhail Azure replied. Floating in the
middle of his private zero-gravity sanctum, he opened his eyes to look
calmly at the Captain of his warship.

"I have completed my assessment," Wong told him, standing just
inside the door of the room, holding onto the edge of the door as he
return his master's gaze. "I have identified our destination."

"Our destination is the *Blue Jay*," Azure told him, his eyes sharp
as he tried to read the other man's inscrutable pose.

"Perhaps I should say the *Jay*'s destination," Wong said, unfazed.
"They made a point eight light year jump to an uninhabited star
system."

"Then prepare the ship for jump," the crime lord instructed. "You
do not need me for that, Mister Wong."

The old Tracker remained standing in the door, silent, for a long
moment before speaking again.

"You know, My Lord," he said quietly, "that there are things from
my old life that I am not permitted to speak to you of. Oaths I have
sworn that are not superseded by my vows to you."

Azure considered. He vaguely recalled that Wong, previously one
of the most dangerous bounty hunters in the galaxy, had warned him of
such things when he had entered Azure's service. The man had
delivered two decades of loyal and valuable work since, and the crime
lord had mostly forgotten.

"You would not be reminding me of this without a point," he said
softly.

"I am privy, through the Hunters, to information that would be of
immense value to your operations," Wong said calmly. "Certain codes,
certain ciphers, certain markers are known to me, and I have kept my
eyes and ears open. My oaths to my brothers have kept me silent until
now, but with the opportunity now before us I would betray my oaths
to you if I kept silent."

A flicker of power brought Azure's feet to the ground and he
crossed to the wall. He tapped a command, and an image of the stars
outside the cruiser suddenly covered the wall. Azure looked out to the
abyss around them, and drew patience from infinity. His back still to
Wong, he spoke softly.

"What opportunity, Wong?"

240

"Rice has fled to Darkport," the ex-bounty hunter said in a single rush of breath.

Azure looked out at the stars, and a cold smile spread across his face. Darkport – the center of *Casa Nostra*'s power. From that hidden colony, the old Mafia Families stretched their power across the Protectorate, and challenge the Syndicate at every turn. To them, the Blue Star Syndicate – *his* Syndicate, the most powerful crime organization in the galaxy – was a mere newcomer to the scene.

"An opportunity indeed," he agreed. "What do you know of their defenses?"

"They were built to withstand a full squadron of Martian destroyers," Wong told him. "The *Azure Gauntlet* is almost half again that squadron's mass, and double its firepower. An assault on the station itself would be more difficult."

"Do we have the men?" Azure asked, considered the stars. The *Blue Jay* was a more valuable prize than Darkport, but if he could take both, it would be well worth the risk.

"We would need time to prepare," Wong replied. "Most of my crew have combat training, but we would need to refresh them and fabricate arms and armor for them."

"How long?"

"Twelve hours," the Tracker explained. "I did not wish to jump to Darkport without knowing if you planned to seize it or simply pursue the *Blue Jay*."

"Oh, my dear Mister Wong," Mikhail Azure told him as he turned to face Wong, a cold smile on his face. "With your well-timed warning, I believe we can do both."

#

Rice called a staff meeting as soon as he and Damien had returned to the *Blue Jay*. His meeting with the ship parts dealer on Darkport had been even more productive than he'd hoped, and he'd returned to the ship with a briefcase full of details. He'd noticed the young Mage had acquired a similar case of his own, but Damien had been unusually non-committal when asked about it.

The youth had disappeared when they'd arrived back at the ship, but was still one of the first to arrive in the conference room on Rib A. Kellers, Jenna and Mike Kelzin drifted in shortly after the Mage. David waited for everyone to finish seating themselves, and then opened the briefcase to pull out the datachips he'd been provided.

"We have a lot of work to get done in a short time," he told them, "so I'll give you the quick rundown."

"I've acquired several weapon systems we're going to get mounted on the *Blue Jay*," he continued. The cost of said systems was still boggling him, but that wasn't his crew's issue. Thanks to the LMID's payment for the Chrysanthemum shipment, he could afford it, but it was going to gut his reserves.

"First, we're getting two military-grade battle lasers." David pulled an icon over from one of the datachips, flipping a blue highlighted wireframe of the weapons onto the image of the ship on the big screen behind the table. "These are two gigawatt pulse lasers, used by the Navy's last generation of destroyers." He looked at Kellers. "James, I'm assuming we can run them through the radiation cap without too many issues. The specs are on the chips," he gestured towards the pile of datachips he'd dumped out of the briefcase, "so let me know ASAP if that isn't the case."

"Those beams are energy hogs like you won't believe, boss," the dark-skinned chief engineer warned. "I don't know if we can feed them from our current plant."

"I know we can't," David agreed. "The *next* piece we're getting after those two is a new five gigawatt fusion plant, the exact same model as our current reactor. The dealer says – and I count on you tell me if he's wrong – that we can basically bolt the reactor section on as a module at the front of the ship, replacing a bunch of our cargo space. Since we don't have the tanker anymore…"

"We have over a quarter of our cargo pylons free," Kellers agreed. "We'll need to re-arrange the containers we have left."

"My boys will take care of it," Kelzin, the ship's First Pilot, interjected. "I don't know about anyone else, but I *don't* trust this place with cargo."

"I'm unhappy enough trusting them to cut through the rad cap to install lasers," Jenna agreed dryly. "You sure about this, boss?"

"Any work here comes with the implicit warning that if they screw us *too* badly, we can always reveal Darkport to the authorities," David reminded them all. "It's true both ways, and everybody knows it. We'll keep an eye on them, and we don't let them anywhere *near* Damien's simulacrum chamber, but I think we can trust them to do the work cleanly."

"I'm still moving the cargo myself," the Pilot told him, and David laughed.

"Fine," he agreed. "We'll have a new pod arriving this evening too – we're getting a container of Tempest XI smart missiles. Four hundred of them."

"And just what are we doing with fusion-drive kinetic impacters, boss?" Jenna asked.

"We're receiving four ten-bird external racks in the morning," David explained with a grin. "Mount them on the Ribs; we can fire anything from a single missile to all forty of them. No bounty hunter's modified yacht is going to take forty missiles, even kinetic impacters, and keep coming."

"What about targeting?" Jenna asked. "We don't have military-grade sensors, or a missile telemetry suite."

"Hence the Tempests," David told her. "They're fire and forget weapons – we feed them a target at launch and they fly the rest of the way on their own. We'll need to upgrade and integrate some software," he admitted, and then gestured at the pile of chips again. "Software for both the lasers and the Tempests is in the pile."

"LaMonte is our best programmer," Kellers told him. "I'll loose her on it – sorry Damien!"

"I can live with my girlfriend programming the guns that will help keep us alive," the young Mage replied dryly. "That's a lot of things for everybody else. What do you need me to do?"

"Keep an eye on *everything*," David told him. "With your link into the ship, you're the most likely one to catch if the installers do something we don't want. Plus, if any of the hunters decides to ignore the bounty ban – or the Falcones themselves decide we're worth coming after us – you're still our first line of defense."

"I'm looking forward to us having guns," Damien replied. "A defense *other* than me sounds great."

David shook his head at the Mage.

"We'll have our missiles aboard within the hour, and our installers are arriving at nine Olympus Standard tomorrow morning," he told his officers. "That's fourteen hours from now – and we need to be ready. Let's get to it!"

#

Damien was awoken late that night when Kelly finally slipped into the quarters they'd quietly started sharing. It wasn't a large enough ship that anyone *didn't* know they were in a relationship, and his quarters as the Ship's Mage and Second Officer were noticeably larger than those assigned to the most junior of three Assistant Engineers.

The petite engineer tried not to wake him, but with all of the concerns the senior officers had over Darkport, the young Mage was wound tightly and sleeping lightly. When he heard a noise, he flicked the lights on with a gesture and a touch of power, to catch his girlfriend halfway through undressing in the dark.

"What the?!" she exclaimed, but then turned a green-eyed glare on her boyfriend. "Some warning before you do that would be nice," she told him. "I was hoping to let you sleep."

Damien smiled at her as he sat up.

"I don't think I'll sleep decently until we're out of this place," he told her. "There's too much that can go wrong, and the people here scare me."

"Me too," she admitted, settling onto the bed next to him. "I got all of the software for the missiles and lasers installed. It's not some hacked together job to run stolen hardware – the programs they gave me *were* the Navy programs for these guns."

"I didn't think the Tempests were Navy missiles?" Damien asked. To his knowledge, the Royal Navy of the Mage-King of Mars had used antimatter missiles for as long as they'd existed.

"Yeah, but the Tempests are *approved* by the Martians for police, security and armed transport use," she replied. "And the Navy authorizes all of their installs. The software is written by the same people as the big antimatter birds."

"The code we got has some gaping holes in it where the remote shutdown orders were, too," Kelly finished grimly. "The arsenal the Captain has us installing would take down a destroyer if we got close enough."

"So could the amplifier," Damien reminded her grimly. "At least these weapons are obvious, not completely invisible."

"It's easier for me to grasp the missiles as a threat," Kelly admitted. "That these people will happily arm us this heavily – it scares me. I knew the pirates have to come from somewhere, but if it's this easy to get an armed ship, I'm surprised there aren't more!"

"There were, thirty, forty years ago," Damien told her. "Then there were half a dozen ports like Darkport. The Protectorate hunted them out and destroyed them."

Kelly shivered against him.

"And we're on this side of that fight," she said quietly. "The side of the slavers and pirates."

"No, we're not," Damien told her sharply. "We're hiding from the Protectorate, yes. But it's not the Martians we're getting guns to protect ourselves from – it's the 'slavers and pirates.' Sooner or later, we'll be back in the light. I promise you," he said softly, "I will find a way for us all to go home."

He held her for a long moment, both of them drawing comfort from the others' touch.

"It's not all on you, you know," she told him quietly. "It'll take all of us to dig our way out of this hole – and we all put ourselves here knowing what we were getting into."

He thought of the locked case tucked away in his closet, with the skin of a Hand of the King. If he could find a way to get that back to the man's family, maybe that would buy them some leniency. It wasn't as if they'd hurt anyone from the Navy, all they'd done was run away.

"All right," he conceded, "*we'll* find a way."

Kelly's response was interrupted by the beeping of a priority alert on Damien's com. He hit an audio-only channel button.

"Damien," he answered sharply.

"It's Jenna," the ship's XO replied. "We have a *big* problem – a god-damned *cruiser* just jumped into the system."

"And it's *not* from the Royal Navy."

#

The rats ran for their holes, and Mikhail Azure smiled.

The *Azure Gauntlet* advanced on Darkport, making no attempt to conceal their intentions. Around him, Wong's efficient bridge crew went about their duties. The ship's First Officer, the senior Mage aboard other than Azure, stood by the glowing silver simulacrum at the heart of both bridge and ship.

"We have identified multiple small craft launching from the asteroid," one of the junior pirates, a bronze-skinned woman with slanted eyes named Hu, reported. "They appear to be carrying multiple missiles each."

"When will we range on them?" Wong asked. Azure remained silent, allowing the bounty hunter to command his ship – he knew the limits of his own expertise.

"About thirty minutes," the ship's gunner, a man named Monroe with dark skin and a spectacular pink Mohawk, reported. "The missiles appear to be Phoenix Sixes –twenty years older and slower than ours. They won't range on us for ten minutes after that."

"Do you wish to speak to the Falcones, my lord?" Wong asked Azure after considering for a moment. "There are several hunter ships at Darkport and the station itself is well armed. Once we have engaged their pilots, I doubt they will talk again until the dust settles."

Azure settled himself carefully in his chair – the one added for an Admiral to observe the workings of his flagship in the Navy – and nodded slowly.

"Yes, let us see what Julian Falcone has to say today," he agreed softly.

Another junior pirate quickly approached Azure at Wong's gesture, the young woman rapidly setting up the communication recorder on the crime lord's controls.

Looking directly into the camera, Mikhail Azure smiled.

"This message is for Julian Falcone, or whichever of his brothers is currently in charge on Darkport," he said cheerily. "You have twenty minutes to completely surrender the station and all ships docked on it, or I will start blowing things to hell."

The tech gave a worried looking nod to Azure, confirming the message was on its way, and the crime lord leaned back in his chair to wait.

They'd jumped in almost dangerously close to the asteroid port, but it still took time for the radio waves to wing their way across space. It likely took longer to even *find* Julian under whatever rock he'd found to hide behind and deliver the message, but the response was well within his twenty minute warning.

"This is Julian Falcone, of *la Casa Nostra*," the swarthy, heavily-built man in the responding video. "I don't know what you're playing at, Mikhail, but I suggest you drop it and leave. *La Casa Nostra* has been dealing with fools and pretenders for eight hundred years – this station is not defenseless. Even if you took it from us, you would never be able to keep it!"

Mikhail grinned, watching the timer tick down until the *Azure Gauntlet* would range on the first of the Falcone's defenders. He nodded to the young tech to start the recorder again.

"You have eight hundred years of history at being thugs," he agreed mockingly. "That's cute. I have a *battlecruiser*, Julian – and I'm coming for you."

#

"Have you located the *Blue Jay* yet?" Azure asked Wong, turning his attention away from his entertainment to the task of the day.

"There is no jump signature that would match her," the Tracker replied. "I believe she, along with most of the freighters in system, is docked inside the asteroid. Once we have demonstrated our superiority over the Falcone forces, they will attempt to flee."

"You can track her if she does?"

"Of course," Wong answered disdainfully. "With sensor footage of the inevitable explosions, there will be no issues.

"Now, if you will excuse me my lord," he continued in a momentary lapse of subservience, "I need to fight your ship."

Azure settled back in his chair, accessing the controls and bringing up an overview of the space around his warship. Despite the hovering young woman, he actually *had* familiarized himself with the tools available to him, and quickly zoomed in on the immediate dangers.

The Falcones really had prepared for a major assault on the base. The *Gauntlet's* scanners were incredibly powerful when fully active, sweeping the entire system with overwhelming pulses of radar and lidar that allowed them to identify every feature of the pirate port.

Twenty-four missile boats closed in on the *Gauntlet*. The cruiser's computers happily informed him that the Phoenix VI missiles the Falcone defenders carried had a maximum range of ten million kilometers after a seven and a half minute burn – versus the *Azure Gauntlet's* Phoenix *VII* missiles, with a range of eleven million kilometers after a seven minute burn.

"Target two missiles per shuttle, hold tubs forty nine through sixty in reserve for any that survive the first salvo," Wong ordered. "Fire."

Across the front facing edges of the massive spike that was the old cruiser, hatches slid aside to open weapon ports that had never been fired in anger, even in the old ship's years of service in the Martian Navy.

Now electromagnetic coils flared to life, expelling the missiles away from the warship. Moments passed in the silence of deep space, then forty-eight antimatter explosions burst to life and flung themselves forwards.

"Spin up the RFLAMs," Azure heard Wong order. "Some of them will launch, even if they're not in range."

Behind the shuttles, orbiting around Darkport, a fourth armed yacht drifted lazily out from the asteroid's interior hangers. The four hunter ships assumed a loose formation between the *Gauntlet* and Darkport, but didn't move any closer to the cruiser.

"Impact in twenty seconds," Hu reported from the main sensor station. "Targets maneuvering – *they've fired.*"

"Confirm that!" Wong snapped, and then Azure's screen dissolved in static as their missiles hit. Almost fifty antimatter warheads went off within seconds of each other, blotting out every scanner or sensor for a light minute around.

"Systems resetting," the scanner tech reported. "Confirm kills – I see four shuttles."

"I see four left as well," the Gunner confirmed. "Confirm twenty kills. Last four are breaking off, six gees acceleration."

"Let them go," Wong ordered. "Where are the missiles?"

"I've got them," the first tech responded, and Azure's screen lit up as the ship's computers and junior pirates finally resolved the missiles. "Looks like our blast wave gutted their salvo; I'm reading sixty-one inbound, four hundred seconds out and closing."

"Spin up the RFLAMs and engage at one million kilometers," the ex-hunter captain ordered. He stepped over to Azure and looked down at the crime lord.

"They're running on internal sensors," he told Azure. "Between the explosion and the range, they'd need twice that many missiles to be a threat. We'll deal with them, and then move on the station."

"What about your old brethren, the Hunter ships?" the Blue Star Syndicate's master replied.

"Even for this place, they won't fight without money," Wong told him. "If they do, they'll do it under the guns of the asteroid itself. At that point, we will know we've been in a fight."

"And the *Blue Jay*?"

"The asteroid rotates slowly under its own power," the ship captain observed. "The hangar exit will point directly away from us just as we reach range of the rock. The Falcones will try and hold the ships back until then – it will be the safest time for anyone to run. We will track her then," the tiny Asian man said confidently.

"Mister Wong, Lord Azure," the young woman who'd helped Azure with his comms earlier interrupted. "You'll want to see this message."

She threw it up on the bridge's main screen before either of the two men who ran the ship had time to question her. The swarthy image of Julian Falcone glowered out from the screen as he spoke.

"All Hunters in Darkport," he said grimly, "this station is under attack. We will pay one hundred million Martian dollars, plus munitions, repairs, and death benefits, to any crew that engages Mikhail Azure's ship."

The loose formation of Hunter ships Azure had been watching suddenly tightened up, the heat signatures of all four ships increasing as they spun up secondary fusion reactors to power their weapons.

"That's the price of a good-sized starship," Azure observed. "I think we have them scared."

"Scared or not, he's got the Hunters in," Wong told him. "Strap in, my lord. This is about to get ugly."

In the space around them, the *Azure Gauntlet's* laser turrets opened fire on the pitiful salvo that the Falcone missile boats had died to deliver. Without guidance, and with radiation scrambled sensors, even military antimatter missiles fell easily.

A handful broke through the lasers, but the Mage standing next to the simulacrum was ready. In an almost casual display of power, he blotted the remaining missiles from space with a single blast of fire.

\#

David glared at the main viewscreen on the *Blue Jay's* bridge and the relentlessly closed main hangar doors of Darkport. They'd detached from the docking tubes and connectors as soon as Jenna's sensor feed had shown the arrival of the cruiser, but Darkport Control had ordered them to stay where they were.

A single ship – an armed bounty hunter ship, from what the burly Captain could tell – had been allowed to leave. The remaining collection of freighters and blockade runners, over thirty starships, was blockaded inside the massive cavern hangar by immense metal doors he hadn't even realized Darkport *had*.

"You should *see* some of the offers we're getting to carry people away from Darkport," Jenna told David dryly. "We're into buy a small mansion territory – a small mansion in *New York*."

"Let someone with fewer of their own problems take them," David replied sharply. "I just want out of this place. Damien?"

"Before you ask boss, yes, I can probably open the doors," the young Mage told him from his usual spot in the simulacrum chamber. "Of course, the small arsenal the Falcones have strapped to the rock might object."

The *Blue Jay*'s Captain nodded sharply. "Any word on outside?"

"The cruiser just blew away the missile boats," Jenna told them grimly. "Looks like the Falcones have bought the Hunter ships outside – I think they're maneuvering to fight. I'm guessing the exterior launchers and lasers are charging up too. It's going to be ugly."

"And we're stuck in here?" David complained aloud. "I'm about ready to risk that they won't want to shoot at us, even if ..."

"Incoming coms from the station," Jenna told him, then threw the transmission up on the viewscreen, replacing the image of the hangar doors.

"All ships, this is Julian Falcone," the swarthy, heavily-built man in the suit informed them. "In twelve minutes, Mikhail Azure's personal warship will come into range of Darkport. Fortunately for all of you, about thirty seconds before that, the hangar will have rotated to point directly away from him.

"At that time, we will open the hangar doors, and I recommend that you all run for it," the crime lord said bluntly. "We will use the station weapons to cover your retreat. I hope to defeat Azure, in which case you will all be more than welcome to return to the base."

"Uh-huh," someone said into the channel. "We're supposed to believe you'll expend resources to protect us? Right!"

"Oh, we will also be covering a number of *our* own ships," Falcone told the voice dryly, then leveled a hard glare on the camera. "But I am also somewhat old fashioned, and I believe that if a man has paid me for protection, I owe him some god-damn protection."

"If you don't trust me, do whatever the hell you want," he finished, "but I will only attempt to provide *one* window of opportunity. After that, you can dodge the cruiser on your own."

The channel cut off and David looked over at Jenna and the screen with Damien's image.

"I have this sinking feeling that even with thirty other ships around us, that asshole is going to shoot at us," he told his two officers. "Thoughts?"

"I'm not coming up with much beyond 'run like hell,' boss," Jenna admitted.

Damien seemed to consider for a long moment, and the Mage nodded.

"I think so," he said. "If we keep on a relatively steady course and acceleration, I think I can hide us from the cruiser's sensors."

The Captain stared at his Mage in shock for a moment. "You're kidding me, right?" he asked bluntly.

"I couldn't do it in empty space," the youth admitted. "But we're going to be in an area with explosions and a bunch of ships firing their engines. I can split up our heat signature to attach to everything around us and mis-direct their radar and lidar." He hesitated. "I don't think I'll be able to do it for long, but I think I can get us far enough out to jump."

"Get ready then," David ordered, before his doubts solidified. "Any edge we can get," he reminded himself and Jenna aloud. "We need out of this system – and away from that cruiser!"

#

Azure watched as the four Hunter ships formed into an even square facing the *Gauntlet*. The modified yachts starting moving towards the Syndicate cruiser, their acceleration slow for no reason he saw.

"Should we be slowing down to board Darkport?" he asked Wong, quietly so as not to betray his ignorance to the rest of the bridge crew.

"We'll be firing retro-thrusters shortly," his Captain told him, "but to actually be able to *dock* with Darkport, we'd need to start full deceleration, which would have us pointing our engines at the station – and three-quarters of our weapons *away* from it."

"We'll make a slow firing pass of the station and remove most of the weapons with our forward batteries, then return once we've neutralized their batteries and defenders."

Azure nodded his understanding. The Crime Lord knew the limits of his skill-set, and fighting a space battle was well beyond them.

"What about the hunters?"

"The four of them could probably take a pair of Navy destroyers," Wong observed, watching the defenders' formation. "They know what they're doing, too – that square clears both their offensive and defensive lines of fire, but lets them support each other too."

The pirate captain shrugged, and flashed his boss a bright grin. "Not enough," he concluded, turning to his crew. "Monroe!"

The ship's gunner turned to face Wong. "Yeah, boss?"

"Once we're in range, pick a target and give her the full forward battery," Wong ordered. "Rinse and repeat until we need to start shooting at the rock."

"Gotcha."

"How long to range?" Azure asked quietly and Wong shrugged.

"Five minutes for us to range on the hunters," he said. "Eight for us to range on the station. If they have the same missiles as those shuttles, the hunters will range on us as we range on the station."

"And Darkport?"

The asteroid flickered in Azure's display as a highlight settled on it, marking the weapons bases they had identified so far.

"I expect them to have heavy ground-based missiles," Wong admitted. "They'll range on us when we range on them."

Wong walked away from Azure, checking in on other stations as Azure began to run through the various displays on his chair's console. One of the video feeds was from a recon drone that had settled in to watch the hangar bays.

Those doors stayed resolutely shut as the timer in the corner of the screen ticked down, and Azure was starting to wonder if the Falcones were planning on letting *anyone* out when Monroe's sharp announcement cut through his thoughts.

"Range on targets, firing one through sixty," he declared aloud. A moment later, the entire multi-million ton mass of the *Azure Gauntlet* shivered as her main weapons fired.

"Time to impact, seven minutes and counting," the spectacularly haired gunner continued. "Time to reload, ninety seconds."

"Bandits are firing!" another pirate tech suddenly announced. "I'm reading seventy-two missiles inbound, Phoenix VIIs."

"I guess they're feeling spendy on Falcone's dime," Wong told the bridge crew with a teeth-baring grin. "Monroe, keep pouring it on. Kelsier, run the turrets and keep us clear. Hu, if Darkport launches, I want to know *yesterday*."

Azure sat back, watching the crew of his ship fight for him. There was little he could do other than watch his screens now.

Ninety seconds after the first salvos launched, Monroe sent a second salvo blasting into space. Twenty seconds after that, the hunters returned fire. Azure noted the slower reload time, but evaluating the competence of the hunter ships was outside his purview.

Before the third salvo launched, though, there was movement on the screen from his recon drone. He pinged the sensor tech immediately, in case Hu hadn't seen it.

"They're opening the hangar to release the freighters."

"Keep your eyes peeled, that means the station is going to launch again!"

A third salvo blasted clear of the pirate cruiser, and Azure watched the scans of the ships fleeing Darkport carefully.

"Holy *mother of devils*," a voice cut through the buzz of the bridge, and Azure's gaze snapped to the sensor tech and the image on the screen.

"Darkport has launched," Hu said in a dry voice. "I'm reading one hundred fifty – I repeat, one five zero – heavy missiles inbound."

Azure looked at the screen, taking a moment to interpret the unfamiliar data codes. *Gauntlet* had fired more missiles than the asteroid so far – they had three salvos sweeping out at the Hunter ships, still with over three minutes to go before impact. The Hunters had fired almost as many, with two seventy-two missiles salvos blasting towards *Gauntlet*.

Even he knew that a single hundred and fifty missile salvo was a different kettle of fish.

"I see we're earning our pay today," Wong said after the sharp moment of silence. "Monroe, hold tubes fifty-one through sixty for counter-missile deployment. Begin transferring area denial munitions to those tubes.

"Kill me those Hunters, and then we'll deal with Darkport," the ex-Hunter ordered.

The external cameras on the bridge suddenly dulled, the computers auto-filtering as the first explosions began to light up the space around the stolen cruiser.

Lasers reached out from the Hunter's modified yachts as well, and Azure almost immediately saw the difference between the *Gauntlet*'s defenses and those of the essentially civilian ships. The *Azure Gauntlet* had dozens of Rapid-Fire-Laser-Anti-Missile turrets. The bounty hunter ships had a dozen apiece, and they were weaker and shorter-ranged than the *Gauntlet's* as well.

"Got him!" Monroe shouted as his first salvo ran home. With four of the ships networking their defenses, Azure hadn't been sure for a moment. Of the sixty missiles they'd fired, three made it through the gauntlet of coherent light to impact.

With eight hundred megaton antimatter warheads, three was more than enough.

Of the seventy-plus missiles the hunters had fired back, one made it past the lasers. The Mage at the amplifier flicked it away with ease, his eyes focused on the next salvo.

The second exchange ended the same way, another hunter ship dying in flame. The remaining two ships were withdrawing under the shield of the asteroids defenses now, though. The *Gauntlet*'s third salvo ran into a salvo of counter-missiles from the asteroid that *almost* saved them. Two missiles broke through, and then revealed that Monroe had perhaps grown cocky with his third round.

The missiles split at the last moment, each homing in on a different target. One missile slammed into each of the surviving hunter ships, and two separate explosions lit up the side of Darkport's asteroid home.

"Brace yourself," Wong ordered. With the last of the bounty hunters' missiles gone, the first salvo from Darkport itself was inbound.

"Lord," Hu interrupted Azure's focus on the battle. He turned to face the small Asian woman who was running the sensors. "We can't find the *Blue Jay*."

"What do you mean?" Azure demanded.

"We've identified every freighter that has fled Darkport," she told him. "Your target isn't among them."

"There's no way they'd stay," the Crime Lord objected. "They have to be there."

"I know," Hu said helplessly, clearly anticipating his anger. "We do not see her."

Azure glanced back at the recon drone's footage of the fleeing freighters. Each of them was now tagged with a name, clearly identified by the crew and computers. The *Blue Jay* wasn't among them. There was a pattern, though, and he began to reach for it.

Then the entire ten-million-ton mass of the *Azure Gauntlet* leapt like a startled puppy and his screens crashed with the main bridge lights.

#

The lights flickered back on, along with Azure's screen, after a few moments of pitch black. Some of the consoles stayed on through the blackout, providing an eerie light in the space that Azure was suddenly all-too-aware was basically a large steel coffin.

"What the hell was that?" he demanded.

"Emergency defense override," Wong told him. "The ship diverted all available power to an electromagnetic weave in the hull that's supposed to dissipate antimatter before it annihilates the hull."

"That seems dangerous," Azure observed dryly.

"We took three gigaton-range direct hits and we're still here," his ship captain told him brusquely. "I can live with the inconvenience. Damage report!" he bellowed at his staff.

"All three hit on quadrant two," Monroe told him grimly. "We lost ten tubes and over a dozen laser turrets. Hull integrity... is holding."

The mohawked pirate sounded surprised. Azure *was* surprised – three *gigatons* worth of explosions, and they weren't even breached?!

"They built this ship tough," Wong observed. "Ninety seconds to next salvo. Please tell me we're targeting the launchers."

"An entire salvo on its way, another launching shortly," the gunner promised.

Leaving the battle in Wong's capable hands, Azure turned back to the scan of the freighters and the pattern he'd noticed.

"Ship's Mage," he barked. He hadn't actually learned which of the three was on duty. "Use the amplifier to scan this space," he ordered, highlighting a region in the middle of the gaggle of fleeing starships.

A moment passed in silence.

"It's there," the Mage replied flatly. "That's one *hell* of a thaumic signature – how come the sensors can't see it?!"

"Because he's shielding against those, and didn't realize he'd stick out like a sore thumb to a Mage," Azure told him calmly. "Montgomery's a clever bastard. Wong – can he shield his jump signature?"

The Tracker faced the crime lord and shrugged. "Unlikely," he told Azure. "A Mage remaining behind probably could, but I suspect he would like to leave with his ship."

"Indeed," Azure settled back in his chair. "Then once we have captured Darkport, he will be easy to pursue."

Wong looked uncomfortable. Behind him, missiles exploded in space on the main screen as Darkport's defenses began to shred the *Gauntlet's* attack.

"That salvo hurt us," he told Azure softly. "We're down a *sixth* of our launchers – and we just got less than ten missiles through their defenses with *full* salvo."

"Are you saying we can't take Darkport?" the master of the Syndicate asked slowly, his voice cold.

"No," Wong replied, his voice equally cold. "But we *will* have to close to amplifier range to do so now, which means we *will* get hurt by their missiles and lasers.

"If we take Darkport, my lord, we will not be in sufficient condition to pursue the *Blue Jay*," the ex-bounty hunter laid out flatly.

"I recommend we wait until we have the scan of the *Jay's* jump, and then jump out to our fall-back position. We will be able to make repairs and pursue your prey. We have three Jump Mages to their one – it will only take a few days at most to catch up and capture Montgomery.

"Then, with that bird in the hand, we can return and capture Darkport," Wong concluded. "Every jump capable ship is in that flock of refugees. There will be no help for the Falcones – no reinforcements that can arrive before we return."

"We can still have them both, my lord, but we must leave off the attack today."

Azure turned away from his Captain, eyeing the asteroid ahead of them. Nine missiles had detonated on the rock's surface, gouging massive chunks out of the planetoid and wiping away defensive weapons. Enough still remained that he believed Wong. If they took too much damage reducing Falcone's defenses, they would lose the grand prize.

"Very well," he replied. "But if we lose Montgomery, Wong..."

"We won't."

#

Damien struggled to maintain the cloaking spell. For the first time in a long time, it wasn't his *power* that was the problem but his *concentration*. The spell wasn't overly demanding in terms of energy and even his limited strength could handle it, but tracking all of the complex components of burying the *Blue Jay*'s energy signature in other ships took a lot of focus.

He'd had a moment of hope when he'd watched Darkport's first missile salvo strike home, but when the radiation flare of the multiple antimatter explosions had faded, the massive Syndicate cruiser was still there, still advancing relentlessly on the station.

Around the *Blue Jay*, the other freighters were slowly beginning to scatter. Each of them had a different destination where they would try and lie low before rebuilding their business. Based off what he'd seen on Darkport, Damien couldn't help but hope that most of them would fail and fall into Protectorate hands.

"Darkport is not winning this, Damien," David said quietly over the bridge intercom. "Are we clear to jump yet? I don't like *anyone* in this fight, but I'd like to be gone before Azure has time to hunt us."

Still keeping most of his attention on the stealth spell, Damien checked the space around them. Were they this close to a planet, they wouldn't have been able to, but Darkport had almost no gravity to warp the space flattened by the LaGrange Point.

For most civilian ships, a LaGrange Point wasn't flat enough for jumping. Damien's training suggested he had to be significantly further away from the gas giant than they were. With the amplifier, however, he should be able to push through.

"We're clear."

"Get us out of here," David ordered.

Damien took a deep breath. Releasing the stealth spell, he reached for the magic of the amplifier again as quickly as he could, funneling it into the jump he'd prepared days earlier.

In a collapsing bubble of magic, the *Blue Jay* vanished from the center of the fleeing gaggle of freighters.

#

"There they go," Hu reported, the scanner tech highlighting the sudden appearance and jump flare of the *Blue Jay* from the middle of the fleeing freighters. "Damn, he's jumping in close."

"He has a fully functional amplifier, and has had reason to learn his limits," Wong said sharply. "Monroe, time to next salvo?"

"We'll be loading and firing in thirty seconds," the gunner replied. "Their next salvo is forty five seconds out."

Darkport's salvos were weakening as the *Gauntlet* destroyed their surface platforms, but the cruiser wasn't invulnerable anymore either. Two more missiles had got through, detonating just clear of the warship's hull and searing sensors and weapons from the surface.

"Jourdaine," Wong snapped, turning to the Mage. "Jump us to the rendezvous point as *soon* as Monroe's birds are in the air. We have enough holes to patch up!"

Azure remained impressed by the sheer survivability of the ship he'd stolen. *Five* one gigaton antimatter explosions had happened on or near the *Azure Gauntlet*'s hull, and while they'd lost weapons and surface emplacements, there was only one actual breach. Only fifteen of the cruiser's crew were dead, about the same injured.

"Firing!" Monroe announced, and the ship lurched as another forty-plus missiles blasted away from her.

"*Jumping!*" Jourdaine snapped, and Azure shivered against the indescribable sensation of teleportation.

The screens blanked for a moment, and then returned with the image of deep space, a light year away from Darkport's dead home system.

"Monroe, get on the repair crew – I want to know how many tubes and turrets we can get back online," Wong ordered sharply. "Jourdaine, check in with the other Mages. Hu, go over the sensors – make sure we've got as much of the array working as we can. Once you've done that, send the data on the *Jay*'s jump to my office comp. You know what I need by now."

As his bridge crew jumped into action around him, Wong turned back to Azure.

"My office, my lord?" he asked softly. "The less we hover, the sooner the ship will be repaired."

Azure nodded and followed his ship captain into the small room tucked off of the bridge. The space set aside for the vessel's commander had a viewscreen along one wall that duplicated the main screen outside.

"I apologize for my brusqueness, my lord," Wong said after a moment, taking one of the two chairs in front of the desk.

"You command my ship, Mister Wong," Azure replied calmly. "You have earned my trust in your judgment on *this* matter."

He met his Captain's gaze for a moment before Wong glanced away. Both messages heard and received.

"How long until we can pursue Rice and Montgomery?" he continued.

"I would like to take twelve hours to make sure we can finish most of the immediate repairs," Wong told him after considering for a moment. "I don't expect to get all sixty launchers back without a shipyard, but we should be able to get back over fifty.

"After that, we can pursue them with a jump every four hours," the Captain finished. "If Montgomery thinks his little trick has concealed his path, he will likely hold to the standard three jumps a day. We will catch him inside two days."

"You have three Mages qualified to jump," Azure objected. "We can almost double that time."

"If we had three true Jump Mages like Montgomery, yes," Wong agreed. "If we had Fleet Mages aboard, they would easily be able to jump every six hours each. But finding Mages willing to serve on a pirate cruiser was not easy, my lord. Jourdaine is my only actual Jump Mage. The other two were too weak to qualify, which is how I got them aboard.

"They can jump. But neither can jump more than every twelve hours," the Captain finished. "We can pursue far faster than the *Blue Jay* can run, but we must be aware of the limitations of our crew and vessel."

"And once we bring them to bay?" Azure asked.

Wong shrugged. "Able's plan was solid," he admitted. "We are equipped with precision kinetics capable of severing the freighter's ribs. My and Jourdaine's analysis is that this will disable the amplifier and allow us to board."

"We need the ship intact," the Crime Lord warned.

"There is a risk of the *Blue Jay*'s destruction," Wong told him with a nod. "But we can close to a little over two million kilometers –

outside their amplifier range – which will minimize that danger. Unless they have heavily armed the ship, and I doubt they had enough time at Darkport for that, Montgomery will be no threat to us at that range."

Azure considered the plan. He couldn't see any way of reducing the risk of blowing away his prize without risking getting into a range where Montgomery would strike at the *Azure Gauntlet* with the amplifier.

For all that the ship had survived antimatter warheads meters from its surface; he doubted it would withstand a desperate Mage with an amplifier. There was, after all, a reason the Martian Navy tried to keep amplifiers out of the hands of anyone else.

"Very well, Mister Wong," he allowed. "I am returning to my cabin. Advise me when we are ready to resume the pursuit."

#

The mirror in the sealed room hidden beside Alaura Stealey's main quarters glowed with starlight. The eight foot by three foot piece of glass was wrapped in a silver frame that was covered in meticulously carved runes, none of which would have appeared in a Martian Runic dictionary.

Across the room from the mirror, and taking up most of the space carved out of the *Tides of Justice*'s backup missile magazines, was a full scanner array that wouldn't have looked out of place on the outside of the destroyer.

The magic running through the mirror and its frame allowed Stealey to open a window to a space many millions of kilometers away – almost exactly one light year, in fact.

Right now, the mirror was open onto the co-ordinates Captain Seule had given her for Darkport as her borrowed flotilla prepared for its jump.

A small holograph tank was set up against the only empty wall, showing a three dimensional image of the region the mirror was pulling radiation from. A dedicated computer core collated the data from the sensor array to produce an accurate image of a region of space a full light year away.

Darkport had clearly had better days. Even her unpracticed eye picked out the scars of recent explosions on the asteroid's surface, and new debris fields scattered around the rock.

"Lady Hand," Admiral Medici's voice interrupted from her wrist PC. "The flotilla is preparing to jump. Would you care to join me on the flag bridge?"

The *Tides of Justice* had been built as a squadron command ship by the Navy – the additional communication and administrative equipment was part of why Alaura had 'borrowed' it – and had a small Flag Bridge. Medici, in the interests of not aggravating Castello's ex-Flag Captain, had decided to use the *Tides* as his flagship.

She regarded the hologram for a moment. The situation was very different from what they expected, but not in a way that qualified as a threat. Certainly not enough of a threat to justify revealing the existence of the Star Mirror.

"I will be up momentarily, Admiral," she told him calmly.

#

When the *Tides of Justice* erupted into Darkport's otherwise empty system, the Seventh Cruiser Squadron was already there. Medici had sent the *Rising Sun of Gallantry* and its sister ships ahead to sweep for threats. Their sensor data began to feed into the *Tides* tactical computers as soon as the ship had stabilized from the jump spell, and a complete image of the system took form in front of the Hand and the Admiral.

"It looks like we're a little late," Medici observed as the battered state of Darkport came into view. "Though the radiation makes *finding* them easier."

"We're reading no ships in the system," Lieutenant Harmon reported. Alaura's aide had taken over the console on the flag bridge set up for a squadron tactical officer. Medici's squadron tactical officer had been shuffled to a backup console, but they'd somehow fit everyone into the tiny room.

"It looks like some of the surface weapons platforms are still operational," Harmon continued. "It's hard to say how many there were, they've taken one hell of a pasting. CIC is estimating at least sixteen separate detonations."

"Order the flotilla to advance on the station," Medici ordered. "We'll keep the cruisers forward – even if someone decides to be damned stupid, it doesn't look like Darkport has enough launchers left to threaten a full cruiser squadron."

Alaura activated a communication channel of her own, to one of the three Marine Assault Transports following at the rear of their formation.

"Brigadier Raphael," she greeted the man whose image appeared promptly on her screen. Brigadier Michael Raphael was a bronze-skinned man with a shaven head, his skin color a sharp contrast with the stark white default mode of his battle exo-suit's camouflage plating. "Status of your brigade?"

"Marines clean up after slavers, ma'am," Raphael said bluntly. "I have twenty-four hundred boys and girls just *itching* to clean up the scum more directly."

"It looks like you'll get the chance," she told him. "Azure appears to have beaten us here, so we'll need to secure the station and establish if they have any information on where he or the *Blue Jay* left to. We'll need them alive, Brigadier," she warned cautiously.

Raphael nodded sharply.

"We know the rules of engagement, Lady Hand," he promised. "Once we're in, this is a police operation. Getting in though…"

"Lady Stealey," Harmon interrupted. "We're being hailed by Darkport."

"Getting in may be easier than we hope, Brigadier," Stealey told the Marine. "I'll be in touch." She turned to Harmon. "Put our erstwhile friends online."

The flag bridge's main screen switched from the exterior view to the image of a burly man with swarthy skin turned pale with stress. The image behind him was of some kind of control room, and smoke was visible in the air behind him.

"Protectorate forces, this is Julian Falcone of Darkport," he said simply, his voice quiet. "I am requesting humanitarian assistance. Please respond."

"Time delay?" Alaura asked.

"We're on the cusp of missile range; call it forty five seconds each way."

"Record for me," she ordered and turned to the camera.

"Mister Falcone, this is Alaura Stealey, Hand of the Mage-King of Mars," she informed him. "We both know what this station is and who you are. You'll forgive me if I find a request for aid suspicious."

A minute and a half passed and the flotilla slowly approached the station. At the current pace, it would take them just over hours to reach the station. They'd arrived outside missile range to be safe from the station's weapons, but it made the approach, even at three gravities, frustratingly slow.

The return message opened with a firm, accepting, nod from the Mafia boss.

"My Lady Hand, you can see the damage done to the exterior of the station," he said quietly. "We came under attack by Mikhail Azure in a stolen Navy cruiser, which I assume is the reason you are here."

"The necessity of delivering supplies to generate oxygen required us to place most of this facilities oxygen generating capacity on the surface," he continued. "We have recycling and scrubbing facilities in the asteroid, but it turned out that *they* were more vulnerable to electromagnetic pulses than we thought – as were the reserve generating plants inside the asteroid."

"I have over a thousand wounded, and only four doctors," Falcone admitted. "And unless we get additional air and manpower, a good third of the station is going to lose air before I can get anyone out. The rest of us will run out of air in three days.

"I know what you think of me, Lady Hand, but I have my own code," he said firmly, looking directly into the camera. "These people are under my protection, and if I have to trade my freedom for their lives, that is a deal I am prepared to make."

"I offer the complete surrender of the Darkport station, all databases intact, if you can save these people," he concluded. "My current estimate is that we will need additional oxygen supplies either installed or dug into the aft third of the base within eight hours or people are going to start dying."

The transmission ended, and Stealey looked over at Medici.

"Do you believe him?"

The tiny Admiral considered for a moment, and then nodded.

"His description of their issues is consistent with what I would expect to see," he admitted. "Oxygen supply on a facility like that would be vulnerable, and the EMP from that many antimatter explosions would be devastating to even shielded items as fragile as oxygen processing systems."

"Can we get there in time?" she asked. They were currently much further away than Falcone's eight hour estimate.

"This is a Navy flotilla, ma'am," Medici said dryly. "This is a *crawl*. Harmon!" he barked, and Alaura's aide turned to face him. "Order the flotilla to accelerate at ten gravities. We have some scum to save for the prisons!"

#

As the shocky sensation of jump faded, David looked over at Jenna grimly.

"How long was that?" he asked.

"Five hours," she replied. "Same as the one before. And the one before that – that's five jumps with only five hours rest each."

The Captain of the *Blue Jay* nodded grimly. They were now six jumps and twenty-five hours away from Darkport – a speed that was perfectly fine for a ship with multiple Mages, but for only one Jump Mage…

Damien was trained and normally scheduled around jumping every eight hours. David's experience was that most Jump Mages could jump after six hours rest once or twice without an issue – but five hours rest was pushing it.

And David's Ship's Mage had just done that five times in a row.

"Call Kelly," he told Jenna, extracting himself from his command chair. "Have her meet me at the simulacrum chamber."

"That's low," his executive officer pointed out.

"I'm surprisingly okay with that," David told her.

#

The petite blonde engineer met David at the entrance to the simulacrum chamber, carefully maneuvering herself in the zero-gravity of the ship's core.

"What's this about, boss?" she asked.

"Making sure your boyfriend doesn't kill himself," David told her grimly before overriding the lock on the Chamber and launching himself in.

Damien was floating in the center of the chamber, surrounded by the screens carrying the starlight of deep space to the heart of the *Blue Jay*. The young Mage barely seemed to notice them entering, and David was *on* the platform next to him before he reacted.

"Hey, boss," he said blearily.

"Damien, what are you *doing*?" David asked bluntly.

"Getting us the hell out," the young Mage told him. "Keep going, keep everyone safe." His voice was slurred, and he refused to look at the Captain.

"We're six light years from Darkport, can you stop trying to kill yourself?"

"Everr'one in trouble 'cause of me," Damien slurred. "Gotta keep…"

David grabbed his Mage by the shoulder and turned Damien to look at him. Looking at the youth's face he couldn't keep from swearing aloud.

Damien's eyes were bloodshot, his nose had clearly been bleeding and the veins along his cheeks stood out in sharp relief against the sudden pallid tone of his skin.

"What the hell?! You can't *do* this to yourself!" David snapped at him. His Ship's Mage wavered for a moment, as if trying to muster the energy to argue, and then slumped, his body going limply limbless in the way only fainting in zero-gravity could do.

"Damien!" Kelly shouted, diving across the room to join them. By the time she reached the pair, though, David was already checking the youth's pulse.

"He's alive," he told the engineer. "Looks like a damn near-run thing, I should have stopped him after the *last* damned early jump."

Gently, he shifted the young man's mass over onto Kelly.

"Look, get him to bed," he told her. "I'll set an alert so the ship will tell me when he moves, and make *damned* sure the idiot doesn't try and jump us again for at least twelve hours."

"Will do, boss," Kelly confirmed, shifting Damien's weight so she could move with him.

"When you're done, come see me on the bridge," David instructed as she headed for the door. "If Damien's damn stupid stunt isn't enough, we'll need some way to cover ourselves still. I have some thoughts on that box of missiles we picked up."

#

By the time the *Azure Gauntlet* had finally been ready to go, Mikhail Azure's patience had grown very short. Even he couldn't argue that the six missile tubes and fifteen laser turrets Wong's crew had got back online weren't worth the wait, however, so he had remained silent.

Fortunately for Wong, the old bounty hunter's abilities as a Tracker were sufficient that they had not needed any more data for him to track the *Blue Jay*, and two jumps after their repairs were complete, they had arrived on the fleeing freighter's trail.

After twelve hours of repairs and a full day of jumping, however, he was starting to doubt Wong's abilities. By any reasonable standard, there was no way the *Jay* was still ahead of them – to have jumped as often, as fast, as it would have taken for them to have come this far should have *killed* Montgomery.

"We are ready for the jump, my lord," Wong reported, seemingly unaware of his master's doubts. He stepped up to stand directly beside Azure and continued, too quietly for any but the crime lord to hear. "I have Jourdaine standing by to jump us again if necessary," he murmured. "I do not believe that Rice and Montgomery could have gone further than this in the time available."

"So you are prepared to run?" Azure asked sharply, glancing at his ship's commander.

"For all of my distaste for the man, Able was very good at what he did," Wong admitted. "He died. We know what the *Blue Jay*'s crew did to him, but they have proven themselves very tricky – and no prey is as dangerous as one that knows it's cornered.

"I am prepared for the unexpected, my lord," he concluded. "But if my calculations are correct, we will emerge within missile range of your prey, and this long hunt should soon be over."

Azure nodded slowly, glancing around the bridge of the stolen cruiser. Despite the unexpected strength of their prey, the cruiser had proven valuable beyond his wildest dreams. He wondered, now, why he'd held it in reserve for so long. With Montgomery to build amplifiers for the rest of his fleet, the *Gauntlet* would make a suitable flagship for the conquest that would ensue.

He saw the future of the Blue Star Syndicate stretch out before him, and it was glorious.

"You may jump when ready, Mister Wong," he said aloud.

Reality shivered around him, and the *Azure Gauntlet* was elsewhere. It took precious seconds for her scanners to awaken to their new reality, but when they did they showed the *Blue Jay* dead center in the *Gauntlet's* screens.

#

Damien was on the bridge when the jump flare blasted onto the *Blue Jay*'s sensors. David's idea for making sure he didn't jump early again was apparently to keep a continuous eye on the Mage.

Given the blazing headache the last jump he'd made had left him with, after twelve straight hours of nothing but sleep, the youth wasn't planning on disobeying the orders he'd been given to avoid jumping until twelve more had passed.

Besides, it had been a while since he'd actually been on the freighter's bridge. Normally he was linked in by intercom.

Once the massive cruiser appeared on their scanners, though, he started to regret the situation.

"We have this under control, Damien," David told him, the Captain's eyes on the scanners. "Of course, I'm not going to object if you were to get down the simulacrum chamber at this point," he finished dryly.

"Inbound message," Jenna announced. "I think they want to talk to us."

"Play it," David ordered, and Damien turned, standing next to the exit from the bridge, to watch the recording.

A tall man in a plain black suit appeared on the screen, surrounded by the bustle of the cruiser's bridge. His eyes were a sharp, piercing blue framed by neatly trimmed shoulder-length hair. He wore the gold medallion of a Mage, but without any of the symbols that marked training or degrees.

"I am Mikhail Azure," the man said simply. "I command the *Azure Gauntlet* and the Blue Star Syndicate, and I have now brought you to bay.

"This message is for the Mage Damien Montgomery," he continued. "We both know that you have an extraordinary gift, Damien, and that you are pursued by the Protectorate for its use."

"Today does not need to end in fire. Your Captain knows the value of my word, and I give it to you on this:

"If you surrender, and swear to serve me willingly, I give my word of honor that I will spare the *Blue Jay* and its crew – even your Captain Rice, for all his sins against me and mine."

Mikhail's piercing gaze seemed to hold Damien's across the room and the vast gap of deep space between them.

"I am generous to my employees, Damien, and if you serve me I will make you rich and powerful beyond your wildest dreams. You cannot lose here – and do not think you can escape me if you refuse. You are out of time. I can be magnanimous, but I will not be defied."

The recording ended.

Damien stepped back into the bridge, glancing around at David and Jenna.

"He's right that we can't run," Jenna said quietly, looking at him.

"You got his son killed," Damien said to David. "Would he really keep his word?"

"He's not as trustworthy as Falcone," the Captain replied slowly. "But in this? To buy *your* loyalty? He would.

"Your gift would be worth that to him."

Of course, Damien knew, what Azure would want from him was warships. Dozens of ships like the *Blue Jay* – regular freighters with amplifier, whose victims would never seem them coming. He could save the *Blue Jay*, but only at the cost of thousands of lives.

"May I?" he asked Jenna, touching the communication controls. She nodded slowly, activating the recorder and focusing the camera on Damien.

"Lord Azure, I have considered your offer," he told the camera, "and I have decided that I have no interest in being a low-life murdering scum working for criminals and slavers. You can go to hell, and take your 'offer' with you."

Cutting the recording, Damien turned back to Captain Rice – *his* Captain.

"Please tell me you have a plan, boss."

"After all we've been through?" David asked him with a slow grin. "Of *course* I have a plan."

#

Azure had not actually expected Montgomery to blithely change sides, though he had suspected that Rice might convince the youth to

265

make a career change to save the rest of the ship. There was rejection and there was *insulting*, however.

"I see that Montgomery has already established his opinion of us," he said icily, loud enough that everyone on the bridge of the *Azure Gauntlet.* "I suggest we show him what us 'low-life murdering scum' think of lily-handed Mages too naïve to know a good offer when they see one!"

The answering growl told him he'd hit the right tone. Few of his people had chosen the path they now walked, and to be judged by a man who'd been handed the world on a silver platter the way many of the Protectorate's Mages were stung.

"Take us in to seven light seconds, Mister Wong, and prepare your precision kinetics," Azure ordered, leaning back in his chair.

They'd emerged from their jump twenty light seconds away from the fleeing freighter. The *Blue Jay* was well within the range of the *Gauntlet's* heavy missiles, but those weapons lacked the precision to disable the ship's matrix. A single one of those gigaton warheads would vaporize the freighter.

The Navy's answer to that, decades ago, had been the precision kinetic missile: a light, antimatter-driven missile with no warhead except its own mass. Carefully aimed, the missile could eliminate turrets, break rotating ribs, and similar disabling damage. To carry a low enough velocity to avoid doing critical damage though, the weapon's range was limited – and detailed targeting instructions were required from the parent vessel.

The Snapdragon V missiles carried by the *Gauntlet* had a maximum range of just over ten light seconds. At that range, though, Azure's experience was that even Navy vessels tended to inflict far more damage than intended. The closer they got to the *Blue Jay* before firing, the better – and rare indeed was the Mage who's amplified reach was more than six light seconds.

"We will be clear to fire in less than three hours," Wong reported quietly. Behind him, the Mages at the Simulacrum switched out, the dark-haired youth whose golden amulet actually bore the stars of a Jump Mage replacing one of his illegally trained fellows. "I've had Jourdaine move up," Wong continued, nodding to the exchange behind him. "He's rested for eight hours, so he can jump us after the *Jay* if they run."

"Keep your eyes peeled, Mister Wong," Azure ordered softly, his eyes on the scanners. "Rice is a tricky bastard, and I will tolerate no more surprises from him."

Wong simply nodded and returned to his station, just behind the Simulacrum at the heart of the bridge.

Azure settled into his chair, watching the screens gathered around him and the bridge crew beyond them. They weren't the finely oiled machine of the handful of Protectorate warship's he'd seen the bridge of, but they were more than good enough for his purposes.

Sixty minutes passed while the *Azure Gauntlet*'s massive engines blazed, propelling her towards her prey at fifteen gravities. Without the gravity runes carved into the floor of every level of the ship, the crew would have been crushed to death long ago at these speeds.

"Sir, the *Blue Jay* just dropped a cargo container," Hu reported from the sensor station. "I'm not detecting anything unusual about it, but its drifting free in space. Seems an odd time to be ejecting their garbage."

"The *last* time the *Blue Jay* appeared to be disposing of their garbage, a starship hunting them *died*," Wong observed dryly. "Monroe! Target that container with a heavy missile and blow it to hell."

The brightly haired gunner didn't respond aloud, but moments later a single missile blasted out from the *Gauntlet's* forward tubes. It blasted forward at thirteen thousand gravities, closing in on the innocent-looking cargo container.

Four minutes later, with the Syndicate missile still forty seconds out, the cargo container gracefully came apart. With the *Azure Gauntlet*'s sensors focused on it, Azure was easily able to spot the pre-placed charges that blew out all six exterior panels.

Several seconds passed in silence as Azure found himself holding his breath to see what happened next. Then, with their missile still ten seconds out, the neat racking holding the contents together came apart as well.

The *Blue Jay* disappeared from their screens, hidden behind *hundreds* of threat icons.

"*What the fuck?!*" Azure exclaimed involuntarily.

"The container was full of missiles," Hu answered after a long pause. "It looks like they suffered some attrition to the charges and initial launch, but we have three hundred and seventy eight fusion drives missiles inbound."

Azure looked at the blinking red icons on his screens. The missiles were blazing back at the *Gauntlet* at five thousand gravities, nothing compared to their own missiles, but there were so *many* of them.

"Talk to me, Wong," he ordered.

"Tempests of some variety," his servant explained calmly. "They're self-targeting and very smart. Compared to our own missiles, they're slow, long-burning, and carry pitiful warheads."

"And?"

"And we can stop maybe three-quarters of that salvo," Wong admitted. "Our armor would probably take thirty or forty hits before it gave way. The remaining fifty or so nukes would gut us and end the Blue Star Syndicate in a blaze of nuclear fire."

Azure glared at the missiles as they shot towards him.

"Surprises," he said bitterly. "Do what you must, Mister Wong."

His captain nodded sharply, and turned back to the *Gauntlet's* bridge crew.

"Jourdaine!" Wong snapped. "Get us the *hell* out of here!"

#

"Damn."

The mild curse word from David was among the worst Damien had ever heard the Captain swear, but it utterly failed to cover the disappointment at watching the pursuing cruiser disappear into a jump flash as the massive salvo of missiles bore down on it.

"Kelly, activate the self-destructs," the Captain ordered after a long pause. "No point in leaving a traffic hazard around for the next poor bastard."

A moment later, the screens surrounding Damien in the simulacrum chamber darkened automatically, as over three hundred one-hundred-megaton fusion warheads detonated simultaneously.

"Damien, get us out of here," David ordered after the fireballs faded. "While they *probably* can't jump right back, I'd rather not stick around and find out!"

The only reasons Damien *hadn't* already jumped them away was David's strict orders not to jump without waiting twelve hours from the last time. Once the Captain revoked that order, he settled his hands on the Simulacrum.

Energy flowed through him as he aligned the runes inlaid into his palms with the gaps and the models, and he relaxed into the warming sensation.

"Jumping," he reported, and channeled the spell.

One indistinguishable moment later, and the freighter was somewhere else – and Damien's migraine was back. At least he wasn't bleeding like he'd been after pushing the first six jumps.

"We've bought ourselves at least some time," David told Damien and the others over the intercom. "Everyone get some rest – *especially* you, Damien. In six hours, I need you to jump us again.

"Then, once we've got a bit more space between us and these assholes, I'm calling a staff meeting," the Captain continued. "I'm starting to run out of clever ideas, so I'm planning on stealing all of yours."

Alaura paced her office on the *Tides of Justice* impatiently. She'd configured the one bare wall to show her the view of the asteroid below, and it was a depressing sight.

Darkport had been hammered hard, and it turned out that their main hangars weren't even working anymore. Brigadier Raphael's transports had ended up having to blast their way into the station to deliver desperately needed oxygen resupply.

For all that the second thing the Brigadier's men had done was arrest the entire ruling council of the station – all Falcone Dons, wanted for dozens of crimes across the Protectorate – they'd been greeted as rescuers and heroes. Julian Falcone, who had met the Marines when they boarded and pre-emptively surrendered himself, had not understated the situation.

Raphael's men judged that they'd had less than twenty minutes to spare when they'd blasted new tunnels into the blocked off third of the station and set up field oxygen supplies. There had been fourteen hundred people in that part of the station, and every one of them owed their lives to the Protectorate.

The Protectorate was now in unquestioned control of the notorious station that had spawned a *lot* of black spots on recent history. The last twenty hours were easily described as 'a good day's work,' but Alaura still had a problem.

They had *no* idea where either the *Blue Jay* or Mikhail Azure's *Azure Gauntlet* had gone. Darkport wasn't a place for requiring flight plans on good days, let alone while under attack by overwhelming force.

Now that Raphael's men were in control of the station, he had a cyber-warfare team quietly tearing through the computers. Alaura's hope was that they would find *some* clue that would permit to chase one of the two ships.

A pinging chime from her wrist personal computer interrupted her reverie, and she threw the call up on the wall-screen, superimposing it over the image of Darkport.

"Brigadier," she greeted Raphael. "Do you have good news?"

"Not sure yet, ma'am," the soldier, still wearing his combat exo-suit despite having declared the station secure four hours ago, told her. "I have someone who is insisting on speaking to the 'leader of your tin cans out there', and since she managed to sneak into my command post past half a platoon of *very* capable security types, I figured she might well be worth your time."

269

Raphael gestured, and the camera rotated to show a woman dressed in a dark blue jumpsuit. For a moment, Alaura thought she was a small woman, and then realized that the soldiers flanking her were still in exo-suits. The intruder was easily six feet tall, with short-cropped black hair and dark eyes that were currently unreadable.

"I am Alaura Stealey, Hand of the Mage-King of Mars," Alaura introduced herself calmly. "You've managed to impress my Brigadier. Who are you, and why do you wish to speak with me?"

"A Hand, huh?" the woman repeated in a soft voice. "That works. I am Julia Amiri. You haven't heard of me."

Alaura checked her files surreptitiously.

"You're right," she admitted.

"I'm a bounty hunter," Amiri continued. "I worked with my brother, ran a ship – the *Last Angel*. We tried to stay on the right side of everybody, including the Protectorate."

Alaura gestured for her to continue. She wasn't sure where Amiri was going, but she could at least guess at part of it.

"My brother, idiot that he was, took the *Last Angel* out against Azure," Amiri said flatly. "Mikhail Azure killed him – him and twenty-six other men and women who were the next thing to family to me.

"I want blood, Lady Stealey, and I think you can give it to me," she finished bluntly.

"I'm not sure what you think I can do, Miss Amiri," Alaura said carefully. "I intend to pursue Azure, yes, but I don't see any reason to bring you with me."

"You won't find him without me," the hunter replied. "I can give you Azure. I can even give you the ship he jumped out of here after, since I doubt you care nothing for the *Blue Jay* and its wonder Mage," she continued with a cold smile.

"I'm a Tracker, Lady Hand," Amiri told her. "Get me full sensor read-outs of their jumps, and I can tell you where they went."

Alaura froze.

"That isn't possible," she objected. "No analysis has ever found a pattern to jump flares."

"It's not a pattern," Amiri replied. "It's… a feeling, an intuition. But I haven't been wrong in ten years. And without me, you'll never bring Azure to bay."

The Hand looked the woman up and down frankly. Flanked by two hulking men clad in armor that would allow them to rip her apart with her bare hands, she was tense and on edge – but not afraid.

"Raphael," Alaura said after a long moment, and the camera rotated back to the Brigadier.

"Yes, Lady Hand?"

"Send her to me."

#

When Julia Amiri was escorted into Alaura's office by Mage-Lieutenant Harmon, the size of the woman truly sank home. The young Mage-Lieutenant wasn't a small man by any means, just over six feet and broad-shouldered.

The bounty hunter over-topped him by three inches, was just as broad-shouldered, and had a physique to put legendary Amazons to shame. Harmon looked overwhelmed – though not intimidated – by the woman he was escorting.

"Miss Amiri, Lady Hand," he announced her before bowing out of the room.

Amiri glanced back after him, somewhat amused.

"He's cute," she observed. "Personal aide, huh?"

"Mage-Lieutenant Harmon is on track to command a Navy destroyer before he's thirty," Stealey told Amiri calmly. "His superiors judged that time in service to a Hand would broaden his horizons in a useful manner. He is also a powerful enough Mage that you are absolutely no physical threat to him. Still think he's cute?"

The bounty hunter whistled silently, and glanced back at the closed door.

"Cuter," she admitted, "though in a different sense than I meant before. My apologies, Lady Hand. I am... unaware of the protocol for dealing with a Hand."

"The protocol is what I say it is," Alaura told her. "So it's irrelevant. You said you could track the *Blue Jay* and Azure's ship. What do you need?"

"A three dimensional modeling tank and every sensor scan you pulled from Darkport's computers of the jump," Amiri said immediately. "Privacy to work would be appreciated as well. As you might imagine, it's not a simple task."

"I'm still only barely accepting it as possible," Alaura told her dryly, considering the hunter's request. "How are you at secrets?" she asked eventually.

"Depends on whose and how badly they need to be kept," Amiri replied.

"The Protectorate's, and the kind the crew of this ship doesn't know about," Alaura replied. "If you can do what you claim, I would be interested in employing you after this is complete – and I have tools that would be of value to you then and now."

The statuesque bounty hunter eyed the Hand.

271

"Not much of one for interview processes, are you?" she asked. "Don't know much about what Hands do. Hunt bad guys, keep the peace, right?"

"We are His Majesty's voice, sword and hand beyond Sol," Alaura agreed. "Interstellar criminals, wannabe warlords, pirates, and rebellions – these are our purview. Our Mandate is that of the Protectorate – to keep humanity safe."

"I'll think about it?" Amiri offered slowly. "Once Azure is dead or rotting in a prison."

"Either way, you have the sworn oath of a Guild Bounty Hunter that I will keep your secrets, Hand Alaura Stealey, unto death or your betrayal of our contract."

"Good enough," Alaura accepted. She tapped a sequence of commands on her wrist personal computer and the bookshelves on the wall slid sideways, revealing a small opening into the secret workspace built beside her office. "Come with me."

Alaura led the Tracker into the hidden Star Mirror chamber and gestured her to the computers and modeling tank.

"There's your modeling tank," she told her. "This room is locked, and only I have access to it. No one will disturb you."

Amiri looked around in surprise.

"Why do you have a full-size sensor cluster *inside* the ship?" she asked, her gaze locking on the massive array of scanners that occupied fully half of the room. "And what's with the shiny mirror?"

"Once you have identified the *Blue Jay*'s destination, I will use this to scout ahead," Alaura said quietly. "It's a Star Mirror, and there are very few of them in existence. The skills require to build one are so rare they may as well as not exist, but with it, I can look across the stars to make sure we are not jumping into a trap."

The Bounty Hunter stared at the silver-framed mirror in shock and awe.

"That's *impossible*," she whispered. "Bringing light from a *light year* away?"

"You live in a world of magic and starships that travel by spell; and you find *that* impossible?" Alaura asked dryly. "For that matter, you can track a jump, and many would call that impossible."

"I have hunted Mages, Lady Hand," Amiri told her quietly. "I made a point to know what they can do, and this isn't even in the possibilities I've studied."

"There are artifacts that can be made that are beyond what most believe possible," Alaura agreed. "A small handful of them are available to the Hands of the Mage-King, that we can do his will."

Julia Amiri crossed to the mirror and gently, reverently, touched the corded silver that surrounded it.

"Mirror, mirror on the wall," she muttered, "who's the *scariest* of them all…"

"That would be my boss," Stealey told her. "Now let's find our running Mage."

#

Having slept for six more hours before jumping again, Damien was finally feeling something close to human when he joined the *Blue Jay*'s other senior officers in the Captain's dining room. His own personal clock was sufficiently warped by trying to recover from his six rapid jumps that the Captain was actually serving supper.

The meal wasn't one of David's flights of culinary fancy, but the conversation stayed determinedly on lighter subjects until the last of the pasta had been cleared away. Then, the Captain leaned back and looked at his crew.

"I don't know how much time we're going to have," he said quietly. "We're pushing Damien as hard as we *safely* can, but that cruiser has multiple Jump Mages and has proven they can follow our jumps. They're going to catch up to us, and we have no onboard weapons, no boxes full of missiles. We need a plan."

There was silence around the table. Damien glanced around at his fellows, hoping Kellers, Jenna or Kelzin had a thought or an idea.

"Whatever we do, we have to end this," Jenna said quietly. "Chasing them away again won't save us – we physically cannot hide a starship in the Fringe, and we can't go back into the MidWorlds."

"We can't run either," Kelzin said quietly, looking at Damien with a concern that suggested that he still looked worse than he was feeling. "Damien can't outrun a ship with multiple Mages on his own."

"We can't run, and we can't hide – but we can't fight either!" Kellers objected. "If we'd time to get *any* weapons mounted, maybe we could come up with some kind of trick to get them close enough, but the only thing we have are anti-missile turrets. Those won't even scratch the cruiser's hull."

"Come on people," David said loudly. "There has to be *something*. I refuse to accept that we are going to end up in those bastards' hands."

"We could blow the ship," Jenna said quietly. "If we know we can't run, self-destruct. I, for one," she continued as she looked around at the others, "prefer that to being tortured to death. If this has to end, let's end it on *our* terms."

"No," Damien said quietly, and everyone turned to look at him. "We're not out of options yet."

273

Everyone looked at him in silence, letting him corral his thoughts. He still had the rune pattern in his quarters. So many things could go wrong, but...

"Jenna's right," he finally continued. "This has to end. So let's end it in fire – *our* fire."

"You have a plan," David said flatly.

"It's risky," Damien admitted. "It could easily kill me. But if it works..."

"If you die, we're all dead anyway," Jenna objected, and Damien rounded on her.

"You just admitted we're all dead!" he snapped. "Do you think I *want* to risk blowing out my own damned nervous system?"

"I have a rune," he explained, "that I picked up on Darkport. They took it from the arm of a Hand of the Mage-King, and it was tied to that man's own power. I *think* I can modify it to work for me, and I think it would increase the range I can affect with the amplifier."

David considered for a long moment before nodding.

"Do you need anything from the rest of us?" he asked.

"Faith," Damien said quietly. "Any good luck you can spare, too. This could go very wrong."

#

The plain sheet of portrait board seemed an oddly prosaic piece of backing for a rune whose existence was probably as secret as the possibility you could turn a jump matrix into an amplifier. Next to it on Damien's workstation was the stretched out skin of the fallen Hand, and Damien was slowly recreating the rune in a silver-based paint.

He heard the door open behind him, and the heavy thud of a brawnier person entering the magical gravity field his workshop maintained.

"Boss," he greeted David softly.

"How bad can it really get, Damien?" his Captain asked behind him.

The young Mage considered, studying the weak energy flow in the inactive rune in front of him. He scraped off part of a line, recreating it two centimeters over.

"I'm trying to create a tailored and controlled thaumic feedback loop," Damien finally answered. "If I really screw up, I miss the loop and just feed the energy back into myself. That will be fatal. Painfully so, but quick and contained."

"And the real worst case scenario?"

"I get it *almost* right and lose control of the feedback loop," the Mage admitted. "That would... well, the *Blue Jay* wouldn't survive. It would be even quicker though – no one would ever know something had gone wrong."

David's hand descended on his shoulder in a firm grip.

"You can do this, right?" the Captain asked, his voice very quiet.

"Eighty-twenty," Damien admitted with a sigh. "I can't promise better."

"I trust you," David said. "Is there anything we can do?"

"Tell Kelly where to find me?" Damien asked. "This is about done, and I'm not sure I want to be alone when I do this."

This was 'cut lines in my own flesh and pour molten silver into them.' He was pretty sure he needed moral support for that.

"She's already waiting outside," David told him with a chuckle. "Good luck Damien."

#

"So how are you planning to try to kill yourself to save us all this time?" Kelly asked. The petite engineer, responsible for saving everyone aboard the ship herself at least twice Damien could think of, dropped herself into the single extra chair in the workshop.

"This," Damien pointed to the rune he'd finally finished drawing on the board. "If I've done this right, this rune will increase my own magical abilities around three-fold, allowing me to reach even further with the amplifier and do more damage."

"My lack of strength has held us back before," he admitted. "If this works, it won't anymore – I'll be stronger than any Mage that doesn't have a rune like it."

"If this rune is so powerful, why doesn't every Mage already have it?" Kelly asked, eyeing the silver design with concern.

"Writing in a script wouldn't work," Damien explained. "I had to shape it to my own power, matching it *exactly* to myself. Whoever did this one," he gestured at the case with its preserved skin, "had to be able to see the flow of power, the same way I do."

"So, what, you think the Hands have access to someone who sees like you?" she asked. "I've looked it up Damien – what you describe is *unique*."

"Or secret," he admitted. "So secret even system Guildmasters don't know about it."

"And you're going to tattoo this into your own skin?"

"I *wish* it was a tattoo," Damien told her grimly. "It's closer to an inlay, much as they did on my palms. It's a very specific mix of silver, polymers, and some other materials that I have to pour into carefully aligned cuts in my skin." He showed the runes on his palm to her and she touched it gently, running her fingers over the hard yet flexible ridge of the rune.

"Can I help?" Kelly asked, meeting his eyes.

"I'm going to have to do it with magic," Damien told her. "It's… not going to be safe in here."

"Can I help?" she repeated, smiling at him.

"It would work better if someone else transferred the pattern to my arm," he admitted. "And then, well…" He smiled. "I wouldn't object if you wanted to stay and hold my hand. This is going to hurt."

Kelly moved closer to him, setting up the lights carefully as he laid his right arm out flat for her to work on. With both his arm and the diagram lit, she studied the original skin for a minute, and then picked up with brush he'd been using on the picture.

"There is a tiny amount of silver in the paint," Damien told her. "It's enough to allow me to judge if the rune is correct. What you're laying is a stencil I can use as a target for the magic in a minute – the closer you can match the diagram, the better."

"Damien, I'm an engineer. I was trained in drafting," she reminded him. "Now, shush and let me work."

The workshop was quiet as she slowly, delicately, and carefully duplicated the rune structure on the diagram on his arm. Only the tiniest of trickles of energy flowed through the silver solution, but Damien watched it carefully as it drew sparks from his own energy. In some ways, this was the most dangerous part for *him*.

"It's done," Kelly finally said, leaning back. "What now?"

"Grab the block of silver from the other workbench," Damien asked. Once that was laid beside his arm, he closed his eyes for a long moment. "Now is the part where you just hold my hand," he told her.

Shifting around him, Kelly settled her hand on his left, gently but firmly squeezing. Damien gave her a grateful nod, and then focused his power on the tiny ingot of silver and polymer. Power flickered into it, and it rose off the workbench and began to melt.

He spun it out in thin air, the molten metal warming the air of the room as he drew the pattern of his rune in silver and power. The liquid metal moved smoothly to the commands of his power, and then slowly descended over his arm. This was both the most dangerous part, and the most painful

The rune hovered so close the molten metal was burning the hairs on his skin. Damien took a deep breath, and squeezed Kelly's hand back.

Then, as quickly as he could, he slashed out with his magic. Tiny lines of force flashed along the pattern of energy and silver Kelly had painted on his skin, and blood welled as he cut open his own flesh.

Before the pain could really sink in, he slammed the rune closed upon his arm.

Damien Montgomery screamed. Molten silver sank into the wounds he'd opened in his skin, cauterizing the wounds even as his magic cooled the silver, knitting skin around it. His entire arm was alive with pain, but he focused on the magic, cooling the silver, stretching skin, stitching wounds closed.

Then, suddenly, it was done. The heat in his arm flashed to impossible intensity, and then spread through his body in a tumultuous rush that took his breath away. *Power* filled him, a cascading, looping, growing sense of strength like nothing he'd ever felt before.

Breathing sharply, he controlled it. His new-found strength rippled through him, but he contained it. His entire body felt full of heat and electricity, but he damped it, brought it back down to something resembling normal – as if he would ever be normal again.

He finally opened his eyes, feeling sweat on his skin that hadn't been there before, and met Kelly's worried gaze.

"I think it worked," he coughed, his throat dry.

"Well, you didn't blow up and neither did the ship," she replied. "Think that's a win?"

Damien found a smile through his suddenly cracked and dry lips. "Hell yeah."

#

Mikhail Azure was not a patient man by nature. He had learned patience over the decades while clawing together the largest criminal organization in the galaxy by hook, crook and blood, but it was still a learned skill.

And he was fresh out.

The Crime Lord stalked back and forth behind his chair on the bridge of the *Azure Gauntlet* like a caged panther, his eyes *daring* any member of the crew to so much as breathe in his direction as he waited for Wong to finish his analysis of the latest jump flare.

Finally, *finally*, the dark-skinned cruiser commander rejoined him on the bridge.

"Well?" Azure demanded.

"They jumped three hours ago," Wong said calmly. "I have the location, and they've been jumping every six hours, regular as clockwork, since our last brush."

"Montgomery can clearly push a jump in five," Azure pointed out. "Will we be coming out two hours flight away from them again?"

"We should be emerging at roughly ten light seconds, three million kilometers," Wong replied. "I cannot guarantee closer except by pure luck. It will take us one hour and twenty minutes to close to a zero velocity rendezvous at seven light seconds to allow for use the precision kinetics."

"And if they have another crate of missiles?"

"Alissa is jumping us," the Hunter replied. "Jourdaine is standing by. If they pull that trick again, we will evacuate again. We have time, my lord – they are still a dozen jumps from any inhabited system."

"I see," Azure allowed. "And if they have some other trick we don't see coming, Mister Wong?"

Wong shrugged. "I will have Monroe prepared and update a GOTH targeting plan," he said calmly. "If it appears that we are in severe danger, we will destroy the *Blue Jay*. I presume you would prefer that to your own death."

Azure glared at Captain, but finally took his seat.

"Very well, Mister Wong. Take us after them."

#

"Here they come," Jenna said quietly, the words echoing in the *Blue Jay*'s silent bridge.

David looked at the main screen as the jump flare settled into the disturbingly familiar sharp spike of the Syndicate cruiser. They'd emerged much closer this time, less than three million kilometers from the *Blue Jay*.

If the *Jay* had managed to have the lasers he'd purchased installed, the Blue Star Syndicate ship would have regretted that decision. Instead, all he could do was watch with frustration as the warship's sensors stabilized, and it began to accelerate for the *Blue Jay* at fifteen gravities.

"I'd love to watch those bastards suffer an engine malfunction," he told Jenna, his voice cold. "There's a *reason* the Navy doesn't push their ships to fifteen unless it's an emergency. Engine failures make very pretty white stars, for a few minutes anyway."

"Unless you're counting on being far luckier than we're used to, boss, I think we need to plan for a more pro-active response," his XO pointed out.

David nodded.

"Hell, given the tricks we've pulled on everyone after us, I'm half-tempted to start accelerating *towards* them, just to make them paranoid," he admitted. "It would get Damien in range sooner, *and* make them sweat."

"Boss, making the guys with the multi-gigaton weapons sweat isn't conducive to our long-term survival," Jenna told him. "Let's just keep running, and hope Damien knows what he's talking about."

The Captain nodded, and activated the intercom to Damien's quarters.

"Kelly here," the engineer's voice answered.

"Our friends are here, Kelly," David told her. "How's Damien?"

"Asleep," she replied. "Seems like the jumps are taking less out of him now, but he did just cut himself open and pour molten metal in the wounds."

"We have an hour until the Syndicate is in range for their kinetics. Wake him and get him down to the simulacrum chamber – then get yourself to engineering. At this point," he admitted, "I have no idea how this is going to turn out."

"Will do, boss."

#

"I swear, we missed them by minutes," Medici told Alaura, pacing back and forth on the video screen linking her office to his flag bridge. "That jump flare is *fresh*."

The Admiral was agitated and worn. Twenty two hours and eleven jumps out of Darkport, pretty much the entire flotilla was in the same state. Each jump brought them closer in behind their prey, though, and even Alaura could feel the excitement in the ships she'd commandeered.

Her own focus was on Montgomery, but she couldn't help but agree with the pleasant buzz the crew was enjoying over the thought of finally putting Mikhail Azure down.

"If they're that close, we should be able to catch them on the next jump," she replied. "If Amiri sorts out their destination, how quickly can you jump, Admiral?"

"We've been cycling the Jump Mages hard, but not *that* hard, ma'am," Medici said with a bright flash of teeth. "This close, we can jump as soon as the Hunter gives us a target."

"Understood, Admiral," Alaura told him. "I'll be in touch."

Cutting the intercom, she stepped through the open secret passage into the concealed chamber with the Star Mirror.

"How long?" she asked simply.

"Same as every other jump, Alaura," Julia Amiri said bluntly, her hands and eyes busy on the three dimensional tank in front of her. "Give me an hour, then we can take a peek through your mirror and see what we can find. I want Azure more than any of your crew, trust me."

With a calm nod, Alaura took a seat back at her workstation. It was down to time, and hoping that the *Blue Jay* survived until they got there.

They'd been tracking both ships for most of a day now, and Alaura could do the calculations as well as any of her compatriots. Unless she was wrong, when the *Azure Gauntlet* had left this system, they'd caught up with Montgomery's ship.

"You're a tricky bastard, Montgomery," she whispered aloud. "I'm coming. *Stay alive.*"

#

Damien was too warm. In the eighteen hours since he'd carved the Rune of Power into his arm, he'd been feverishly hot as his body tried to adopt the new levels of thaumic energy swirling through him. The painkillers he was taking probably didn't help, but that was the only way he'd been able to sleep.

He wasn't on painkillers now. He couldn't afford the dulled senses as he watched the Syndicate cruiser bear unswervingly down on his ship and hoped that everything he'd done would be enough. His arm *hurt*, but the heat burning through him suggested he hadn't failed.

"They'll try close to seven light seconds," David reminded him over the intercom. "I'd really like if they didn't make it that close, Damien."

The young Mage rested the runes on his palms on the blank spaces on the Simulacrum meant for them. The power of his new rune and the amplifier linked together, and he looked at the stars through the lens of the *Blue Jay*'s runes.

"I won't guarantee more than eight light seconds," he said softly. "And if I guess wrong, it might be enough for them to realize what's going on – which I doubt we'll survive."

"Let them close then," David replied quietly. They'd been watching the oncoming ship for fifteen minutes now. "You can take him? That ship is heavily armored."

"I have no idea," Damien admitted. "But there's only one way to find out now."

#

Time seemed to crawl as the *Azure Gauntlet* swept towards its prey. So close to victory now, Mikhail Azure was tempted to order Wong to pour on more speed. Of course, since the *Gauntlet* was now decelerating towards zero relative to Rice's ship, that would have been counter-productive, but the almost childish urge ran in the back of his mind.

Instead, he gripped the edge of his chair tightly, watching the range figures drop and glancing around the bridge. Wong had pulled the same main bridge crew who had assaulted Darkport with to this shift for the attack. The petite woman Hu controlled sensors. The mohawked gunner Monroe sat at the weapons console, two separate firing plans laid out on his console, just waiting a command to fire.

Wong sat at the center of the bridge, and now Azure could be mentally magnanimous towards the Tracker. For all of the setbacks, the ex-bounty hunter had delivered Azure's prey to him, and shortly they would return and complete the conquest of Darkport.

Almost an hour had passed since their arrival, and barely twenty minutes and a hundred thousand kilometers remained before they would fire on the *Blue Jay* and capture his prey.

Something shifted. He *felt* magic sweep through the ship, on a level he'd never personally experienced, and then felt the ship lurch.

"What the hell?" Wong demanded. "What's happening?"

Everything seemed to move very slowly, and Azure *knew* what had happened. He could feel the energy rippling through the ship as magic ripped into the mighty cruisers antimatter tanks.

"We have a critical engine breach!" Hu shouted. "Containment is failing!"

Azure reached out with his magic and slammed a single button on Monroe's console.

Behind him, the antimatter fuel tanks feeding *Azure Gauntlet*'s immense engines lost containment. Hundreds of tons of matter met its opposite and disappeared in a flash of white light and unimaginable energy.

In front of him, every one of the *Gauntlet*'s missile tubes fired. Fifty-two missiles blasted into space, seeking revenge for their mothership.

Azure had enough time to be certain the Go To Hell launch had succeeded, and then the antimatter explosion reached the bridge.

#

"Got him!" Amiri announced. "Stealey, get in here!"

The Hand was in the Star Mirror chamber before the Tracker had finished speaking.

"Give me the co-ordinates," she ordered, but Amiri had already thrown them up in the holographic tank.

The Hand took a long moment to review them, committing the distances and angles involved into her mind before crossing to the Star Mirror.

Holding the location in her mind, she laid her hands on the corded silver frame of the runic artifact and focused her power. Energy ran out from her, the Rune of Power on her arm growing warm as it doubled and redoubled her strength, interacting with the Mirror to do what even by magic's standards was impossible for most.

The silver cords lit up, glowing with an inner fire as the Star Mirror opened and showed Stealey the stars a light year way. The sensor behind her whirred as its scanners drank in that far away light and the computers conjured up an image.

The image was easily ten minutes old, and it was terrifying.

The *Azure Gauntlet* was closing on its prey, rapidly approaching the range at which the pirates would be able to use kinetic missiles to carefully disable the *Blue Jay*.

Alaura regarded it for only moments before making her decision.

"Medici," she snapped, opening a channel. "I'm flipping you scan data from our destination – can you arrange the jump so we arrive in a tight enough defensive formation around the *Blue Jay* to protect her from a disabling kinetic strike?"

"I'm not even going to ask how you got this," the Admiral said slowly. "We can – but we'll need time!"

"Do it quickly!" she told him. "The *Blue Jay* may not *have* time!"

#

The Rune had succeeded beyond Damien's wildest dreams. With its power flowing through the *Blue Jay*'s amplifier he'd been able to reach out to the Syndicate cruiser and enhance the *Jay*'s sensor returns. Locating the cruiser's antimatter fuel tanks had been easy, and after that, a tiny spark would have worked.

The fireball he'd conjured inside the warship had been almost overkill – and yet hadn't been enough.

"They're inbound at thirteen thousand gravities, running on internal seekers only," Jenna reported grimly. "We have three minutes, maybe less. I've spun up the RFLAMs, but they'll be coming in damned fast. The turrets can't stop all of them. They might get five."

"Damien?" the Captain asked, looking at the Mage with a scrap of hope.

"If I do everything I can think of, I might stop fifteen," Damien told him. Even with his new power fed into some of the spells he'd learned, there was only so much he could do.

"One getting through is enough," David said quietly. "We're going to emergency acceleration. Do what you can."

Moments later, Damien was crushed against the tiny acceleration platform in the simulacrum chamber as the *Blue Jay* accelerated at its maximum three gravities. It couldn't do much, but even the tiniest bit of evasive maneuvering bought them time. Precious fractions of a second could let Damien or the turrets take out a few more missiles.

It wasn't enough, and they all knew it. Damien glanced at the intercom screen, but there was nothing to say. The three of them were the only ones with enough information to know they were all doomed. Even if he could reach Kelly, to try and say something – anything! – it wouldn't be fair to fill her last moments with fear.

"I'm sorry," he said quietly. "I tried."

"You did all you could – hell, you did more than anyone else could have, and then some more," David told him. "It's been a good run, kid. I'm sorry we dragged you into all of this."

"Came in with both eyes open, Captain," Damien replied. "I didn't think you were desperate for a Mage for no reason, after all."

He laid his hands back on the Simulacrum and reached out with his power. He could start trying to pick off the missiles from here – might only take out a few more, but it was worth a shot. Any spell he could think of that would wipe more than one or two from space would wipe him out completely even now.

Pulses of coherent light began to flicker through space as Jenna opened up with the laser turrets, and Damien sank into the amplifier, flickers of fire lashing out into the emptiness around them. Missiles began to die, but only by the ones and twos – and the survivors grew closer.

At a hundred thousand kilometers, with the missiles barely thirty seconds away, Damien reached for the attack spell he'd used in Excelsior against the boarding pods. He might get dozens of them – but there were dozens *left*. And it was all he had. He reached for his power, and then –

"*Jump flare!*" Jenna shouted, and the white radiation flare of multiple jumps blinded Damien as the sky around him lit up.

Seventeen ships materialized out of nowhere – eight monstrous cruisers, each a match for the *Gauntlet* he'd just destroyed, and nine more destroyers. An entire *fleet* of Protectorate warships burst into existence around the *Blue Jay*.

Seconds passed, ticking away as Damien stared at the impossible ships in shock, and their sensors stabilized.

Then *their* turrets opened fire. The *Gauntlet*'s missiles died by the dozens: the salvo that had utterly doomed their modified freighter vanishing like ice in sunlight.

Damien stared at his screens in complete shock, and then a visual transmission popped up. He wasn't sure if someone had overridden the *Blue Jay*'s systems or if Jenna had just accepted it without saying anything.

An older woman, clad in a black uniform and a golden chain with an open-palmed hand, stood ramrod straight, staring levelly into the screen.

"I am Alaura Stealey, Hand of the Mage-King of Mars," she said calmly. "I am here to speak with Damien Montgomery."

"We are not your enemies, but I *will* prevent you from jumping," she continued. "I will board your ship with one companion. Please meet me in your shuttle bay."

#

Alaura recognized David Rice from the case files from his encounter, long ago, with the Blue Star Syndicate that had triggered much of the current mess, though age had not been overly kind to the heavyset Captain. Damien Montgomery, on the other hand, didn't look like he'd changed in the slightest from the photos from his imprisonment in Corinthian. Until you met the youth's eyes, anyway.

Both were waiting for her at the exit from the *Blue Jay*'s shuttle bay as she and Mage-Lieutenant Harmon disembarked from the Navy shuttle that delivered them to the freighter. She had decided to allow Amiri to accompany them after the Hunter started making paranoid noises, though the younger woman was remaining in the shuttle as a most-likely-unnecessary security precaution.

Years of practice allowed her to reach the two men without any undignified flailing, and she greeted them with a calm nod.

"Is there somewhere private we can discuss?" she asked. "This may be a long conversation."

Rice nodded carefully, one hand keeping him stable in the microgravity. "Follow me," he instructed.

The trip deeper into the trip was silent. Alaura had no intention of playing any of her cards yet, and the two men seemed a little shaky. Twenty minutes ago, she suspected, they had known they were going to die. Now a complete stranger held their fates in her hands.

Rice led them onto the elevators that linked to the ships rotating ribs, and Alaura breathed a concealed sigh of relief as the rotational pseudo-gravity took hold. She did *not* like microgravity, and it would have been rude to use magic to provide her own footing on someone else's ship.

Finally, they reached a plain conference room, the type found on any merchant ship for staff and business meetings. Rice led the way in and took a seat at the head of the table, with Damien at his right hand. Alaura remained standing, looking at the two men and considering.

"I take it from the absence of the *Azure Gauntlet* that Mikhail Azure has met with an accident?" she asked.

"He did," Rice replied calmly. "He attacked us, and we defended ourselves. I believe that is still our right under Protectorate law?"

"Your right, Captain?" Alaura asked. "Your privilege! We owe you a debt of gratitude. Azure has been a thorn in our side for years."

"Dropping a few charges would go a long way to showing that gratitude," Damien murmured, and Alaura raised an eyebrow at him.

"I guess I should clear that up to begin with," she told them. "You are not facing any charges in the Protectorate – I had the charges with regards to the *Blue Jay*'s modifications struck as soon as I arrived in Corinthian. Those related to breaking Mr. Montgomery out of jail I had dropped after I realized how much effort you'd put into preventing casualties – successfully, I might add."

"After today, I doubt any of the galaxy's crime lords will be chasing you either. My count is now *four* major crime lords that have ended up either dead or in jail after crossing your path," she continued. "You are probably safer than you've been in years."

"Four crime lords?" the Mage asked, surprised.

"James Azure, some five years ago now, died resisting arrest after Captain Rice directed us to him," Alaura pointed out. "You intentionally left Alistair Carney to catch the fall on the Spindle. He was taken alive, and will be spending the next twenty years a guest of a Martian jail. Julian Falcone surrendered Darkport to my forces to gain assistance saving his people, and will be facing a court on Saratoga shortly. And now, Mikhail Azure has very directly died by your hands."

"That's a track record many of our investigators would envy," she added. "But it does lead us to why Azure and half a dozen bounty hunters were chasing you."

"The *Blue Jay* has a fully functioning amplifier," Damien admitted. "I converted the jump matrix."

"I know," she said calmly. "Unfortunately, I am assured by those who understand these matters that any competent Rune Scribe, given a few weeks, could duplicate what was done to the *Jay*. She represents a template that any of the galaxy's crime lords could use to manufacture a fleet of undetectable raiders."

"The *Blue Jay*, bluntly, represents an unacceptable risk to the peace of the Protectorate," Alaura told them flatly.

"You just saved us, and now you want to destroy *my ship*?" Rice snapped. "Who do you think you are?!"

"I think I am a Hand of the Mage-King of Mars," she replied. "Captain Rice, the Protectorate owes you and your crew a deep and abiding debt for allowing us to remove Darkport and for removing Mikhail Azure. I am prepared to compensate you well above market value for this ship. Indeed, I believe we would be able to hand one of the Navy's *Archon* transports over to you as a replacement vessel."

That shut the Captain up. An *Archon* was one of the largest freighters built, mustering a *fifteen* million ton cargo load – five times the *Blue Jay* – and carrying a limited but effective suite of self-defense weapons.

"Please Captain," she pleaded gently. "I do not want to take away your livelihood or your hard built equity. But I *cannot* allow the *Blue Jay* to sail away. You must understand."

"She's right, boss," Damien Montgomery said quietly. "Any ship I did that to… it's why everyone has been chasing us for the last six months. She's offering you the best she can."

Rice nodded choppily. "Can we at least evacuate our things?"

"Of course," she agreed. "All of your personnel and possessions will be transferred to the cruiser *Rising Sun of Gallantry*. They will transport you to the Tau Ceti fleet base, where the Captain will make sure you take possession of your new ship."

"If the *Blue Jay* is a threat, what guarantee will you need that Damien won't do the same to another ship?" Rice asked, and Alaura sighed.

"Mister Montgomery has an exceptionally rare gift," she said, turning to look the Mage in the eyes. "I assume that to destroy the *Gauntlet* you have marked a Rune of Power on yourself. Show me," she instructed.

Slowly, uncomfortably, the young Mage rolled up the sleeve of his turtleneck, revealing the lines of silver she'd expected.

"Untrained and unaware, you are a worse threat than the *Blue Jay*," she said quietly. "You also, when in possession of the perfect raider, believing yourself wanted for crimes you hadn't committed, and chased to the edge of civilization, still acted with honor and integrity."

"Because of this, if you insist, I *will* let you go," she promised. "But I have an offer for you."

Montgomery gestured for her to continue.

"You are a Rune Wright," Alaura explained. "Only a Wright can see the flow of magic, and only a Wright could have turned a jump matrix into an amplifier."

"You have *no* idea what you can truly do with that gift," she continued. "There is only one person in the Protectorate who can teach you. If you come with me, I will take you to him."

"And then what?" he asked.

"Most likely? You would be assigned to the Hands to assist us, if not made a Hand yourself," Alaura admitted. "With your gifts and our support, you would be in a position to do good few others could match."

"Unfortunately, I need you to decide now," she told him.

The conference room was quiet for at least a minute, the young Mage looking down at his hands as Alaura watched him, hoping he would make the right choice. Finally, he looked back up at her and nodded once.

"I will need to say goodbye," he said quietly. "But then, I am yours, Hand Stealey."

#

The *Rising Sun of Gallantry* turned out to have an observation deck, a massive slab of magically transformed transparent steel that allowed people to look out onto deep space. As Damien and the rest of the crew of the *Blue Jay* occupied that deck, however, the ship had been turned so it faced the *Jay*.

Even at four kilometers distance, the massive freighter was clearly visible. The Ribs were no longer rotating, but the running lights were still on, outlining the ship against the black of the space between the stars.

"Scanners confirm no life signs," a voice carried over the intercom. The ship's Captain was piping an audio feed from the bridge to the observation deck, a small courtesy Damien appreciated.

Everyone was off the *Blue Jay*. Their hundred kilograms of possessions each had come with them. The ship's cat was apparently sharing Jenna's quarters aboard the cruiser, though she hadn't brought the animal to the observation.

"All ships confirm minimum safe distance," another voice reported. "We are fully clear."

"Fire tube one," the soft contralto of the *Gallantry*'s captain ordered.

A flash of light struck out from the cruiser. At thirteen thousand gravities, the missile crossed four kilometers in a blink of an eye, a bright streak that didn't, quite, connect the two ships.

Then the warhead detonated. A filter automatically darkened, shading the watcher's eyes from the glare of a one gigaton antimatter explosion.

When the light faded, nothing remained of the old ship, vaporized in a single moment.

Damien blinked away tears, and felt Kelly cuddle up to him.

"It's sad," she said softly. "It'll be better when we get to Tau Ceti and see the new ship the Captain's been promised."

"I'm not coming to Tau Ceti," Damien admitted. Evacuating the ship had been a rush. Now was the first moment of relative quiet he'd had with Kelly, for all that he knew it was probably the worst possible time.

"You're not?" Kelly sounded a lot calmer than he'd been afraid of.

"I'm going with Stealey," he told her awkwardly. "She knows someone who can train me in my gifts, and then I think I'm going to be working with her. Trying to make the Protectorate a better place."

The engineer turned away from him, and he laid his hand gently on her shoulder.

"I'm sorry," he whispered.

"We're spacers, Damien," she told him after a long pause. "I always knew we would never last forever. Always figured you'd find some cause that would drag you away – you're that type. I just hoped we would have more time."

"Me too," he admitted. "I always seem to be leaving people behind, wherever I go. I'm going to miss you."

"But not enough to stay." It wasn't a question. She laid her hand on top of his and squeezed hard. "I get it, Damien." Her voice was choked with unshed tears. "I get it. But with everything else, it hurts."

He wrapped her in his arms.

"I know. I'm sorry."

#

Damien walked through the unmarked stone corridors Alaura had led him to in silence. The walls pressed in on him oppressively, and he honestly wasn't sure where they were. The underground facility they had entered was *immense*, but it wasn't as if the Protectorate didn't have dozens of facilities that would meet that description.

They'd spent sixteen days jumping, so they could be almost anywhere in the half of the Protectorate on this side of Sol. Alaura had taken an almost childish delight in *not* telling him where they were going, and they arrived on planet via a Marine drop shuttle – which noticeably lacked such amenities as windows.

Now the Hand led the way through the tunnels with calm assurance, while Damien tried not to be distracted by the complex twists of silver runes snaking across the walls and roof around them. They moved too quickly for him to read them, but they seemed to be an amplifier matrix of a scale he could barely comprehend.

The runes and the Hand led him to the same place, and they stepped out into a single massive chamber at the heart of the mountain, and Damien gasped in shock.

The air above them was filled with a scale model of a star system. Everything from the sun at the center, to the three massive gas giants, to the asteroid belts and even, he was sure, the tiniest of ships was duplicated in floating molten silver sand that carried every minutiae of the reality of the system. It was a simulacrum, but unlike anything he'd ever seen.

"It affects most people who see it for the first time," an amused deep voice told him, and Damien looked up to see the only occupant of the room. He was a tall man, with silver hair but an unlined face, and he stood before a throne carved from the solid stone of the mountain – a throne that all the runes of the amplifier and the simulacrum ran to.

"This is the man I meant," Alaura Stealey said softly. "The only person who could even begin to train a Rune Wright."

"Damien Montgomery, be known to my master: Desmond Michael Alexander the Third, Protector of Man, and Mage-King of Mars."

###

Author's Note

Starship's Mage began as an experiment in short story writing sometime in 2012. My agent, Mike Kabongo, liked it and suggested I expand it. The story could quite neatly become a novella, but to turn it into a novel I was going to have to add a lot of content, which would in some ways be completely separate arcs.

At the same time, I was starting to read a lot more self-published fiction, and had come across several serials of novellas and novels that caught my eye and gave me the idea of releasing Starship's Mage as a series of novella length episodes.

I also figured that writing what was basically a full novel in multiple shorter pieces would be easier to find time around work for. As it turns out, announced release dates were also good motivators!

The first month that "Starship's Mage: Episode 1" was out, I sold twenty novellas. In October 2014, ten months later, I sold over *two thousand*.

This Omnibus is the culmination of the year of effort that went into the Starship's Mage serial, fuelled by the interest of you, the readers. Getting to this point took the help of more people than I can quickly name, but at the top of the list are the crazy souls who have been my beta readers throughout: Russell Rokos, Meg Anderson, Stef Herrel, and G. W. Renshaw. Right next to them on the list is my wife and cover artist, Jack Giesen, without whom these books would be much less pretty!

It's been a whirlwind journey for both myself and poor Damien, but this isn't the end of the story for either of us. A month before the release of this Omnibus, I put my first full-length novel, *Children of Prophecy*, out into the world in both e-book and paperback forms. Next year will see me release two full novels—and yes, one of them will advance Damien Montgomery's story.

You can find *Children of Prophecy*, an epic fantasy about destiny, love, and duty—along with a threat that might completely destroy everything the Kingdom of Vishni seeks to defend—on Amazon now.

Space Carrier Avalon, a space opera about cold war, honor, and the prices soldiers pay to defend their countries, will be released in May of 2015.

In *Mage-King's Hand*, the next Damien Montgomery novel, the young mage must master his unique gifts in the service of Mars. The book will be released in September of 2015.

Thank you for joining me in the journey so far, and I hope you continue to read and enjoy my work!

-Glynn Stewart

Damien's story will continue in:

Mage-King's Hand

Coming September 2015

If you liked the novella, please leave a review!

Follow Glynn Stewart on Twitter @faolanspen

Or on his blog at www.glynnstewart.com

Join the mailing list at www.glynnstewart.com to be notified of new releases.

Also check out:

Children of Prophecy – Released November 2014
An epic fantasy of coming of age, love, duty and honor.

Space Carrier Avalon – Coming May 2015
A space opera about cold war, honor, and the prices soldiers pay to defend their countries

49020725R00166

Made in the USA
Lexington, KY
21 January 2016